ANOTHER TIME,
ANOTHER SEASON

'When you investigated my son Patrick last year, you found nothing unusual about him? You are positive he had made no connections with any of the Irish organizations?'

'Nothing Ma'am. I think I told you then, you were worrying yourself unnecessarily ... Why, has something come up ...?

'I have a feeling ...' Katherine said slowly. She looked up at Michael. 'Perhaps you should have him watched again. I want to know his every movement for the next two weeks. I want to know where he goes, who he meets ... everything.'

'Something is bothering you,' Michael Lee said softly, looking carefully at Katherine.

'A feeling. I know when someone is lying to me ... If I find he has any connections with Ireland, I'll kill him.' Katherine Lundy snapped, and Michael Lee suddenly realized that he didn't know if she was serious or not.

Also by Anna Dillon in Sphere Books

SEASONS

ANOTHER TIME, ANOTHER SEASON

Anna Dillon

SPHERE BOOKS LIMITED

A SPHERE BOOK

First published in Great Britain by Sphere Books Ltd 1989
Copyright © Anna Dillon 1989

Photoset in North Wales by
Derek Doyle & Associates, Mold, Clwyd.
Printed in Great Britain by
Richard Clay Ltd, Bungay, Suffolk

ISBN 0 7474 0183 7

Sphere Books Ltd
A Division of
Macdonald & Co. (Publishers) Ltd.
1 New Fetter Lane, London EC4A 1AR

A member of Maxwell Pergamon Publishing Corporation plc

CHAPTER ONE

London, 21st January, 1919

There was the nightmare – always the nightmare.

In the dream, she saw the knife coming towards her face. It was moving slowly, so slowly. In the dream she lifted her right hand and stretched out her arm, the tiny pistol almost lost in the palm of her hand, pointed it at the man who had once been her lover – and shot him dead.

The sharp crack of the pistol always brought her awake, cold and shivering. But the bottle helped then, helped dull the pain, helped quell the shivering, helped ease her back into a dreamless sleep.

The bottle helped ...

It was a little after noon when Katherine Lundy awoke, her head pounding, her mouth foul. Turning her head slightly she looked at the cut-glass decanter on the bedside table – it was a little less than half full, which meant that she had drunk three ... no, four glasses of whisky at some time during the night. She half-remembered awakening around dawn, the light vague and grey against the heavy drapes, but she had no recollection of drinking four glasses ...

She sat up slowly in the bed ... and immediately amended her count to three glasses; she had spilt most of the contents of the fourth down the front of her muslin pyjamas and onto the lace coverlet. But the sudden movement set her head pounding, and she squeezed her eyes closed, attempting to shut out the dancing varicoloured slivers of light. She remained still and unmoving for a few moments, allowing her head to settle, listening to the muffled noises from the house,

1

the only recognizable sound the squeal of laughter from her daughter's room further down the hall. She was sure if she listened hard enough she would be able to hear the creak of the rocking-horse the girl had been given as a Christmas present a month ago.

Easing back the stained coverlet, Katherine slowly swung her legs out of bed, and then remained motionless for a few moments, resisting the urge to throw up. She looked down at her new French muslin pyjamas, the corners of her thin lips turning up in a rueful smile, wondering if the whisky stains would come out – and deciding that they probably wouldn't. She reached out and turned the clock towards her, blinking at the small ornate face, attempting to focus on the figures, trying to work out if it was twenty past twelve or twenty past one, finally deciding it was the earlier hour. The calendar beside the clock was turned to the 21st January, 1919 – but was that yesterday's date or today's; had she changed it before she went to bed last night?

Katherine Lundy shook her head savagely, digging the palms of her hands into her eyes and rubbing hard. This was the part she hated, the feeling of stupidity, the loss of control, and the fear and loathing it left in its wake. But it was the nightmare – she needed the drink to cope with the nightmare, and because the nightmare was an image from her past it was all the more powerful, the images and details razor sharp.

It had been three years since Katherine Lundy had shot the man she had once loved. She had shot him for all the things he had done to her and her husband, shot him because, in the end, she still loved him, and it made his ultimate betrayal all the harder to bear. She had shot him without a qualm of conscience, without a second thought, and walked away without even looking back.

She had thought that would be the end of it. It was an episode of her life she was finished with. Katherine had left Ireland almost immediately afterwards, spending a little time in Cornwall with her children before

2

travelling up to Scotland to stay with friends there. Some months later, when she judged that things would have quietened down, she had come down to London and had set about re-establishing her business. The following year had left her with little enough time for dreams, let alone nightmares. But once the business had been established and the initial problems of setting it up had been dealt with, she had found herself with a certain amount of time at her disposal, time to relax, time to remember. And that was when the nightmares had started.

Everything had been fine until the nightmares. If she had been a religious person she would have put it down to retribution for her sins, but she had lost whatever faith she had had in her years as the Madam of Dublin's most fashionable brothel. But Dublin was long ago and far away; the city she had known had changed irrevocably on that Easter Monday three years ago when a handful of men, including her husband Dermot, had walked out to do battle with the might of the British Empire.

Katherine stood up quickly, her head spinning, bile rising in her throat. Another effect of the drink was to make her maudlin. That life – the Dublin days, she called them – was gone forever. She had made a new life for herself now in London, a better, much more successful life than Dublin. And she didn't need reminding of the 'good old days'. They had not been so good to her; she had lost too many things, too many friends, too much of herself.

Katherine crossed to the window and pulled back the heavy drapes, squinting against the pale January sunlight. It had snowed again during the night. The snow showed no signs of melting; it was piled at least four inches deep on her window ledge and against her windows, and there were deep bird tracks patterned across it. The park, directly across from her house, was completely obliterated beneath the snow, the bushes now little more than vague mounds, and the trees

3

standing stark and forlorn. The street below was quiet, little traffic braving the snow and ice even at this time of day – but then Mayfair really only came alive at night, when the various hostesses entertained. And no-one entertained more lavishly, more sumptuously, more successfully than Mrs Katherine Lundy.

Smiling at the idea, Katherine turned away from the window, unbuttoning the pyjamas, heading towards her bathroom.

The bathroom – which was lavish even by Mayfair standards – was all glass and cool, muted blues, which had looked lovely when she had put it in, but which she now thought was cold and vaguely forbidding, and as she pulled off her pyjama top, she thought it made her flesh look white and dead. The mirrors had been a mistake also. Too many mirrors, too many reflections.

The years had been reasonably kind to Katherine Lundy – or at least had been until she had begun drinking heavily. She was thirty-nine now, and it was only in the past two years that she had put on weight. It showed around her face and on her stomach. She touched her soft cheeks, the once-proud cheekbones lost beneath a covering of fat and pulled down the sagging flesh beneath her bloodshot eyes; she had never been beautiful, now she was merely plain. Her hair, which had always been her most attractive feature, was now lined with grey, and she had given up dying it black. She touched it; it was dry and coarse to her touch. She ran her hands down her body, over her small breasts, now beginning to sag, her fingers coming to rest on her stomach. The rich food and drink showed there. She had recovered her figure after the birth of both her children very quickly, but now it looked as if she was four months pregnant. She swore – yet again – that she would leave off the rich food, forget the drink, but even as she was making the promise, she knew she would not be able to keep to it.

She washed quickly, the water barely lukewarm, but the tepid water helped clear her muzzy head, and she

4

began running through her plans for the day – if she kept herself busy she could avoid the drink.

Today was … Tuesday, the 21st of January. There were still bits and pieces left to organize for the coming weekend, when she was hosting the first major social gathering of the new year. Lloyd George, recently re-elected, had been issued an invitation, but it was unlikely that he would attend, but certainly Austen Chamberlain, the Chancellor of the Exchequer, and Winston Churchill, the Secretary of State for War might attend. There were some minor foreign royals who had attended the Christmas celebrations in the palace who might also be prevailed upon to come – they would provide a little exotic colour. She wasn't sure whether there were any artists or writers in town at the moment, but there were bound to be one or two back in the city after the Christmas recess. Politicians, royals and artists – the perfect mix for an entertaining evening.

Katherine wandered back into her bedroom and lazily sorted through her wardrobe, before finally settling on a simple gown of heavy blue satin that was at least two seasons out of date, but which served to hide her fuller figure as she refused to wear a corset. In her years in the brothels in Dublin, she had seen far too many girls with their bodies twisted and scarred by the constricting corsets. She wore no jewellery except for a simple band around her wedding finger.

As she opened the door to her room, she heard the first gong warn that lunch would be served shortly. The last reverberations of the gong were still vibrating on the still air when a door down the corridor burst open and a young girl raced out onto the landing, heading for the stairs.

'Senga!'

Katherine's voice cracked as she called her daughter's name, and she repeated herself, more softly this time. 'Senga?'

'Mama.' The young girl stopped and turned back. 'I did not see you there.'

Katherine smiled proudly; the voice, the accent and the poise were English, three years of the best schools and governesses had completely eradicated the Dublin accent.

'You are well, Mama?' Katherine bent her head and the young girl kissed her cheek.

'I am a little tired ... the festivities ...' Katherine said vaguely.

Senga Lundy nodded, but said nothing; she had smelt the stale odour of drink on her mother's breath. She was eleven years old, with a smooth oval face, and deep, dark brown eyes that at the moment seemed far too big for her face. She had also inherited the lustrous black hair that had once helped to make her mother so attractive.

'And what did you do with Miss Powers today?' Katherine asked as they began to descend the gently curving marble staircase.

'We began with history, and covered the early years of Queen Elizabeth, and we were to have some music practice, but I persuaded Miss Powers to leave that until later this afternoon, lest it disturb you.'

Katherine squeezed her daughter's hand affectionately. 'Thank you. And how are your language studies?'

'Fine. My French is improving, so is my Latin, but the Greek ...' She shrugged, allowing the sentence to trail. She knew she would never be able to master the Greek language.

'I have been considering finding you a tutor in another European language,' her mother continued. 'German perhaps ...'

'Mama, surely not German!' The expression of distaste on the girl's face was almost comical.

'We will discuss it later,' Katherine said absently, stopping on the last step, her eyes sweeping along the broad expanse of highly polished hallway, automatically checking the corners, beneath the lacquered Chinese table, around the edges of the mirror, and finally the glass on the print and picture frames. She had been a servant herself once, and she knew all the shortcuts. Satisfied that everything was to her satisfaction, she crossed the hall and entered the sitting room behind her daughter.

The room was warm, a sparking, crackling fire blazing in the hearth, and comfortably cluttered with furniture that conformed to no particular taste or style; this was the family's private sitting room, where the image that Katherine Lundy worked so hard to maintain to the brittle world of Society London could be dropped, where she and her family and close friends could be completely at ease. French doors opened out onto an enclosed patio which overlooked a long, sloping back garden.

Katherine sat before the fire, and began sorting through the morning's post, which had been left on a small silver tray on the side-table beside her chair. She flicked through the envelopes, sorting them into two piles; the first would be opened immediately, while the second could wait until after she had eaten. Generally, invitations and the like fell into the second category. She glanced at her daughter as she reached for the silver letter-knife; Senga was standing before the French doors, looking out at the snow-piled garden. It had backed up against the patio, completely concealing the ornate wall and steps that led down onto the gravelled walks. The girl's face was set into rigid lines, her deep dark eyes reflecting the white light from the garden, robbing them of all expression. How serious she is, Katherine thought, she reminds me of myself at that age. She looked up at the clock, wondering if there was time for a pot of tea before lunch, but deciding that the second gong would sound soon, and she could wait.

She returned to the letter in her hand, turning it over in her slender fingers before opening it. It was postmarked Manchester, the paper was poor, and the writing scrawled and dipped across the stained envelope. She frowned slightly; it wouldn't do to have

7

letters like this arriving here, she would make arrangements today for a discreet postal address. One of the reasons she had survived in business was because she had always been so careful. Crumpling the envelope in her hand, she tossed it into the fire, watching intently while it blackened and burned before returning to the single sheet of cheap paper. The letter was brief, and couched in the most guarded terms; it reported a half-yearly profit to the end of December, but also added that there had been some deterioration in the product and requested a fresh consignment, preferably of foreign origin.

Katherine made a brief expression of annoyance; this was the third time Lumley had requested fresh stock – she would have to do something about it, and him. She made a tiny note with a gold Swan pen on the note-pad on the table, 'Manchester stock'.

There was a similar letter from Glasgow; this time the writing was marginally more educated, and the paper of slightly heavier stock, but the letter was crouched in the same guarded terms: a half-yearly profit that was a substantial increase on the same period last year. There was also a note to the effect that a suitable premises, with stock, had been offered at a reasonable price, in a similar location to her present premises.

Katherine tapped the letter several times with her fountain-pen. She was looking for the opportunity to extend her holdings in Glasgow, but she was unsure if she wanted to expand her business in the same district as her first premises – perhaps she ought to move upmarket, rather like her London operation. But was there a market in Glasgow for a quality product; should she be thinking of Edinburgh instead?

A sudden thought struck her and she began to laugh. Senga looked at her quickly, before turning away – perhaps there had been something amusing in one of Mama's letters. She hoped so; Mama rarely laughed these days.

Katherine wiped a tear from her eye with a lacy

handkerchief. She was beginning to think like a shopkeeper.

Katherine Lundy's trade was in flesh. She ran one of London's exclusive brothels. Situated in Mayfair, directly across the park from her own house, its clients were drawn from the highest echelons of society. She also owned a brothel in Manchester and one in Glasgow; however, both were considerably downmarket, catering to the middle and working classes.

'Mama?'

'Yes, dear?'

'Do I have to learn German?'

'I said I would think about it. I think you should have another European language rather than French.'

'But no one will speak German now that the war is done and they have been defeated,' the girl said seriously.

Katherine glanced up as she slit open the third envelope. 'The Prussians are hard workers, dedicated people. I would imagine it will not take them too long to become a world power again.'

'Surely not, Mama?'

Katherine nodded. 'I am convinced of it.'

'Were you ever in Germany, Mama?'

Katherine looked across at her daughter and smiled briefly, remembering. 'Yes, once, for a little while, a long time ago.'

'What did you do there?'

Before Katherine had a chance to answer, the second lunch gong sounded followed, seconds later, by the jangle of the hall bell. 'That will be Patrick!' Senga shouted and dashed out into the hall, almost colliding with Gerard, the butler 'That's Patrick,' she said quickly, 'he said he would be back in time for lunch.'

'I'm sure it is, Miss Senga, I recognize his ring.'

Katherine heard the voices fade and lifted the third letter. There was no name, no return address and although the paper was cheap, the writing was firm and rounded, educated certainly.

9

'There will be an auction of some Irish Glass lost in '07; the Greek has details.'

How very curious.

Wondering who had sent it, Katherine turned the letter over in her hands, and then held it up to the light, looking for a watermark – anything which would indicate its origin. There was nothing.

The Irish Glass lost in '07 could only be the Irish Crown Jewels. They had been stolen in 1907 causing both the British and Irish authorities much embarrassment, especially since they had vanished on the eve of a royal visit. Katherine's lips moved in a grim smile as she recalled some of the details – it had been quite a scandal. And she was unsure whether she wanted to become involved with them again; the jewels were not actually worth that much, and the very fact that they were of Irish origin was enough to turn her away from them.

When she had fled Ireland, Katherine Lundy had sworn she would never again have anything to do with the country. Ireland had caused her nothing but trouble, and not only her, but those she held dear. Her father had been maimed while on duty in Ireland, and she herself had been sold into virtual slavery there, where she had been seduced and made pregnant. When that was discovered she had been thrown out on the streets, and subsequently forced to live in a brothel. She had lost her husband and all those she had loved because of Ireland.

If Ireland was a woman – as the poet Yeats kept saying – then she was a banshee, a fairy woman, who brought with her nothing but death and despair.

The subject of Ireland was banned in her house; she employed no Irish servants, imported no Irish goods – although she used Irish girls in her brothels – allowed no Irish books or papers into her house. Katherine Lundy was determined that her children would grow up unaffected and untainted by the cursed country. All she had taken out of Ireland when she had fled had been the money she had made there and her trade – and her trade was that of a Madam.

Hearing voices approach down the hall, she threw the paper and envelope into the fire, and then stood up as Senga reappeared, leading a tall serious-faced young man. Although there was nine years between them, there was no doubt that they were brother and sister; they each had the same deep intense eyes that were their dead father's legacy, and Patrick had inherited his father's square chin, and wiry black hair.

'Mother.' Smiling, he came forward, rubbing his hands to his glowing cheeks.

'Patrick …' Katherine turned her cheek for his kiss, and then immediately ushered both children towards the dining room. 'Where were you, Patrick?'

He held open the door for his mother and sister. 'I went to the Charing Cross Road to buy some books I'm going to need for my studies.'

Katherine nodded, satisfied. Patrick was studying medicine, and it was her wish to set him up in a practice of his own one day. She stood at the head of the small table, waiting for her son and daughter to seat themselves on either side of her and then sat down. 'Did you get what you were looking for?'

He ran his fingers through his hair, brushing it back off his high forehead, and nodded. 'A *Gray's Anatomy* – a good second-hand copy, and some works by Doctor Freud.'

'You bought second-hand books!'

Patrick shrugged in embarrassment. 'Only the Gray's. It was an excellent copy …'

'Patrick, I've told you before. You don't need to buy anything second-hand. I have worked long and hard to ensure that my children want for nothing.'

'Mother … Mother …' Patrick held up both his hands in surrender. 'I bought a second-hand copy deliberately, and not just because of the price …' He fell silent as the door to the dining room opened and one of the maids entered with the first course. When she left, he continued. 'I bought a second-hand copy because it had been very usefully annotated, the notes alone will save

11

me hours of work.'

Satisfied, Katherine nodded. 'Eat your lunch,' she said shortly.

Patrick bent his head to his soup and hid a smile.

Patrick Montgomery Lundy was almost twenty, but looked older, and he had no interest in medicine. He had braved the bitter weather to go down to the bookshops on the Charing Cross Road not just for the chance to get some books – he could have bought them any time – but principally to meet Joseph Hyde and hear the latest news from Dublin.

Patrick had grown up in the Dublin that his mother now worked so hard to forget. He remembered his father, Dermot Corcoran, the man whose name was never mentioned in the house, the man whose name they no longer wore. He distinctly remembered the Monday morning his father had gone out, dressed in the green uniform of the volunteers, carrying his rifle. A week later he was dead, but by that time they had both been shipped off to England.

And while his mother may have forgotten Dublin and his father, who had given his life to make it a better place for his children to live in, Patrick had not.

Initially, he had bucked against her restraints, often asking her direct questions about her previous life, about his father. Almost inevitably, questions about Dermot sent her into a rage – and she usually soothed that rage in a bottle. Patrick didn't need to be a doctor to know that his mother was drinking herself into an early grave. She had banned everything Irish from the house, burnt any newspapers or pamphlets that he brought home, and even searched his room for unsuitable material. In the end he had relented, and agreed to take up the career she had chosen for him. If the truth were known, he had only acceded to her wishes because it took him away from her, allowing him access to libraries, bookshops and students of all races and creeds – many of them Irish.

Patrick Lundy had made many friends amongst London's large Irish community, his parentage, and especially the fact that his father had fought and died in the General Post Office, making him welcome. And chief amongst these was Joseph Hyde, an ardent Nationalist who had actually known his father and mother in Dublin, but who now worked in Webbs, one of the bookshops on the Charing Cross Road.

Patrick didn't like to think what would happen if his mother ever discovered his association with Joseph. He especially didn't like to think what would happen if his mother ever discovered that he was going to sneak out of the house to attend an illegal meeting a few days hence.

Joseph had been tremendously excited when Patrick had strolled into the dusty bookshop that morning. The small Irishman had just sprinkled the wooden floor with water to keep down the dust and was briskly sweeping the warped boards with a long-bristled broom when Patrick arrived. The shop was empty, few people having braved the chilled and icy streets, and Joseph had simply dropped the brush and dragged Patrick to the back of the shop.

'There's trouble brewing at home,' he said breathlessly, pushing his wire-frame glasses back onto his face.

'What sort of trouble?' Patrick asked, feeling his heart beginning to pound. Ireland – home, as Joseph called it – had been a powder keg since the Easter Rising three years ago. The situation had been compounded during the elections in the previous month when the Nationalist had taken seventy-three seats out of a total of one hundred and five, and out of those, forty-two of those elected were in jail for various offences related to their opposition of the British presence in Ireland.

'The new government sits today,' Joseph said hurriedly, 'and there'll be trouble, mark my words.'

'What sort of trouble?' Patrick asked again.

Joseph glanced around, his eyes darting, and Patrick suddenly realized just how nervous the man was. 'There'll be war – mark my words.'

Patrick could only shake his head.

'There'll be war,' the older man insisted. 'Civil War. We'll not let those who fought in the Rising die in vain.'

'I'm not sure I understand ...'

'They're being betrayed – what they fought for, what they died for, they're being sold out.'

'You're not making sense,' Patrick said reasonably.

'But we'll not betray them – we'll make Ireland free, by force of arms if need be!'

Patrick sighed. He had heard the speech often, not only from Joseph, but from those like him, committed, embittered men with a vision that even Patrick with all the wisdom of his twenty years, knew would never be achieved in his lifetime. He touched Joseph on the shiny sleeve of his coat and nodded towards the large-faced clock on the wall above the door. 'I've got to go, Mother is expecting me home for lunch. You know what she's like.'

Joseph nodded absently, still wrapped in his thoughts.

'I'll see you soon.'

'They'll need young men, men of conviction,' Joseph said suddenly, as Patrick headed towards the door. The young man stopped, his hand on the door. Joseph picked up a small parcel and walked down the length of the shop to hand it to Patrick. 'Take these; an annotated *Gray's Anatomy*, some Freud – at least it'll prove you were here for a reason if nothing else.'

Patrick smiled his thanks, and slid his hand beneath his heavy overcoat for his wallet, but Joseph put his hand on his arm and shook his head. 'A gift ...' he began and then hurried on as Patrick started to shake his head. 'Well, an investment then. You can treat me for free when you're a doctor.' He pulled open the door and peered out into Charing Cross Road, which was virtually deserted, the slush packed high and filthy against the kerb. 'There'll be snow again.'

Patrick nodded and pulled up his collar. He stuck the brown-paper bundle under his arm and stuck his hands deep into his pockets. 'I couldn't go back,' he said softly. They both knew he meant Ireland.

Without looking at him, Joseph said, 'Why not?'

'Mother …' the young man said eventually.

'You've got to make the break sooner or later. It's your country – it could be your fight. If your father was alive – what do you think he'd do, where do you think he'd stand, eh? And if you think you owe his memory anything, you'll know where you should stand.'

'Why does my mother hate Ireland so much?' Patrick said softly.

'Have you ever asked her?' Joseph said glancing up at the serious young man.

'Often; she says she doesn't want to talk about it.'

'Ireland took a lot from her, including her husband. She's bitter,' he shrugged. Without looking at Patrick, he said very quietly, his eyes on a tram lumbering slowly and cautiously down the street, 'There's a meeting in the usual place on Saturday night. You should come. There'll be some people from home with all the latest news.'

Patrick patted the books under his arm, and then deliberately pointed to the window, as if he was speaking about a book. His eyes were on the street, scanning the few passers-by. The bookshop was often watched by the British Authorities because of its known association with Irish sympathisers, but in this weather, with so few people about, any observer would be sure to stand out. 'Saturday … yes, Mother's giving a party, I should be able to slip away. What time?'

'The usual, eight or thereabouts,' Joseph said, barely moving his lips. 'Think about going back. I could arrange it, if you wanted to return. Give you the right introductions …'

Patrick smiled vaguely. 'It would be lovely. And in a year or two perhaps I might be in a position to take you up on it.'

'It might be too late then,' Joseph said slapping Patrick on the shoulder, before turning back into the

15

shop and closing the door.

Patrick Lundy stood on the street for a few moments, staring unseeing into the windows, and then he turned away and headed back up to Mayfair.

And if he was quiet and preoccupied during lunch, neither his mother nor sister seemed to notice. They were each wrapped in their own thoughts.

Katherine Lundy sat back in the darkened sitting room, her eyes on the deep red glow from the fire, the only sound the soft hissing of the burning coal and the solemn ticking of the clock. There was a half-full glass of pale sherry standing beside the notepad and pen resting on the arm of the heavy leather chair. When a thought occurred to her, she quickly noted it on the pad.

The house was almost completely silent. The children had gone upstairs after lunch, Senga to continue her lessons with Miss Powers, her governess, Patrick to pursue his studies.

Katherine was still vaguely annoyed because he had bought a second-hand book, and she also had the feeling that he was being evasive. No, it was more than a feeling – she knew he was lying. All she wanted to know was why.

Patrick was nearly twenty now, and she couldn't hold on to him forever, she realized that. But she only wanted the best for him; he had a start in life that she never had; why, when she was his age she had already had one child, and was working in Dublin's most exclusive brothel.

No, not true, not quite true! By the time she was twenty, she had already travelled across Europe, visiting the brothels of London, Paris and Berlin. Her thin lips curled in a rare smile – one might say she had been pursuing her own studies. She could look back on that time with a great deal of fondness; it had been one of the few times in her life when she had been truly free – there had been no one, neither family, friends nor employer – to make demands on her.

Good times, yes, they had been good times …

The muffled jangle of the bell disturbed her reverie, and she glanced up at the clock – it lacked a few minutes to three – her visitor was punctual as usual. She was already rising to her feet when Gerard the butler tapped on the door before opening it.

'Mr Lee, Ma'am.'

'Thank you, Gerard. Some tea please.'

The butler bowed slightly and retired, and although his face was expressionless, Katherine could almost feel his displeasure towards the man who now stepped into the room.

'Ma'am,' he bowed stiffly, almost reluctantly.

Michael Lee, although he dressed, talked and had the manners of an Englishman, was a half-caste – it showed in the vaguely Oriental slant to his features, and the slight pigmentation of his skin. Officially, he was Katherine's business consultant, in reality he was the manager of her London brothel.

'Your message sounded urgent,' he said directly.

She nodded. 'It is.' She returned to her seat and he sank languidly into the chair opposite. She made no attempt to light one of the gas bowls and the vague glow from the fire did little to brighten the dimness of the room. Michael Lee was well used to Katherine's preference for darkened rooms; when he had first started to work for her, he had done some research and discovered that when she had operated in Dublin, she had never appeared in public during the daylight hours and always met her business associates in darkened rooms, where she was known only as Madam Kitten. He waited patiently for Katherine to speak. Lee had inherited a little of his father's Oriental patience – although he had never met his father, who had apparently run one of the infamous Opium Dens in Whitechapel – and was quite content to sit, absorb the heat, and listen to the soft ticking and creaking as the house settled, content in his own company.

Michael Lee had grown up in London's dockland at a time when prejudice towards the Chinese seemed to be at a height – and especially half-caste Chinese children, and there were few enough of those. His mother was a common prostitute, working the wharves, the cheap gambling clubs, and the dens. An addict of the pipe herself, she had little time for her son – the only one of three to survive – and left his rearing to her own mother. By the time he was eight, Michael Lee was an accomplished thief, and successfully touted for business for some of the street-girls, usually those who were either too ugly, raddled or diseased to approach a customer themselves. Lee would pick out a suitably drunk customer, extoll the virtues of his 'sister,' and then lure the man into a nearby darkened alley where, more often than not, the customer was attacked and robbed of everything he had on him, sometimes even his clothing. The young boy quickly became an authority on who received and dealt in stolen goods in London, who specialized in watches, clothes, foreign money, rings.

By the time he was fifteen, he was an accomplished fence himself, often dealing as a middle-man between the thief and the fence. He also had a small stable of girls working the docks, specializing in the new boats to put into harbour, and the girls had their instructions to discover details of the shipment ... and there was always a bonus if they discovered an interesting cargo. Interesting cargoes had a tendency to go missing.

Katherine had come in contact with him three years previously through her contacts in the London underworld. Her proposition had been simple and direct – if he were to work for her, she would make him wealthy and ensure him a place in society.

And, although she never actually put it into words, she had made it perfectly clear that she would put him out of business if he didn't agree to her terms. With little option, Michael Lee went to work for the Madam.

But in the three years he had worked for her, she hadn't deceived him. He had wealth, position and authority, and by nature of his association with Mrs

18

Katherine Lundy, he was invited to some of the best parties in London society. The half-caste prostitute's son had come a long way.

Katherine made a tiny note on her pad and then looked across at Michael Lee. She opened her mouth to say something, when there was a knock on the door and Gerard re-entered, carrying an ornate silver tea service on an equally ornate tray. He stood in the doorway, blinking in the dimness.

'Your tea, Ma'am. Shall I turn up the light?'

'No,' Katherine said immediately, 'I don't think that will be necessary; neither Mr Lee nor myself will be reading nor writing, I don't think we will need a light.'

'I find the afternoon twilight very restful,' Michael Lee said quietly, concentrating on keeping the accent he had perfected to hide his East End slang.

'Very good, Ma'am ... sir ...' The butler placed the tray down on a table close to Mr Lee and with infinite care poured the tea. Both Katherine and Michael Lee preferred it black. Gerard handed Katherine her cup, and Mr Lee took a certain small pleasure in allowing him to pass over the second cup, even though he could have easily reached out and taken it. Although the butler had never said or intimated anything untoward, Michael had grown up with prejudice long enough to recognize it for what it was.

'If that will be all ...?' Gerard bowed slightly and left, closing the door softly behind him.

'He doesn't like me,' Michael remarked.

'That worries you?'

He smiled, showing surprisingly white teeth. 'Not at all.'

'He is everything a butler should be, and a good butler is essential to one's position; moreover he is discreet and, as far as I can determine, without a vice.'

'Every man has his vice,' Michael said softly.

Katherine nodded. 'Granted, but I have not yet discovered his.' She sipped her tea and grimaced. 'Now, I asked you to come over for several reasons. I received some letters this morning which are of interest.' He nodded, a vague movement of his head. 'Lumley reports a half-yearly profit, but is in need of stock again.'

'Again?'

Katherine nodded. 'I think perhaps you should investigate. This situation is extremely annoying, though. I fear Lumley may need replacing. If he does, I would prefer it if he were to emigrate.'

Michael Lee smiled broadly. Katherine's two main rivals in London when she arrived had both mysteriously and suddenly decided to 'emigrate' when she started her operations. One was later found in a shallow grave in the New Forest, the other – his body wrapped in chains – was at the bottom of the Thames.

'There was a letter from Glasgow, again reporting increased profits, and giving details of a nearby establishment for sale.'

'I will investigate that also. On principle I am against owning too many establishments dealing in the same merchandise in the one town. If one falls, the others are likely to fall alongside it.'

'That is true, but you must also bear in mind that premises offering a similar service often feed off one another … at least that was my experience in Dublin.' Katherine sipped her tea. 'Well, visit it anyway, and see what you think, we can discuss it again.' She placed her cup down on the side table and folded her hands together. 'There was a third letter, this one unsigned and undated, the paper poor, but the writing was educated. It said – and I quote – "There will be an auction of some Irish Glass lost in '07; the Greek has details." Unquote.'

'Irish Glass …?'

'Jewels,' Katherine murmured.

'The Irish Crown Jewels?' Michael Lee asked.

'I believe so.'

'Are you interested?'

'I'm more curious than interested. I can remember

when they were stolen, and the investigation which followed. From what I learned of their disappearance at the time, I never believed they would re-surface intact. Their monetary value was not great, neither as individual stones nor as pieces of work. However, contact the Greek ... find out what you can.'

'Of course.'

'Now, finally. There will be a fancy-dress party here on Saturday evening. It will be the first grand event after the Christmas and New Year celebrations, and I am determined to make it a success. Here is a copy of the guest list. I want you to go through the list and then supply some girls who will be unknown to any of the people here.'

Lee grimaced. 'You realize that is getting harder and harder to do. As the house becomes more and more popular, we are attracting quite a select clientele – some of whom I feel would be on yours and every other society guest list.'

Katherine smiled thinly. 'Either that says a lot for the quality of guests, or for the reputation of the house.'

'Do you want me to bring in outsiders?'

'No,' Katherine was emphatic. 'I want no cheap tarts masquerading as ladies. Use only our own girls and warn them to be on their best behaviour. Give them the standard aliases. Also, on no account are they to conduct their activities here in this house.'

Michael nodded, dipping his head to hide his smile; Katherine Lundy was so conscious of her reputation. If his guests picked up some pleasant female company at her party then that was fine ... as long as they didn't enjoy that same female company on the premises.

Katherine sighed. 'That is really all I wanted to see you about.'

The tall, thin young man stood up, realizing that the interview was at an end. 'If that is all ...'

Katherine nodded absently. 'When you investigated my son Patrick last year, you found nothing unusual about him? You are positive he had made no connections with any of the Irish organizations?'

'Nothing, Ma'am. I think I told you then, you were worrying yourself unnecessarily. My agents could find no connection between him and any Irish organization or group. The closest to Ireland we came were a few students in college, and even they seemed to have no interest in politics.' He paused and added, 'Why, has something come up ...?'

'I have a feeling ...' Katherine said slowly. She looked up at Michael. 'Perhaps you should have him watched again. I want to know his every movement for the next two weeks. I want to know where he goes, who he meets ... everything.'

'Something is bothering you,' Michael Lee said very softly, looking carefully at Katherine.

'A feeling,' she repeated. 'I know when someone is lying to me,' she added with a thin smile.

'Might it be nothing more than a girl?'

'Patrick has never exhibited any interest in girls,' Katherine said quickly.

'A boy then?' Lee said seriously.

Taking no offence, Katherine thought about it, and then finally nodded slowly. 'It is possible – just possible. He has grown up surrounded by women. I suppose it is possible he has formed an affection for some boy,' she conceded.

'It does not bother you?' Michael said cautiously. One of the reasons he was able to run his brothel so successfully was because he was homosexual, and therefore had no interest in the stock.

'No, it doesn't bother me,' Katherine said, keeping her face impassive. Although Michael Lee concealed the fact very well indeed, Katherine was well aware of his leanings. And then she suddenly wondered if her son and Lee ... she dismissed the idea equally swiftly; she would know. She picked her employees very carefully, and then she watched them equally cautiously; there was little she didn't know about them, from the girls who worked in her houses, to the scullery maid who worked in the kitchen.

'It doesn't bother me – perhaps it should, but then that is what this business does to you. You get used to seeing so many things, you become immune to what would normally be considered perversions. If Patrick was homosexual then it might sadden me, but it wouldn't shock me.'

'He would be in very good company,' Michael Lee said with a sly smile, 'all the best people are.'

'The very best of company,' Katherine agreed.

Michael Lee bowed slightly as he prepared to take his leave. 'I take it you would be happier if your boy was effeminate than if he were somehow connected to some Irish political group.'

'If I find he has any connections with Ireland, I'll kill him,' Katherine Lundy snapped, and Michael Lee suddenly realized that he didn't know if she was serious or not.

Dimly, Patrick Lundy heard the governess' shrill voice repeat – yet again – a line of verse. All he could distinguish was the sound rather than the words, but he could tell by the tone of her voice that Senga wasn't taking it in.

The thin young man was standing by the window of his bedroom, his hands deep in the pockets of his dressing gown, looking out over the park. Dusk was drifting in over the park, covering the snow in gritty grey shadows, bringing the houses around the park alight almost simultaneously. His thoughts were spinning, mulling over what Joseph had said to him earlier. Deep in his heart he knew he just didn't have the nerve to give up everything – his home, his family, his fortune – to return to a country he thought he loved. He knew he hadn't the nerve to face his mother's wrath. Joseph Hyde said Ireland had taken too much from her, but was that enough to account for her hatred of the country? There was a mystery there.

He heard the hall door directly below the window slam closed, and a slim dapper man stepped carefully down the clean-swept steps, the ferrule of his cane tapping the steps. He paused on the bottom step to turn up the heavy collar of his overcoat, before striding off down the street, his breath pluming before him.

Now there was a mystery – how had his mother ever got involved with a shark like Michael Lee, a miserable jumped-up half-caste, with his too soft handshake and his ice-cold calculating eyes?

Mysteries, all mysteries, but no answers. The only answers, he knew, lay back in Dublin. And he wondered if he would ever discover them.

He wondered if he wanted to.

CHAPTER TWO

Saturday, 25th January, 1919

In the still pre-dawn silence, Katherine awoke. She lay in her bed, her eyes moving across the ceiling where the snow piled outside her window reflected vague purple-grey patterns into the room.

It came almost as a shock to realize that her night had been peaceful – there had been no dreams, no nightmares, and the bottle by her bed remained untouched.

It might have been an omen.

But Katherine Lundy didn't believe in omens; she imagined her untroubled night's sleep was due to nothing more than complete exhaustion. She had been up until close to three the previous night, putting the finishing touches to the preparations for this evening's grand dinner. She was determined it would be a success.

This would be the first party since the Christmas and New Year round of celebrations, and it would set the tone and standard for the rest of the year. But because it was the first, it naturally left itself open to criticism.

Katherine lay in bed, listening to the floorboards outside her door creak and the hurried whispers of the servants as they made their way down from their attic quarters; it was a little before six then. In her days in service, the fires would have to have been cleaned and lit by six. But times had changed, the Great War had seen to that.

She snuggled deeper into the warmth, idly reviewing the plans for the evening. It had to be a success – she knew she would only be allowed one failure. Too many people had resented her abrupt intrusion onto the

London society circuit, and while she might have gained some measure of respectability, she knew the resentment remained. She had appeared out of nowhere three years previously, with money and connections, and had almost immediately established herself as one of the city's leading society hostesses. Her sudden, almost overnight, success had not been without its problems however. Initially, she had been ostracised in some quarters, and on several occasions when she had arranged a soirée, rival parties had been arranged for the same night. But somehow Mrs Lundy's were always better, and invitations to her gatherings were soon eagerly sought after. Eventually, those waging their campaign against her found they were losing, and furthermore, they quickly realized they couldn't afford not to be seen at a Katherine Lundy party.

Tonight the theme was an anonymous – but not a fancy-dress – ball; no names would be used and everyone would be masked. Katherine smiled; the idea appealed to her. There would be enough celebrities to keep the guests guessing ... and it would also allow her girls to mingle unnoticed in the crowd. Lee would pick the girls for the evening and she would approve his choice. Much would depend on that choice.

Katherine Lundy ran two similar, but quite separate, operations. There was the high-class brothel, managed by Michael Lee, which operated out of the house across the park from Katherine's own home, and then there were the dozen or so girls – the pick of the brothel girls – who worked the society parties. Their task was simple; they would entice a given target with their charms or education, whichever was appropriate, holding out the possibility of a night together. If the ruse didn't work the first time, it invariably did on the second occasion. The idea was to get the target hooked, and once he was hooked, he could be played along – very successfully and lucratively – for presents. These usually took the form of cash, but were more often clothes, furs and jewels – all of which Katherine's

26

organization had a ready outlet for. And of course, each girl was the mistress of more than one man.

But the success of the operation depended on the girls Katherine and Michael Lee chose. Each girl was then carefully suited to the target, tailored to his likes and dislikes.

Tonight, four of Katherine's special girls were working the party, each one fully acquainted with her target. There would also be a dozen girls from the brothel in attendance, they would provide colour, and nothing more. Tonight, they were young ladies of quality, they were not whores.

The food was ready, the rooms prepared, the entertainment laid on. It was going to be a very successful night indeed. Katherine threw back the covers and swung her legs out of bed. She reached for her silk dressing gown and pulled it on; she felt good, it had been a long time since she had awoken feeling so alive. It boded well for the night.

At the other end of the corridor, Patrick Lundy was also thinking of the coming night. He was wondering how he was going to slip out for a few hours without alerting his mother.

Last week, when he had left Joe Hyde in the bookshop, he had more or less made up his mind not to attend the meeting of the Irish sympathisers planned for this night.

But that had been before he had heard of the shootings. Two Irish policemen had been shot dead at Soloheadbeg last Tuesday by fellow Irishmen: it looked as if Joseph Hyde's prediction about Civil War might become a reality all too soon. Patrick had heard various stories and rumours about what had actually happened on the lonely country road from Tipperary town into Soloheadbeg Quarry when a shipment of gelignite – or dynamite – had been intercepted and the guards shot. On his way home from college, he had managed to slip into the bookshop and grab a few quick words with Joe

27

on the pretext of asking for a book, but the small, stout man could only tell him more or less what he already knew. He had mentioned that they would have the full story on Saturday and that had changed Patrick's mind for him. Now he was committed to attending the meeting; Joseph would have his disguise ready and would vouch for him. All he had to do was get out of the house.

He wasn't actually sure why it was important for him to discover the facts. On the face of it, the shooting looked like another bloody event in Irish history, but perhaps it was its timing – on the same day that the government had sat for the first time – that intrigued him, or perhaps it was Joe's words: that his father and the men like him who had died for Ireland were being betrayed. Perhaps it was nothing more than idle curiosity.

Patrick pulled his hands out from beneath the covers and clasped them behind his head, his eyes on the ceiling. Unlike his mother, who slept with the curtains drawn, Patrick preferred them open, and the wan dawn light reflected off the snow and created a ghostly, sparkling pattern across the high ceiling. Tracing the glittering lines of light, he idly wondered how he was going to get out tonight. Occasionally his mother allowed both Patrick and Senga to attend one of her functions, but obviously tonight's grand affair was not to be one of them. If they had been invited it might have made it easier, since it would have allowed him to slip away unnoticed. Tonight, he would have to try another ruse ...

Although Patrick Lundy was almost twenty, Katherine still considered him a child and treated him accordingly, and often it was easier to go along with her rather than risk an argument. He could of course simply walk out on some pretext – visiting a friend. Some other students – but he knew from experience that his mother would want all the details, and he clearly remembered the time he had slipped out for an evening to meet a girl

– the only girl he had ever really liked. He had given his mother a false address that time. The following day she had been able to tell him that he hadn't been there, and had demanded the truth. With no choice, he told her and while he never discovered what she did or said to the girl or her parents, the girl never spoke to him again, indeed, never even looked in his direction. At the time he had assumed that she had simply contacted the address on some pretext and discovered that he hadn't been there, but it was only later, when the argument had blown over, that he remembered that the address he had given his mother had been vacant. Which meant that he must have been watched … and that made him wonder was he still being watched? And why?

Which brought him back to tonight.

Patrick threw back the covers and hopped out of bed. Unlike his mother's room which was fully carpeted, his floor was of plain though highly polished wooden boards. In the summer, with the sun slanting in through the window, with the deep tan wallpaper, and the overall colour scheme of tan and creams, it looked lovely, but in the depths of winter it looked vaguely soiled, and depressingly dull. He dug his feet into his slippers and dragged on his heavy dressing gown, feeling the chill air nip at his flesh.

He pulled open his door and hurried down the landing towards the bathroom. He could hear the pipes chugging and banging together and from below came the rattling of pots in the kitchen, and the faint smell of a freshly lit fire.

The combination bathroom and toilet was bitterly cold, and the water was freezing, hot water not having come through yet. Shivering, he splashed cold water on his face and washed his hands and then hurried back to his own room, trying to decide whether it would be better to go back to bed, or to get up, get breakfast and do a little study before Senga was up and about. There was no school on a Saturday and she would probably demand that he take her skating on the frozen lakes in the park – and in all honesty he didn't want to disappoint her. There was little enough fun in her life; she had no friends, she rarely left the house and on the few occasions she did, it was never on her own and her only contacts were with her mother, the tutors, some of the servants and Patrick. Patrick couldn't help wondering what had occurred to make his mother so possessive of her children, so overly-protective to the point of obsession. He stood in front of the window, looking out across the snow-locked road and smiled wryly. He was twenty – well twenty this June – and he still hadn't walked out with a girlfriend, and yet his mother was moving in very exalted circles, where it should have been possible for him to meet the pick of the debutantes. When he had broached the subject – tentatively – he had been turned down with surprising sharpness. He could understand his mother – any mother – not wanting to lose their children, but she was carrying it too far.

Some day, he promised himself, he would discover the reasons for his mother's obsessions. When he had graduated, but before he had established a practice, he would return to Dublin and retrace his mother's steps. The answer to his questions lay in his mother's past, in Dublin.

Patrick dressed quickly, his teeth chattering in the chill air, and then hurried down to the kitchen. His mother would have disapproved, he knew, but at the moment it was the warmest, cosiest room in the house.

Patrick tapped softly on the kitchen door with the tips of his fingers and then turned the handle and poked his head in. 'Morning!'

Four of the eight servants in the Lundy household were seated around the scrubbed kitchen table, drinking tea, finishing their breakfast. Gerard the butler sat at the head of the table, facing Mrs James, the cook, while the two maids, Jane and Sarah, sat beside her. They all looked up, startled, and Gerard started to come to his feet.

'Stay where you are,' Patrick said quickly, stepping into the room. 'I've only popped down for a cup of tea.'

'I could bring it up to you, sir. The fire should be lit in the dining room,' the butler said stiffly.

'Not at all; it will still be freezing up there. I'll have it in here with you – if you don't mind that is,' he added quickly.

'Don't mind him, you sit down and warm yourself,' Mrs James said quickly, glaring at Gerard. The cook looked at one of the maids, 'Jane, will you fetch Master Patrick a cup and saucer please.'

Patrick thanked her and sat down facing the second maid, Sarah. Her eyes met his and she immediately dropped her gaze, colouring slightly. She and Jane were sisters, but while Jane was slender and dark, Sarah was broader, and lacked her younger sister's intense dark beauty.

Aware of the growing silence, Patrick looked at Mrs James as she poured the tea. 'I'm surprised to find you in so early.'

'Aaah, it's this party tonight, I want to make sure everything's ready.'

'I'm sure it will be,' Patrick said, smiling his thanks as she passed across the cup and saucer.

'You're up early yourself, sir,' Jane said softly, ignoring the butler's glare of disapproval.

'Oh, I've some studying to do, and I thought I'd get it in now while the house is still quiet.'

'And how are your studies coming along, sir?' Gerard asked, politely, although it was plain that he considered Patrick's presence in the kitchen as an intrusion. In the old days – the good good old days – a member of the family would never even consider entering the servants' quarters or the kitchens.

Patrick sipped his tea. 'Oh, they're coming along slowly. There seems to be so much to learn, so much to absorb. And there are new techniques being discovered every day – why, the Great War alone brought us many new methods of surgery and medicine.'

31

'And you'll make a grand doctor some day,' Mrs James said with a quick smile. She was aware of the butler's discomfort and enjoying it. She took a great deal of satisfaction in seeing the pompous old ass upset. He was a sour one, and no mistake …

'I think it will be a long time before I'm qualified,' Patrick said with a smile.

'Well, when you are you can treat my rheumatism. This damp weather kills me.'

'I could suggest some liniments …' Patrick said with a smile.

'You wait till you're qualified. You don't want to go practising on me!'

The two girls fell into a fit of giggling, more at the butler's outraged expression than anything else.

Patrick finished his tea. 'But we need bodies to practise on,' he grinned, 'we're always looking for volunteers.' He stood up, pushing away his empty cup. 'Thank you for the tea – and thank you for allowing me to join your table.'

'Do you want some breakfast … it's no trouble?' Mrs James asked.

'No, not yet, thank you. I'll wait until my sister or mother come down, and I'll eat with them. The tea was perfect – just what I needed. Thank you again.'

'It was our pleasure, sir,' Gerard said quickly.

I'm sure it was, Patrick grinned as he walked down the corridor and climbed the half-dozen steps from the servants' quarters up to the hall; he had seen the look on the butler's face, and knew how uncomfortable it had been for him. He toyed with the idea of reading in the drawing room, but he could hear one of the junior maids moving about in there and decided to go back up to his room instead. He was standing on the bottom stair when he heard footsteps coming up the back stairs from the kitchen and then Jane's large dark eyes peered through the banisters at him.

'You've quite scandalized Mr Gerard,' she whispered.

'And hasn't he little enough to worry about,' Patrick

32

smiled, the accent and phrase coming straight from his childhood.

'He's giving out to Mrs James for making so free with you.'

'I didn't realize she was making free with me,' Patrick grinned at the thought.

'He didn't think it was proper for her to tell you about her complaint.'

'Oh, her rheumatism. She should have let me prescribe for her; I know an excellent liniment ...'

'She's right,' the maid grinned, 'you are just looking for a body to practise on.'

'Well ...' He looked at her speculatively, wondering at the expression in her dark eyes and then said very slowly and carefully, 'Well ... it is true, we do need bodies to practise on ...'

Colour touched her cheeks but she looked him straight in the eyes and was just about to reply when the kitchen door opened and Gerard's solid footsteps sounded along the hall. Without a word, Jane turned and fled into the sitting room, leaving Patrick alone on the stairs, wondering what her reply might have been.

The first guests were due to arrive around eight, which actually meant that they would begin arriving anytime after nine. The house had been polished, checked, and then double-checked, first by Gerard and then later by Mrs Lundy herself. The large dining room which had been airing for the past week had passed its final inspection although Mrs Lundy had insisted that the maids cleaned the windows and French doors one more time.

Earlier that afternoon, Katherine had stood before the French doors and watched her son and daughter playing in the snow outside. She would lose Patrick soon, she suddenly thought – all that was keeping him with her now was because she kept a very tight control of the purse-strings: he had no money of his own. But he would be twenty next birthday, a young man certainly, but not mature – certainly not mature. Although he had been brought up in a brothel, Katherine had ensured that neither of her children knew the true function of the house, and while they might suspect where some of her money came from – especially Patrick – they were in no position to argue about it. That same money had given them everything they possessed, including their fine education. So, she would lose Patrick, first to medical school and then later to a practice – and she would ensure that it would be one of the finest in the city – and then she supposed there would be a wife and children ... and the intensity of her sudden anger surprised her.

She might not be able to keep her children forever – but she would try. They were all she had; everything else was transient – the money, the position, the power – but her children were tangible proof ... proof of what?

'Madam ...?'

Katherine turned, her eyes vacant.

'The musicians for tonight's entertainment,' Gerard said stiffly.

Katherine turned her back on the window – and immediately forgot about her children.

Patrick watched his mother walk away from the window and turned back to his sister. 'Senga, listen to me for a moment. I need your help,' he said slowly, putting the finishing touches to the snowman he was building for his sister. He glanced back up at the house, where warm orange light spilled out from the dining room into the grey afternoon.

Senga turned large adoring eyes on her brother. 'What do you want me to do?' she breathed, dropping her voice to a conspiratorial whisper. Patrick took his sister's hand and led her further down the garden, out of sight of the house, and then he squatted in the snow and stared into her deep, dark eyes. She would never be a great beauty, he knew, but she had a natural charm and personality that lent an extra depth to her character, and he imagined that this would have been how his mother would have looked

34

at a similar age. 'I need you to do something for me,' he said, his breath white on the bitter air.

'What?'

'I need to slip out tonight ...' he began.

'Where?'

'It doesn't matter where. I won't be long.'

'It's a girl, you're seeing a girl. What's her name, what's she like?'

'I'm not seeing a girl,' Patrick insisted with a grin, his sister was as eager to see him married off as his mother was against the idea. 'I just need to see some friends ... from college.'

Senga frowned. 'Why don't you ask Mama ...?'

Patrick shook his head. 'She won't let me go – you know that. No, I'll have to sneak out while she's tied up with the party. But listen, when we go in now, I'm going to say I'm not well and then I'll go up to bed. If you're asked, will you say that I was sneezing out here?'

'Well ...' Senga began doubtfully.

'Please?'

'Oh, all right, I suppose. But I hope you won't go getting yourself into trouble,' she added, and Patrick burst out laughing: the phrase and the accent were his mother's.

As Patrick and Senga strolled into the house a few moments later, Katherine suddenly heard her son sneeze explosively. Frowning slightly, she hurried across the highly polished floor back into the dining room, and was in time to see Patrick sneeze again and then again. He was fumbling for a handkerchief as she hurried up.

'Patrick's not well, Mama,' Senga said immediately. 'He's got a cold.'

Katherine looked at her son's streaming eyes and nodded. 'To bed,' she said decisively, 'I'll have some tea sent up in a little while.'

'Mother ...' Patrick protested ineffectually, bringing up his handkerchief again to hide his smile.

'Bed!' she insisted, 'I don't want you falling ill and missing classes.'

'Yes, Mother,' Patrick said, and sneezed.

Senga took her brother's hand and led him out into the hall. 'How did you do that?' she hissed, as they climbed the stairs to his room.

'Do what?'

'Sneeze.'

Patrick winked. 'Snuff,' he grinned.

Katherine came to visit Patrick a little later. She found him sitting up in bed, a score of his medical texts and notes scattered across the heavy coverlet. The fire had been lit in the bedroom, and Senga was sitting curled up in the rocking chair beside the fire quietly reading aloud from the latest issue of the 'Girls Own Paper.'

'Senga – you shouldn't be disturbing your brother. He should be resting.'

'I'm fine mother,' Patrick said, pitching his voice low and adopting a nasal twang.

'Yes, I'm sure you are,' Katherine said slowly, something about the expression in her son's eyes or the way her daughter lifted her paper a little higher to hide her face, making her suspicious. She crossed to Patrick's bed and rested her hand on his forehead; it felt hot and his cheeks were certainly flushed – but perhaps that might be nothing more than the heat in the room. Dismissing her fears – her whole life seemed to be ruled by fears, both from within and without – she bent her head and kissed Patrick's forehead briefly. 'Now, you must rest. Tea will be up shortly, and then I want you to try and get some sleep. Hopefully, the noise from below won't disturb you too much.'

'I'm sure it won't, Mother.'

Katherine looked at her daughter. 'Senga, now you run along ...'

'Can I come down tonight?' Senga asked hopefully.

'No, I'm afraid you cannot. You can watch the guests arriving from the window, if you wish. But that's all; I want you in bed early.'

'Mama!' Senga said in exasperation.

36

'Senga!' Katherine said warningly.

The young girl lapsed into sulky silence.

'Now, run along to your own room. I'll see you in the morning' she added, looking back at her son.

'Good-night Mother, enjoy your party.'

Katherine smiled slightly, and then ushered Senga out of the room before her. She paused at the door before closing it. 'I want you to stay in bed Patrick, let's try and get rid of that cold before morning.'

'I'm sure it'll be gone by then,' Patrick mumbled, hiding a smile.

The fire had died down to a dull glow and Patrick was just beginning to doze off when there was a soft knock on the door, and it opened to admit Jane, the younger of the two maids, carrying a large tea tray.

'I heard you were unwell, Master Patrick. I'm sorry about that.'

'Its just a touch of a cold,' Patrick said, smothering a huge yawn. 'What time is it?'

'Just gone six.' The young woman put the tray down on the table beside the bed and began gathering up the books and papers off the bedspread. 'You looked very well this morning,' she added, glancing sidelong at him.

'I only sneezed a couple of times … but you know what mother is like,' Patrick said defensively.

'Yes, I know.'

Something in her voice made Patrick look up. 'What do you mean?' he asked quietly.

'Nothing … nothing, sir,' she said quickly, knowing she had said too much.

'Come on,' Patrick reached out and grabbed her hand. 'Tell me. I won't say anything.'

'I've seen the way she treats you, sir … like a child,' Jane blurted out. And then realizing he was still holding her hand, she gently disengaged it.

'She is a bit over-protective,' Patrick admitted.

'You shouldn't let her. Look at you – a few sneezes and she pops you into bed like a six year old.'

'Hold on now.' Patrick threw back the covers and

swung his legs out of bed. For some reason, he felt he had to explain himself to this dark-eyed, intense young woman. 'I didn't just let her send me to bed – I wanted to go to bed.'

'Oh … yes?' Jane said, looking him up and down. She handed him his dressing gown and then knelt to add some coal on the fire.

Patrick tied on his gown and sat down in the chair beside the fire. For a few moments he was content to look at the maid's face and the way the orange firelight lent it strength and mystery. She turned her head to look at him, her eyes twinkling red-gold with the firelight, a touch of a smile curling her lips.

'Look, the thing is, I want to go out tonight, but my mother wasn't likely to allow me …'

'Oh, seeing a girl, eh?'

'No, not a girl,' Patrick said in exasperation. 'There is a meeting of an organization my mother disapproves of.'

'It must be Irish then,' Jane said shrewdly.

'It is.'

'So you told her you were sick and now you're going to sneak out, hoping that you'll be back before the party is over.'

Patrick nodded. 'Exactly.'

'And I suppose you're going to slip out the kitchen door,' she continued, 'which you might be able to do if you time it right and both Mrs James and Mr Gerard are distracted – but how are you going to get back in?'

Patrick opened his mouth to reply and then closed it again. 'Ah!'

Jane nodded. 'Exactly. By the time you get back most of the staff will have retired; Mrs James will certainly have gone home, but Gerard will still be up until after the last guest has gone. And there's no way you're going to get past him.'

Patrick nodded glumly. 'You're right, of course. But I've got to go to this meeting …'

Jane smiled archly. She stood up, dusting off her

hands and stood before Patrick. She smiled down on him. 'What you need now is someone in the basement who might just leave a window open for you …'

Patrick suddenly smiled. Jane and her sister shared the basement rooms off the kitchen, unlike the other two maids whose rooms were at the top of the house. Playing along with the game, he asked, 'And do you know anyone who might be prepared to leave a window open …?'

'I might …'

'And would there be a payment involved do you think?'

'There might.' The speculative look in her eye was unmistakable.

Suddenly conscious of the pounding of his heart and the raw burning at the back of his throat, Patrick stood up. 'And what do you think that payment might be …?'

The maid stared into his eyes for a long moment and then suddenly turned away. 'Well, we will just have to wait and see, won't we?' She stopped by the door. 'Your tea's getting cold.'

'And the window?' he asked.

'It'll be open.'

The first guests began arriving just before nine. Patrick stood by his window, fully dressed, but still wearing his dressing gown, watching an elegantly dressed middle-aged couple alight from a gleaming Rolls Royce. Even as the car was pulling away, another was swinging in around the Green. Secure in the knowledge that his mother would be fully occupied for the rest of the evening and the butler would be busy introducing the guests, Patrick pulled off his dressing gown and slipped down the back stairs to the kitchen.

He stopped outside the kitchen door and carefully cracked it open a fraction – and looked straight into Jane's wide eyes. She moved her head fractionally and mouthed the word, 'No.' And then Patrick saw Mrs James moving behind her.

39

'Do you not think it's very hot in here?' the maid suddenly asked the cook.

'It is a bit; will you open the back door for a few minutes and let in a breath of air?'

Jane flashed a grin at Patrick and turned away to open the door. A gust of cool air swept through the kitchen, setting the steam swirling, drawing it out the door.

'That's better. Now, I need some butter,' Mrs James said, and passed behind Jane again, heading for the larder.

Jane nodded quickly and Patrick immediately dashed through the kitchen, squeezed Jane's shoulder as he passed, and was then out through the open door. When Mrs James returned moments later with a slab of yellow butter, Jane was just closing the door.

'It was getting chill,' she said. From where she was standing, she could just about make out the shape of Patrick's cap as he hurried down the back lane.

CHAPTER THREE

Patrick made his way to Joseph Hyde's digs in one of the backstreets almost directly behind the bookshop on Charing Cross Road. From the window of his room on the top floor of the tenement building, Joe could see down into old Mr Webbs' office at the rear of the shop, and the outline of scores of books were clearly visible piled up against the filthy windows.

Hyde's room was small and squalid, hot and stuffy in summer, cold and damp in winter. He had to share a bathroom with the four other tenants on the floor, and the room itself consisted of little more than a single bed pushed up against the wall to one side of the room, a wood-wormed wardrobe and a single gas ring for cooking. Although Joseph Hyde had occupied the room for nearly eight years, he had done nothing to personalize it. Patrick had once remarked that if Joe were to pack his bags and walk out, there would be nothing of him left behind, no hint, no trace. The small, stout man had smiled and said, 'That's the idea, my boy.'

Joseph had just stepped out of his room and was pulling the door closed when Patrick came panting up the stairs. Joe squinted short-sightedly at the shape in the dimness. 'It's you,' he said, automatically lowering his voice. 'I was beginning to think you weren't coming.'

'I had a few problems getting away.'

Joseph nodded; he knew what Katherine Lundy was like. He put the key back in the lock and opened the door, and then ushered Patrick through before him. He paused for a moment, checking the hall and stairs before stepping into the room and closing the door behind him. He locked it, and then turned on the light.

'You best hurry up, otherwise we'll be late. The

clothes are in the usual place,' he added.

Patrick opened the wardrobe and pulled out an old army kit bag. It held his 'disguise' – a limp, old round-necked sweater, and a pair of stained work trousers. There was an oily cap on the top shelf of the wardrobe and a pair of much worn and down at heel working boots under the bed. Patrick stripped off and changed quickly, trying to ignore Joseph Hyde's too intense stare; he had long suspected his friend's preferences for young men – although to be perfectly fair, he had never seen him in any company other than those who supported the Irish movement.

Patrick brought the jumper to his nose and then winced. 'Don't you ever wash this?'

'I never wear it,' Joseph remarked with a grin. He turned off the light and crossed to the window to stand and stare out across the back of the houses.

Patrick finished dressing in semi-darkness. 'Why do I have to wear this stuff?' he complained.

'You're the one who wanted your identity kept a secret,' Joe reminded him.

'Yes, I know. But I think this is taking it too far.'

Joseph smiled. 'Well, it's a bit late now. People are used to seeing Paddy Montgomery at these meetings; if Patrick Montgomery Lundy were suddenly to appear, questions would be asked. And you don't want that – do you?' He turned, the light from outside silhouetting his face, robbing it of all expression.

Patrick squirmed uncomfortably in the jumper and the trousers, which were at least two sizes too large for him – he felt as if they were going to fall down at any moment. He popped the cap onto his head and pulled the brim down over his eyes. 'I'm ready.'

Joseph moved away from the window. 'Now remember, keep those finely kept hands of yours in your pockets; I guarantee they'll be the softest hands in the place tonight – and that includes the women!'

The Queen Victoria was deep in the heart of dockland, a

quayside pub that catered mainly to the wharf trade. Its clientele was drawn from every part of the world, and the owner was a tiny German whom everyone called Fritz, although that wasn't his real name. He ran the pub with his wife, an Irish woman who was known as Mrs Nora, and whose reputation along the docks had been assured the day she had broken up a brawl between a huge Turk who had just knifed two men, and a dozen of the wounded men's shipmates. While the pub had been emptying of its customers, and Fritz had been cowering down behind the counter, Mrs Nora had grabbed a broom and, holding it in both hands like a bat, had waited until the Turk had turned to face her – and then cracked him across the forehead. He had gone down without a sound – and by the time he had woken up, his ship had been two days out into the Channel.

The Queen Victoria sold cloudy beer, bad gin and passable whisky, but the main source of its revenue – especially when the docks were quiet – came from the rent it received from its rooms. Although the Victoria was not an especially large establishment, it backed onto an old warehouse that had at one time been split down the middle and then divided up into a series of small rooms that all opened onto a single long corridor. There were forty rooms in the warehouse, twenty on either side of the corridor and Fritz let the rooms to the street girls who worked the docks. If a boat was in, each room might see between eight and ten customers a night, and could earn him anywhere between ten shillings and a pound a night. The German's rates differed from girl to girl, and with some he had an arrangement that he received a commission rather than a rent per room; the advantage here for the girls was that they could pay him at the end of the night, rather than each time they used the room. And to ensure they didn't even think about cheating, he employed a 'caretaker' whose job was to keep a tally of the girls and their customers.

But Fritz wasn't too perturbed what his rooms were used for – so long as he was paid, and many factions and organizations, both political and criminal, operating in London used the Warehouse Hotel, as it was called, for their meetings. Amongst its advantages were a series of paid watchers who warned of approaching police, as well as numerous exits out into the warren of houses and warehouses that backed onto the Thames.

And in one of the these rooms at the rear of the long warehouse, the group of Irish sympathisers had gathered. Although the room was nearly twice the size of any of the other rooms, it was uncomfortably crowded with the dozen men packed into it.

As Joseph and Patrick squeezed in, nodding to the faces they recognized, Tom Rooney, the most senior of their group was finishing speaking.

'... who'll give us all the latest news from home ...'

A sharp-faced young man immediately stood up and looked, unsmiling, at the other men in the room, suspicion evident in his eyes. He stuck his hands in his belt pulling back his coat, allowing them all to see the butt of a revolver protruding from the inner pocket of his coat.

Patrick leaned forward and whispered to Joseph. 'Who's he?'

The bookseller shook his head slightly. 'Don't know, never seen him before. Cocky young pup though by the look of him.'

'Suspicious bastard too,' a tall bearded man beside Joseph murmured with a grin. 'Don't know whether he's showing us the gun because he's afraid of us, or so that we'll be afraid of him.'

The young man pulled forward the chair he had been sitting on and lifted one leg up on it. He then leaned forward, resting his right forearm on his raised leg.

'Reckon he took his time getting the pose right,' the bearded man added in a broad Cork accent, and the men standing around him laughed quietly.

'Brothers,' the young man said softly, 'I've news from home.' His voice was soft, the Dublin accent immediately evident, and Patrick immediately placed

44

him as coming from one of the city centre tenements – one of the great breeding grounds for revolutionaries. 'On Tuesday last, January 21st, we struck another blow for Irish freedom. But before I start, I should tell you that Mick Collins sends you all his regards and thanks you for your efforts on his – and our behalf.' There was a quick murmur of appreciation around the room, after the execution of Patrick Pearse and the other leaders of the Easter Rising of 1916, Michael Collins was the most active and charismatic of the leaders of the Cause.

The un-named young man smiled, showing broken, discoloured teeth. 'Aye, the Big Fellow is active again you'll be pleased to know; perhaps we might see some results soon. We'll certainly see some action.'

'What happened on Tuesday?' someone from the crowd asked impatiently.

The young man's eyes narrowed as he tried to identify the speaker. 'On Tuesday,' he said slowly and distinctly, 'seven men of the south Tipperary Brigade of the Irish Republican Army under the command of Seamus Robinson captured a consignment of gelignite ...'

'Hang on there a minute,' the bearded man beside Hyde said suddenly, 'what's this Irish Republican Army, eh?'

The young man straightened up and put his hands on his hips, staring at the man. 'And your name?' he demanded, his lip curling into a sneer.

The bearded man pushed his way through those in front of him until he was standing not more than six inches from the young gunman. 'I'm Dan Brady, and I've served the Cause both here and at home since before you were born ... so I'd take that look offen your face before I take it off for you.'

The young man's hand moved fractionally closer to the butt of his pistol.

Brady smiled, showing his teeth. 'And if you touch that gun, boy, I'll take it off you, and shove it down your throat.'

45

'Gentlemen ... gentlemen ...' Tom Rooney pushed his way between the two men. 'Gentlemen, we're all on the one side remember. Our enemies will divide us soon enough without us doing it for ourselves. Now Dan, why don't you calm down. This young man has come from Dublin to answer all our questions, and I had a letter from Mick Collins himself telling me that this young man would assist us in every way possible ...'

Patrick was watching the gunman's face when Tom Rooney had mentioned the Big Fellow's name, and was surprised to see the reaction it brought. The man either feared or greatly respected Michael Collins.

'I won't be threatened by a young pup ...' Dan Brady said belligerently.

'I'm sure there was no threat intended, now was there?' Rooney asked, looking at the younger man.

He shook his head slowly. 'No ... none intended I'm sure.'

Joseph Hyde tilted his head back and Patrick leaned forward to catch what he was saying. 'That's taken the wind out of his sails.'

'Now why don't you tell us about this Irish Republican Army,' Tom Rooney said to the gunman.

'It was decided to change the name of the loyal volunteers to the Irish Republican Army.'

'Why change the name?' Joseph called out.

'Because we're an army now, fighting for the cause.'

'We were always an army,' someone else shouted.

Tom Rooney raised his hand. 'We seem to be drifting away from the point here. Let's forget about the name for a moment, and perhaps we'll get to hear what happened last Tuesday.'

There was a general murmur of agreement.

'Tell us first,' Dan Brady called out, 'were you there, young man?'

After a moment's hesitation, the gunman answered. 'No, I was not: I'm not a member of the South Tipperary Brigade, but I heard the details from one of the lads there, and they've since been confirmed by the

Big Fellow himself.' He brought his leg back up onto the chair and resumed his original pose. 'There was a shipment of gelignite heading into the quarry at Solo-headbeg, and the Brigade had orders to capture it ...'

'Orders from whom?' Rooney asked.

The young man looked puzzled. 'Dublin, I suppose.'

The old man shook his head. 'They deny it. But go on ...'

'There's little enough to tell. The boys captured the gelignite ...' His small dark eyes darted around the smoke-filled room, looking for a friendly face, but they were all closed and impassive. There were no youthful revolutionaries, they were all, in the main, mature men – some of whom had fought in '16 – and all of whom had advanced the Irish cause either with funds or arms down through the years. 'And there were two of the constabulary shot in the process,' he finished quickly.

'How many guards ...' someone asked.

'Just the two ...'

Patrick stifled a yawn. He desperately wished he could glance at his watch, but knew he couldn't risk it; it was late ... it must be sometime around ten. And he was going to stink of smoke.

He would change back at Joseph's digs, but the smoke would linger in his hair and on his skin. He would have to bathe early tomorrow morning – before his mother was up, but that shouldn't be too difficult. With luck, she should – if she followed her usual pattern – remain in bed until around noon. He only hoped Jane had remembered to leave the window open – otherwise he was rightly stuck. He had no key to the house; he had asked his mother for one, but she had said it wasn't necessary – there would always be someone there to let him in. He wondered what he would do if he couldn't get into the house ... well, he supposed he could go back to Joseph's place, spend the night there and then hurry home at first light, when the servants would be up. But then there was every possibility that his mother would get to hear of it, and he didn't want that ...

47

There was the sudden sound of clapping, and Patrick automatically joined in, abruptly realizing that the meeting was over.

The men began moving restlessly when the young gunman raised his hand. 'One final thing,' he said loudly, 'the Big Fellow needs people like you; loyal, committed people ... so if any of you feel like joining us, you'd be very welcome.' He looked from face to face, but no one said anything. Most of the men there had families or commitments in England, and while they would support the Irish cause in word and sometimes in deed, no-one ever seriously considered leaving everything to go and fight for the cause. They had already done their bit. 'Aye ... well, if any of you change your mind, you can contact me through Tom here.'

There was a gradual movement towards the door and Patrick allowed himself to be carried with it. Joseph Hyde tugged at his sleeve. 'Well, what did you think?'

'Yes ... interesting, very interesting,' Patrick said, his voice carefully neutral.

Joe looked scornful. 'Two policemen – Irish policemen too – dead, and killed on the same day as the first sitting of the new Irish parliamentarians. You can't tell me that was accidental. It does our cause no credit.'

Patrick smiled and shook his head. 'No, I suppose not.' He was only half listening to the bookseller. His eyes were on the numerous doors lining the corridor, and he couldn't help wondering what went on behind those doors. Occasionally, he caught a snatch of sound – a moan, a groan, the creak of springs – which fired his curiosity even further. Although he had a reasonably good idea of what went on between men and women, so far he had never even kissed a girl.

There was a small queue at the rear exit as the men waited to slip away into the night. Tom Rooney was standing by the door with his pocket-watch in his hand, allowing his men out in regular intervals. It was raining outside and the gusts of cold, damp air were refreshing after the stale smokiness of the room. Joseph and Patrick joined the end of the queue and patiently waited their turn. 'What time is it Tom?' Patrick asked as they drew level with the old man.

'Half ten son; why, are you in a hurry somewhere? Off to meet a girl, I shouldn't wonder, eh?' Tom Rooney knew Patrick Montgomery's identity; like Joseph Hyde he had also known the Madam in Dublin and was all too aware of her reputation.

'Something like that,' Patrick grinned. Half ten! Well, he would be home in an hour; the dinner party would be in full swing and if his luck had held he wouldn't even have been missed. He didn't want to think of what would happen if his mother discovered that he had been out of the house.

Katherine Lundy closed the door to her son's room. Her face was set in grim lines and beneath her make up, she was white with rage, her lips drawn in a thin line. On impulse she hurried down the corridor to her daughter's room and carefully opened the door a fraction. A long sliver of light fell across Senga's bed, sparkling off lustrous black hair. Senga slept curled up in a ball, her long-fingered hand splayed across her cheek. Suddenly conscious that she had been holding her breath, Katherine pulled the door closed and then leaned back against the wall, aware of the pounding of her heart. Her one great fear had always been that she would lose her children – they were too precious to her, they had cost too much to lose now.

But Patrick had deceived her – and that was unforgivable. Katherine Lundy operated in a world where deceit was accepted – indeed, expected, and she survived in this world because she herself had learned her lessons in one of the toughest schools of all – in the fire and revolution of Dublin before the '16 Rising. But she expected – she demanded – complete honesty from her children.

Coming to a decision, she turned and hurried down

the stairs. Below, a door opened and there was a brief swell in the volume of conversation and laughter as Gerard stepped out into the hall. He stopped when he saw Katherine sweeping down the stairs. 'Ma'am – is everything in order?'

'Yes – everything. Why do you ask?' she demanded suspiciously.

'You look a little pale, Ma'am,' the butler said quickly.

'A touch of a headache.' She stopped on the bottom stair and pressed taut fingers to her throbbing temples. 'Who locks up at night, Gerard?'

'Why, I do of course.'

'I want you to make doubly sure everything is locked and secure tonight.'

'I always do,' Gerard said, sounding slightly affronted.

Katherine recognized the tone and smiled placatingly. 'I'm not doubting you, but the thought struck me that a gathering of this type might attract some unwarranted attention, and perhaps encourage unwanted visitors.'

Gerard bowed slightly. 'Of course, Ma'am.'

'Now,' she continued changing the subject, 'is Mr Lee still inside?'

'He is, Ma'am; I passed him a moment ago and he was talking to Mr Churchill.'

'Would you be so good as to ask Mr Lee to step out here please. I have a few words for his ears alone.'

The butler nodded and stepped back into the grand dining room, only to reappear almost immediately with the tall, thin figure of Michael Lee following him, his face impassive.

'That will be all Gerard,' Katherine said immediately, 'you may return to your duties.' The butler nodded and was about to turn away, when Katherine added, 'Oh, and Gerard, ensure that we are not disturbed. We will be in the sitting room.'

'Of course, Ma'am.' Although the butler's face registered nothing, his eyes flickered from Lee to

Katherine and back to Lee. He would gladly have given a year's salary just to know what exactly was the relationship between these two.

The sitting room was dark, and the fire that had blazed earlier had died down to grey-ashed coals. The only light in the room came from the street lamps which vaguely illuminated one corner of the room but left the rest in shadow. Without turning up the light Katherine crossed to stand beside the window, leaving Michael Lee to close the door and move gingerly into the centre of the room. He made out the high-backed chair to one side of the fire and sank into it, sitting tall and erect, careful not to crease his dinnerjacket.

'Patrick has disappeared,' Katherine said without preamble, glancing around, barely able to make out the seated figure of the man beside the fire.

'What do you mean, disappeared?' Lee asked, taken aback.

'He went to bed earlier today because he had a cold coming on – or so he said. When I went up to check on him a few minutes ago, his bed was empty and cold; it hadn't been slept in. His clothes and wallet are also missing.'

'His keys?'

'He has no keys,' Katherine said shortly.

'Have you any idea where he might have gone?' Michael Lee asked softly. He found it difficult to have any sympathy for Katherine Lundy in this instance; this situation was entirely of her own creation.

'He's obviously gone some place he knows I would disapprove of – which probably means something involving the Irish sympathisers ...' Katherine turned back to the window. 'I want you to find out where he went, who was there and what they discussed.'

'I don't think ...' Lee began, coming to his feet.

'And I want to know by morning.' She turned back and faced her manager. 'By morning, I want to be able to tell my son where he was. I want him to know how futile it is for him to try and escape my influence ...'

'I think you're making a mistake; I think you'll probably lose him …'

'I don't give a damn what you think!' the woman snapped. 'You're paid to do as I say.' Her voice dropped, turning low and vicious, and not for the first time, Michael Lee realized how cold and calculating, how vicious and cunning she was. 'I want that information by mid-morning.'

'I will attend to it myself.'

'Do that!' The woman brushed past Lee, leaving the essence of expensive scent and the faintest hint of perspiration on the air. He was almost surprised to find no trace of alcohol. Lee rubbed his long-fingered hands together; he wondered where to start. Start with Patrick. Now just whom did he know in the Irish organizations? The bookseller Patrick Lundy associated with, he had strong Irish connections, hadn't he? Now what was his name …?

It was close to midnight by the time Patrick reached the house in Mayfair. He had been delayed by Joseph Hyde who had wanted to discuss the night's events again and again, working out possible and probable courses of action; from experience, Patrick knew the stout bookseller would do nothing.

He had left as soon as he could, leaving Joe to consume half a bottle of whisky while he raced through the backstreets, slowing to a walk only when he spotted someone approaching. He was propositioned twice by ragged and wretched young women in the alleyways and a drunk rising up from a pile of papers frightened him into shouting aloud.

He was delighted to find the house still a blaze of light: that meant the party was still in full swing, which meant that Gerard would be busy … and that meant that he should be able to creep in through the kitchen door. He moved around to the back of the house, and then ducked into the laneway that ran behind it. Taking a deep breath, he then walked slowly and sedately down one side of the lane, keeping to the shadows, praying that none of the neightbours would report a suspicious man creeping along the back of the houses. He paused at the wooden gate to his mother's house, squinting against the glare thrown out from the uncurtained kitchen window. The kitchen seemed to be empty. Holding his breath, Patrick lifted the gate slightly to prevent it scraping along the ground and then pushed it open.

A shadow crossed the kitchen and he froze, recognizing Gerard. The man reappeared, picked up something and then moved from sight again. Patrick guessed he was bringing a tray into the sitting room, which gave him a few moments. Bent almost double, he darted towards the kitchen, pressing himself against the wall. His heart was throbbing painfully, and he was controlling his breathing with the greatest of difficulty ... but he also realized that he was enjoying it. When he finally reached the house, he risked a quick look inside. The room was empty. Bending double, he ducked beneath the window and was moving towards the door ... when a long man-shaped shadow moved across the bar of light thrown out onto the paved pathway. Gerard had returned.

Moving as quietly as possible on the gravel, Patrick moved away from the kitchen, and then continued on until he came level with the basement windows. He wondered if Jane had remembered her promise; if she hadn't, he was in serious trouble. Treading carefully so as not to walk in the flower beds that were almost directly beneath the window, Patrick pressed two fingers against the glass, just over the lock and pushed ... and the window opened. Breathing a sign of absolute relief, Patrick Lundy scrambled inside ...

And a hand touched his arm!

'Jesus Ch ...!'

'Sssshh, it's me.' The voice was soft and feminine, coming from the shadows directly in front of him.

'Jesus, but you frightened the life out of me,' Patrick

whispered hoarsely, climbing down off the window ledge.

'Sign of a guilty conscience,' Jane giggled.

Now that his eyes had adjusted to the light, Patrick could just about make out the vague shape of the young woman before him, her face a dim grey against the paler shape of her nightdress.

'Thanks for leaving the window open. Have you been waiting long?' he asked then.

'Not long.'

'Where's Sarah?'

Teeth flashed in the gloom. 'Oh, it was agreed earlier that Mr Gerard would only need one of us to assist after the coffee was served, so I pretended to have a headache.'

Patrick manoeuvred around the bed which, along with a wardrobe and a chest of drawers were the only pieces of furniture in the room. 'Look, thanks again for helping me, I really do appreciate it.'

'Your mother called Mr Lee out of the party and spoke to him privately in the sitting room,' Jane said suddenly.

Puzzled, the young man stopped, not sure what the girl meant, but a vague uneasiness settled into the pit of his stomach.

'I overheard Gerard tell Mrs James that she had come down stairs with a "face fit to murder",' Jane continued, doing a passable imitation of the butler. 'Then she sent him in to get Mr Lee and they spent about five minutes in the sitting room.'

'Do you think she knows I wasn't upstairs …?'

'I don't know, but you better have some story ready just in case.'

'There's no story going to get me out of this one.'

'You could of course just tell her the truth,' Jane suggested. She took a step closer to Patrick and laid her hand on his arm. 'She'll be angry, but she won't want to lose you. She won't do anything rash.'

Patrick shook his head, not quite so sure.

Jane squeezed his arm, and the young man abruptly – shockingly – realized just how close she was to him. He could feel the heat from her body and he was quite sure that, beneath the long cotton nightdress, she was naked.

'This could be the opportunity you've been waiting for,' she said slowly, her eyes black shadows in her face. Her lips curled in a smile, and Patrick wondered if she knew what effect she was having on him – and then realized that she probably did. 'You could invent an argument with her – and have a huge blazing row – and then you could demand your freedom.'

Patrick nodded, although he wasn't really listening. Jane had now taken hold of both his elbows and was gripping them tightly as she stared into his face.

'You can't stay tied to her forever,' she insisted.

Patrick nodded.

And then she kissed him. There was a moment's shocked resistance and then he melted against her, his arms curling around her back, feeling her flesh soft and warm beneath the thin cotton. Her fingers slid into his hair pulling his face close to hers, and her tongue and lips moved against his.

And then she abruptly pulled away and held him at arms' length. 'There's a lot to be said for being free,' she panted. She twisted away from him and backed over to the door, and then cracked it open, and peered out into the hall. 'All's clear,' she whispered.

Patrick suddenly fround himself standing in the hallway, his heart tripping frantically, his breathing too fast to be comfortable. Still in a daze, he made his way to his bedroom.

When Katherine Lundy opened her son's bedroom door less than an hour later, the bar of light fell across the sprawled figure of Patrick, the sheets rumpled and curled around him. She smiled grimly, let him sleep, let him get all the rest he could – he was going to need it.

'Joseph … Joseph … open up …'

Joseph Hyde opened his eyes, blinking rapidly until

he realized that the room was in darkness and the lighter grey square to his left was the window. Gradually, he reassembled the room and added the events of the previous night. He was sitting propped up against the end of the bed with his back to the wall, still fully dressed. He had come back from the meeting with Patrick, and he had opened a bottle of whisky ... automatically his hand reached for it, found it between his legs, and he was raising it to his lips when the hurried knocking shook the door again.

'Joseph ... Joseph ... open up.'

His mouth worked, but nothing happened, and he took a quick swig of whisky. 'Who ...?' he croaked.

'Patrick,' the urgent whisper came back.

Joseph eased himself off the bed, and staggered across to the door. His head was pounding and he vaguely wondered what time it was, and as he began to unlock the door he wondered what had brought Patrick back.

'For Christ's sake, what's wrong ...?' he demanded.

The blunt end of a pickaxe handle smashed into his stomach, sending him reeling backwards, choking and gasping. He hit the edge of the bed and slid to the floor, holding his stomach, desperately resisting the urge to vomit.

There were three of them, two were large, well-built men, obviously nothing more than the muscle, while the third man, tall and thin, was the boss. Through a haze of pain, Joseph Hyde wondered who the hell they were, British or Irish?

A hand wrapped itself into his collar and hauled him to his feet, and then his arms were pinned behind his back in what felt like two huge fists. The second thug was standing to his left, holding the long pickaxe handle in his right hand, tapping it against his left palm. The blunt end of the club suddenly came up and pressed against his cheek, and then moved around to rest against his teeth. Without a word being spoken, the message was plain.

The third man spoke then; his accent was wharfside

London with a touch of something else, some unidentifiable accent. 'Now, Mr Hyde, I will ask you certain questions, and you will answer them. You will do so quietly and clearly, and you will tell me the truth. Lie to me, and the gentleman behind you will probably break your fingers one by one, and very possibly the gentleman with the club will take a certain delight in knocking out your teeth.' He paused, and his own teeth flashed in the gloom. 'Do your understand me?'

'You can go to hell!' Joseph spat.

The club struck him in the stomach again, dropping him to his knees, and there was a sudden crack that seemed unnaturally loud in the silence. It took a moment, while he fought the fire in his stomach and throat to realize that his left hand was completely numb. He couldn't feel his fingers.

'You really don't have much use for a little finger anyway,' the thin man said. 'Now, every time you lie to me, or prove difficult, we're going to break a finger, and then next time you'll lose a tooth – I promise you. Do you understand me?'

Iron-hard fingers dug into Joseph's thinning hair and pulled his head back until he was forced to look at the soft spoken man. He nodded briefly.

'Good. Now, was there an Irish political meeting tonight?'

Joseph nodded.

'Where ... where?' the man repeated, his voice dropping ominously when Joseph remained silent. From the corner of his eye the stout grey-haired man saw the thug shift his grip on the club.

'The Warehouse Hotel,' Joe muttered, using the common name deliberately.

'At the back of the Queen Vic?' the man asked immediately.

Joseph nodded.

'And what was discussed?'

Joseph started to shake his head – when the club struck him full in the mouth. His two front teeth shattered, and he choked on a sudden spurt of blood. He was suddenly kicked in the groin, and as he struggled against the excruciating pain, the thin man put the question again. 'And what was discussed?'

Joseph spat and spluttered blood. He had lost the two centre top teeth, and with the tip of his tongue he could feel that the two on either side were also loose. 'The ... the Irish situation,' he lisped, his tongue huge in his mouth. 'The killings last week at So ... So ... So-lo-head-beg,' he said the last word slowly, his tongue constantly finding the gap between the teeth. They were British Intelligence, he decided, Scotland Yard detectives investigating the Irish Brotherhood.

'Who was there?'

'I don't know all the names. Security reasons,' he gasped.

'Was Patrick Lundy there tonight?'

And in that moment, Joseph suddenly knew who the three men were; only Katherine Lundy's men would be enquiring after Patrick. He didn't know the thugs' identities, but he guessed that the tall thin man was Michael Lee.

'I asked you a question,' Lee – if it was Lee, and he was convinced it was – said softly.

Eventually, reluctantly, Joseph Hyde nodded.

There was another flash of a grin. 'Good; now we're getting somewhere.'

A sudden thought struck Katherine Lundy and she suddenly sat up in bed. How had Patrick managed to creep back into the house? Gerard and Sarah the maid were in the kitchen, the hall door was locked, and besides, Patrick had no key. But how had he got in? He had help certainly – well, God help them, whoever they were!

CHAPTER FOUR

Patrick awoke again as the church bells all across London were tolling noon. He lay in bed, surprised that he had remained undisturbed for so long. He remembered coming awake some time earlier, when the hall door had slammed and high heels had clicked down the steps, passing beneath his window. He had guessed then that it was his mother – with Senga in tow – heading off to ten o'clock Mass in the nearby church.

Patrick turned over in the bed, and discovered that there was a fire burning in the grate and a breakfast tray on the small side-table beside the bed. He reached out and pressed his fingertips against the teapot. It was cold. Wondering why he hadn't been awakened for his breakfast, he contemplated snuggling down beneath the covers for another few moments when he heard the door bell ring. Moments later he heard his mother's voice, and then quick footsteps tapped up the stairs. There was a scratching on the door and a small bonneted head peered around.

'You're awake,' Senga stepped into the room, closing the door with her heel. 'I looked in earlier but you were asleep.'

Patrick sat up in bed, and ran his fingers through his wild hair. 'I hate sleeping in so late,' he mumbled. 'How's mother?' he asked. He needed a bath and quickly, he imagined he could smell smoke and the sour stench of sweat from his skin.

Senga pulled off her bonnet, and tossed it on to the chair beside the fire. 'I don't know,' she said slowly, 'she's in a strange humour.' She actually had a fairly good idea of what was wrong with her mother, but was wondering how to approach Patrick, without alarming him ... although in this case, it was probably better to alarm him.

'She's probably just tired after the party ...' Patrick suggested.

Senga went to stand before the window. Looking out over the snow-covered park, she could still see her brother's reflection in the glass. 'Mr Lee met her outside the church,' she said slowly.

Patrick turned to look at his sister. 'And ...?' he asked eventually.

'They talked for a few moments, and then he handed her an envelope and walked away. She didn't speak a single word to me all the way back here, and she's in foul form downstairs at the moment. She's just snapped at both Gerard and Sarah for no real reason.'

'What did Lee say to her?'

Senga shook her head. 'I don't know. She asked me to stand by the gate while she spoke to him.'

Patrick rubbed his sweating palms on the blanket. 'Do you think she knows?'

'Well ... something's put her in bad form ...' Senga said very slowly. 'I'm just saying this to you so that you can be prepared.' She turned to look at him, her oval face pale and serious. 'What will you tell her if she knows?'

He shook his head and shrugged. 'If she knows, then there's nothing I can tell her, but the truth,' he said lightly, desperately hoping it wouldn't come to that.

Katherine sat in her chair at the head of the table in the dining room. She was still wearing her Sunday clothes, black coat over a long dress, with matching gloves, hat and bag; every Sunday she remembered those dear to her who had died – every Sunday she mourned. At the moment, the gloves and hat were placed side by side on the gleaming wood of the table before her and her hands were folded in an attitude of prayer – although her humour was anything but reverent.

60

Standing in a row down the left hand side of the table were Gerard, Mrs James, Jane and Sarah, the maids, only the two skivvies had been excluded.

None of them – except possibly Mrs James, the cook – looked comfortable, Katherine mused. Even Gerard, whom she probably suspected the least, looked as if he had something to hide.

'I have asked you here,' she began without preamble, 'because something has happened which has caused me deep hurt. My trust has been betrayed,' she said dramatically, watching their faces intently, looking for a reaction.

Gerard coughed discreetly. 'May I ask in what way, Ma'am?'

'Someone here has gone against my will, has connived with someone else to deceive me. Now, they know who they are, and I would like them to come forward and admit their guilt.'

Gerard frowned. 'Perhaps if you could be more specific ...' he suggested.

'No!' Katherine snapped, her eyes beginning to glitter dangerously. 'No, I will not be more specific. But what I will say,' she added, her voice falling to little more than a whisper, 'is that if that person does not step forward, it will go badly for all of you. Is that understood?' she snapped.

No one moved; no one said anything.

'Fine.' Katherine looked at each face in turn. 'Well now, I want you to go away and think about this very carefully. If I do not know the identity of the person who assisted ... who deceived me ... by the dinner bell tonight, well, then you're all dismissed – without references.'

'I must protest ...' Gerard began.

'I don't give a damn what you do!' Katherine hissed. 'But if I don't have that name you'll walk the streets too – and you know how difficult it will be to find another position without references.'

'Impossible,' Gerard admitted.
'Exactly.'

Katherine was waiting for Patrick when he eventually plucked up enough courage to come downstairs. His mood throughout the early afternoon had swung sharply between apprehension of the inevitable scene and a certain amount of self-disgust at his fear of his mother – after all, he was twenty.

Surprisingly, no Sunday lunch was brought up to him, nor was there any tea, and it was only around three in the afternoon that he realized he had had no visitors since noon. He dressed quickly, all the time arguing fiercely with himself, working out possible conversations with his mother, and what he would say to her, the devastating arguments he would present ... and all the time he knew that she would say her piece and he would agree. And he hated himself for it.

He found his mother and sister in the family sitting room, both silent and seemingly absorbed in their own tasks. His mother was leafing through a huge pile of correspondence, the wire-framed spectacles perched on the end of her nose threatening to fall off at any moment, while Senga sat beneath the window, copying verses from an open Bible.

They both looked up as he came quietly into the room, and he knew – immediately and instinctively – that his mother knew everything. His sister's face was pinched, her eyes large and dark against the paleness of her skin, and she looked for all the world like some sort of trapped animal. His mother's expression was cold, her expression set, her lips pursed. Without saying a word she began to gather up her pieces of paper.

Patrick hovered around the door for a few moments and then finally decided to brazen it out. Taking a deep breath, he walked slowly across the room and sat down in the easy chair directly facing his mother.

'You are recovered,' she said eventually.

'I am much better thank you.'

'A remarkable recovery,' Katherine said softly, removing her spectacles.

Patrick nodded, unsure what to say.

In the long silence that followed, the solemn ticking of the clock seemed very loud indeed. Patrick squirmed beneath his mother's scrutiny, her gaze was direct and unblinking – like a snake, he realized, and he wondered where she had perfected that trait. He dropped his gaze and concentrated on his hands, examining his clean and perfect nails. He could sense the gathering storm in the room, and knew it was only a matter of time ...

Fully ten minutes went by before Katherine spoke. When she did, her voice was soft, but tightly controlled, the words clipped, and it was obvious that she was holding her temper in check with the greatest difficulty.

'Perhaps it is time for a little truth. A little honesty. Would you care to tell me about your sudden cold, Patrick? Would you like to tell me where you went last night? What you did? And while you're at it, would you like to tell me who let you back into the house?'

'Mother, I don't ...' Patrick began.

'And don't even think about lying to me,' Katherine whispered, her voice sending a chill through him. 'You two are my children,' she continued, her voice abruptly returning to normal, 'you are all I have, the only things that are truly mine. I will give you everything – everything you want and need, everything I never had – but in return I want, I demand, perhaps not your love, but certainly your respect. And with that respect, your honesty.' She looked from Patrick to Senga. 'Do you understand me?'

'Yes, Mother.'

'Yes, Mama.'

Katherine turned back to Patrick. 'Now the truth.'

He started to shake his head. 'There's really nothing ...'

Katherine's expression turned stark, her face hardening to a mask. 'Well then, let me tell you,' she hissed. 'Let me tell you what you did, and whom you saw.'

'Mother ...'

'Be quiet,' she snapped. With the forefinger of her left hand, she slid out a single sheet of paper from the pile at her side. Holding her glasses before her face she glanced down at it. 'It seems you went to see your friend Joseph Hyde first,' she said softly, very softly, 'and then, having changed your clothes, you accompanied him to a public house called the Queen Victoria where you attended a secret meeting of the Irish Republican Brotherhood, of which apparently, you have been a member for some two years.'

'Since I was eighteen,' Patrick said defiantly.

Katherine ignored him.

'Following the meeting, you returned with Hyde to his rooms where you changed back into your clothing ...' She stopped as a sudden thought struck her and she looked up, removing her glasses. 'Are you homosexual?'

Shocked, surprised, Patrick shook his head. 'No.'

'But your friend Hyde is; you do know his preference is for young men?' she asked with a sly smile.

'I know,' Patrick said defiantly, realizing what she was trying to do, 'I've known that for a long time.'

Katherine glanced at her notes again. 'It seems you returned here sometime around eleven or so ... and someone let you into the house.' Katherine looked up and removed her glasses again. 'And I would like to know who let you in.'

'I want to know where you got all that information,' Patrick demanded.

'It doesn't matter.'

'It matters to me. I want to know why you're having me watched, why you need to know every move I make, why you must have control over everything I do.'

'I am your mother,' Katherine said simply.

'That's not good enough,' Patrick snapped, surging to his feet.

'Sit down! Just remember who you are and who you

are talking to. You may lie to me, deceive me in my own house, turn the servants against me, but you will not shout at me!'

Patrick subsided into his seat, thoroughly alarmed now at the expression on his mother's face. It was hard and set, her jaw clamped shut, the muscles rigid, her eyes staring.

'Now, I don't want to know what was discussed at the meeting; if I did I could find that out easily enough. But I am forbidding you ever to attend another of those meetings. Is that understood – you will stay away from these Irish organizations.'

'My father was a member of the same organization,' Patrick said defiantly.

'And he's dead now – thanks to the same organization,' Katherine said, bitterness like bile in her throat.

'But at least he died for what he believed in!'

'No … no he did not,' Katherine said, her voice falling to a hoarse whisper. She opened her mouth, as if she were going to say more, but then closed it again. 'You will not see Hyde again. You will not attend any more meetings of the Irish Republican Brotherhood. Is that understood?' she snapped.

'I hear you.'

'But are you listening to me?' Katherine hissed. 'Stay away from Hyde, stay away from IRB.' And this time the threat in her voice was quite implicit. Katherine shuffled her papers together and turned away. Patrick took the opportunity to stand up. 'There are two more things,' his mother said very softly, her voice almost gentle. 'You will never again leave the house without my permission … and I want to know who let you back in last night.' She looked up quickly. 'Now, I don't expect an answer just now, but if I don't know by dinner tonight, I am dismissing the entire staff without references. I will do so in your presence of course,' she added. 'You may leave.'

Moments later, Patrick Lundy slammed the hall door

shut and hurried down the path, and Katherine, speechless with rage, could only watch him race down the street, still pulling on his coat. That boy needed a lesson – well, perhaps it was time he got one.

Although he partially guessed that Joe Hyde would not be in the shop, Patrick stopped long enough to check the window. When Joe was in the shop, the first thing he did every morning was to place a copy of *Irish Fairy Tales*, by W.B. Yeats, in a corner of the window; when he left in the evening or for lunch, the book was removed. It was a simple code whereby his friends were able to determine his presence without attracting attention to themselves by actually going into the shop. There was no book in the window today.

Patrick's next impulse was to race around to Hyde's digs, but something like caution held him back. His mother must have had him watched last night; perhaps he was still being followed. Automatically he glanced over his shoulder – and was startled to discover two bulky men in long overcoats standing some distance away – both very obviously watching him. Startled, and by now more than a little frightened, Patrick headed for Foyles, hoping to lose his followers in the bookshop's maze of nooks and corners. It was only when he reached the closed doors that he remembered that it was Sunday. And that of course also accounted for the fact that there was no book in Webbs' window. He was so scared that he wasn't even thinking straight. He glanced over his shoulder again, and discovered that the two men were nowhere to be seen – it had been nothing more than his imagination. Shaking his head in annoyance, Patrick strolled down the street and turned to the left, heading up towards Joe's digs. He was whistling tunelessly, annoyed that he had allowed his mother to so unnerve him. He would be seeing shadows around every corner next.

Behind him, two men in long overcoats stepped out from the shadow of a doorway and watched the young man turn to the left again, heading up the main backstreet that led to Joseph Hyde's flat.

The door was ajar and Patrick could see movement inside the room. He stopped on the stairs, all his old fears returning, feeling his heart beginning to pound. In all the time he had known Joe, he had never seen anyone else in his room; indeed he had never seen him in company, except at the meetings of the IRB. His immediate reaction was to turn and walk away, but to date, his life had been spent turning and walking away, allowing his mother to have her own way, to do things her way. Taking a deep breath he moved up a step. He could hear voices from within the room now, three – possibly four – accents, and they all sounded either Irish or Dublin. Stepping up onto the landing, he was about to walk over to the door when a large hand dropped onto his shoulder.

'Christ!'

'There's no need for that.' The voice from behind him was Irish – a broad flat Dublin accent – that Patrick thought sounded vaguely familiar. 'Now, what're you doing here, eh?'

'I'm a friend of Joe's,' Patrick began, without turning around.

'Oh.' The grunt was expressive, and Patrick immediately knew what sort of friend the man thought him to be. The hand tightened on his shoulder, the stubby fingers biting into the muscle. 'Well, now, Mr Hyde isn't receiving any visitors today; come back another time.'

'I've got to see him ...'

'And I said no!'

The door to Joe's room swung open and a man stepped out into the landing. 'What's going on here?' he demanded. His accent was soft, but also Irish.

'One of Joe's friends,' the Dubliner behind Patrick grunted derisively, 'looks like he'll have to fall downstairs.'

'Take it easy,' the newcomer advised. He stepped

forward and Patrick suddenly recognized him. 'Tom ... Tom Rooney? It's me, Pat, Patrick Montgomery.'

The old man stopped in surprise and then craned forward, squinting in the dim light coming through the grimy fanlight. 'Why, so it is. What are you doing here?' he asked, but before Patrick could reply, he glanced at the man holding him. 'Its all right, he's one of our own.'

The hand dropped from his shoulder, and Patrick glanced around, massaging his stiffened muscle, to see a broad, stout man grinning at him. The man smiled sheepishly. 'You can't be too careful, you know?'

Patrick nodded. He looked back at Tom Rooney, one of the leaders of the IRB in London. 'What's wrong? What happened?'

The older man stepped aside and ushered Patrick into the room before him. It was made tiny by the three men standing around the bed, but Patrick only recognized the bearded Dan Brady. The men parted to allow him to see Joe Hyde lying on the bed.

'Jesus Christ,' Patrick breathed.

Joseph Hyde had been beaten up; systematically, and by someone who knew what they were doing. His face was a mass of purple bruises, his lips swollen and split and his eyes lost behind puffy tissue. His hands, resting on top of the blankets were swathed in bandages, and there were further bandages showing around his chest, beneath his striped pyjamas.

'Joe ...?' Patrick whispered, his voice catching.

'As far as we can determine there were three men, two with clubs who did the beating and one other,' Tom Rooney said quietly. 'One of the neighbours found him this morning – luckily someone loyal to the cause. They contacted me rather than the police, and we've had our own doctor patch him up.'

'He should be in hospital,' Patrick said immediately. He crossed to the bed and knelt beside it, touching Joe's hand lightly with his fingertips.

'That would attract attention,' Dan Brady said gruffly.

'It might save his life!'

'He'll live, he's tough,' Brady said confidently.

Patrick peeled back the blankets, examining the bandages; they had been professionally and properly tied and applied. He lifted Hyde's right hand; the fingers had been set and splinted and individually wrapped. 'Well at least it looks like you had a good doctor ...'

'We did; Harley Street, with an accent and a school behind him,' Brady winked, 'but his parents were Galway born and bred.'

Patrick touched Joe's face and the man winced. 'Joe, can you hear me? Joe ... Joe? Who did this? Joe, who did this to you?'

Joe's swollen lips moved and Patrick bent his head, bringing it close to his friend. He could smell the copper stench of blood on his breath and wondered about internal injuries.

'Joe?'

Hyde's lips moved again, and then he breathed a single word. 'Lee.'

And Patrick Lundy suddenly understood.

Both Tom Rooney and Dan Brady realized that they were being followed at about the same time. They were walking Patrick Lundy down Charing Cross Road, the two men supporting the younger man, who was ashen-faced and shivering. Whatever Hyde had told him moments before had obviously terrified him.

The big bearded man had dipped his head slightly and, still looking straight ahead, said in Irish, 'We've got company.'

'I know,' Rooney replied in the same language, 'how many do you count?'

'Two. Big men in coats.'

'Police?'

'Unlikely.'

'Following who I wonder; us or the boy?'

'The boy; they weren't there when we went in; nor were they around on the two occasions I checked the

69

street, nor were they there when I accompanied the doctor to the cab.'

'Now, I wonder why they're following the lad?' Rooney said, almost to himself.

'Did you want me to discourage them?' Dan Brady asked with a smile.

'Not yet; let's get a sup of tea into the lad and ask him a few questions. I think Joe told him the name of his attackers, and it's obviously someone ... someone ...' Rooney's voice trailed off to a whisper. Pieces of the puzzle suddenly clicked together. He knew Katherine Lundy's reputation in Dublin, knew what she was, knew how she had achieved her reputation there and how she had carved herself a slice of the London underworld. He also knew her feelings towards Ireland in general, and the IRB in particular. Now, what was it Hyde had told him, 'two men and one other.' The two were just muscle, but the third man could well have been Michael Lee, Katherine Lundy's notorious henchman. 'Here,' he turned into a pub off the Strand and pushed open the door. Because it was Sunday, it was practically empty and silent. 'Keep an eye on our friends,' he muttered and while Brady took up position beside the door, Tom helped Patrick over to the bar. 'There's been a death in his family,' Tom said to the barman who was looking curiously at the pale, wide-eyed young man.

The barman nodded sympathetically. 'What'll it be then?'

'Two whiskeys – Irish,' Tom said, 'and look ...' he slid a coin across the counter, 'could you do us a favour and get a cup of tea for the lad. Strong and with plenty of sugar.'

The barman looked at Patrick and nodded. 'Sure.' He nodded at a corner booth, 'I'll bring it over.'

'I'd be grateful to you.' Tom picked up the two whiskeys and manoeuvred Patrick into the corner, pushing him into the seat first so that he was up against the wall. It also ensured that Patrick was in the deepest

70

shadow and not immediately visible from the street. Moments later Dan Brady slid into the seat opposite. Tom looked at him without saying anything.

'They're across the street, standing in a doorway … and it's starting to snow,' he said with a smile.

They sat in silence, the two older men drinking their whiskey, until the barman arrived with the tea. 'The missus made it,' he said, pushing the big cup towards Patrick, but looking at Tom as he spoke, 'strong and sweet as you said.'

'I'm grateful to you.'

'If there's anything else …?'

'No, you've been very kind.'

When the barman had disappeared behind his bar, Tom Rooney pushed the steaming cup in front of Patrick. 'Drink!' he commanded.

Patrick started to shake his head, when Dan Brady leaned over and glared at him. 'Drink.' The young man lifted the cup to his lips, sipped the strong dark tea and grimaced. 'Too sweet.'

'Now tell me what poor Joe Hyde told you back there,' Tom Rooney said quietly.

Patrick's face immediately lost all expression. 'Nothing,' he said defensively.

'He said something that upset you.'

'There was nothing,' Patrick insisted.

'Well then, let's try it this way,' Tom said patiently. 'Would he have told you the name of one of his attackers, and might you have recognized that name …?'

Patrick concentrated on the foul tea.

'Three men attacked Joe – and we've been racking our brains trying to figure out a motive. There's neither rhyme nor reason for it; Joe isn't active enough to attract that type of attention. Then we thought it might have been something criminal – but Joe is clever enough to steer clear of anything illegal, the last thing he needs is investigation by the police. Finally, we thought it might have been a lovers' quarrel, but now I'm not sure …'

'It was Lee,' Patrick said suddenly. 'He told me Lee was there, and Lee is ...'

'Oh, we know who Lee is,' Tom said glancing over at Dan Brady; the bearded man nodded grimly.

'But it was my fault,' Patrick continued, wrapping his hands around the cup, bringing it up to his lips as if to hide his face. 'It was my fault, all my fault. My name is Patrick Montgomery Lundy – Katherine Lundy is my mother ... a powerful woman. My mother wouldn't allow me to go to the meeting last night – you know she despises anything Irish.' Both men nodded. 'So I pretended to be ill and went to bed. She had a party you see, and I knew she'd be busy, and I hoped she wouldn't be able to check up on me. But she must have found out somehow. She confronted me with it this afternoon and she had all the details – even the name of the pub where the meeting was held.'

'Were you followed last night?' Dan Brady asked.

'No, no, I'm sure of it. And don't forget, Joe was with me, and you know how careful he is. Lee was at the party and one of the maids told me that she took him out of the party and spoke to him for a few minutes. She must have been giving him instructions to find out where I was last night. And my sister told me that she met with him after Mass this morning and he gave her an envelope.' He drank some more of the sweet tea. 'And then when Joe said Lee, I immediately knew ...'

Dan Brady nodded. 'They beat it out of him,' he said grimly.

'It's not his fault,' Patrick said quickly.

'We're not saying it is, lad. Nor is it yours.' He ran his calloused finger around the rim of his glass. 'And at least we know why Joe was worked over, and that's a relief of sorts.'

'That's not all though,' Pat added. 'My mother is threatening to dismiss all the staff unless I tell her which one of them admitted me back into the house last night. I've no key, you see.'

'And who let you in?' Tom Rooney asked.

'One of the maids.'

'Will she own up?'

'Probably.'

'Where does your mother keep the keys?'

Pat started to shake his head. 'I don't ... no, I do know!'

'And could you have borrowed one for the night?'

Smiling in understanding, Pat nodded quickly. 'Of course.'

'I think lad,' Dan Brady said seriously, 'it's time for you to leave the house. She'll smother you if you remain.'

'I've no money, no place to stay ... I've nothing. She controls everything.'

Both men smiled, but it was Tom, the older man who spoke. 'You're a member of the organization now – and we take care of our own. Remember that, if you ever need a place to stay, we'll be there, waiting.'

'Thank you – I'll remember that. But what do I do about Joe? And why would she do such a thing, how could she?'

Tom finished the last of his drink, and edged the empty glass over towards Dan. The taller man grinned, 'My turn, I suppose,' he murmured, and headed over to the bar to order another round of drinks.

Tom Rooney looked at Patrick closely, his pale eyes squinting in the dim light as he attempted to make out the younger man's expression. 'Tell me,' he said, very softly, 'what do you know of your mother's past.'

Patrick's expression was suddenly wary. 'What do you mean?'

'Do you know how she earned her living in Dublin?' Tom asked gently.

'I ... I'm not sure ...'

'You needn't try to hide the truth from me, boy, I know all about your mother. Katherine Lundy Corcoran ran a brothel ... aaah, but I see you knew that. Did you also know that she had connections with the Dublin and London criminal underworlds? Did you know that she dealt in stolen goods, arranged thefts and

73

then fenced the goods, did you know she arranged insurance for many of the smaller shopkeepers – her kind of insurance? No ... I see you didn't. Your mother was one of the most powerful women in the Dublin underworld. Everyone went in fear of the mysterious veiled Madam Kitten.'

Dan Brady slid back into his seat, and pushed a glass across to Tom. 'They're still out there,' he remarked, dipping his head in the direction of the door. 'Good and cold they look, too.'

Tom nodded. 'I was just telling Pat about his mother.'

'Ah, the mysterious Madam Kitten,' Dan grinned, 'not a nice lady at all.'

'If she was so mysterious, how do you both know about her?'

'Your father was one of us, remember? When he joined the organization, and later, when the meetings of the high command were actually held in your own house, we made certain inquiries. Your father, Dermot told us a lot of course – I'm sure your mother would have been none too pleased, if she knew, but his first loyalty was always to the cause. Coupled with what he had told us and what we already knew, the rest was easy.'

'And now?' Pat asked. 'What does she do now?' he asked, although he had already guessed the answer.

'The same,' Tom murmured.

'People who cross her, have a habit of ending up dead,' Dan said, without looking at Patrick. He was sitting at an angle which allowed him to watch the door.

Tom Rooney nodded. 'When she was setting up her business in London, several of her opponents disappeared.'

Patrick shook his head savagely. 'I can't believe I'm hearing this!'

'Lee is one of her brothel masters. He's a sadistic man – he must have taken great pleasure in working over Joe last night.'

'But why?' Patrick breathed, 'Why?'

'You defied her, tricked her. She couldn't take out her anger on you, so she probably instructed Lee to make Joe an example ...'

'A warning you mean!'

Tom nodded silently.

'What about the two outside?'

Dan Brady grinned. 'Lee's henchmen, more n'like, sent to keep an eye on you, report where you were, who you've seen. Don't worry about them – this pub has a side door!'

Patrick finished the last of the cold tea and stood up quickly.

'Where are you going?'

'What are you going to do?'

The two questions came together.

'I'm going to have a talk with my mother.'

CHAPTER FIVE

Patrick re-entered the house by the back door – and was surprised to find the kitchen empty. Immediately, instinctively, he knew something was wrong; the kitchen staff should have been busy with preparations for dinner. Something cold settled into the pit of his stomach. With damp palms he opened the door that led up into the hallway. Moving as quietly as possible he climbed the stairs from the kitchen quarters.

Voices echoed flatly down the long hall.

He recognized his mother's first – harsh, raucous and demanding. There was a second voice – sharp, abrasive – and it took him a few moments to identify the second voice as belonging to Jane, the maid. Most of what she said was muted, but three words rang out clearly.

'... spiteful old woman ...'

In the stunned silence that followed, Patrick raced up the stairs and down the hall and had the door open and was actually in the room before another word had been spoken. Shocked, everyone turned to look at him, and he briefly registered the faces and the expressions – his mother's, the butler's, the cook's and the two maids' – before Jane turned and brushed past him, her face set, her eyes hard and glittering.

Patrick saw something settle down behind his mother's eyes, something like satisfaction, and the anger that had burned within him since he had discovered the identity of Joseph Hyde's attackers, turned cold and brittle. Stepping to one side, he looked at the three remaining servants, and said, 'That will be all, thank you.'

It was the first order of its kind that Patrick had given, but both Mrs James and Sarah immediately moved towards the door. Only Gerard lingered, looking at Katherine questioningly.

'You may go, Gerard,' Patrick insisted coldly.

Katherine nodded fractionally, and the butler bowed and moved silently from the room, not looking at the younger man.

Patrick nudged the door closed with his foot and turned back to his mother. 'I think you and I need to talk.' He crossed to the easy chair facing his mother and sank down into it.

'I think you owe me an explanation, young man,' Katherine snapped, looking at her son over the rim of her wire-framed glasses.

'I owe you an explanation?' Patrick whispered. 'What do you owe me, eh?' he demanded, and then, realizing that his voice had risen, allowed it to drop again. He knew if he allowed her to anger him, then he had lost; at all costs he had to control his temper. 'I am nineteen years old, I am capable of forming my own opinions, making my own decisions. I will not have – I will not tolerate – your interference anymore.'

'You forget to whom you are speaking, young man. It would be better if you did not anger me.'

'Oh, I'm not forgetting that, I can never forget that. And if I do anger you, what are you going to do with me, eh, have me beaten to an inch of my life? Your hired bullies did a good job on poor Joe Hyde last night ...'

'I don't know what you're talking about,' Katherine said quickly.

'Oh, I'm sure you don't. I'm sure you didn't order Lee and his men to find out where I'd been and who I had seen. Are you aware how they carried out your orders, eh? They went to Joseph Hyde – probably because he was the one connection they had between the Irish organization and me, and then they nearly beat him to death just so Lee could make his report to you. But I don't suppose you care,' he added bitterly.

'And where were you?'

77

'I was at an IRB meeting,' Patrick said defiantly.

Katherine's lips tightened into a thin hard line. 'After all I said ...'

'You don't own me. I'm not one of your working girls!'

In the long silence that followed, Katherine looked at her son closely, realizing – for the first time – that whatever chances she had had of keeping him, had just disappeared. 'I don't know what you're talking about,' she said eventually.

'Oh, but you do,' Patrick said aggressively. 'You ran a brothel in Dublin, and you've continued your foul trade here – but only on a grander level. I often wondered where the money came from. Now, I know; my mother is a brothel-keeper!'

'Be quiet!' The colour had drained from the woman's face, leaving it mask-like, the eyes hard and dark against the paleness of her face. 'How dare you speak to me like that. I did what I had to do in Dublin – you'll never know what I had to do to survive. And when I had nothing else, I had my children – and all that I did, I did – and continue to do – is for my children.'

'And does that include running a brothel and dealing in stolen goods?' The anger was eating into him, and although he knew he was going too far, saying too much, he couldn't help it. 'My father would have been proud of you,' he spat, 'did he even realize the half of what you did, eh?'

Katherine's expression crystallized into something hard and ugly. 'Your father!' she spat. 'Don't talk to me about your father,' she whispered very softly, 'you don't know what you're talking about. And I don't think you want to know!'

'Mysteries ... more mysteries. Your whole life is nothing but a mystery,' Patrick raged. 'Everything's a mask, layer after layer of lies and confusion. You know,' he hissed, 'I used to wonder why my father left you to go out and fight against the British, I used to wonder why he sacrificed everything ... but the more I learn about you, the more I realize why!'

'You don't know what your talking about,' Katherine began, experiencing a deep burning rage that she hadn't felt for a long time, a rage all the more intense because she knew she could do nothing about it.

'I used to think he gave up his life for Ireland because he wanted a free country ...'

'Your father didn't die for Ireland,' Katherine snapped, silencing him, and even as the words were tumbling out, she was regretting them. 'Your father hated Ireland and the Irish!'

'That's a lie,' Patrick whispered aghast, 'my father fought and died in the Rising ...'

'Dermot Corcoran fought and died in the Rising, but Dermot Corcoran was not your father!'

There were other words, harsh, angry bitter words, but later Katherine could never remember exactly what she had said, nor could she recall her son's replies. All that remained with her was the look in her son's eyes, a look of absolute loathing and hatred, a look of betrayal.

And in those few moments he looked so much like his father, Major John Lewis, the man who had first taken her virginity, and later betrayed her husband. The man she had killed.

Katherine sat in the sitting room, memories creeping in with the shadows. She rarely thought about Ireland now – she had deliberately suppressed it, and usually it was only in her dreams that it rose unbidden to haunt her. But the ghosts were very clear this afternoon.

Katherine stood up quickly and crossed to the drinks cabinet, her fingers tracing the metal discs on the cut-glass decanters ... and for the first time in many months thought about Dermot Corcoran, her late husband.

He had been a young man when she had met him back in 1898. He had been a year older than herself, almost painfully shy, but even then passionately interested in the plight of the working classes in Dublin, and determined to do something – although even he didn't know what – for them. He had been a reporter then and it was some time after their first meeting that he had begun his campaign to highlight the plight of the poor.

She remembered those days with a special clarity. There had been times in her life when she had been – if not happy, then content. She had only recently arrived in Dublin, a servant girl in the house of Captain and Mrs Lewis. Alone and friendless, she had struck up a casual friendship with Dermot as he showed her Dublin. And when, some months later, Katherine had become pregnant by Captain Lewis, Dermot had offered to marry her. She had refused – even though it would have offered her an easy way out, and then circumstances had intervened and she had ended in the brothels in the notorious Monto.

Eight years were to pass before she encountered Dermot Corcoran again.

The years had changed them both, matured them too – Katherine more so than Dermot. By 1907, she was the madam of the most luxurious of the Dublin brothels, and she had travelled extensively across Europe. She also did a lucrative sideline in stolen goods and peddled information to the Dublin underworld, and she was reputed to be one of the most powerful and certainly one of the richest women in Dublin.

Dermot was then a respected reporter, with a growing reputation amongst the poor of Dublin. He had championed the cause of the poor for many years in a series of investigative articles, and had highlighted the terrible conditions in which a large proportion of the ordinary Dublin people lived. And while his experiences had hardened him, he still retained the ideals of his youth.

Fate brought them back together, fate, and a shared interest in the whereabouts of the recently stolen Irish Crown Jewels. And when Dermot Corcoran stepped back into her life, it seemed almost natural that Captain – now Major – Lewis should reappear also. With the wheel turned almost full circle, it seemed almost inevitable that Dermot Corcoran and Katherine Lundy should marry. The fact that she was pregnant with his child made the decision easier to make.

And Patrick Lundy, then seven years old, never questioned that the man his mother married was not his natural father. As he grew older, he simply assumed that he was Dermot Corcoran's child, but conceived outside wedlock ...

She had always intended to tell him the truth, but somehow the time was never right ...

And now he knew.

Katherine put down the empty glass with a start, she hadn't realized that she had been drinking. And then of course there was Major John Lewis, Patrick's real father ...

Katherine turned away quickly, suddenly chilled. For a brief moment, she had seen herself raising the tiny silver gun and pulling the trigger, once and then again, the blood appearing like a diseased flower on Lewis's soiled shirt.

The tall hard-faced woman stood by the fire, watching the small flames flicker on the dying coals, and then, with a deliberate effort of will, she dismissed the thoughts and memories. She murmured her motto, 'What's done is done, and cannot be undone,' and then returned to her present problems.

The maid would have to be dismissed of course ... the girl had brazenly admitted allowing Patrick back into the house, and Katherine wasn't sure which annoyed her more – the fact that the boy had managed to creep back into the house or the fact that he had been alone in the girl's bedroom. She wondered if she should have Lee teach the girl a lesson, but decided not to – for the moment. Later, perhaps the girl could have an accident. Katherine liked to believe that she wasn't vindictive, but she did have certain rules, certain standards, both for her house and her business, and one of the reasons she had been so successful both in Dublin and now in London, was because she applied those rules rigorously. And she couldn't have it put out that a servant girl had defied her and then abused her to her face, now could she? No, the girl would be taught a lesson. She could go now – but later she could fall under a tram.

And Patrick – what was she going to do about Patrick?

She would have to give him a certain amount of freedom she supposed, there was no way around that. But under the strictest supervision, of course. There was no real way of keeping him away from Irish friends ... unless of course, he were to have an accident too – something that would keep him at home for several months preferably. A broken leg perhaps?

She reached for the bell rope beside the fire and pulled gently. Gerard appeared almost immediately. The butler's usually impassive expression was still creased with worry. He regarded Katherine warily.

'I would like some tea brought up, Gerard.'

'Of course, Ma'am. Will that be all, Ma'am?'

'The maid is to be dismissed without references,' Katherine continued in the same tone of voice. 'She is to leave immediately. If her sister so wishes, she too can leave – also without references. That will be all – oh,' she added, as the butler turned to go, 'will you have Master Patrick step in please.'

Gerard bowed and backed from the room.

Katherine had barely had time to pull off her wire-framed pince-nez and press the palms of her hands to her eyes before Gerard had returned. The butler was ashen-faced and his face was sheened with sweat.

Katherine was on her feet before he had spoken. 'What ...?'

'They're gone Ma'am, both of them. They've gone!'

When Patrick had stormed out of the room, his head pounding, bile in his throat, he had started for his room, but then he had thought of Jane, and he had turned and headed back down the hall towards the room she shared with her sister. He rapped gently on the wood. When there was no answer, he turned the handle and looked in.

'Oh, I'm sorry ... I didn't realize ...'

Jane was standing in her shift, her maid's uniform thrown casually across the bed. A flower-print dress was draped across the back of the chair, and there was a brown battered suitcase on the floor at her feet, which looked as if it had been pulled out from beneath the bed. 'Well, come in and close the door.' She picked up the dress and slipped it over her head.

'You're leaving ...' Patrick began.

'When herself calms down she'll dismiss me,' Jane said quietly, her voice surprisingly calm. When she had left Madam Lundy's presence earlier she had been shivering with reaction, but that had now passed, leaving her calm, her options clear.

'I'm sorry ...'

'I'm not. I'm glad I'm going. The atmosphere in this house is suffocating – if you'll take my advice, you'll leave before it stifles you too.'

'You're the second person to say that to me today,' Patrick murmured. 'Where will you go?'

Jane shrugged. She sat down on the edge of the bed and pulled off her flat shoes. Reaching into her case she pulled out a pair of ugly buttoned boots. 'I suppose I could try and get some waitressing work ...'

'Will my mother give you a reference?' Patrick wondered.

Jane glanced up at him, her face expressionless. 'What do you think?'

'Have you any relatives you could go to?'

'There's none alive here, though my mother's youngest sister – my aunt – lives just outside Dublin, in a place called Kingston. I haven't seen her in years, I'm not even sure if I'd recognize her ...' she finished doubtfully.

'Have you any money?'

She shook her head without saying anything.

Patrick went and sat on the bed beside her. He put his arm around her shoulder and hugged her unconsciously. 'I'm sorry I got you into this. It's all my fault. I was going to tell her I had taken her keys and let myself back into the house,' he added, 'but I arrived too late. You had already said your piece.'

'She's going to make your life miserable, you know that?'

Patrick nodded. 'She had a friend of mine beaten up just to find out where I was,' he said softly. 'I was followed today – and it's not for the first time, either.'

Jane turned to look at him, her dark intense eyes large in her face. 'Leave,' she said earnestly, 'leave with me now. There's nothing left for you here, nothing but misery. Come away with me, we'll find some money, maybe make our way to Ireland ...'

Even as he was shaking his head, Patrick could hear Tom Rooney saying to him, 'You're part of the organization now ... we look after our own,' and then he remembered the young gunman's statement, 'We need people like you ... if any of you feel like joining ...' He could go to Ireland and join up with the Republican Army, and carry on the fight his father ... no, not his father, but the man he loved as a father ... had started. And while he was there, perhaps he would be able to solve the mystery of his real father. Yes he could do it. He would do it. There was nothing holding him here, except ...

'What about Senga?' he asked finally.

'You can do nothing for her now. But once you've established yourself, made some money, you can come back and take her away with you.'

'How will we get out without being seen?' Patrick asked.

Jane looked at the window – and they both burst out laughing.

'Where did he go?' Katherine demanded, glaring at her daughter, who was standing before her.

'I don't know Mama, truly I don't. He called me into his room a few moments ago and said he was leaving. He said he'd suffocate if he remained in this house. for another hour. He told me ...' Senga blinked back tears, 'he told me he loved me and that he'd come back for me when he'd made his fortune and could afford to take me away.'

Katherine's expression was a mask, a terrifying rigid mask. 'And what else? What was he doing while he was talking to you?' she said tightly.

'He was packing a small case.'

'Was there anyone with him?'

'What do you mean?'

'Was the servant girl Jane with him?' she snapped.

'No ... no one.'

'Did you see her?'

Senga shook her head. She was still confused and shaken by the day's events.

Furious, Katherine stormed away. It was obvious what had happened. This girl, this Jane Bradley, was evidently far more involved with Patrick than she had suspected. She had obviously enticed Patrick to run away with her – were they sleeping together, she wondered briefly? But they wouldn't get far. The girl would have had little if any money, and Patrick had none. And London wasn't big enough to hide them.

She met Gerard on the stairs. 'Contact Mr Lee; tell him it's an emergency.'

The same guard was still lounging outside Joseph Hyde's door when Patrick and Jane arrived there less than an hour later. The man moved to stand at the top of the stairs, barring their way, and then he recognized the young man. 'Back again, eh?'

'We may have been followed. You might have company,' Patrick panted. He knew that they hadn't been followed, but he also knew that as soon as his mother discovered that he – that both of them – had gone, the first place she would head for would be Joe Hyde's flat.

The guard tapped his coat pocket significantly. 'I'm ready.'

'Is anyone inside?'

'Dan.'

Concealing a sign of relief, Patrick tapped on the door and then gently turned the handle and poked his head around. The room was unlit and in the gloom the large man was almost invisible. Joe's rasping breathing was the only sound.

'Dan ... Dan ... it's me, Paddy Montgomery.' He felt Jane start beside him, and he squeezed her arm reassuringly. 'It's how they know me.'

There was a sharp metallic click and as Dan stood up, Patrick saw him slip the heavy pistol back into his pocket. The big man's bearded face was serious. 'What's wrong?' he asked, looking at Jane.

'I've left ... I've left home and mother and ... and everything. Jane's coming with me. She's the girl who let me into the house last night ... She's lost her position because of it ... and so we're going to Ireland, but we've no money and no place to stay, and ...'

Jane squeezed Patrick's arm just above the elbow, the sudden pain silencing him. He realized he had been babbling.

'We would like to go to Ireland,' Jane said quietly, 'Patrick would like to join the fight over there. I would like to go with him if I could.'

Dan Brady smiled quickly. 'We cân arrange that.'

'Patrick was also worried that his mother might send men here, because she knows that this is the only place Patrick could run to.'

Dan smiled again. 'Do you think she'll send men here?'

'I'm sure of it,' Patrick said tersely.

'Have we much time do you think?'

'A little – but not much though.'

'All we need is twenty minutes – have we that, d'you think?'

'I think we've that – why?' Patrick wondered.

Dan Brady winked. 'You don't need to know that.' He nodded at the guard waiting patiently outside. 'You go with Pete now, he'll take you to Tom Rooney, an' Tom will make the arrangements to get you to Dublin.'

'It won't be easy, my mother will be looking for us …'

'She'll never find you,' Dan promised.

'I hope so,' Patrick breathed.

'Nothing.' Michael Lee turned to look at Katherine. 'My men have scoured every cheap hotel and doss house. I've had the stations and ports watched, I've kept a permanent watch on all those locations usually associated with the Irish movement, and I've turned up nothing.'

Katherine sat back into the heavy leather chair, watching the tall, thin man, her face hard and impassive. 'Have you traced Hyde yet?'

Lee shook his head quickly. 'He's vanished also. He hasn't been in contact with the bookshop …'

'Well, he's hardly likely to be after the beating you gave him. What about the hospitals?'

'I've checked. I've had men go through the registers but with no success. Our own men are still on the critical list,' he added, but Katherine wasn't interested in the condition of the two men who had gone to Hyde's rooms two days ago looking for her son. Patrick Lundy hadn't been there, neither had Joseph Hyde, but half a dozen men armed with pick-axe handles had been. The only words spoken during the brief attack had been: 'This is for Joe.'

It was unlikely that either men would ever walk properly again. One of them might never walk at all.

In the two days since Patrick had left the house with the maid, Katherine had had her men take London apart looking for them. She had offered a substantial reward for information which led to the capture of either of them, and had used what contacts she had with the London constabulary to have them both placed on their wanted lists – officially they were sought in connection with the 'murderous attack' on two of her employees. If they were caught it could all turn out to be a mistake of course. But Katherine also realized that the longer it took, the more chance there was of them leaving the country. She looked up at Lee, still standing before her, like a disobedient schoolboy. 'What contacts do we have in Ireland?'

The sallow skinned man shrugged slightly. 'Few at the moment, but money buys us a lot of friends. Why; do you think he's gone there?'

Katherine nodded silently. She looked down at the notes on the small side table, and then pulled off her wire framed pince-nez. 'It's the only place he would go. The various Irish organizations would probably take care of him – it depends on how deeply involved he is, and he's obviously deeply involved if they're shielding him.'

'Do you want me to send some men to Ireland – they could watch the ports, make some inquiries?'

'You'd be wasting your time – if he's made it to Dublin, then he's vanished. But no,' she shook her head savagely, 'he's in London. He has to be.'

'But where?' Lee asked.

'Find out,' Katherine said ominously.

Lee nodded and turned away. He had done all he could, but the boy was gone – he couldn't say he blamed him – and if the Irish Republican Brotherhood were sheltering him, then there was no way he was going to be able to make contact with him. Since the 1916 Rising in Dublin, the organization, which had always been prone to spies and informants, had grown very security conscious. They now operated in cells, and even if Patrick and Jane were being sheltered, only a very small number of people, perhaps no more than two or three, might be aware of it. Still, he wondered where the boy was ...

Patrick was receiving last minute instructions from

Tom Rooney in the sitting room of his three room flat in Kelly Street off the Kentish Town Road. Jane was in the tiny kitchen talking quietly to Mrs Rooney, a tiny white-haired woman, who spoke with a broad Scottish accent.

The two men sat facing one another beside a small fire, a bundle of papers on the floor between them. Cups of half-finished tea were on the floor beside their chairs.

Patrick and Jane had remained in the flat in Kelly Street since they had been brought there two days ago, they hadn't ventured outside the door and had remained quiet and away from the windows. Even the neighbours were not aware that they were there. And now that an end to their confinement was in sight, they were both eager to be away.

'Now, we've arranged that you will travel as a newly-wed couple. I think there's less risk of you being caught then – Lee's and your mother's people are looking for either a single man and woman or two unrelated young people; it seems as if they think it's inconceivable that you should have remained together. You're going to Ireland for your honeymoon. Now ...' he rooted through the papers on the floor, 'now, here's your marriage certificate, it's made out in the name of Paddy Montgomery ...'

'I thought you would have changed that?' Patrick interrupted.

Tom shook his head, adjusting the glasses on his nose. 'No; unfortunately too many people in the organization over here know you as Paddy Montgomery; if someone from Dublin wants to check up on your credentials – as they surely will – then we need to use your established name. We've changed Jane to Janet – I hope she doesn't mind.

'You'll be met when you step off the boat in Kingston, and taken to a safe house, and then you'll be absorbed into the organization at some level. Your medical training might come in very useful indeed, and they might allow you to continue your medical training

– it is always handy to have a fully qualified doctor to call on if the need arises – if you take my meaning.'

Patrick nodded, remembering the Harley Street doctor who had attended to Joseph Hyde. 'What about Jane?' he asked.

Tom shrugged. 'She can go her own way if she wishes. If she wants to work for the organization I'm sure we'll find something suitable for her.'

'She did lose her position because of me, I'd like to see her fixed up with something.'

'We'll see she has a job, don't worry.'

Patrick nodded. 'I feel responsible for her.'

'Don't be. She made her own decision,' Tom said, reaching into his pocket for his pipe. He pulled out his tobacco pouch and pulled the drawstrings open. Without looking at Patrick he said quietly, 'You know she's smitten with you?'

Patrick thought about feigning surprise or shock, but knew the older man would see through him. 'I know,' he said eventually.

'And how do you feel about that?'

'Why?' Patrick wondered.

Tom concentrated on stuffing his pipe with strands of dark tobacco. 'From what I've seen of her, she's a strong-willed independent young woman, who knows what she wants, and is not afraid to say so. She stood up to your mother, and I've known very few people who have had the pluck to do it.' He struck a match, and pulled strongly on the pipe.

Patrick nodded into the silence, wondering where the conversation was leading.

'I just think that she might prove to be somewhat difficult to dispose of ... oh, don't look so surprised. You're heading off into a grand adventure, you might not want additional baggage.'

'She might become dependent on me, you think?'

'Possibly,' Tom shrugged. 'I'm just giving you a friendly warning. Have you ever slept with a woman?' he asked suddenly.

Surprised, Patrick replied without thinking. 'No …'

'Don't sleep with this one. If you do, she has you. And while she's a likeable enough girl, be wary of her tricks and wiles. Never pick the first fruit,' he said mysteriously, and then continued when he saw Patrick's puzzled expression. 'A handsome young man like you will find you'll never be short of female companion-ship.'

The door to the kitchen opened and Mrs Rooney, followed by Jane, came into the room. 'And what are you both looking so serious about?' Moire Rooney asked with a gentle smile, and Patrick immediately knew that she had been deliberately keeping Jane in the kitchen while Tom spoke his piece. He looked at the young woman, noticing now how her eyes rested possessively on him, and he couldn't help wondering if they were right.

Tom Rooney turned back to Patrick. 'You're leaving tonight. You'll be in Dublin tomorrow.'

CHAPTER SIX

It was raining when Patrick Montgomery Lundy, followed by Jane Bradley, stepped onto Irish soil, and he suddenly remembered his mother telling him that it had been raining on the day she had first come to Ireland, in the May of 1898.

And for the first time, the realization of what he had done – severed all ties with his mother, his inheritance and all the creature comforts of his home in London – sank in. The last few days had seemed like a dream, but now, with the soft rain damp on his face, that dream had ended ... and become a nightmare.

'Mr an' Mrs Montgomery?'

Patrick whirled, half-expecting to find himself confronting – what? Police? His mother's and Lee's men? Instead he found he was looking at a short, rather stout middle-aged man.

'You are Mr an' Mrs Montgomery, Mr an' Mrs Patrick Montgomery?'

Patrick nodded cautiously, and the small man beamed. 'Excellent. I'm here to take you to your hotel.' Patrick breathed a sigh of relief; the man was the representative of the IRB. 'Well now – and this is your luggage.' He picked up the two grips and the empty suitcase Tom Rooney had given them to lend credence to their story. 'A real honeymoon couple would have at least one suitcase' he said with a grin.

Jane linked her arm through Patrick's and together they followed the small man. 'Now,' he continued, not looking at them, 'the two men standing on either side of the gate in front of us have been there since morning. They seem to be watching the passengers. It might be nothing; they might be police ... or they might represent those who are chasing you, so say nothing as we go past.' As they approached the gates, their guide continued talking, but his voice was now meant to be heard. 'Yes, your father sir, was most anxious that I meet you ... and of course, he's looking forward to meeting you, ma'am.' The men lounging beside the gate didn't even give them a second a glance. The small stout man grinned at Patrick. 'Works every time. Welcome to Ireland,' he said with a broad smile.

'Welcome back to Ireland,' Patrick corrected him. 'It's good to be home,' he said, sounding much more sincere than he felt.

'Mama? Mama?'

Katherine started awake, confused for a single moment, images of the dream in which she had shot John Lewis still vivid behind her eyes – except now when she raised the gun and pulled the trigger, it was her son who spun away, red blossoming on his shirt.

Senga waited until she was sure her mother was awake and then asked softly, 'When's Patrick coming back?'

Katherine straightened up in the chair. She had fallen asleep sitting before the fire and she was stiff, her joints aching. 'I don't know,' she said tightly. 'Soon, I hope.'

'The man said he was safe ... safe from what, from whom?'

'What man?' Katherine looked up, startled. Her daughter was standing just inside the door, wearing her coat, hat and walking shoes. Her cheeks were red and she exuded chill air. 'When was this?'

'The man in the street ... a few minutes ago.'

Katherine shook her head quickly. 'Start again, tell me everything. Where were you – was Miss Powers with you?' she asked suddenly.

Senga nodded.

'Would you ask her to step ...'

The door opened and Miss Powers peered in, pale

grey eyes matching her expression. She squinted nervously into the room.

'I was just about to send for you,' Katherine said, her voice harsh and uncompromising. 'My daughter said she was talking to some man in the street. Is that true – can that be true?' she asked incredulously.

Miss Powers, a tall thin woman of indeterminate age shuffled reluctantly into the room.

'It is true, Ma'am. I had taken Miss Senga into Hyde Park with the intention of showing her some of the winter birds, and the park is so beautiful at this time of the year, what with the snow piled up.'

Katherine's expression made the governess hurry on. 'We were approached by a man and woman – a settled couple, I would have said – and as they passed, the woman suddenly spoke to me, calling me by name. I stopped naturally. She professed to have been a cook in a house where I was once governess. I confess I did not remember her at all, but I have been in so many houses, I suppose it is only natural ...'

'The man,' Katherine snapped, 'what was the man doing while you were chatting to this woman?'

'Not chatting – surely not chatting, Ma'am. He spoke to Miss Senga who had stepped off the path to look at a snowman. I thought he had passed some inconsequential remark, but when the couple had walked on, Miss Senga informed me that the man had relayed a message from Master Patrick. As I understand it, he said that Master Patrick had asked him to advise Miss Senga that he was safe and would be home in a year or two.'

Katherine turned to look at Senga. 'What were his exact words?'

'That's what he said.'

'What did you do then?' Katherine turned back to Miss Powers.

'As soon as I had realized what he had said I returned home again immediately.'

Katherine nodded. 'You will not leave this house again with Senga without my express permission, even for the simplest task – is that understood? When you do leave the house, I will ensure that you will be accompanied at all times. You will admit no strangers to this house. That will be all Miss Powers,' she finished sharply. She waited until the governess had hurried from the room, her eyes sparkling with tears. 'Senga, you will not talk to strangers unless it is within my presence. You will not go out without my permission, and when you do go out, you will be accompanied by one of the servants.'

'But why, Mama?'

'These are dangerous times my girl, and we would be perceived as being wealthy. There have been several kidnappings for ransom recently and I'm just taking precautions to ensure that nothing will happen to you. Now, run along to your room and change, I'm sure it's nearly time for tea.'

Katherine remained seated, listening to her daughter's footsteps hurry up the stairs and then the ceiling creaked as she entered her bedroom which was directly above the sitting room.

A cold insidious anger began to seep into her. It was made all the more intense because it was directed inwards. She should have anticipated that Patrick would try to get some sort of message to Senga – they had always been very close. But it had also been brought home to her with chilling clarity how easily he might have snatched her. She had lost one son – lost him truly, for she realized that he must be in Ireland now – but she was determined that she would not lose a daughter. Senga would never leave her – she would make sure of that. She leaned over and rang the bell for Gerard. She would issue the new instructions regarding strangers and then she would have to see Mr Lee about a permanent bodyguard here in the house, someone who would blend in ... a manservant. They needed a servant to replace that girl Jane who had betrayed her trust. She wondered where she was, and if she had gone with Patrick. But somehow she doubted it; she was certain her interest in him would have vanished when she discovered he had no money.

Patrick and Jane had been put up in a room in the Shelbourne Hotel which faced St Stephen's Green. Patrick had been interested to see that all traces of the damage the insurgents had wrought in the Green – the trenches they had dug, the trees they had felled – had vanished, and the only evidence of the 1916 Rising were the bullet holes in the stonework of the hotel where the rebels had fired on the British troops positioned on the roof and in some of the upper rooms.

The small stout man had kept up a constant chatter as he accompanied the two young people into Dublin city on the train. But although he had a seemingly endless supply of small talk, he asked no questions and Patrick wondered how much he knew. When the train pulled into Amien's Street Station, Patrick had asked the man – who didn't volunteer a name and they didn't ask – where they were going. But his secretiveness extended to not even telling them that, and they had to be content to accompany him as he turned left at the foot of the steps that led up to the station entrance and headed for the quays.

'Where are we going?' Jane murmured. Her right arm was linked through Patrick's and her left hand was also closed over his arm; he felt he was in a vice.

'Some hotel I suppose,' he said softly. The small stout man had marched on ahead, and was now humming happily to himself.

'Where?'

'Could be any of a dozen,' Patrick said distractedly. Jane's constant chatter was beginning to annoy him. He had endured the days in hiding in London and then the boat trip across listening to her talk. Part of it was nerves and excitement, he knew, but at this stage he knew nearly everything there was to know about the girl. Several times over.

Deliberately ignoring her, Patrick concentrated on his

surroundings. It felt strange to be back in Dublin, to be home, the city both familiar and alien. He resisted the temptation to turn around and look back up the street to where he knew the turn for Montgomery Street lay. How many times had he come down here with Mickey – dead now, killed in the Rising – to watch the trains come steaming in?

A sudden thought struck him, and he realized that before he had left Ireland, his mother had insisted that he was accompanied everywhere ... maybe that was why it felt strange to be here without a chaperon. He looked down at the two hands locked onto his arm and then at the small man hurrying on ahead, and realized that he still had his chaperons, and once again they were not of his own choosing ...

Their guide turned left across Butt Bridge, heading towards Great Brunswick Street which would bring them up around by Trinity College ... Patrick frowned, wondering where they were going.

At the bottom of Great Brunswick Street, they swung left around by the main entrance to Trinity. Partially to silence Jane's chatter, Patrick began quietly pointing out some of the landmarks, the memories coming back with the names. He was somewhat consoled to find that she seemed to be genuinely interested.

If Patrick had been expecting the small man to head up Grafton Street, then he was disappointed; the guide continued on past the bottom of the crowded street, passing Yeates & Son, the opticians with the giant spectacle frame hanging outside the shop, heading into Nassau Street and then he turned right into Dawson Street.

As they neared the top of the street, Patrick slowed as they neared the Royal Hibernian Hotel, but their guide continued on ... and that left only one major hotel in the vicinity. 'The Shelbourne?' he asked.

Their guide nodded. At the top of the street, he turned left, heading towards one of the more expensive hotels in Dublin. Patrick touched his arm. 'I've no money,' he said gently, as they neared the ornate portico of the white stone building.

He stopped outside the hotel. 'All that's taken care of. Only the best for you boys. Now, you're booked in under the name you're using now. You'll remain in your room for the rest of today and all day tomorrow – if you want anything, order it, and have it brought to your room. You're a honeymoon couple, so the staff won't think it unusual. The day after tomorrow you'll receive a visitor, and everything will be sorted out then.' The man tipped his hat to Jane and then he darted across the road, heading into St Stephen's Green, leaving Patrick and Jane standing before the hotel.

'Shall we, Mrs Montgomery?' Patrick asked more lightly than he felt.

'It doesn't look as if we've any choice, Mr Montgomery,' the young woman grinned.

The room was not the best the hotel had to offer, but it was still magnificent by any standards. It was on the top floor and its two large windows looked out across St Stephen's Green and the College of Surgeons was clearly visible across the tops of the bare trees.

As Jane wandered around the room, poking in the cupboards, examining the small but luxurious bathroom, Patrick stood by the window staring absently into the Green. As he looked across the now peaceful Green, he found it was surprisingly easy to imagine it filled with men and women in uniform fighting for a cause they truly believed in. Men and women had fought in the College of Surgeons opposite and British soldiers had fired upon them from the roof of this very hotel. He was surprised at the intensity of his memories, surprised at the bitterness he felt. And yet he hadn't directly experienced the fighting in the city; at the first sign of trouble his mother had packed Senga and himself off to England. He pressed both palms flat against the cool glass, resting his forehead against the window.

Some of the memories were almost too painful to dwell upon. He remembered the last time he had seen his father – Dermot Corcoran, he corrected himself – alive. Why had he walked out on that bright Monday morning in April 1916, knowing that his chances of Corcoran returning were very slim indeed? What would have made an intelligent man do that?

And then the questions which had arisen so few days ago arose unbidden, and this time, instead of forcing them away, he forced himself to face them – and the principal question of course was, just who was his father?

He had little enough to go on: someone anti-Republic, anti-Irish, his mother had said, but who? And more importantly, was he still alive?

'You're very quiet.' Jane had come up behind him, standing so close he could feel the heat from her body, close but not touching.

'Just thinking, remembering.'

'Do you regret what you've done?' she asked, moving around so that she was able to look at his face.

'No,' he said immediately, surprising himself to find that he actually believed it.

'No regrets?'

'No ... well, only one.' He looked into her wide dark eyes. 'I'm so sorry I ever got you involved.'

'Don't be.' She moved closer to him. 'I got myself involved.' She reached out and plucked a thread from the lapel of his coat. Patrick flinched.

Jane stepped back in surprise. 'What's the matter with you?' she demanded, her voice rising. 'When you crept into my room less than a week ago, you weren't so shy about touching me. But I've noticed that in the last few days you've been careful not even to come close to me. Why did you wait until I was asleep before coming to bed on the boat on the way over? Just what did you think I was going to do to you – rape you? Or do you prefer boys?' she asked suddenly, her eyes widening. 'Your friend Joe Hyde preferred boys, didn't he?'

'No, no, there's nothing like that,' Patrick attempted a smile. Her outburst had surprised and confused him. 'It's just … it's just … I respect you too much.' He took a few steps away and sat down in one of the room's elegant easy chairs.

'You make a poor liar.' She turned her back on him and stared through the window. It had started to rain again, and the streets below were deserted. 'Let me tell you what I think,' Jane said slowly and evenly. 'You think I'm an opportunist don't you, latching onto you as some sort of meal-ticket. You think I'm trying to get you into bed so I can have some sort of hold over you. Isn't that it?' she snapped, turning suddenly, catching the surprised expression on his face. 'That is it. Well, you're wrong, Mr Lundy. I used you to get to Ireland, that's true, and if your friends in the organization can get me a job, then so much the better, but that's the last you'll see of me. And I don't think that's using you. I think that's due to me in payment for having lost my job. At the moment, Mr Lundy, you have nothing, no money, no friends, no family. Why would I want to have anything to do with you, eh? What do you have to offer me?'

'I'm sorry,' Patrick said eventually into the long silence which followed. He was thoroughly confused now. Had he been completely misreading her intentions?

'So am I,' Jane said. 'Perhaps I should have let that precious mother of yours catch you sneaking back into the house.'

'Why did you help me?'

Jane folded her arms beneath her breasts. 'Because I liked you, I genuinely liked you. I felt sorry for you. I wanted to help you.'

'Look!' Patrick surged to his feet. He took Jane by the elbows and looked directly into her eyes. 'Look, I'm sorry, I'm sorry. I've never been with a girl, I don't know how to react around one. I was given some advice about you – advice which I took against my better judgement, but it seems that advice was wrong.'

'What sort of advice?' Jane asked seriously.

'Tom Rooney told me to beware of you, not to end up in bed with you. He said I'd never be rid of you if I did.'

The young woman threw back her head and laughed aloud. 'Oh, Patrick, sometimes you can be so stupid, so naive. Can't you see that he was just worried that you would betray some of the organization's secrets in a moment of passion? And to an English girl at that. No wonder he was worried.' She unfolded her arms and wrapped them around his waist, pulling him closer. 'Patrick, I'm not a virgin, I've slept with men before. So you needn't worry, I'm not going to fall madly in love with you ...' She stood on her toes, kissing him quickly – and then pushed him away. 'I'm going to have a bath, I feel grimy after the boat and train.'

Patrick nodded dumbly as she walked away, working on the buttons on her cuffs. 'You could order dinner,' she called as she kicked the bathroom door closed.

As the room slowly slipped into darkness, the lowering skies bringing on an early evening, Patrick sat by the window, staring out onto the streets below, listening to the noises in the bathroom as Jane gently hummed to herself. He was confused. He had grown up living in a web of deceit, he was used to his mother's machinations, had grown accustomed to her lies. He had grown up with the impression that women's motives were suspect, and so when Tom Rooney had given him his advice he had found it so easy to believe, because it was what – subconsciously – he expected. It was difficult to accept that Jane had no ulterior motives. Patrick smiled ruefully; he was nineteen going on twenty – what right had he to assign motives to a woman?

Dinner arrived on a trolley escorted by two servants. Swiftly and with the minimum of noise, they laid the small table with heavy silver tableware and spread out the various dishes. There was also a bottle of wine, 'with the compliments of the management'. If the waiters were curious about the room being in darkness, they neither said nor did anything which indicated it; they had been in the hotel business for far too many years now to be surprised by the antics or activities of the guests. When they had left – and Patrick had the grace to look embarrassed because he had no money with which to tip them – he went and tapped on the bathroom door.

'Dinner.'

'I'll be a minute.'

'It will get cold.'

'What are we having?'

Patrick peered under the dish covers. 'Breast of turkey in an orange sauce, vegetables marinated in …' he sniffed, breathing in the mouthwatering aroma, 'marinated in some sort of alcohol …' He picked up the bottle of wine. 'There's also a bottle of wine with the management's compliments. I wish I knew more about wine, but it looks like a good year.'

'That's champagne, you idiot.'

Patrick nearly dropped the bottle with fright. Jane was standing right behind him. She reached out and took the bottle from his hand and turned it around to examine the label, while he simply looked at her in amazement.

Patrick had always seen Jane as a maid, she walked, talked and acted as a maid. And when they had been hiding out in Tom Rooney's house, they had still fallen into the roles of master and maid, and on board ship Patrick's attitude, influenced by Tom's warning, had been stand-offish. Now, he saw her simply as a woman, and a surprisingly beautiful one at that.

She was slightly smaller than himself, slender and compact, with an intense, almost exotic beauty about her features. Her face was oval, and her expression seemed to be constantly challenging. Beneath an open, high-necked, long-sleeved cotton dressing gown, she was wearing a simple white cotton nightdress, which stuck to her still damp body, and she smelt of soap and steam. Her hair, damp from the bath, had been pulled back from her face, giving it a very youthful expression.

'Dinner's getting cold,' she murmured, smiling at his startled reaction; he hadn't been aware that he'd been staring.

Over dinner, they chatted together easily, casually, the conversation drifting. Jane had shown Patrick how to open the bottle of champagne, and they drank it slowly, neither of them enjoying the sharp fizzy taste, but neither willing to admit it. They chatted about their respective childhoods and, while Patrick had wanted for nothing, he found himself envying Jane's childhood freedom as the daughter of a groom and maid in service in a large country house just outside London.

'You could say I grew up in service – and so it seemed almost natural that Sarah and I should go into service.'

'I didn't think servants were allowed to marry,' Patrick remarked.

'It was unknown in the past, and in the larger houses in town it was unheard of, but in the country it was not unknown. It was felt that married servants – especially if both servants worked in the same house – tended to be more stable, and have a stabilising effect on the younger, unattached members of staff.'

'And what will happen to you now, do you think?'

Jane shook her head. 'I'll have to wait and see what your friends can do for me – if anything.'

'I won't see you without a job,' Patrick said quickly.

'Don't fret yourself about it. I'll always find a job.'

'Where?' Patrick demanded, 'you've no references.'

'There's always the streets,' she said with a cheeky grin – which immediately faded when she saw Patrick's expression. 'What's wrong – it was only a joke.'

'Nothing … nothing's wrong.'

'There must be something wrong,' she persisted. 'Tell me.' Patrick shook his head stubbornly.

Jane reached out and rested her fingers on the back of his hand. 'Tell me,' she insisted.

'Well, I don't suppose there's any harm in you knowing now.' He took a deep breath and sipped some of the flat champagne. 'When we lived in Dublin, my mother ran one of the largest brothels in the city. Apparently, she had been taken in by the Madam who ran the house, a woman called Bella Cohen, who adopted her almost as her daughter, but personally, I always found it hard to believe myself.'

'I'm sorry ... I didn't realize ...'

'You weren't to know. I didn't know myself until relatively recently. It's just ... it's just ...'

'What is it?'

Patrick ran both hands through his hair and buried his head in his hands and stared at the fine linen table cloth. 'Shortly before I left – the last argument I had with mother – she told me that Dermot Corcoran wasn't my father. I had grown up believing that my father had been a great patriot who had died for Ireland, but she told me that Dermot wasn't my father, and that my father was someone who hated the Irish and the idea of Irish independence.'

Jane reached out, covering his hands in hers.

'She wouldn't tell me who my father was.'

Her fingers tightened on his hands, hearing the anguish in his voice. 'Have you any way of finding out?'

He shook his head. 'No ... I don't know.'

'It must be someone in your mother's past, someone reasonably close to her. Perhaps someone who knew Dermot.'

Patrick nodded numbly.

'Perhaps if you were to start looking into your mother's past, you might find some lead.'

'It's a long shot.'

'It's all you have.'

Patrick looked up, his eyes glittering with moisture, and smiled gratefully at her. 'Well, it's something – thank you.'

'For what?'

He turned her hands, bringing her fingers around to his lips. 'For everything. For giving me the courage to do what I did.'

'You would have done it sooner or later,' she smiled,

her eyes deep and dark, the single light they had lit
earlier on which kept the room partially in shadow,
lending her face a slightly mysterious air.

'Later might have been too late. If I had left it any
later, she would have completely dominated me.' He
kissed her fingertips again. 'It's been quite a week. I've
learned a lot.'

Jane stood up and moved around the table to stand
before him. She shrugged off the dressing gown and
stepped closer to Patrick. He could feel the heat from
her body, smell the soapy scent from her skin. He could
clearly see the outline of one side of her body through
the cotton nightdress she wore, her nipples dark spots
against the pale cloth.

'Perhaps you can learn a little more,' she whispered.

Patrick awoke briefly during the night and lay awake,
confused and troubled for a few moments until he
realized where he was. He moved slightly in the bed,
and felt the warm, naked body beside him and smiled,
remembering the last few hours. He slid back beneath
the covers, hugging the woman's body close to his, his
arm around her waist, and fell into a deep and dreamless
sleep.

Jane smiled in her sleep, contented.

It was early morning when Patrick awoke again, and
this time he came fully alert. His arm reached out for
Jane – and touched only the still-warm sheets. He sat up
in bed, just as she came out of the bathroom, rubbing
her hair with a towel, unselfconsciously naked. He sat
back in the bed, pulling the sheets up around him.

'What are you looking at?' she teased, 'have you never
seen a naked woman before?'

'Not before last night.'

'But you lived in a brothel,' Jane said, disbelief in her
voice, sitting down on the edge of the bed and rubbing
vigorously at her hair.

'I was very young …'

Jane snorted rudely.

'… And mother, for all her faults ran the house with a rod of iron. I don't think I ever saw a nude woman in the house – certainly there were women in various states of undress … but never nude.' He reached out and ran the back of his hand down her thigh.

'Why don't you start with the brothel then?' she asked, watching him closely.

He looked at her uncomprehendingly.

'You wanted to trace your father, didn't you? Well, then start with the brothel where you lived – you can find it again?' she asked.

'I can find it.'

'Perhaps someone there might remember something … or do the staff at these establishments change quickly?' she wondered.

'Some of the women were there so long I used to call them aunty.' He leaned over and reached for her, his arms wrapping around her waist, but she slapped his hands away.

'Not now – later. I thought we were expecting visitors today.'

'Tomorrow,' he said.

'Let's go for a walk then,' she suggested.

'We were told to stay in our rooms,' Patrick said doubtfully.

Jane crossed to the windows and stood staring down into the street. They were quiet at this early hour and the cobbled stones still glistened from the night's rain. Patrick hopped out of bed and came up behind her, wrapping his arms around her waist, resting his chin on her shoulder. 'What's wrong,' he murmured.

'Do you always do what your told?' she asked sharply.

Patrick turned her around and looked down into her dark brown eyes. 'What would you like to do?' he asked.

'I'd like to go for a walk in that park over there,' she said quietly.

'It's called St Stephen's Green, or more usually just the Green.'

'I'd like to go there, just you and me, no one watching over us, no-one minding us, or guarding us, or whatever. I'd go myself,' she added, 'except that the hotel staff would think it strange if one half of a newly married couple should go for a ramble on her own.'

'We were told to stay here ...'

'Well, if you don't tell, I won't ...' she smiled and then, tilting his head down in her small hands, kissed him.

Less than an hour later, Mr and Mrs Montgomery strolled out of the Shelbourne Hotel and into St Stephen's Green.

Within the hour, a telegram was on its way to London claiming the reward for information as to the whereabouts of Patrick Lundy and his female servant.

CHAPTER SEVEN

'Just what the bloody hell do you think you're playing at?'

Patrick stepped back from the door in shock as a tall, broad shouldered man pushed his way in. A second, smaller man followed. He immediately closed the door, turning the key in the lock, and leaned back against the wood, arms folded, an expression of unconcern on his face.

'You were told to remain in your room.' The man strode into the centre of the room and tossed his hat onto a chair. He ran his hand through his thick black hair and glared at Patrick.

Patrick's initial shock was now turning to anger. 'Now look here ...'

Jane laid her hand on Patrick's arm, squeezing slightly, silencing him. 'What is the problem?' she asked the dark haired man.

He looked at her and smiled slightly, the smile lending his face a certain boyish charm. Here was a man who would have no trouble with women, Jane thought, strong and handsome, but cruel – perhaps cruel was too harsh a word, but hard certainly, it showed in the set of his mouth.

'The problem, dear lady,' he said quietly, his accent more pronounced now that he had calmed down, 'is that a certain Madam Lundy was sent a telegram yesterday informing her of the whereabouts of a certain Patrick Lundy.'

'Oh no,' Jane whispered.

Patrick visibly blanched.

'You two were spotted on your little perambulation

around the Green – very civilised, I must say, very stupid.'

'What are we going to do?' Jane asked, her voice calmer than she felt. From the little Patrick had told her, and from what she already knew of the woman, she knew Madam Lundy was quite capable of having them killed as a lesson.

'Nothing,' the broad Irishman grinned. 'I said Madam Lundy had been sent a telegram – I didn't say she had received it.'

Patrick shook his head, thoroughly confused now. 'I don't understand.'

'One of our men in the post office pulled it. Luckily he had been one of those we had briefed and he remembered the name. Oh, and my name, by the way, is Michael Collins.'

Patrick started, although only twenty-nine, Michael Collins was one of the prime movers in the Republican Movement now. He had fought with Pearse in the GPO in 1916, where he had acquitted himself honourably, and he had risen swiftly through the ranks. He shared Pearse's ideal of a Free Ireland, but his methods were slightly more pragmatic. He was tall and broad, with a square strong face, his eyes hard and sharp, and when he shook hands with Patrick, his grip was firm and dry.

'It's an honour,' Patrick gasped.

'It is an honour for me to meet the son of Dermot Corcoran,' Collins said immediately. 'I knew him briefly in the last days before the Rising, but I know of his work of course. He was a great man.' He turned to Jane. 'But you must excuse my manners, Miss. You must be Jane Bradley?'

Jane curtsied, charmed by the man's old world manners.

'You'll forgive my rudeness, but I am naturally concerned for your welfare, not only because of your father's memory, but because Tom Rooney requested it – and I have a great respect for Tom. The movement needs more men like him.' As he was speaking he was looking Patrick up and down. 'And Joe Hyde speaks highly of you too.'

'How is he?' Patrick asked quickly.

Michael Collins shrugged. 'Coming along, but slowly. A bad business …'

'My fault,' Patrick said immediately.

'Let's not apportion blame. What's done is done – and at least the men responsible for it have paid their dues.' He looked around the room. 'Now, come on. Your bill is paid, you've got to be out of the room by noon.'

'Where are we going?' Jane asked quickly.

'Somewhere safe; somewhere Madam Lundy won't find you – I hope.'

Jane grinned. 'I hope so too.'

Michael Lee hated the city.

He hated the people, the smell, even the sounds. It was foreign, alien, and he felt very much out of place. This wasn't his world – and Madam Lundy knew that – and he knew that his chances of finding the boy and girl were very remote indeed. At least in London, Manchester, Birmingham, Glasgow or Edinburgh, he had contacts he could exploit, although, he reflected ruefully, his contacts in London hadn't borne much fruit. But whatever chances he had of finding them in London, he had none in Dublin.

Michael Lee had arrived in Dublin barely four hours ago – he checked his watch again – but already it felt like a lifetime. He had immediately checked into the Shelbourne, one of Dublin's premier hotels, and spent the next hour soaking himself in a bath, washing away the grime of the rough sea-crossing. Michael Lee, although born and reared in squalor on London's wharves – or perhaps because of it – was now fastidiously clean. As he soaked in the warm, slightly scented water, he ran through his options. Madam Lundy had given him a list of possible contacts in Dublin, people she had known in her days here; some owed her favours, others had exploitable vices or indiscretions. Lee privately doubted that the majority of these contacts would be useful: favours had a way of being conveniently forgotten, and vices and indiscretions tended to lose their edge as the years passed. Also, some of the people on her list might no longer have the connections he needed.

A police inspector in Scotland Yard who owed him a favour – a slight matter of some indiscreet letters – had supplied him with a list of known criminals in Dublin, as well as a separate listing of all known Republican sympathisers. Therein lay his best chance, he felt; Patrick Lundy would be sure to make his way into the organization.

And assuming he found him – what then? Madam Lundy's instructions had been explicit. He was to bring Patrick back, any way he could, but the girl – if she was in Dublin – was to be taught a serious and possibly fatal lesson.

Lee sank deeper into the bath, wisps of white steam rising lazily into the heavy air, and he wondered where Patrick Lundy and the girl were.

... less than ten feet away Patrick Lundy and Jane Bradley, followed Michael Collins down the carpeted corridor, while behind them the silent bodyguard carefully locked the door after them.

It had rained again, leaving the streets dark and shining, and the wheels of the car hissed across the damp road. They were driving around the Green and the smell of damp earth and undergrowth was rich, overlaying even the sharp car fumes. It was silent in the interior of the car, Patrick and Jane sitting close together, across from Collins who seemed intent on the street scene. The bodyguard drove, cut off from them by a sliding glass panel.

'Do you remember the city?' Collins asked suddenly.

Patrick started. 'No ... well, a little.'

'Where did you live? I'm afraid I only got the briefest details on you,' he said by way of explanation.

'In Monto.' He saw Collins' look of surprise and hurried on. 'We lived on the top floor of number eighty-two, Tyrone Street, Lower.'

'I've heard of the address,' Collins said shortly.

'Some of the 1916 leaders met there,' Patrick said quickly, catching some disapproval in the older man's voice.

'Aye.' He shifted uncomfortably in the seat, and then turned his head away.

Patrick glanced out the window and caught sight of a troop of British tommies marching around the Green towards them, on the opposite side of the road. There was silence until the soldiers had passed, and Collins slowly withdrew his hand from his coat pocket; glancing through the sliding glass panel, Patrick saw the driver do the same.

'I'm told you're a doctor?' Collins continued as if nothing had happened.

'I'm still a student.'

'But you know a little?' he persisted.

'A little, yes.'

Collins nodded. 'Good, we've always use for medical men.'

'Then you'll take me into the organization?' Patrick asked excitedly.

Collins smiled slightly. 'Do I have any choice? I'm just wondering where we can put you. With your mother chasing you, we've got to keep you out of sight for a while.'

'How about a disguise?' Jane asked, startling them both.

Patrick snorted rudely, but Collins looked interested. 'What sort of disguise?'

She shrugged. 'Nothing dramatic. Change his hair, colour it, give him a beard — it would all help to age him, and Madam Lundy's men will be looking for a young man.'

Collins smiled warmly. 'That's an excellent idea, young woman.'

'Jane, Jane Bradley,' she said quickly.

'Of course,' he said apologetically. He turned to look at Patrick again. 'Yes, I think we could do that.' He leaned back to tap on the glass partition and then slid it open. 'Take us around to see Eddie.'

The driver nodded. He swung across two lanes of traffic and turned left into Grafton Street. Jane sat mesmerised at the array of expensive and exclusive shops that lined the narrow street – this was not how she imagined Dublin. This street would not look out of place in London's most fashionable shopping district. Patrick too was watching the shops go by, remembering the last time he had walked down them, it had been early in 1916, and he had gone out with Mickey – God Rest Him – to buy his mother an Easter gift. He had never found a suitable gift, and there hadn't been an Easter that year, the only gift many families had received had been blood and fire.

At the bottom of Grafton Street, the driver swung around to the left into College Green. Patrick looked out at Trinity College on his right and the Parliament buildings on his left, but neither seemed to have been scarred by the Rising. Further down the street, in Westmorland Street, some of the shops bore the scars of the fighting, and many were still under repair. However, it was only when the driver turned to the left up the quays that the real damage wrought by the 1916 rising could be clearly seen. Many of the old buildings had been gutted, while others still bore the starred and shattered glass of the explosions that had rocked the city.

Just past the Ha'penny Bridge, the driver turned to the left into Lower Fownes's Street and stopped before the first building on the right hand side. The man alighted and checked the street first, his hand deep in his pocket, before finally opening the door. Patrick climbed out first and then helped Jane down; Collins was the last man out, and Patrick heard him murmur to the driver, 'Around the block the long way, only stop if you see us on the street.'

113

Patrick turned to look at the street, wondering what had brought Collins here; but it seemed just another poor tenement sidestreet. He squinted to make out the figure above the nearest open door, but it was completely encrusted with grime; the name and number above the next building however, was Number Two.

'Let's not hang about,' Collins said, ushering them both into the darkened hallway. Patrick had grown up in the tenements and immediately recognized their peculiar odour – the smell of cabbage and urine, of burnt food and unwashed humanity. Although his mother's house had always been spotless, and was considered to be one of the most exclusive brothels in the red-light district, it too had managed to capture some of the essence of the tenements, a lingering miasma that no matter how often the skivvies scrubbed and washed the floors and walls still managed to seep into the house.

The hallway was dark, but Michael Collins made his way without hesitation to the first doorway on the right hand side and tapped once, then twice and once again in an obviously prearranged signal. The door was opened almost immediately by a tiny grey-haired woman, who looked past Collins to stare hard at the two strangers standing behind him.

'They're with me,' Michael Collins said gently.

The woman nodded eventually and stood back, allowing Collins, followed by Jane and Patrick, to enter. She immediately closed the door and snapped two heavy bolts across it.

'It's been awhile Michael,' she said, her accent broad and sharp, pronouncing his name in the Irish language as Mee-hawl

'You're looking well, Eddie,' he said, smiling fondly. 'How have you been?'

'Getting old,' she grumbled, moving past Patrick to stand before Jane. 'A pretty lass,' she muttered.

'This is Eddie,' Collins said, introducing the woman. 'Eddie has worked in most of the theatres not only in

London but all across Europe as well as our own National Theatre.'

'I was wondering where the postcards came from,' Jane said. She was staring at the far wall of the small room, which was completely covered in postcards and photogravure cards from just about every city in Europe. There were also framed pictures of theatrical personalities and playbills on the walls. Otherwise the small single room was almost bare; a bed in one corner, a dresser before the single window, a small table with two chairs flat against the far wall. There was a coal fire beside the bed – dangerously close – with no more than a dozen coals piled one atop the other, more smoke than flame.

'This is Patrick,' Collins said, 'and Jane. They are on the run from some particularly nasty people in England who, we have every reason to suspect, have followed them here. Patrick will join us in the organization, but for him to be able to work effectively, he will need to be able to move around freely.'

The tiny woman, her sharp face a mass of wrinkles, gripped Patrick by the arms and spun him around to face her. 'How do you intend to use him?'

'He has some medical training, and we won't want to waste that. He has a good education and will be able to mix with the upper classes.'

'Nothing too rough then,' Eddie muttered. She ran her frail fingers through his nondescript hair, brushing it off his forehead. 'We can lose some of the hair, deepen the colour, and then add a little silver,' she said to Collins and then looked back at Patrick, 'how old are you boy, eighteen, nineteen ...?'

'Nearly twenty,' he said quickly.

'Nineteen. Well, when I'm finished with you, you'll look closer to thirty.' She looked at Jane. 'Now you sit him down over there and wet his hair.' She nodded first to the table and then to the ewer on the window ledge.

Patrick looked wide-eyed at Collins, wondering what was going on, but the big man smiled genially and

nodded. 'Eddie knows what she's doing. She's the best
– trust her.'

Patrick nodded doubtfully. He allowed Jane to sit him
by the table and then damp down his hair with water –
ice cold and brackish! – from the ewer. She squeezed his
shoulder comfortingly and stepped away as Eddie
reappeared with a cloth wrapped bundle. She rolled out
the towel on the table, revealing two scissors, one large,
the other tiny, a score of combs and brushes and a razor.
Picking up a comb and the larger scissors she turned
back to Patrick, looking critically at his hair.

'How often do you shave, boy?'

'Well … ahem …'

'Not often, I'll wager. Well, when you do shave in
future, don't shave so high,' she touched his cheeks
below his ears, 'and allow your locks to grow and
thicken. It will help change the shape of your face. Now
…' she ran her fingers through his dampened hair, 'close
your eyes.'

Patrick obediently closed his eyes, feeling the sun
warm and orange on his eyelids, hearing the click of
the old woman's scissors, feeling cold strands of hair
drift occasionally across his face. He felt the blade of the
open razor scrape against the back of his neck and again
on his forehead. When the scissors stopped, the old
woman dragged the comb through his hair several
times, trying different styles, and he heard Jane
murmur, 'That's amazing.'

'We're not finished yet, my dear,' Eddie said quickly.
She tapped Patrick on the shoulder. 'Keep your eyes
closed now. This might sting,' she added.

Patrick was just about to ask what she was going to
do when he felt something cold touch his scalp – and
then it was as if his head had caught fire. Eddie splashed
more of the liquid against his temples, brushing it back
and then rubbing it in with a comb.

'More water, dear,' she asked, and then, obviously
speaking to Patrick, whose eyes were now squeezed
tight with pain. 'This is only water.' The liquid against

his burning scalp was like balm, and then Eddie rubbed his head briskly with a rough towel, before damping it again, and then brushing it back. 'You can open your eyes now.'

Patrick carefully opened his eyes to find the three faces staring at him; the look of satisfaction on Eddie's face, contrasted sharply with Collins' look of admiration, and Jane's shocked expression. The old woman picked up a spotted mirror and held it before his face. Patrick blinked in astonishment. He raised a hand to touch his face, not believing what he saw. Eddie had cut away most of his thin nondescript hair, cropping it close to the skull, and she had also cut back the hair on his forehead, giving him a pronounced widow's peak. She had then bleached his hair along the side and at the temples ... and the results, as she had promised, added ten years and more to his age.

'We could give him a pair of spectacles,' Eddie suggested.

Michael Collins wrapped his arm around her shoulder and squeezed affectionately. 'You've worked wonders, as usual.'

'Perhaps you should let me do something for you,' she suggested. 'You're far too noticeable as it is.'

'Some day,' he promised.

'Some day soon,' she said.

'Soon.'

Collins ushered Patrick and Jane back out onto the street – just in time to see the car come chugging around the corner. It had barely stopped before Collins had the door open and had bundled them inside.

'Where to now?' Patrick asked.

'Somewhere safe.'

'Where?' Jane wondered.

Collins nodded. 'It's not far,' he said evasively.

Michael Lee checked the address on the scrap of paper and then the name plate pinned high to the wall of the tenement. 'Tyrone Street Lower.' Methodically tearing the paper into tiny pieces, he casually strolled up the gently sloping cobbled street, looking for number eighty-two.

Although it was early afternoon, the streets were empty, and Michael Lee was conscious that he was probably attracting much unwarranted attention. This district, with its decaying tenements, its cobbled streets shattered and stinking, the pervasive odour of massed humanity, and their filth, reminded him with almost terrifying clarity of the wharves where he had grown up. This was more what he had imagined Dublin to be; he had been surprised to find it so obviously wealthy and cultured. This area – even if he had been a total stranger to the city, and known nothing of its history, would have immediately advertised itself as the red-light district – even the very air seemed tainted by the smells of cheap perfume and sex.

He found number eighty-two close to the top of the street, looking just as derelict as the rest of the tenements on the shabby street. And yet this was the house run by the notorious Whore mistress, Bella Cohen, and later by the woman known only as Madam Kitten but who was, in reality, Katherine Lundy. The reputation of number eighty-two was widespread, and prior to the outbreak of the Great War, it ranked as highly as any of the European brothels, and was reputed to number amongst its clients the very highest in the land.

The steps to Number Eighty-Two were worn, and Lee smiled, wondering how many eager feet had climbed those steps. Lee's inclinations led in other directions, and he found it difficult to comprehend how men were so easily led by a woman.

The tall thin man paused on the top step, looking casually up and down the street – too many years on the street having taught him what to look for – but he saw nothing suspicious. He knocked quickly, tapping out the code Madam Lundy had given him. She hadn't known if it had been changed – it was unlikely – but if nothing else it would help to gain him admittance.

There was no reply.

Lee knocked again, and this time the door was immediately opened and he found himself staring down into the large black barrels of a sawn-off shotgun.

'Step inside and no tricks now, or they'll be scraping you off the street.'

Suppressing a smile, Michael Lee stepped into the darkened hallway. It took a few minutes for his eyes to adjust to the dimness, and he remained still, blinking hard, making out the man standing directly in front of him holding the shotgun, while on the stairs to his left another person – a woman? – was also holding what looked like a small pistol on him.

'The only person likely to use one of the old codes is a police officer.' The voice was female, Dublin, and came from the stairs to his left.

Lee turned slightly towards the sound – and immediately heard the double click as the hammers on the shotgun were pulled back.

'Stay where you are.'

'Are you a police officer?'

Lee grinned. 'Well, I'm hardly likely to admit it if I was now, would I?'

'Who are you then?'

'I don't think …'

The man with the shotgun hit him with the butt of the weapon, driving it deep into his stomach, doubling him over, dropping him to the floor.

'Answer my question,' the woman continued, as if nothing had happened.

'The Madam taught you well,' Lee gasped, suppressing the urge to throw up.

'Who are you?' the woman said once more. 'I won't ask you again.' The woman came down the remaining stairs and stood before Lee, so close that he could smell the perfume – expensive and subtle – off her.

'My name is Lee, Michael Lee. The Madam sent me.'

'Who?'

Lee straightened painfully, his hand massaging his

bruised stomach. 'Madam Kitten, Madam Katherine Lundy who ran this house until Easter week, three years ago. She sent me.'

'Proof?'

'There's a letter in my inside pocket.'

The woman stepped back, and Lee was roughly turned over, and the shotgun pressed into his throat. The Londoner found himself staring into the expressionless face of the tall and broad, blond-haired, blue-eyed bouncer.

'Meet Jem,' the woman said conversationally, 'short for Jemmy. He's from Germany originally; he doesn't speak much English, but he understands well enough. His real name is James, or Jim, but he doesn't pronounce it too well,' she continued, as the man deftly extracted the thick envelope containing one of the notes Katherine had written for Lee on the day of his departure. She had written four introductions to her old cronies in Dublin, in the hope that one, at least, might prove useful.

The woman in the shadows read the brief note. 'Let him up Jem, he's all right.'

The bouncer – bullies, as they were called in Dublin – stepped away from Lee, and eased the hammers down on the shotgun. However, he still managed to keep the weapon pointing loosely in his direction. He made no attempt to help Lee to his feet.

'So Madam Lundy is still around. I wondered when she would ever return to Dublin – I presume that's why you're here.'

'You're wrong.' Michael Lee scrambled to his feet. 'Madam Lundy will never be returning to Dublin. Are you Nuala?' he asked eventually.

The woman turned and walked up the stairs without replying, and for a moment, Lee stood undecided. Then, glancing quickly at Jem, he slowly climbed the stairs, feeling his bruised stomach muscles protest with every step.

He followed the woman into a room on the top floor.

Compared to what he had seen of the rest of the house, this was luxurious. Heavy, ugly furniture rested on a blood-red carpet, which matched the flocked design in the off-white wallpaper. The prints on the walls were dark and undistinguished, and the large, gilded mirror on the wall over the marble fireplace was speckled. There were numerous gaps in the bookcase at the end of the room, and Lee wondered what had happened to Madam Lundy's collection of books. The room was exactly as Katherine had described it – only shabbier, neglected.

Lee turned his attention to the woman.

What he had first taken for height he soon realized was a product of high – very high – heels, and he guessed that without the lifts she would be around five foot, pleasantly featured, with a round face and perfectly round brown eyes that looked almost serene until he realized how hard they were. Her chestnut coloured hair – recently coloured too, he guessed – was tightly curled around her face and her figure was hidden beneath the drapes of an ugly housecoat.

'Sit, please,' she said, her Dublin accent more noticeable now. 'Drink?'

He shook his head.

Nuala crossed to the window and perched on the ledge looking down into the street below. Glancing around at Lee, she said, 'Tell me about the Madam.'

Slightly off-balance by the speed of the events, Lee floundered for a few moments. 'Well, eh ... well the Madam is fine. She has continued her business interests in London, and now runs one of the most successful houses in the city, indeed in the whole country. She also has business interests in Manchester and Glasgow.'

'But she won't be coming back to Dublin?' the woman asked, and Lee suddenly realized where this line of questioning was leading.

He shook his head emphatically. 'The Madam will have nothing to do with either Dublin or Ireland. This country cost her too much; indeed, she has gone so far

as to refuse to discuss the topic. No, you may rest assured
– this house is yours, Madam Lundy does not want it
back.'

The woman smiled, and moved away from the
window. 'I was somewhat concerned,' she admitted,
crossing to the fireplace and pulling the ornate sash that
hung down beside it. The door opened almost immediately and Jem appeared, without the shotgun this time.
'Some tea for our guest.'

The man nodded and silently disappeared.

Nuala sat down facing Michael Lee. 'When the Madam
gave me the keys and deeds of this house in Easter week,
1916, she said that it was mine, that she had no further use
for it. But somehow I always feared that one day she
would return to claim what's hers. I've worked hard for
this house over the past three years. Maybe I haven't kept
it up to her standards but I've done my best.'

'You've done a good job,' Lee said quickly, recognizing the woman's insecurity. 'This house is yours,
she'll never want it back, and from what I've seen, I think
you've done her proud.'

'You think so?'

Lee nodded quickly. 'I run a similar institution for the
Madam in London, but I wouldn't be ashamed to say I
ran this one.'

Nuala positively glowed, and for a few moments she
looked like a child who had been given a present. But
then the smile faded. 'If you are here though, it must
mean trouble.'

'It does, but not for you. The only reason I came here
was because the Madam gave me your name and said that
with your underworld connections you might be able to
help me find someone.'

'She looking for someone for a job?'

'Not quite. She's looking for a young man and
possibly a young woman. Runaways from England.'

'And why would the Madam be interested in
runaways?' Nuala wondered, looking up as the door
opened and a young woman appeared carrying a tray.

Lee waited until the girl had placed the tray down on a small side table and backed silently from the room. 'One of the runaways is her son, Patrick. And she wants him back.'

'Master Patrick ... yes I remember Master Patrick,' Nuala smiled fondly.

'Following the events of 1916, Madam Lundy's control over her children quickly became complete,' Lee said, watching Nuala pour tea from a fine silver teapot. 'Eventually, they became almost prisoners, answerable for their every movement.'

'You don't approve?'

'I have spoken to the Madam about it. I knew it would lead to trouble. The boy's nearly twenty now. He should be able to take care of himself – and yet she won't even let him out of the house without demanding to know where he's going, who he'll be with and what time he'll be back.' He shook his head quickly, his lips a thin, hard line.

'The Madam always loved her children,' Nuala said, remembering how proud Katherine had always been of them.

Lee sipped his tea from a cup of pale fragile china and shook his head. 'Well now she's just possessive. It's bad for business. It takes her mind off other things,' he said savagely, remembering the note the Madam had received offering her some of the stolen Irish Crown Jewels. When this affair with Patrick and the servant girl had blown up, she had forgotten all about the stones. They were gone now – sold to some Russian apparently. What a waste.

Nuala smiled automatically, re-evaluating the man. When she had seen him first, she had marked him as a 'bully', one of those who kept the brothel girls in line. In her years working with the Madam and then running her own brothel she had come to know many, and she could usually spot their type. And Michael Lee was that type: aggressive, cunning, smooth, dangerous, and probably homosexual too, she shouldn't wonder.

She had initially thought he might have come to reclaim the Madam's brothel – in which case he was going to have a mysterious and fatal accident. But when he had been speaking of Katherine's children, her opinion of him had begun to change, it sounded as if he did have a genuine sympathy for them and their plight. But he had revealed his true colours now – he considered that the Madam's overwhelming interest in them was merely bad for business. Nuala decided she didn't like this smooth, sharp man.

'So how can I be of assistance to you?' she asked, fixing a professional smile to her face, the same smile she used when dealing with difficult customers or when fixing the amount to be paid out in bribes.

'In any way you can. If you could put the word around that a substantial reward will be paid for information leading to the boy's capture.' Lee settled the cup on the saucer. 'And of course, if there is any other information you think might be useful to me. Perhaps you might even allow me to borrow one of your people as a guide around the city. I don't know Dublin at all.'

Nuala nodded. 'Of course,' she said quickly, her professional mask never slipping. 'And of course, if you had any clues as to where the boy might have gone …'

'We know he has Nationalist sympathies …'

Nuala smiled, showing surprisingly white teeth. 'So has half the city … that gets you nowhere …'

Lee shook his head as she offered more tea. 'Where would a young man and woman go – assuming they landed in this city with little money and no contacts.'

Nuala shrugged. 'This is a big city. And they could just as easily have hopped on a train to any other part of the country.'

'I would imagine they have very little money,' Lee supplied.

'Would they have any compunction about acquiring more?'

'If you're asking me would they steal for it, well then I don't know. The boy I know has been brought up to want for nothing, and has been raised a staunch Catholic. The girl I'm not so sure about.'

'There are a few cheap hotels close to the stations ...' Nuala mused, 'I'll have someone look into it.' She finished her own tea and put down the cup. 'I think you're wasting your time, to be honest. It will be like looking for a needle in a haystack. Far too many young people arrive from England every day – they're just another young couple, there's nothing special, nothing remarkable about them.'

'Madam Lundy doesn't think so.'

Nuala nodded. 'And that's the only reason I'll help you look for them.'

CHAPTER EIGHT

'And this time stay here,' Michael Collins said for the last time as he pulled the door closed behind him, leaving Patrick and Jane alone in the small, dark room.

Patrick had opened his mouth to ask a question, but Collins was abruptly gone, the large man moving surprisingly silently down the bare stairs of the empty house. He turned to look at Jane, but she simply shrugged and looked away. She knew as much as he did.

When they had left Eddie's, they had driven up the quays in silence. They turned right onto the bridge when they came to Kingsbridge Station and then immediately left and right into Parkgate Street.

'Where are you taking us?' Jane asked as the car began the drive up the long sloping street.

'We have a safe house on Conyngham Road,' Michael Collins said, not looking at her, his eyes now on the street outside. There seemed to be more than the usual number of soldiers about. 'We don't use it much,' he continued gently, 'because it's so close to the barracks.' He jerked his head to the right towards the high wall surrounding the Phoenix Park. 'But since you're not wanted by the police it should be all right. Now listen to me, both of you,' he continued sternly, turning to look first at Jane and then settling on Patrick. 'Don't leave the house. Don't answer the door. If either I or any of my men have need to visit, we have our own key. Stay in the house,' he said slowly and distinctly. 'Disobey me, and I'll walk away and you can fend for yourselves. Is that understood?'

They both nodded obediently.

'Now, we'll be here in a moment. Once the car stops,

get out immediately and walk up the steps directly in front of you, as if you own the place. We don't want to stay too long, it might attract too much attention …'

'What's going to happen to us?' Jane asked.

'I'll find you a position in service somewhere, if that's all right with you,' he said quickly, watching her, 'and I would like to think that Patrick will join us eventually …'

'What do you mean "eventually"?' Patrick demanded, 'I thought I was already one of you …'

Jane smiled and squeezed his arm. 'I think he means when you've proved yourself,' she explained.

Collins grinned, but said nothing. Seconds later, he tapped on the glass with the back of his fingers. 'We're here.'

Now that they were alone in the house, they became aware just how silent the place actually was. It was a three-storied redbrick house over a basement, set a little way back from the road and boasting a tiny square of a front garden and an equally large back garden. From the grimy upper windows they could see the Phoenix Park, and Patrick could see Jane looking longingly at the greenery.

'Don't even think about it,' he warned.

'I wasn't.'

Hand-in-hand they wandered through the house, starting at the top where Collins had left them. Obviously the house had been used as a hide-out for men on the run. There were blankets piled high in one corner of the room, as well as pillows and a half dozen mattresses, some of which had certainly seen better days. The rest of the rooms were deserted, the floors bare, the walls stained, pale squares marking the positions of old pictures. There was a mirror in one of the larger rooms – a bedroom – ancient and spotted, cobwebs coating it in grey. Jane glanced into the mirror and quickly looked back again – the image that had looked back at her was that of an old, old woman. It took another startled look to realize it was nothing more than a trick of the light and the filthy glass.

'What a cheery place,' Patrick said, his voice a whisper.

'It gives me the shivers,' Jane nodded, her own voice a thin, reedy whisper.

'Why are we whispering?' Patrick smiled.

'So give me something to shout about.' She tiptoed over to where he was standing looking out the window onto the road, now busy with traffic. She slipped her arm through his, and rested her head on his shoulder.

'I don't suppose we'll have to stay here too long anyway,' he said absently.

'I hope not,' she said feelingly.

They completed their circuit of the house, but didn't descend into the cellars; when Patrick had pulled open the door that led downwards, the stench that had wafted up had been of something long rotten and foul, and the squeaking of rats had sounded far too loud to be comfortable. Shaken, they made their way back to the top of the house, where Patrick dragged out two of the old mattresses and laid one beneath the window which looked down onto Conyngham Road. He placed the second flat against the wall, and then covered it with all the available blankets.

Jane meanwhile had wandered through all the rooms on the top floor and had returned to stand by the door watching Patrick.

'It's all dust and spiders,' she said quietly, much of her natural cheerfulness gone now. 'There are four rooms on this floor as well as a cupboard. There are some tins in the cupboard – but we've no tin opener,' she added.

She sounded so morose that Patrick took her into his arms, squeezing her tight. 'Look, don't worry about it; they won't forget about us.'

'I hope not.'

'I only wish mother would.'

Jane grinned ruefully. 'You know she won't.'

'I know.'

Now it was Jane's turn to smile at Patrick's mournful expression. 'Cheer up … it could be worse!'

Their laughter sounded very hollow in the empty house.

If the house was lonely by day, then by night it became almost frightening. Conyngham Road began to quieten down by early evening, and by eight o'clock, it was almost completely deserted. Night came early to Dublin; it was a cold chill night, with the sky clear and sparkling, the streets quickly taking on a metallic glitter.

It was bitterly cold in the house and Jane and Patrick huddled together beneath the bundled blankets for warmth. Conversation had flagged as dusk was falling. Eventually Jane broke the dusky silence.

'Why couldn't he have left us in that nice hotel; why did he have to bring us here?'

Patrick shook his head. 'I don't know, do I?' he snapped, the chill of the night and his own frayed nerves making him tense.

'Well, he's your friend,' she retorted.

'I've never met him before in my life. I only know him by his reputation.'

'Well, I'm cold,' she grumbled.

Patrick pulled her close, wrapping his arms around her shoulders. She was shivering. 'I'm cold too,' he said quietly, his voice muffled against her hair.

'Why did they take us out of the hotel?' she muttered. Ten minutes later she was asleep.

'Obviously the first place they would start looking would be the hotels,' Collins explained about two hours later, as he watched Patrick and Jane eat the hot soup he had brought. 'The only way to find you is by trial and error – the easiest way would be to start with the hotels; failing that, they would then move on to the cheaper boarding houses,' he grinned, 'they would have caught up with you eventually.'

'How long will we have to stay here?' Patrick asked, watching him over the rim of his bowl.

The big man shrugged. 'I'm in the process of sorting that out now. I've made a few inquiries, and I think I can find Jane a position in a house on the north side. The people there sympathize with our cause, and all we need to do is to explain that you are on the run from England – which is partially the truth anyway – and they'll be happy with that. Will you be?' He arched his eyebrows, looking at Jane. She nodded sleepily.

Collins then turned to Patrick. 'You present me with a little problem though,' he said slowly. 'I have the greatest respect for the memory of your father – and I know that the leaders of the Rising held him in just as high regard ... but you ...'

'I'm an untried quantity,' Patrick supplied.

Collins nodded.

'My belief in the Cause is what has landed me in this position,' Patrick said quietly. 'I believe in the Cause my father fought and died for just as strongly as he did. I've given up everything – an easy comfortable life, an assured future, wealth and all that it brings – to be here, to fight for the Cause. How many of your men can say the same?'

Collins rocked back on his heels, laughing silently. 'That's a grand speech. Did you make it up yourself?'

'It's true,' Patrick, slightly abashed at the outburst.

'I've no doubt about it,' Collins grinned. He spread his large hands. 'Well, what can I do? I'm not a gambling man – but I do follow my instincts.' He held out his large rough hand and Patrick shook it. 'So that there will be no acrimony amongst the men, I'm taking you into my own group. No one will ask any questions and you'll be accepted all the easier. But you'll be expected to do whatever you are asked. Do you understand me?'

Patrick nodded quickly. 'I'll do whatever I'm told to do.'

'Even if you disagree with it?'

He nodded quickly.

Michael Collins shook his head sadly. 'If only you knew what you were agreeing to.' He stood up quickly,

130

brushing off his hands, dusting his trousers. 'Someone will come for you in the morning.' He looked down at Jane. 'I don't expect I'll see you again, but then, I don't expect Patrick will either.' He looked at the young man again. 'You realize that by taking up with me and my men, you lose the right to call yourself a free man, you lose the right to family, and friends. You may have felt trapped in London, but by God that's nothing to the feelings you'll experience here. You'll end up trusting no one but the men you work with.'

'It's what I want,' Patrick said quickly.

'We'll see. I'll ask you again in a couple of months maybe,' Collins walked away, moving assuredly through the darkened rooms.

Patrick and Jane spent the remainder of the night together talking quietly, discussing everything but their futures, and it was only as the dusty windows were beginning to burn with the gold of the dawn that Patrick brought up the subject.

'If we don't see one another again ...'

'We will,' Jane said quickly.

'Collins didn't seem too sure.'

'Perhaps he was only trying to scare you off – see if you were going to change your mind ...'

Patrick shook his head. 'I wish I could believe that. He sounded sincere.'

Jane said nothing. She didn't believe it either; Collins had been trying to warn Patrick in his own gentle way about just what he was getting into. But Patrick was either too stupid or too blind to see that. And Jane couldn't help wondering why Michael Collins, who was on the wanted list of every policeman in Ireland, and who had obviously survived so long because of his caution, should take on a stranger so easily. Was it just because of what Patrick's father had done before and during the Easter Rising? Was it that – or was there another reason, she wondered?

'You're pleased you're joining Collins and his group?' she ventured.

131

Patrick nodded happily. 'It's a great honour to be allowed to fight with his group. They're the elite. It'll give me a chance to fight for my country's freedom ...'

'Like your father?'

He nodded.

'Your father was killed,' she reminded him gently, very gently.

'I know that!' He stood up quickly and crossed to the window to look down onto the street, still sparkling with the night's frost. He rubbed the flat of his hand against the glass; it was iced up on the inside.

'I don't want to see you killed,' she said softly.

Patrick leaned his forehead against the chill glass. 'I won't be,' he said tightly.

Jane took a deep breath, attempting to quell the anger she could feel bubbling up inside her; anger at his stupidity, his obstinacy. 'So what makes you invulnerable – what made your father invulnerable?'

She knew she had said too much when she saw the look on his face. His lips were drawn to a thin white line and his eyes had hardened; looking at him, she could see his mother's face, cold and pitiless.

'You will never speak about my father again. You never knew him, you don't know what he was like.'

'Do you?' she snapped, and from the look of betrayal on his face she knew she had hit a nerve. 'Do you know who your father was, what he was? Well, do you? Tell me about your father, Patrick Corcoran,' she persisted venomously.

But Patrick no longer heard her – all he could hear were his mother's bitter, angry words as she destroyed all his childhood illusions ... 'Your father didn't die for Ireland ... Dermot Corcoran fought and died in the Rising ... Dermot Corcoran was not your father ... not your father ... not your father ...'

'Patrick ... Patrick ...' Jane's voice was beginning to break; the distant expression in his eyes had been truly frightening. They held such pain, such hurt ... and such anger.

His eyes blinked and he focused on her again, his voice tired and defeated. 'You're right. I don't know anything about my father ... but I intend to find out!'

Jane shook her head. 'What are you talking about?'

'I'm talking about my father, my real father. Dermot Corcoran was not my real father – that piece of information was my mother's parting gift to me. I don't know who my father was – but I'm going to find him!' A sudden noise distracted him, and he looked down into the street below to see two men alight from an old and battered car. One remained by the car, while the second walked quickly up the path where he disappeared from Patrick's sight. Moments later they heard the key turn in the lock and footsteps echoed down the hall and thundered up the stairs.

'Hello ... Hello ...'

They were waiting for him on the top landing, and he seemed as much startled by their appearance as they were by his. He was wearing the garb of a priest. He grinned at their surprised expressions. Touching his collar, he said, 'Yes it is real and I am entitled to wear it.' He looked around, searching for something. 'Have you got everything ... no bags?'

Jane shook her head. 'Nothing.' They had left the bags Tom Rooney had lent them with Collins; he had assured her that they would find their way back to Tom in time.

'We're ready to go,' Patrick said.

The priest nodded and turned away without another word. Without speaking, the young man and woman followed him out of the empty house.

'Nothing?' Michael Lee said in astonishment, 'nothing at all?'

'If they were here, then they've vanished from the face of the earth,' Nuala said, walking away from the Englishman to stand before the small lake. Nuala had taken him walking in the Green; the day, although bright, was bitterly cold, and the park's leafless trees and

133

muddy walks had attracted few strollers, allowing them a great deal of privacy. Nuala recalled wryly that it had been one of the Madam's favourite places.

'But were they seen here?' Lee asked.

Nuala smiled. 'They were two doors away from you in the Shelbourne at one time,' she grinned. Lee's expression soured and she added quickly, 'But I don't think we need tell the Madam that, eh?'

Lee smiled tightly. 'Maybe not. What about the Republican Organizations?'

The woman shrugged. 'Since the 1916 Rising they're as tightly closed as a …' she stopped, and it was Lee's turn to smile.

'I'm sure I've heard the expression – and hundreds like it. But I take your meaning. Have you no one on the inside?'

Nuala turned away from the water and walked towards him, her hands now buried deep in her stole. The thick ocelot fur coat had its collar pulled up, obscuring most of her face. 'Some months ago, I attempted to place a man on the inside, someone close to Michael Collins …'

'Why?' Lee asked, surprised.

'Collins is worth a lot of money – dead or alive. And if the Madam taught me one thing – it was the value of information.'

'What happened?' Lee wondered. He offered her his arm and together they walked down the cinder and gravel path, avoiding the muddy pools of leafy water.

Nuala shrugged. 'I don't know. Officially, he got drunk, fell in the river and drowned.'

'You don't believe that?'

'He was a Pioneer,' she said, and then, seeing his puzzled expression, continued, 'he was a member of one of the total abstinence organizations that seem to flourish in Ireland and nowhere else. He had taken a pledge before a priest never to touch alcohol. He had taken this pledge when he was fifteen, and in forty years, he had never touched alcohol.'

Lee nodded. 'So he was discovered and disposed of.' He shrugged. 'They're ruthless, we know that. Well, we can be ruthless too when the need arises.'

'What are you suggesting?'

'Are you sure they're with Collins and his people?' he asked.

She shook her head, wondering where the questioning was leading. 'No, not exactly sure, but I think – in view of what you've told me about the boy – that it's more than likely.'

'Do you have the name of anyone in the organization who might be in a position to know?'

She considered for a moment. 'I know one or two runners, I suppose they might know if something unusual was happening.'

Lee grinned, showing his yellowish teeth. 'Have your people pick one of them up – I'll ask the questions, and we'll see what answers we get then.'

'No killing,' Nuala said immediately. 'I'll have no killing. We can't afford the publicity or the attention either by the police or the politicals.'

Lee patted her arm. 'Don't worry. I'll ask my questions politely and they'll only be too eager to answer. I've done this before,' he said. 'And I'm very good at it,' he added, sounding almost proud.

I'm sure you have, Nuala thought, and you sound as if you enjoy it. Aloud she said, 'We'll try and find someone this evening. It shouldn't be too difficult, they usually drink in certain pubs.'

Lee's tongue, wet and glistening, touched his lips. 'Sooner the better,' he said dreamily, and then, as if recollecting himself, said quickly, 'I don't want to keep the Madam waiting too long. You know what she's like when she's angry.'

Nuala nodded automatically. But somehow she didn't think Michael Lee had the Madam's best interests at heart, and she wondered if he was one of those who liked to inflict pain. Looking at his face, with its stone-hard eyes and thin cruel lips, she thought it more than likely.

Tommy Nolan stood outside Guiseppe's the fried fish shop in Great Brunswick Street and contemplated the steamed up windows. The aroma of freshly fried fish drifted out onto the smoky night air from inside, briefly dispelling the heavier, fouler odours of the city and the river. He dug into his pockets, wondering how much he had left: a piece of fish – cod perhaps – in batter, would go very nicely indeed. He examined his change with a drunken man's care, sorting through the farthings and halfpennies and pennies – no silver – to discover that he possessed the grand sum of fourpence. It was enough, a pennyworth of fish went a long way.

A hand passed before his face, an open hand with a guinea in the callused palm. Mesmerized by the glitter of silver he followed it.

'It can be yours.' The speaker was a short stout man with an accent that was vaguely Irish. Although his face was in shadow, he was reasonably well-dressed, and his shoes – always check the shoes first – were polished. That decided Tommy; only people with servants could afford to keep their shoes that well.

Taking a deep breath and straightening himself, he said slowly and distinctly, 'What can I do for you, sir?'

The stranger leaned forward. 'I've just come to town and I was looking for someone who could show me where a man might find a little entertainment.' He paused and added with a grin. 'If you know what I mean?'

Tommy Nolan grinned, showing his bad teeth. 'Indeed I do sir. And, if I may say so, you've made a very wise choice.' In his drunken state, he didn't pause to consider how he had come to be chosen. 'Now, what sort of entertainment were you looking for, eh?' he winked.

'A little drink perhaps – and not this watered swill they serve in the pubs – I'm looking for a real drink, a proper drink. Why, where I come from, we make our own.'

'I know just what you're looking for.'

'A little gambling perhaps, nothing too strong, you understand. I'm feeling lucky tonight.'

Tommy nodded happily.

'And perhaps a little female company ...' the stranger suggested diffidently.

'I know just the place,' Tommy said happily.

In his drunken state, it took Tommy nearly half an hour to lead the now uncommunicative stranger to Monto, and it was only as they were entering the red-light district that the stranger spoke again. 'I've heard Number Eighty-Two is a good house.'

Tommy nodded. 'One of the best – the best! – but it's expensive,' he warned.

'I'm not worried about the cost,' the man smiled.

'Number Eight-Two it is then.'

Monto was quiet that night. The bitterly cold January weather kept a lot of the regular clients at home, while the uncertain political situation didn't exactly encourage people to be on the streets, and now Monto was being patrolled – if that was the right word – by the Legion of Mary, whose self-appointed task was to save the fallen women and keep the streets of Dublin clean and free. And very few of Monto's regular clientele wanted to meet up with any of the Legionnaires. After the noise of the rest of the city, Monto was unusually quiet, but it was still relatively early, and the houses wouldn't usually open for business until late into the night, and then run all night on into the morning.

At the bottom of the steps leading up to Number Eighty-Two, Tommy turned to the stranger. 'Well, here you are,' Light from the arched fanlight fell on his face, washing away the years and the pain, leaving the face of a child in its place. His eyes too were like those of a child, wide and innocent in their drunkenness. He could do a lot with a guinea.

'You ring for me ... I've never done this sort of thing before.'

Tommy grinned as he climbed the steps. In truth, he had never visited a brothel before himself – for lots of reasons and not all of them religious, but he had lived long enough on the streets to know the score. He pulled the heavy brass bell once, and then again, and was turning back to the stranger when the door opened.

There were two surprises for him then: the stranger – and his guinea – were gone, and he was suddenly yanked backwards into the house. He turned to protest – when he was hit on the side of the head with something hard. Sickened with the blow he turned, shadows hovering around the edges of his vision ... and was hit again. This time the darkness was complete.

Tommy Nolan awoke with icy water streaming down his face, the chill so intense it almost burned. He attempted to stand, but suddenly realized that there was something wrong with his feet ... and his hands ... They had been tied to a chair.

Sober now, stone-cold, ice-cold terrifyingly sober and thoroughly frightened, Tommy realized he was in trouble. His first thought was the police – they had lifted him and were either going to beat a confession out of him, or make him sign a confession they had written. And then he realized that the police wouldn't have gone to so much trouble to lift him – they would have just snatched him off the street. And suddenly he was even more frightened.

A face swam into view, a thin, hard face with something vaguely foreign about it, the eyes slightly slanted and startlingly blue, the skin vaguely yellow, like that of an ill man. His accent was English.

'I'm going to ask you a few questions – answer them and you'll walk away. Lie to me and you'll never walk again.'

Tommy concentrated on his surroundings, ignoring the man. He was in a cellar somewhere – probably in the cellar of Number Eighty-Two. It smelt damp and the air was tainted with the odours of something rotten mingled with the sweeter smell of the oil lamp.

'I'm not going to hit you, I'm not going to beat you ... what's the point in that?' the man continued amiably.

'I'll ask you a few questions, and every time you deny me or refuse to answer, I'll cut you …'

There was a knife before Tommy's face. A long thin blade, double-edged, the edges glittering as if they had been recently sharpened.

'Perhaps even castrate you,' the man said, and he laughed then, a high-pitched, terrifying giggle. He rested the flat of the blade against Tommy's unshaven cheek and moved it slightly, a fraction of an inch, but Tommy felt his face burn, and knew he had been cut. Moments later he felt the itchy crawl of blood on his neck.

'What do you want to know?' he asked softly, his voice barely above a whisper, his throat constricted.

'You've run with the Nationalists, you know their ways. Has anything unusual happened recently?'

Tommy frowned. 'What do you mean by unusual?'

'Comings and goings,' the man shrugged, 'strangers perhaps …' he suggested.

Tommy shook his head … and the knife drifted before his eyes again.

'The Big Fellow has been busy with visitors … important visitors, but I don't know who,' he added quickly.

'When did they arrive?'

'A few days ago – I'm not sure when.'

The cold sliver of steel pressed against his cheek again. 'How many?'

Nolan started to shake his head, and then cried out as the knife gouged his flesh. 'Not many,' he panted, 'one, two, three … no more than that, but no one knows for sure.'

'Men or women?'

'I don't know.'

'Guess!'

'Both.'

'Anything else?' the sallow skinned man hissed.

Tommy thought about it for a moment, and when he felt the knife begin to move on his cheek, he said quickly, 'Well, the Big Fellow spent a lot of time with them, so they must be important. And I think he was arranging for one of them to stay with an old couple loyal to the cause who live on the northside of the city – so they must be on the run.'

'Good,' Lee breathed, 'you're doing very well indeed.'

'That's all … I can't remember any more.'

Lee stepped back into the shadows, well satisfied. He had a good idea just who Collins' special guests were – undoubtedly Katherine's dead husband's name opened many doors – and now all he had to do was find them.

'This house on the northside. What do you know about it?'

'I've brought food to it in the past when they were sheltering men on the run. I brought supplies to it yesterday evening.'

'Enough food for one or two people?'

'I don't know.'

'And where is this house?' Lee demanded.

'I don't know!'

Lee looked at him in amazement. 'But you've just told me you brought food there yesterday, you must know where it is.'

'I know where it is, but I don't know the name of the road or street. I'll have to take you there.'

For a moment Lee contemplated killing him, and then he leaned forward, pressing the knife into the soft flesh beneath Tommy's chin. 'You don't want me to kill you, do you?' he hissed.

Tommy blinked quickly.

'Double-cross me and I'll kill you without a second thought,' Lee warned. 'Bring me to the house and if one of the people I'm after is there, you can walk free.'

Tommy nodded slightly – although he didn't believe it for a moment.

CHAPTER NINE

When he had no further use for him, Michael Lee killed
Tommy Nolan without a second thought. He had what
he wanted; he had found Jane Bradley.

Tommy Nolan had led Lee across the city at first light
the following morning, heading out into the suburbs of
Cabra on the north side of the Liffey. The small
Irishman had been discreetly handcuffed to Lee, and the
Englishman had cut him – slightly – with the knife
as a reminder to behave. Tommy Nolan needed no
reminders; he knew if he didn't bring this terrifying
hard-eyed Englishman to the house, he would be killed
– and if he did bring him ... what then? All he had was
the Englishman's promise that he wouldn't be harmed
... and he could guess how much faith he could put in
that. All he could do now was to try and escape at the
first opportunity ... all he needed was that opportunity,
but it didn't look as if Lee was going to give it to him.

The house was tucked away off the Cabra Road, in a
small, almost secluded cul-de-sac. There were about
twenty-two houses in a semi-circle around a neatly kept
green; Nolan had pointed to the last house on the block.
'That's it ... the pale yellow door,' he said, and then
added hopefully, 'can I go now?'

Lee simply looked at him, and Tommy shrugged.

They stood beneath a small stand of trees watching
the house for the best part of an hour, Lee seemingly
impervious to the biting cold, but Tommy was soon
shivering so badly he could barely stand. Eventually,
their patience was rewarded and the chintz curtains
flickered in the bedroom that looked down onto the
cul-de-sac, and Lee had a glimpse – a brief momentary
glimpse – of a girl's face ... Jane Bradley's face. Without

a word or a backward glance, he walked away, dragging Tommy with him.

'Can I go … please let me go. I've got children, a wife. Look I haven't seen you … I wouldn't even recognize you if you stood in front of me … I don't know where you've been …'

Lee walked in silence, retracing the route Mickey had taken them to Cabra, through Phibsborough and onto Constitution Hill, down on to Church Street and out on to the quays in sight of the Four Courts. They walked out on to Father Mathew Bridge, and almost in the exact centre of the bridge, Lee stopped and unshackled Tommy. The small man rubbed his wrists and smiled nervously. 'Look, I meant what I said; I've never seen you … I wouldn't know you again.' Lee nodded, seemingly distracted by the sight of the pale wintry sunrise coming up further down the river. Tommy followed his gaze. 'It's a grand sight …' he began.

It was his last sight of this world. Lee hit him on the back of the head with the shackles which he had wrapped around his fist in a makeshift knuckleduster. The man pitched forward, and Lee toppled him over the edge of the bridge and down into the filthy water below. He entered the water in an explosion of foul-smelling liquid, and didn't rise. Lee walked away quickly, already forgetting the man, concentrating on the next task. Now that he knew where the girl was, it should be a fairly simple matter of getting the boy. He wondered if he was in the same house …

On the morning Michael Collins had brought Jane to the house in Cabra, he had taken Patrick across the city to a house on the south side of the Liffey, in Ballsbridge, almost facing the Royal Dublin Society, and left him in the charge of a man he simply addressed as the doctor. 'The doctor looks after the boys when they've taken a wound,' Collins had explained simply, 'I'm sure he will find some use for you.' And without another word, he walked away, leaving Patrick alone with the small, stout, red-faced man, who was looking at Patrick suspiciously.

'So you're Patrick Lundy,' the man said, his educated English accent taking Patrick by surprise.

The young man who had been looking around the book-lined study, turned back to the small man. 'You know me?'

'I know about you ... you're Katherine Lundy's boy.' The doctor returned to the large leather chair behind the desk and sank down into it, the leather hissing and sighing like a live thing. He indicated a seat with nicotine-stained fingers.

Patrick sat, eyes still on the doctor. 'You knew my mother?' he asked carefully, remembering that Katherine's reputation in Dublin meant different things to different people.

The doctor nodded. 'And your father too ... though I think you favour your mother,' he added, looking at Patrick from beneath yellow eyebrows, while reaching for a slim silver cigarette case and extracting a slightly crumpled hand-rolled cigarette. He offered the case to Patrick.

'I don't.'

'Sensible,' the doctor gasped between puffs as he lit up. He coughed once, and Patrick winced with the harsh sound.

'Did you know my father well?' he asked casually.

The doctor smiled, showing strong teeth stained yellow. 'I knew Dermot Corcoran.'

'What was he like?' Patrick asked quickly, unable to keep the eagerness from his voice.

The doctor didn't seem in the least surprised at his question. 'What's happened boy; time begin to wipe away the memories, eh? Well, it does that. I remember when my own father died, soon I couldn't remember his face ... frightened me, that did. And then one day ...' he shrugged, 'I could see him as clearly as I see you now. So, if it's any consolation to you, the memories come back, clear and clean – and you can only remember the good things.'

143

'I can remember him,' Patrick said quietly. 'But I only saw one side of him and, as far as I can see, he meant different things to different people. It's ... it's just, I wonder how others saw him,' he added quickly, seeing the doctor frown. 'I mean, I can remember him walking out on that Easter Monday morning, and knowing – and I'm sure he knew – that he wasn't going to come back. I've often wondered what made him do that.'

'He believed in the Cause he was fighting for,' the doctor said gently. 'Like most of the others, he believed in the dream of Irish freedom. He believed that there would have to be a sacrifice – a blood sacrifice – to achieve that freedom.'

'Was he right?'

The doctor shrugged. 'Time will tell. If you're asking me what I think today – then, I'm bound to tell you no, I don't think it was. But we'll see.' He finished his cigarette, and ground out the remains in a brass ashtray that was a relic of the Boer War, and leaned forward, all business now. 'The Big Fellow tells me you're a medical student.'

Patrick nodded.

'How good are you?'

Patrick shook his head. 'I'm not sure what you mean ...'

'Any practical experience?'

Patrick started to nod and then shook his head. 'None.'

The doctor sank back into the chair with a sigh. 'So ... does blood bother you?'

'Not at all.'

The doctor remained silent for a while, his watery grey eyes fixed on Patrick's face. The young man found the scrutiny unsettling and took the opportunity to look around the room. Aside from the mass of books – and Patrick was sure Joseph Hyde's bookseller's heart would have missed a beat – the only other feature of the room was the framed certificates that adorned one whole wall. In the dim light it was difficult to make out any details, but from the little he could see, it seemed as if the doctor had trained in at least a dozen schools and universities and had acted as physician to two European monarchs, and numerous heads of state. The young man shook his head in astonishment.

'Is something wrong?' the older man asked quietly.

'The certificates ... your qualifications ...' he said.

The doctor dismissed them with a wave of his hand. 'Paper, just paper, but they impress my patients, and allow me to charge an exorbitant fee.'

'Then they're all genuine ...?'

The doctor smiled affably. 'They are.'

'Then why are you doing this?'

'Doing what?'

'Working for Collins.'

The man shrugged. 'I'm doing what your father did – I'm doing something I believe in,' he said with a smile. 'Now, I'll take you on as a "junior partner" – or at least that's the story we'll put out. You can attend some of the consultations with me, and you can take care of the dressings and simple cuts and bruises ... things like that. The clientele here is predominantly wealthy and English, or Anglo-Irish – that's one of the reasons I've kept my accent,' he added with a wry grin, 'and you've enough of an English accent to satisfy them. Naturally, you'll come out with me if we're called to an "accident".'

' "Accident?" '

The doctor nodded. 'If one of the boys has an accident ... we go out.'

'Do you know what's going to happen to me – eventually?' Patrick asked.

The doctor shook his head. 'Not yet. I was asked to take care of you for a few weeks, possibly a month or two ... after that I don't know.'

'Will I have any time to myself?' Patrick asked carefully, watching the doctor.

'I don't see why not. Eddie's done her work on you –

so you shouldn't be that recognizable. My surgery hours are between ten and twelve on weekdays, ten and one on Saturdays; there's late surgery on Thursday, seven to nine. Aside from that your time's your own.'

'You've no objections if I go out?'

'None at all. Just be careful not to meet anyone who knew you three years ago.'

'I didn't know anyone then. I just want to see the old places, revive some old memories.'

'You'll be surprised at the changes.'

'I'm sure I will be.'

'I've found the girl!'

Nuala's lips twisted in annoyance. The Madam had been slowly and painfully reading down the list of the month's expenses, noting the figures for further checking at a later stage. Reading and numbers had always been difficult for Nuala, and she hadn't learned to read until she had neared her twentieth birthday and even now, nearly twelve years later, she found it a slow and painful task. She threw down her pencil in annoyance and looked across the room to where Michael Lee was slouched in the couch, a newspaper before his face, a thin curl of grey smoke drifting up from behind it.

'What did you say?'

Lee folded the paper and dropped it to the floor. 'I said I've found the girl.'

'How?' the Madam wondered, her opinion of the man changing slightly. For a stranger in a strange city – especially one as clannish as Dublin – he had done remarkably well to find the girl so quickly.

Lee shrugged, a smile twisting his thin lips into a sneer. 'I asked my questions in the right places.'

'Obviously. What about the boy?'

'I've no sighting of him yet – but he may very well be in the house with the girl.'

'And where is the girl?'

'In a house in Cabra … I have the address here.' He tossed a piece of paper on to Nuala's table.

She touched it with her painted fingernails but didn't open it. 'And what do you want me to do?'

'I want to get the girl. If I have the girl I'll be able to find where the boy has gone.'

'You seem very confident.'

'If I ask someone a question – they answer me,' he said with a ghost of a smile. 'Sooner or later, they answer me.'

Nuala looked at him but said nothing. Her first impressions about the man were slowly being confirmed. Here was a man who enjoyed inflicting pain.

Lee leaned forward, resting his elbows on his knees. 'Will you give me the men?'

Nuala thought about it – and then shook her head. 'No, not yet.' She saw Lee's expression change and hurried on. 'We don't know how many people are in the house – it could be full of armed IRA men for all we know – and we don't even know if the boy is in there. And it is the boy you are principally after, isn't it?'

He nodded.

'Then do some more work – find out how many people are in the house, find out if there's a young man in there, find out if the girl ever goes out. If we mount a major raid on the house, it will cause too much trouble, excite too much interest. The police will blame it on the IRA and the IRA will blame it on the police – either way there will be bloodshed, and there's been too much of that already. I'll not be a party to any more. When you have your information come back to me, and we'll decide what to do next.'

'And what happens if the girl has gone? What happens if this place is just a temporary resting spot for them before they move on to someplace else?'

'You've found them once – you'll find them again.' She looked across at Lee, as a sudden thought struck her. 'Tell me, how did you find the girl?'

'I told you – an informer.'

'Who?'

'I don't know – I never learned his name.' Lee surged

to his feet with a suddenness that startled her and left the room without another word.

Twenty minutes later, Nuala learned that Tommy Nolan's body had been fished out of the river.

'The report says he drowned, but I want to know the truth.' Michael Collins handed a copy of the medical report to Patrick Lundy, and then took the doctor's arm and led him down the long tiled corridor that led to the hospital's mortuary.

Patrick followed on behind reading the single sheet report in the brown manila envelope. The facts were few enough: the body of a male, of between forty and fifty years old, had been pulled out of the river just below the Ha'penny Bridge. There was a gash on the back of his head, but that could easily have happened when he fell into the river. A preliminary examination indicated that although alcohol was involved it was not the cause of death. The subject's liver showed extensive damage, so the man was not unaccustomed to drink. Cause of death was listed as 'drowning'. Foul play was not suspected. Patrick returned the sheet to its envelope, wondering if this was how his father had ended up – a single sheet report in someone's file. The idea came to him so suddenly that he stopped. Why hadn't he thought of it before? There must be a file on his father somewhere … on Dermot Corcoran, he corrected himself. Would there be a clue to his natural father in that file? His mother had suggested that they knew one another, and if their paths had crossed, then there would be a note of it somewhere. All he needed was the file.

'Patrick …?'

He realized Michael Collins was standing at the door of the mortuary, looking at him. 'Is everything all right?'

'Yes … sorry, I was miles away.'

'If you don't want to go in …' Collins suggested.

'I do. No, it's not that,' Patrick protested with a smile. 'I've seen dead bodies before.' He looked up into

148

Michael Collins' clear eyes. 'Can I talk to you later?'

'Of course.'

Patrick looked into the room to where the doctor was walking around a naked body on a table. 'Who was the man?'

Collins walked into the room, and Patrick followed him, their footsteps echoing on the tiled floor. 'He was called Tommy Nolan ... I knew him. He was one of us; and he fought alongside De Valera in Boland's Mill in '16. He was trustworthy, never inquisitive, and so very useful for carrying messages. I want to know how he ended up in the river.'

'Drink?' Patrick suggested.

The doctor shook his head. 'I knew Tommy too – I treated him on a few occasions. He had been drinking, but not nearly enough for it to have led to his death.'

Patrick stood back while the doctor moved around the body, working silently and efficiently. He found he could look at the corpse without any feeling at all, no revulsion, no disgust. In some curious way, he was aware of himself standing beside the table, watching the doctor work, aware of Collins in the background, arms folded across his broad chest, watching them both with a curious intensity.

The doctor looked up and nodded to Patrick, drawing him closer. The old man lifted the corpse's head and pointed to the ugly gash at the base of the skull. 'That's the killing wound. But see how regular it is – two straight lines with the indentation between them ...'

'A bar ... a stick ...' Patrick suggested.

The doctor nodded. 'Something like that.'

Collins strode forward. 'So you're saying ...?'

'It looks as if he was hit on the back of the head by something hard and then pushed into the river. There's not enough water in his lungs for him to have drowned,' he added very softly.

'Murdered,' Collins breathed.

The doctor nodded.

Patrick walked over to the sink to wash his hands, leaving the two men alone together. Their voices were still clearly audible.

'Police, G division?' the doctor suggested.

Collins shook his head. 'A bit too subtle for them. They'd just as likely shoot him on the street for "resisting arrest", rather than do this. No,' he shook his head, 'this is something else ...'

'Was he involved in anything unusual lately?'

'Nothing.'

'Anything out of the ordinary happen recently?'

'Not that I can think of.'

'Would he have had access to information that might have proved useful to an individual or group?'

'I don't think so ...'

'What has he been doing over the past few days?' the doctor persisted.

Collins shrugged. 'A few odd jobs ...' his voice trailed away and he turned to look at Patrick as the young man moved away from the sink.

'What's wrong?' Patrick asked, something in Collins' expression alarming him.

'Tommy delivered food to the safehouse in Cabra.'

'What safehouse ... what's that got to do ...?' Realization sunk in suddenly. 'Jane!'

Lee rapped on the door, and then turned away to examine the quiet cul-de-sac. It was a little after one and the street was deserted, most people at their lunch, the thin, sleety rain that had begun to fall a little earlier helping to keep them indoors. He turned back to the door when he heard movement in the hall. The door was opened by a woman who was into her late seventies, with ice-white hair and the ruddy cheeks of a countrywoman. 'I've come for Patrick,' Lee said, dropping his voice, watching the woman carefully. He saw the flicker of puzzlement behind her eyes and she started to shake her head. 'And Jane too,' he added.

The woman had opened her mouth to cry out when Lee produced the knife. The blade was broad and flat and double-edged. He stepped closer to the old woman and rested the knife against her stomach. The woman stepped backwards and Lee followed her inside, closing the door behind him with his foot. 'Give me the girl and nothing will happen.'

'Who was it …?' The doorway at the end of the hall opened and an elderly man stepped out. He stopped in confusion seeing the stranger in the hall. 'What's going on? Who are you?'

Lee's grip tightened on the old woman and he spun her around, so she was now facing her husband. He brought the knife up until it was resting against her throat. 'I want the girl,' he said quietly.

The old man started to shake his head, but Lee pressed the point of the blade against the woman's wrinkled throat and a tiny glistening bead of blood appeared. Her eyes widened in horror. 'The girl?' Lee whispered.

'Leave them alone.' Jane stood on the stairs, her coat thrown over her arm. She was arranging her hat and there was a pair of shoes in her other hand.

'Going somewhere?' Lee smiled.

'Looks like I don't have much choice, now do I?'

'Not really. Where's the boy?'

'I don't know … truly I don't,' Jane shouted in alarm as Lee bent the old woman's head back, stretching the muscles in her throat. 'I don't. We were separated; neither of us knew where the other was going.'

Lee relaxed his hold on the old woman. 'I believe you. Now, here's what happens,' he continued, looking at the old man. 'You can have the girl back in exchange for the boy. It's as simple as that. Tell the boy he can leave a message at his mother's old place. He'll know where.' He glanced back up the stairs at Jane. 'Let's see how much he cares for you, eh?'

She walked down the few steps to stand before him. 'And what happens if he wants nothing to do with the deal?'

Lee shrugged. 'I've got to bring something back to the Madam. You'll do – you'll be second-best, but you'll do.' He pushed the old woman down the hall, towards her husband, and his iron-hard fingers wrapped themselves around Jane's arm. 'And perhaps it would be better if I were to kill you here than let you fall into her hands,' he smiled. 'She's mad, you know that?'

'She's obviously in good company,' Jane said tightly, gritting her teeth as his grip tightened painfully.

Michael Collins walked slowly up the path, his right hand deep in his overcoat pocket clutching a pistol. He stopped, looking at the door which was slightly ajar, and looked back over his shoulder at Patrick who had remained by the gate. He shook his head slightly and then stepped off the path and with his left hand, gently pushed the door open. When nothing happened, he risked a quick look inside ... and found himself facing a shotgun.

'It's me ... it's Mick.'

'Mick?'

'Put down the gun ...' He heard the double-click as the shotgun hammers were let down and risked another quick glance inside. The old man was leaning against the kitchen door, the shot-gun held loosely in his right hand. Michael Collins darted inside. 'What happened?' he demanded.

The old man shook his head, suddenly overcome with emotion. He started to shake so badly now that the gun fell from his nerveless fingers. The Big Fellow squeezed both his shoulders, lending him strength. 'What happened?' he asked softly, slipping into the Irish language, as Patrick's shadow fell across the door.

The old man looked up as Patrick stepped into the hall, and his eyes tightened in anger. 'So, you're the cause of this,' he snapped in Irish, and then repeated it in English for Patrick's benefit.

Patrick looked from the old man to Collins, and Michael shook his head slightly, warning him to say nothing.

152

'This man forced his way into my house.' His voice was trembling, sounding shrill and reedy. 'He put a knife to my wife's neck, cut it, cut her neck with his filthy knife, and then took the girl away. And he left a message, yes he left a message. The girl in return for you.' He was nodding quickly now '... yes, the girl in return for you. And you could leave a message for him in your mother's old place ... he said you'd know where it was.' The old man turned back to Michael Collins slipping back into the Irish language. 'Why did you get us involved in this? Nothing like this has ever happened before. My house has never been invaded before.'

The door leading in to the kitchen opened and the old woman appeared. There was a broad white bandage around her throat, but she seemed more composed than her husband. She put an arm around his shoulder and laid her hand gently on Michael Collins' arm. 'Pay him no heed. He's upset, you can see that.'

'I'm sorry for bringing this on you ...' Patrick began, but the woman shook her head.

'It's not your fault lad ... you've nothing to worry about on that score. But find the girl, she's a nice lass, and you bring her back safely.' She looked from Patrick to Collins. 'But be careful of that man. He's a bad one.'

Michael Collins bent and kissed the old woman gently on the cheek, and Patrick saw his lips move as he quickly whispered something to her, and he saw her smile and then nod briefly. Collins walked away and ushered Patrick back outside, pulling the door shut behind him.

'What did you say to her?' Patrick asked as they walked down the snow-locked path.

'I thanked her, told her we needed more brave women like her.'

'She was the one Lee threatened ... but it was her husband who was the more upset,' Patrick said, shaking his head.

'Her husband was also threatened, but in a different way. He found himself in a situation where he was unable to help his wife. Naturally, he was angry.'

153

'What are we going to do now?'

'We make contact with your old home and try and work something out.'

'And if that doesn't work?' Patrick persisted.

'Let's take one step at a time,' Collins said gently.

'You've gone too far this time,' Nuala raged.

Lee, who was sitting by the fire, sipping tea from a pale china cup, didn't even bother to look up.

'Now, listen to me, Lee …' Nuala sat down facing him and clasped her hands together, the knuckles showing white with tension. 'You don't seem to realize just how serious this is. Let us say they don't want anything to do with the girl — what's to stop them reporting her as being kidnapped to the police? We can't afford a police raid on this house. Are you listening to me!' Her hand lashed out, knocking the cup from his hand, shattering it against the fire. Immediately Lee's thin hard fingers closed around her wrist, tightening into a painful vice … only to release them again immediately as a large hand wrapped itself into his hair, twisting his head upwards and a sawn-off shotgun was pushed in under his chin. Lee found himself looking into the broad impassive face of Jem, Nuala's bouncer.

'I think you forget just where you are … just who you are,' Nuala said coldly, rubbing her bruised wrists. 'This isn't London, you don't have the authority here that you may have there. Now you've placed me in a very awkward situation.' She sat back into the chair. 'I think it would be better if you were to remain in your room for the next few days.' She looked up at her servant. 'Jem, will you see to it that Mr Lee is made comfortable in his room.'

The man released his hold on Lee's hair and stepped back, the shotgun still pointing in Lee's direction. Lee ignored the man and rounded on Nuala. 'You can't do this to me. The Madam …'

'… is in London,' Nuala said firmly. 'Now, you will do as I say, and I will try and sort out this mess. Take him away, Jem.' She sat back and watched Jem lead a sullen Lee towards the door. 'Oh, and Jem,' she said softly, 'if Mr Lee decides he would prefer not to stay in his room, see to it that something happens to him that ensures that he will.' Jem nodded silently, his face expressionless.

The hard-eyed woman sat back into the heavy leather chair, attempting to work out the ramifications of Lee's action. The last thing she needed now was trouble with the IRA, or the police. The situation in Monto was beginning to become untenable. Business was not as it had once been; the days of the great flash houses were gone. The English and Anglo-Irish gentry who had supplied the houses with so much of their business were already beginning to drift away: the events of 1916 and subsequent years having disturbing them and their ordered way of life. Also, many of the young men who had frequented the houses – many of whom had had their first experience with a woman in one of the houses – had perished in the Great War. And of course, there was the Legion of Mary, a fervently Catholic religious group that was making efforts to save the street girls – many of whom had little enough interest in being saved – but their very presence on the streets was enough to embarrass the fainter hearted of their customers. All in all, it was not a good time to be a madam in Monto.

And now this.

From what Lee had told her, he had left a message that he could be contacted here at this house. He had intended to lure Master Patrick – she still thought of him as a young boy – here, but she had an idea that Patrick might very well arrive backed up by dozens of armed IRA men, and they would have a score to settle.

As the afternoon drifted towards dusk, Nuala came to a decision …

It was possibly the most frightening thing Patrick Lundy had ever done. Walking down the street had been like walking into his past. Looking at the tall redbricked houses, he found it easy to ignore the more recent signs of decay and see them again as they had been only a few years previously ...

The houses hadn't been much different then, merely cleaner ... more alive, the streets that had once buzzed with life day and night – especially at night – were now quieter, almost deserted. And now the decay, both real and imagined, was more evident, reminding him of the old whores who walked the cheaper end of the street, wearing the clothes and make-up of a younger woman. Montgomery Street had assumed that same air. The steps up to number eighty-two were as he remembered them, perhaps not so clean as they had been in his time, and the varnish on the door was beginning to flake and peel. The numbers – in solid brass – were tarnished and unpolished, but the house still looked to be in better shape than any of the others on the street. Taking a deep breath, he quickly mounted the steps and rapped on the knocker which was shaped in a snarling lion's head, the clapper clenched between its teeth. In the silent street, the noise sounded thunderous, and he had to resist the temptation to turn and look over his shoulder. Michael Collins had told him that his people would be in position by the time the Angelus bell rang ... and the church bells had rung out six o'clock barely five minutes ago.

He could feel the tension inside himself like a coiled spring. Part of it was fear, he knew – fear of his mother. Even here, in Dublin, supposedly away from her influences, she had managed to find and control him. He had gone to the trouble of running away, assuming a false persona, disguising himself, putting not only himself, but also Jane and Michael Collins and his friends, in danger and to what end ...? She had still caught up with him, still managed to reel him in like a hooked fish. Would he ever escape her?

He lifted the knocker and rapped again, louder this time.

There was movement inside, approaching the door,

and almost instinctively he placed his finger over the tiny spyhole he knew existed just above the lion's head. Listening carefully, he heard the scrape as the spyhole cover was pulled away. He smiled, imagining their frustration when they discovered that they could see nothing.

And the bolts were pulled back – top and bottom – and the key turned in the lock. The heavy door swung open.

For a moment Patrick almost expected to see Mickey standing behind the door ... and while it wasn't Mickey – Mickey had died alongside his father in the GPO in 1916 – the man standing behind the half-open door was cast in the same mould. He was a brothel 'bully', one of the hard men employed to keep both the girls and the patrons in order. Only one hand was visible and Patrick wondered what he was holding in the other hand ... stick, knife, gun? The man looked down at him, but said nothing.

'My name is Patrick Montgomery Lundy. I was left a message by a Mr Lee. He said I would find something of mine here.'

The man nodded and moved back, allowing Michael to step into the hall, and he immediately closed the hall door. When Patrick turned around he found the man was holding a sawn-off shotgun, the ugly weapon looking like a child's toy in his large hands. He gestured with the gun towards the sitting room, but remained standing by the door until Patrick had entered the room and pulled the doors closed behind himself.

The room was exactly as he remembered it – only shabbier. This was where the girls would assemble every evening, wearing their working clothes, awaiting the 'gentlemen callers'. As a boy he had never been able to understand the ritual, but now – along with so many other things – it made sense. When the girls had been chosen they would go up to the rooms on the second floor with their partner.

A fire had been lit and Patrick went to stand with his

back to it, warming his hands against the sparking flames, looking around the room, the memories – good and bad, but mostly good – came flooding back. He had never been allowed downstairs after seven in the evening, and so he had never seen this room at night, but in the morning it had always smelt of stale perfume, cigars and cigarettes and old drink. And then one of the maids would come in and throw open the windows, and flowers fresh from the market would help dispel the smells ...

There were flowers here now, but they were a few days old, and wilting, curling petals scattered around the vase.

He turned as the door opened and a woman entered quickly, closing the door behind her, but not fast enough as Patrick caught a glimpse of the bouncer taking up position outside the door. She turned and smiled at him. 'Hello Master Patrick, it's good to see you again.'

For a moment Patrick looked at the small woman, taking in the round, smiling face, the tightly-curled chestnut coloured hair, the deep brown eyes. And then recognition dawned, and he gasped, 'Nuala ...?'

She sat down on the long couch facing the fire and nodded. 'The same.' She smiled at his bemused expression. 'Why, whom did you expect to find?'

'I don't know ... I'm not sure ...'

'Once a servant does not necessarily mean always a servant,' she said, smoothing the folds of the deep russet coloured evening gown she wore. 'You of all people should know that.' He shook his head uncomprehendingly, and she continued, 'Your own mother started out as a servant,' she reminded him.

Nuala looked at the young man carefully. He would be close enough to twenty now, ten years or so younger than herself, and while he was not handsome, he was too thin, too gaunt for that, and his prisoner's haircut didn't help, his features were not unpleasing. He had his mother's intense stare, but his lips were thinner, lending

158

his face a slightly cruel cast. In a few years time, with a little meat on his bones, however …

'How much is my mother paying you?' he asked suddenly.

Nuala sat back into the couch, folding her hands in her lap. 'There has been some misunderstanding …' she began.

'You don't need to lie to me. Lee said he could be contacted through here.'

'I'm not denying my association with Lee,' the woman said quickly, 'but if you'd be prepared to listen for a few moments, I think we could sort out this misunderstanding.'

Patrick looked around the room suspiciously, and then stared pointedly at the door, before finally turning back to Nuala.

'Jem is there to ensure that we will not be disturbed,' she explained. 'Now sit, please. This isn't a trap.'

Patrick sat stiffly in a straight-backed chair. 'I have friends outside …' he said, attempting to keep his voice from trembling.

'I'm sure you have. But you will not have to call on them.'

'If I'm not out of here by half six …'

'You will be.' Nuala nodded towards the long tasselled rope that hung down by the fire. 'If you'll ring, we'll have some tea.'

Patrick obediently pulled the rope, imagining he could hear the distant jangling of the bell in the kitchen below. He turned back to the Madam. 'What have you done with Jane?' he asked evenly.

'Jane is upstairs, resting. She will be down shortly and you can both leave then. I don't want any trouble.' She concealed a smile at his surprised expression. 'Lee came here with a letter from your mother, requesting help tracing her missing son. Lee said you had run away with this servant girl – gave me to understand that she had seduced you, perhaps tricked you.' She looked up as there was a gentle tap on the door. It was opened almost immediately by Jem to admit a small, rather plain-looking servant, carrying a heavy silver tray. The maid set the tray down on a small side-table and then looked at Nuala.

'Will there be anything else, Ma'am?'

'Not for the moment Mary; that will be all.' She waited until the young girl had left the room, before lifting the heavy silver teapot and pouring two cups. Patrick recognized the tea service; it had been a gift to his mother from the working girls in the house on her fifth wedding anniversary in 1913.

Nuala sipped her tea, drinking it without milk or sugar, and continued, 'I helped Lee because I owed a lot to your mother ...' She smiled wryly and shrugged, 'In fact I owe her this house. When she left in '16, she gave it to me to keep in trust for her.'

'She'll never be back,' Patrick said quickly.

'Oh, I realize that now. But when Lee arrived ... well, I wasn't sure. I allowed him to stay here, use my contacts, as well as those the Madam – your mother – had given him. But Mr Lee is ... resourceful. He decided to use methods of his own. And his methods included murder!'

'Tommy Nolan!' Patrick said suddenly.

Nuala nodded. 'Lee forced him into revealing Jane's whereabouts – and then killed him.'

Patrick finished his tea in silence, and then looked at Nuala. 'That still doesn't tell me why you've decided to have nothing more to do with him.'

'Murder is bad for business, and the murder of an IRA man doubly so. It brings down trouble, IRA trouble, police trouble. I don't need any of that.' She put her cup down and looked into Patrick's dark eyes. 'I've known your mother to do many things, but I never knew her to order a killing. Maybe she's changed now, I suppose things are different in London. But murder isn't done lightly here.'

'She's changed,' Patrick said into the silence which followed. 'She employs people like Lee.'

Nuala nodded, but said nothing. She had long ago learned the value of allowing someone to talk.

'She's changed; she's become hard, cruel, bitter. She hates the Irish and everything Irish, blaming them for having taken everything from her. She's possessive – unnaturally so. She didn't want me to leave, and when I eventually did leave, she wanted me back. But if I hadn't left when I did ... then I don't think I ever would. She wouldn't let me have any friends of my own, she wouldn't allow me to attend meetings I was interested in. She wanted to know where I went, whom I was with, what I did, and what time I would be home at. She drinks too much too,' he added softly.

'She has changed,' Nuala said. Watching Patrick carefully, she asked. 'Why did you leave?'

He shrugged uncomfortably. 'We ... we had an argument. I wanted to attend an IRA meeting, but I knew she wouldn't let me go, so I pretended to be ill and then crept out later that night. Somehow she discovered that I'd been missing during the night, and then of course she demanded to know how I'd got back into the house – I've no keys you see. She knew one of the servants must have helped me, but when none of them owned up, she threatened to fire them all without references. Eventually, of course, Jane admitted that she let me back into the house via her room.' He couldn't hide the bitterness in his voice as he continued. 'In the meantime, she had Lee and a few of his friends beat one of my few friends in London – a quiet gentle man, whose only crime was that he had introduced me to the IRA supporters in London. Lee and his bullies damn nearly crippled him too so that she could find out where I'd been. My mother and I had an argument – in the course of which I learned that Dermot Corcoran was not my real father.' He saw Nuala's startled look and nodded quickly. 'She told me that Dermot was not my father and furthermore that my real father had no interest in things Irish. When I came to Dublin, one of the things I was determined to do was to discover my father's true identity.'

'Are you sure you want to?' Nuala asked quietly.

'Why, do you know something?'

She shrugged, unwilling to commit herself. 'Possibly.'

'Well?' Patrick demanded a few moments later, when she had still said nothing.

'It's half six,' she said gently, 'first things first. Let's get you and Jane sorted out and then we'll talk – tomorrow.'

'But ...'

'But nothing. I've a business to run. We'll talk about your past tomorrow.'

CHAPTER TEN

The four IRA men Michael Collins had posted to keep watch on Patrick were beginning to move in when the door to number eighty-two opened and Patrick and Jane appeared. The young couple hesitated, obviously talking to someone in the darkened hallway behind them, and then they turned away and walked down the steps, walking down Montgomery Street, heading for Parnell Square. Unsure what to do now, the four men fell into position around the couple, keeping a safe distance, but close enough to act if the need arose. They were all wondering just what was going on; they all had their own theories – and none of them were even close.

'Thank you for coming.' Jane slipped her hand into Patrick's and squeezed lightly.

'Why, did you think I wouldn't?' he asked with a smile.

'No, I always knew you would,' she lied.

'You're all right ... you weren't harmed?' he asked anxiously.

'No, not at all. That man Lee was none too gentle, but once we reached the house, I was taken away from him and treated with every courtesy ... much to Lee's disgust, it seemed.'

Patrick grinned. 'He's in a bit of hot water himself with Nuala, the madam of the house.'

'I've no sympathy for him. Anyone who would threaten an old woman like he did deserves only contempt. I wonder what will happen to him,' she continued.

'I suppose he'll be sent home. And if he doesn't have either you or me with him, he'll be in trouble with my mother ... and goodness knows what she'll do to him …' He spotted the waiting cab and guided Jane towards it. The door opened as they neared and a hand reached out to help Jane inside.

'It went well then?' Michael Collins asked.

'It went well,' Patrick agreed. 'Nuala is inclined to side with us – especially since she discovered that Lee killed Tommy Nolan.'

Collins leaned forward eagerly. 'He admitted it, did he?'

Patrick nodded. 'That's what changed Nuala's mind.'

'Tommy was a good man,' Collins stated flatly. 'Your Mr Lee owes us. And he'll pay – mark my words, he'll pay.' He leaned forward and tapped on the glass separating them from the driver. With a stuttering roar the cab lurched forward, black fumes billowing around it.

'Where are you taking us?' Patrick asked eventually, when Michael Collins showed no signs of breaking his reverie.

'Tonight, you'll both stay with the doctor, and then in the morning, you're off to Cork, my girl, and then we were thinking of putting you on the boat for America. What do you think?'

Jane smiled happily. 'I've always wanted to go to America.' She turned to Patrick. 'You could come with me …'

Patrick shook his head, and then, realizing that she might not be able to see him in the cab's dim interior said, 'Later, I'll join you in America later. But first I've some work to do here.'

'What sort of work?'

'I want to continue my father's work for the Cause, and I want to talk to Nuala about my father. She indicated that she might have some idea just who he was.'

'Do you really want to know?' Michael Collins asked suddenly.

'I don't know … but I have to find out for myself.'

They rode in silence down the ruin that was

O'Connell Street. When the rebels had taken over the GPO three years previously, the British authorities had brought in a gunboat which had shelled the centre of the city. The rebels had surrendered, but the city centre had been gutted. Even now, three years later, re-building was still only in its early stages, and it would obviously be years before it returned to something like its former magnificence. Patrick leaned his forehead against the cool glass, looking at the shadow through the window, half-remembering what the city had looked like at the height of its beauty. It had once been the second capital of the Empire, the city where many of the English gentry spent the summer months, and where most had a second home. No longer.

He shifted in the seat and looked across at Michael Collins, his strong profile outlined against the glass. 'Would you have any objections if I moved out of the doctor's house?' he asked softly. Collins turned towards him but said nothing. 'I mean now that the threat from Lee doesn't exist anymore, then there's no reason for me to hide, and if you're sending Jane away, then she'll be safe too,' he continued quickly.

'Do you think your mother is going to give up so easily?' Jane said immediately, looking from Patrick to Collins for support.

'The young lady is correct.'

'But ...'

'No buts,' Collins said firmly, 'and in any case where would you stay, eh?'

Patrick looked surprised. 'Why, in Number Eighty-Two of course, it is my home ...'

'It's a brothel,' Jane snapped, suddenly angry.

'I spent the first sixteen years of my life there,' Patrick said, his voice sounding almost sullen.

Collins smiled in the darkness. 'We'll discuss it in the morning. We've all had a hard day – a long day. Let's not make any decisions now ... and let's not have any arguments between ourselves, eh?'

'I'm sorry,' Patrick said immediately, 'it's just ... it

was just being in that house today ... it brought back so many memories. It was my home, still is, I suppose.'

'Your future's not there,' Collins said softly. He leaned forward and looked out into the night. 'We're nearly there.' He sat back into his seat, the shadows swallowing his large frame. 'Jane, someone will call for you tomorrow evening, so be packed and ready to go. We have supporters in the States, someone there will put you up, find you a job ...'

'Thank you ...' she began.

'Yes, thank you ...' Patrick added.

Collins grinned, a flash of white teeth, 'We look after our own – and it would be a bad show indeed, if we didn't look after Dermot Corcoran's son.'

'Was my father really so important to the Rising?'

'Important enough to go around Dublin city with Joseph Plunkett in the months beforehand planning our defences. And there are few now living in the slums who will forget the work he did on their behalf. He was responsible for highlighting the problems of the slums and the slum-dwellers. The ordinary people of Dublin owe him a lot.'

'I never knew,' Patrick said softly.

The cab drew to a halt, and Michael Collins leaned over to open the door. 'Sometimes it's very easy to be blind to the faults or virtues of those closest to us.' He waited until Patrick had climbed out and helped Jane down. 'Good night.'

The doctor lived alone in a house that had once held a family of eight and four servants comfortably. Now, only a daily woman came in to keep some semblance of order. He was a quiet, reserved man of solitary habits, who enjoyed his privacy, and whose life and interests revolved around the practice of medicine and whose love was the ideal the IRA were fighting for.

The door opened even as Patrick and Jane were walking up the path, and closed again the moment they had stepped inside. There was no light in the hall and they followed the small, stout man down the corridor and into the sitting room. Crossing to the fire, he poked it to a sparking blaze and then turned to face them. He seemed genuinely pleased to see Patrick and the girl. 'So this is your young lady, eh? You've brought her back safe and sound.'

'This is Doctor Montague Meredith,' Patrick made the introductions, 'and doctor, this is Jane Bradley, who has been more than a friend to me.'

'I'm delighted to meet you young woman. I was somewhat concerned when I learned about the events in Cabra earlier today.'

'Lee is an animal,' Patrick snapped.

'Few animals inflict pain and kill for no reason,' the doctor said quietly, 'no, Lee I'm afraid, is all too human.'

'He killed Tommy Nolan.'

'Ah,' the doctor nodded, but said nothing. 'But sit, sit, please, both of you – you must be frozen. You'll have something to drink?' he looked at Jane.

'I'd love a cup of tea,' she ventured.

'Nothing stronger?'

Smiling, she shook her head, 'Tea would be lovely.'

'And you?'

Patrick nodded. 'For me also.'

'I'll be just a moment.'

The couple sat in silence, while the doctor clattered down into the kitchen below, and they heard pots rattling. Patrick sat back into one of the easy chairs, staring deep into the fire, watching the flames dance across the wood, the memories the house in Montgomery Street had brought back drifting behind his eyes. He was determined to go back, no matter what Collins or Jane said.

Jane sat back into a corner of the settee and allowed the tension to seep from her. Now that she was safe – or as safe as she was ever going to be in Patrick's company – she could afford to relax. When Lee had snatched her earlier that day, she had been terrified that he would kill her; certainly he had the potential to harm her without cause or reason. And then when she discovered that she had been taken to a brothel, she had feared the worst. She hadn't in all honesty thought that Patrick would come for her – why should he give up all he had achieved so far for a simple servant girl – and yet he had. He had walked into what he thought was a trap for her. She glanced across at him. He was lost in thought, his thin face painted red and orange by the flames. He was a person of such contrasts, weak and indecisive one moment, strong-willed and determined the next.

Patrick glanced up and spotted her looking at him. 'Ha'penny for them?' he asked quietly.

She shook her head. 'Thanks for coming for me,' she said eventually.

'You would have done the same for me,' he said with a grin.

But Jane wasn't so sure.

'I've been thinking,' Patrick continued. 'I think you should go to the States – you'll be looked after, I know that. Collins will make sure that you'll want for nothing. And in a few years time, I'll join you.' He was talking quickly now, not looking at her. 'I'm going to continue my studies in medicine here – I'll see if I can join the College of Surgeons – and when I'm a qualified doctor, I'll come over and join you. We'll set up a clinic together …'

Jane stopped listening. What she was hearing was nonsense of course. Patrick was becoming too involved with the IRA and their struggle to continue his studies; soon he would have to make a choice … and she didn't think medicine was going to rank too highly at that stage. She was also mature enough to realize that as soon as she was out of the country, he would forget about her – oh, there might be a letter or two or three in the beginning, and then there would be a card at Christmas or something like that, until finally nothing.

'You'll like America,' Patrick said awkwardly, realizing he had lost her.

'I've always wanted to go there,' she said truthfully. What she didn't add was that she realized she was being got out of the way; she was an embarrassment. She was Patrick's, unmarried, unchaperoned, unaccompanied female companion, and in staunchly Catholic Ireland that just would not do.

'I'll write,' Patrick added.

'Tea!' the doctor announced. 'My, what glum faces,' he said, looking from Patrick to Jane. 'You should be rejoicing. You're together again.'

'Jane is off to America soon,' Patrick said.

The doctor nodded. 'I know.' He looked at the young woman. 'And how do you feel about that?'

'I'm looking forward to it,' she nodded.

'She's always wanted to go there,' Patrick supplied.

'Ah good, good,' Dr Meredith said vaguely. 'Now, come along, drink up, and then to bed. You must be exhausted, both of you.'

Jane nodded. 'It has been a very long day.'

'I've made up the bed in the spare bedroom, and a fire's been going in the room since early afternoon, so it should be very cosy now.' He looked at Patrick. 'And there's a fire in your room also.' He stood up, rubbing his hands together. 'I shall go up now, if you don't mind. I'm sure you would appreciate a little time together.' He looked at Patrick. 'Perhaps if you wouldn't mind settling the fire and checking the lights ...'

'Of course ...'

'And I will wish you a good night, young lady ...'

'Thank you.'

They sat in silence while he climbed the stairs, and then waited until they had heard the door to his room close and the floorboards creak in sequence above their heads.

'He seems a nice man,' Jane said.

'He's very devoted to the IRA cause.'

The young woman turned to look at him. 'And what about you, Patrick, how devoted are you to the Cause?'

Patrick looked at her for a moment and then shook his head. 'I don't know yet.'

She sipped her tea and grimaced – it was dark, strong and bitter. 'And what about your future?' she asked, watching him over the rim of her cup. 'Mine seems to have been mapped out for me. But what about yours?'

'I've been thinking about that,' he said cautiously. 'I'm going to move back into my old home. It is mine,' he said immediately, defensively, expecting an argument. When none was forthcoming, he continued. 'I'm going to do a little research into my background. I want to find out just who my father was.'

'Are you sure you want to know?'

He shrugged. 'I don't know. It's something I have to do. I'm going to continue my studies and become a doctor, and I'm going to fight for the cause of Irish freedom.'

Jane finished her tea. 'And what are you going to do in your spare time?' she asked, sarcastically.

Patrick frowned, missing the reference, and Jane shook her head. 'Forget it – it's not important. Look, you have your life to lead, and you must make your own decisions. Just try not to make them all at once and in such a rush. Give yourself a little more time to grow up.'

'I'm nearly twenty ...' he protested.

She finished the tea and stood up. Looking down on him, she said, 'Patrick, you haven't lived. You've been sheltered since birth, you're still a child in many respects. Now, I'm for bed ...' She saw the look in his eyes and smiled slightly. She touched his cheek with the back of her fingers. 'I've had a very long day,' she said gently, 'and tomorrow promises to be even longer.'

He turned his head slightly to kiss her fingers. 'You're right, of course. Good night, sleep well.'

'I shall.' She hesitated when he showed no signs of moving. 'Are you coming up?'

'In a moment. I'll just finish my tea.'

Jane nodded. 'Well, don't stay up too late. Tomorrow promises to be a busy day.'

Shortly after two-thirty an argument broke out between

one of the girls and a customer. The sounds carried clearly even through the thick tenement walls – a man arguing in what sounded like French, the woman in a flat Dublin accent. It was something to do with money – it seemed as if the man had caught the women going through his pockets – and it ended in a sudden sharp crack of flesh on flesh. In the moment's silence that followed Michael Lee pulled on his coat and darted over to the door, pulling back the heavy curtain draped over it to help deaden the sounds, pressing his ear against the flesh-warm wood.

The woman began to scream, a long drawn-out wail which Lee felt she must have practised. It set his teeth on edge and grated along his nerves ... and the guard standing outside his door raced off down the corridor towards the banshee wail. Lee immediately opened the door and stepped outside into the corridor, pulling the door closed behind him. And in all the confusion that followed, he simply walked out of the house.

The hand over Patrick's mouth brought him suddenly, terrifying awake. When the single moment of fear dissipated, he immediately thought it was Jane, until the voice hissed in his ear. 'It's me.'

Patrick struggled to sit up, rubbing sleep from his eyes. 'What time is it?'

'A little before four,' Meredith whispered. 'Listen to me; a messenger arrived a few moments ago. Nuala sent a runner to the Big Fellow about an hour ago to say that Lee has escaped.'

'No!'

'I'm afraid so.'

'What's going to happen?'

Meredith shrugged, the movement vague in the dim light. He crossed to the smouldering fire and coaxed a few dancing flames from it. 'I don't know. He hasn't got this address, so you're safe enough, and there's some guards on the house in Cabra, just in case. There's also some men at the station and at Kingstown, so I don't think he's going to get very far …'

Patrick sat up in bed. 'Why bother? Why not just let him go?'

The doctor looked back over his shoulder. 'He's killed a man.'

'I don't see …'

'He owes us,' he said simply.

'What happens now?'

The doctor stood up. 'Now, we wait. Perhaps you might like to get dressed. We'll probably be called out if they find him.'

'Why?'

The doctor smiled slightly. 'Why, to certify his death of course.' He stood and dusted off his hands. 'I'll make some tea.'

Patrick dressed hurriedly. There was a pounding at the back of his head and a sour taste in his mouth that he vaguely recognized as fear. Although the doctor had said they would be safe there, Patrick wouldn't put it past Lee to have somehow discovered their whereabouts – after all, he had found Jane.

He stopped outside the door to her room and pressed his face against the wood. There was no sound from within and he gently opened the door. The shaft of light fell across the bed; asleep, she looked like a child. Smiling, he closed the door.

The doctor had poured tea and the two men sat in the kitchen, drinking silently together. When the clock chimed the half hour – startling them both – the doctor got up and left the room. When he reappeared, ten minutes later, he had dressed, and was carrying his medical bag. He put the bag down on the kitchen table and opened it.

And handed Patrick a small revolver.

The young man looked at it as if it was some species of venomous snake.

'Take it.'

'I don't want it,' he said quietly.

172

'You can give it back to me when I return,' the doctor said with a slight smile.

Patrick looked up in surprise. 'Why, where are you going?'

'I'm going to try and find out what's happening.'

'Stay here,' Patrick said quickly.

'I won't be long.' He pointed to the pistol on the table. 'It's fully loaded with six rounds. Simply pull back the hammer and squeeze the trigger. But I don't suppose you'll have any cause to use it.'

'I hope not,' Patrick said fervently.

'I won't be long,' the doctor repeated. 'Now, I've my own key, so there's no reason for you to answer the door to anyone. If it's one of our boys ... well, you know the signal.'

Patrick nodded. 'Two rings and then a single knock?'

Patrick Lundy sat at the kitchen table and listened to the hall door bang solidly shut. The house suddenly felt very lonely. He looked at the small pistol on the table before him, and realized just how far he had come since he had walked out of his mother's house ... how long? ... a week, two weeks ago now?

Michael Lee waited in the shadows, lounging against a wall, his hands deep in his pockets. On the ground beside his feet was a broken bottle; to a casual observer, it was just another broken bottle, but it had taken Lee four tries with four different bottles to get just the shape he wanted. Now, he had the weapon – all he needed was the victim.

When Michael Lee had been growing up on the London dockland, he had learned one lesson very early – to survive, one needed to be absolutely ruthless.

When Madam Lundy had come to London, he had recognized something in her – something familiar. It didn't take him long to discover that she too possessed a streak of absolute ruthlessness. As he had grown to know her, he had never quite worked out where she acquired her callousness. His own was a product of his youth and the need to survive, and hers, he decided, must stem from something similar, although she never spoke of her early years in Dublin. In the years he had worked with her, he had lost some of his crude edges, and had acquired a patina of respectability. Occasionally – very occasionally – that veneer slipped and Lee reverted to the savagery of his youth. Few things could cause that change – fear was one of them. And Michael Lee knew what Madam Lundy would do to him when she discoverd that he had failed.

Well, if he couldn't bring the boy and his girl back ... then he had one alterative. A smile touched his thin lips – he decided he preferred the alternative.

Paul Timms had been a Sergeant in the Guards during the Great War; he had fought in Flanders and on the Somme, and had been one of the lucky few to escape with mind and limbs intact. His prospects as a career soldier had looked very good indeed – until he had beaten a woman to death in an unnamed town on the Belgian border. In the trial he claimed the woman had been a prostitute who had attempted to kill him for his money – and the fact that he had several stab wounds along the palms of his hands where he had defended himself, helped save him from a firing squad or the rope.

When he had been demobbed, he found it impossible to find work in post-war England, even for an ex-army serviceman and so, on the advice of a drinking friend, he took the boat to Ireland, where he joined the Royal Irish Constabulary.

Timms enjoyed the RIC. The uniform was respected in most quarters of the city, and feared in others – it lent him both power and authority. It also allowed him to make a few shillings on the side, and enabled him to sample the favours of several of the flesh houses in Monto at no cost ...

Yes, altogether it was an easier station than the army ... there was less chance of ending up dead for one thing ...

He spotted the man lurking in the shadows.

'You!'

The man looked up bleerily, his head coming forward into the light, his eyes attempting to focus. He took a step forward, his feet crunching on glass and then sat down suddenly.

'Drunken bastard,' Timms muttered. Probably been sampling too much of the Monto brew. He looked well-dressed though. He stepped up to the man and prodded him none too gently with his foot. 'You can't lie here, sir …'

'Robbed …' the man muttered, 'robbed, beaten …'

The accent was undoubtedly English, and Timms squatted down beside the fallen man, the ground sparkling with broken glass. None too gently, he lifted the man's head forward into the light. Curiously, there didn't seem to be any blood.

He never even saw the jagged bottle that came up and took him in the throat, severing vocal cords, larynx and jugular.

By the time he had bled to death on the filthy street, Michael Lee had walked away with the man's regulation police baton and handcuffs.

Patrick was still sitting in the kitchen, the remains of the cold tea and the pistol on the table before him when the doctor returned. As soon as he saw his face, Patrick knew that something was badly wrong.

'Wake Jane, get her dressed. Collect your belongings and be ready to move in an hour!' The doctor's usually red face was pale and sheened with sweat.

'What's wrong, for God's sake?' Patrick demanded.

'A policeman's just been found in Monto with his throat torn out. They won't like that – there'll be a rigorous investigation and probably reprisals.'

'Who did it?'

The doctor shook his head. 'Not one of our boys. Come on now – let's get you moving.'

'But I thought you were safe – I thought they couldn't touch you,' Patrick protested.

'In normal circumstances yes, but I've sailed close enough to the wind on a number of occasions now for them to have their suspicions. And with something like this they will investigate every possibility. If they do come here, I just don't want you involved …'

The kitchen door opened suddenly startling them both – and Jane found both the doctor and Patrick pointing guns at her. 'What's wrong?' she demanded, fear making her voice shrill.

'We have to go,' Patrick said quickly. 'We've got to get away – there might be a visit from the police.'

'Get dressed,' the doctor said gently, 'I'll make some tea.' He was about to turn away, when he stopped. 'You'll find some of my late sister's clothes in the front bedroom. She was about your size – and you're welcome to whatever you want. They may not be in fashion at the moment,' he added with a smile, 'but you're obviously not a follower of fashion.'

Jane shrugged. 'This was all I had.' She was wearing one of Patrick's shirts as a night-dress. Even though she had it buttoned up to the neck, and the sleeves rolled down to her wrists, it still ended – indecently short – just above her knees.

Patrick followed Jane down the hall, too preoccupied even to admire her bare legs. 'What's going to happen?' she asked, startling him.

Patrick shrugged. 'I don't know.'

'Am I still going to America?'

He shook his head again.

'If we can't stay here, then where will we stay?'

Patrick said nothing.

They climbed the stairs in silence, but on the landing, Patrick stopped and turned Jane around to face him. 'Lee's escaped,' he said quietly.

'He's a dangerous man,' she said eventually.

'I know. He's vindictive too. He's been made to look a fool – he'll want revenge of some sort.'

'Does he know where we are?'

Patrick shook his head. 'The doctor said no, but he did find you in Cabra.'

Jane nodded. She looked into Patrick's face, her dark eyes troubled. 'Let's get out of here,' she whispered, and suddenly shivered.

Patrick drew her to him, holding her tightly, feeling the warmth of her body through the thin shirt. 'It'll be all right. Things will quieten down in a day or two and then we can slip away.' He eased her away from himself. 'Come on, let's get you dressed.'

Patrick sat by the bedroom window, and looked down onto the cold early morning street. There had been a sharp frost during the night and the cobbled streets sparkled with frost, while the windows were cobwebbed with intricate designs. Behind him, Jane rummaged through the collection of women's clothes, wrinkling her nose at the stale smell of perfume and lavender, eventually choosing a simple dress of heavy tartan and a thick tweed coat. She laid out two cotton blouses, and an ivory-coloured silk chemise that had once been white. She dressed quickly, unembarrassed by Patrick's intense scrutiny. The clothes were a little too long, but their slightly old-fashioned appearance added at least ten years to her age. She saw Patrick attempting to suppress a smile, and warned, 'If you say one thing …'

'I wasn't …'

'You were …'

Doctor Meredith was almost quivering with anxiety when the couple reappeared in the kitchen twenty minutes later. The contents of his medical bag were spread out on the table before him, alongside the pistol he had given to Patrick earlier and another, slightly larger pistol. There was a small red box of ammunition on the table beside the gun.

'Where's the tea?' Patrick asked with a grin.

'You'll have to take the guns,' Meredith said abruptly. 'I can't afford to be caught with them.'

'And what happens if we're caught?' Jane protested.

'You won't be!'

'We might!'

'Please. If you're stopped, tell them you're a newly-married English couple on honeymoon here. Your accents and age will help carry it off. You won't be searched.'

'And what are we supposed to do?' Jane demanded, vaguely annoyed at the old man.

He began sorting through the contents of his medical bag. 'Spend the day in the city, see some of the sights, and then I'll meet you – if I can – at the foot of Nelson's Pillar at ... let's say six this evening.'

'That's twelve hours we've got to kill!' Patrick protested.

'I'm sorry ...'

'This is January,' Patrick said softly. 'You can hardly expect us to spend the day on the streets, now can you?'

'I can't help you. I daren't give you an address in case it's visited. The RIC will take this city apart looking for the man who killed one of their own, and you cannot afford to be caught in an IRA house.'

'There has to be an alternative,' Jane snapped. 'Look at that sky. It's going to snow.'

'There are theatres,' the doctor hissed, 'museums, galleries, hotels. Use them. Now go. Go – before it's too late.'

Patrick touched Jane's elbow. 'Come on – let's go!'

She rounded on him. 'Go! Go where?' she asked bitterly. 'We're being thrown out onto the streets!'

'It's for our own good. Listen to me,' he whispered, bring her face close to his. 'We need these people – let's not antagonise them.'

'But ...' she began.

'No buts,' he said firmly, and turned and walked away. 'We'll see you later,' he called back to the doctor.

The young woman remained standing in the kitchen, lost and undecided. Finally, with no other choice open to her, she followed Patrick up the steps into the hall.

She didn't bother saying goodbye to the doctor – and he was too absorbed to even notice her.

'Don't say a thing,' Patrick warned as she strode down the hall towards him, her face set and angry. 'I know what to do.'

'Well, that'll be for the first time in your life I imagine,' she snapped.

'Very possibly,' Patrick agreed with a grim smile, opening the door and allowing her to precede him out into the sharp early morning.

'We're closed.' The man standing in the doorway was easily the largest man Patrick had ever seen, although most of it seemed to be fat. 'Come back later.'

'We want to see the Madam.'

'She doesn't want to see you.'

'Tell her it's Patrick Lundy.'

Something in the man's expression changed. It seemed to harden, and his watery grey eyes locked onto their faces, almost as if he were memorizing them. But without another word, he stepped aside and allowed them inside.

Patrick and Jane stood in the dim hallway. After the chill of the morning air, it felt pleasantly warm and had been scented recently with something sharp and astringent.

'They're upstairs in Madam's sitting room,' the fat man said and turned away, heading back down towards the kitchens at the back of the house.

'I know the way,' Patrick said unnecessarily, and headed for the stairs.

'It's very quiet,' Jane murmured, her voice falling to a whisper as they climbed.

'All the working girls are sleeping, and the servants will have finished tidying the house after last night's visitors, or else they're out at market buying in food for tonight,' Patrick explained.

'I thought you didn't know your mother was running a brothel,' Jane accused.

'I didn't. That was the routine in my mother's day, and since Nuala was trained by my mother, I don't see any reason why she should have changed.'

At the all too familiar door – now in need of painting – Patrick knocked lightly.

'Who's there?' Nuala's voice was strained, sounding tired.

'Me, Patrick Lundy.'

'Ah …' There was a moment's silence, and then she said, 'Come in.'

Patrick opened the door and, followed by Jane, stepped into the room. Nuala was standing directly in front of him, before the fire, pale as a sheet, her eyes wide and dark in her head. Patrick stopped – and there, reflected in the mirror over the fire – was Michael Lee, standing behind the door, a sawn-off shot-gun clutched in both hands. His teeth were bared in a triumphant grin.

Patrick hit the door hard, slamming it back into Lee, pinning him up against the wall. There was a shot – the sound tremendous in the confines of the room – that tore a chunk out of the top of the door. Lee surged forward, pushing Patrick back. It was only a matter of seconds before he got out from behind the door and fired again …

And then the doctor's pistol was in Patrick's hand, flesh-warm, skin-smooth. He pressed the barrel against the wooden panelling and pulled the trigger. The gun bucked in his hand, and flame scorched the wood … and then a tiny tendril of blood trickled through the ragged bullet hole!

CHAPTER ELEVEN

By the time Doctor Meredith arrived at the house, accompanied by a silent young man who kept his hands deep in his greatcoat pockets, all signs of the killing had disappeared.

Less than ten minutes after Patrick Lundy had fired the shot that had taken Michael Lee through the heart, the body had been disposed of, the blood hastily and effectively mopped up and two of the men who doubled as servants during the day and bouncers at night, had removed the broken door from its hinges and replaced it with a door from the next floor.

Jane watched how efficiently and methodically all signs of the killing were removed and looked at Nuala. The Madam saw her look and smiled crookedly. 'There have been accidents in the past,' she said quietly.

Jane nodded, but said nothing. She was perched on the arm of the chair Patrick was slumped in, her arms around his shoulders.

When he had stepped away from the door, and Lee had fallen face forward onto the carpeted floor, a gaping hole in his back, the wall behind him splashed with blood, Patrick had begun to shake. He had acted instinctively, he didn't even remember taking the gun from his pocket, and if he had been asked moments before where the gun was, he was sure he wouldn't have been able to answer. He was still shaking when Jane took the pistol from his frozen fingers and helped him across the room and into the chair. Ignoring the body, Nuala had produced a rug and handed it to Jane, and while she was wrapping it around his shoulders, the Madam poured three Irish whiskeys. The two women drank theirs quickly, but Patrick had to be force-fed his.

The alcohol brought some colour back to his cheeks, but he quickly lapsed back into a daze in which he heard the explosive shot and saw the blood trickling through the scorched hole in the door.

'Shock,' Nuala said to Jane. 'He'll be all right.'

Jane ran her fingers through Patrick's tousled hair. 'I didn't think he had it in him,' she admitted. 'That's twice he's surprised me. I didn't think he'd have the guts to come here for me … and now …'

'He's his mother's son alright,' Nuala said. 'A ruthless streak when pushed,' she explained. 'You took your bloody time,' she exploded as two servants came running up. Both held pistols. 'Now clean up this mess. Oh, and you'd better set Jem free. This bastard tied him up and locked him in the cupboard. Oh, and bring Paddy in here please.' The Madam then turned back to Jane, as the servants wrapped the corpse in a rug and carried it from the room. 'I'm Nuala,' she said, 'we weren't properly introduced earlier.'

'Jane Bradley.' She looked around the room. 'This is your house.' There was just a hint of condescension in her voice.

'I'm the Madam here,' Nuala said, looking her in the eye. She had been too long in the house to feel any shame about it – especially not to some jumped up servant girl.

The two women were still attempting to size one another up when two men entered the room almost together. One was the hugely fat man who had opened the door to Patrick and Jane and the other was broad-shouldered, blond-haired and blue-eyed, and carried a sawn-off shotgun. The blond-haired man came over and stood beside Nuala, his face impassive, his eyes roving around the room, taking in the shattered door, the blood-stained wall and the bullet-marked ceiling.

'Paddy,' Nuala said to the fat man, 'Paddy was the man who let Lee into the house earlier. Money undoubtedly changed hands …' Paddy started to shake his head, beads of sweat running down his cheeks to drip off his chin, but Nuala pressed on, 'and Paddy was the man who brought Lee to this room.' She glanced sidelong at Jane and continued, speaking for her benefit now, but looking at the fat man, 'Paddy was also responsible for calling Jem in here, and when Lee hit him on the head with his baton and tied him up, Paddy here dragged him to the cupboard down the hall and locked him in. And Paddy watched while Lee took Jem's gun and put it to my head and threatened me, and Paddy smiled while Lee described what he was going to do to me ... he was an evil man,' she added bitterly. She looked at Jem and then turned away. The manservant lifted the shotgun, pointed it at the fat man and pulled the trigger.

Paddy fell back into the hallway screaming like a wounded pig, clutching his face, his stubby fingers clawing at his eyes.

Jane, who had squeezed her eyes shut at the last moment, opened them again, expecting to find the room splotched with blood. But there was none.

Jem strode across the room and pulled the door shut behind him. The screaming continued until a blow was struck – the sound dull and meaty – and then there was silence.

'Sand,' Nuala explained. 'Jem uses sand or sometimes salt.'

'But that could blind,' Jane protested.

Nuala shrugged. 'And lead could kill.'

The smelling salts brought Patrick around, coughing and hacking, his eyes streaming. Liquid was forced past his lips and seared its way down his throat, and when his vision cleared he found he was looking into Doctor Meredith's watery grey eyes.

'So you're back with us, eh?' Patrick attempted to stand, but the doctor pushed him back into the seat. 'Stay where you are for the moment. Tell me, what's your name?'

'Patrick Lundy.'

'And where are you now?'

Patrick blinked at him. 'Home ... well, number eighty-two Lower Tyrone Street.'

'And what are your last memories?'

Alarm flared in his dark eyes. 'Lee!' he gasped.

'Lee is dead. Shot through the right ventricle if you're asking my opinion. He was dead before he hit the floor.' He glanced over his shoulder and smiled at Jane. 'He'll be all right.'

She nodded, surprised at the relief she felt.

'Perhaps if you could make up some soup ...' Doctor Meredith looked at Nuala, and she nodded silently. The doctor closed up his bag and looked around for his coat. Jane handed it to him, holding it while he slipped his arms into the sleeves. He nodded his thanks. 'Now, I think I'll be off home, just in case we have visitors ...' He looked at Nuala again. 'And Mr Lee?' he asked quietly.

'Mr Lee will be taken care of.'

The doctor nodded again and then shook hands with Patrick, pressing him back into the chair when he would have risen. 'No, stay where you are. Rest awhile. You've had a nasty shock – mind you, not half as nasty as Mr Lee's eh?' he smiled wickedly, bringing a wan smile to Patrick's colourless lips. 'You take care of him now – both of you.' He looked from Jane to Nuala, and both women nodded, looking at one another.

'Jem will see you down,' Nuala said, 'thank you for coming so promptly.'

'When I heard there'd been a shooting I feared the worst,' he said quietly, pulling his muffler tighter around his throat.

'He saved our lives,' Nuala said, walking the doctor to the door. They shook hands briefly, and then he was gone, following Jem down the softly lit corridor, followed by the hard-eyed young man who hadn't spoke a single word while the doctor had examined Lee and then tended to Patrick.

Nuala leaned back against the door looking from Patrick, who was still slumped in the chair to Jane, who had moved away from the fire to stare down into the street below, watching the doctor make his slow and careful way down the cobbled streets, still slick with ice. Nuala saw her head move and knew she was being watched in the reflection of the glass.

'What ... what happens now?' Patrick asked suddenly, startling them both. His eyes had sunk into his head and were rimmed with red.

Nuala crossed to the fire and sat in the chair opposite him. Reaching out she took both his hands in hers, marvelling at the pale soft skin, and the cleanly manicured nails.

'The police ...' Patrick said.

'This is Monto,' Nuala said, looking straight into his eyes. 'We keep our own laws here. And nothing happened in this room today ... do you understand? Nothing happened.'

'But Lee ...'

'I've never heard of Mr Lee,' Nuala said flatly, 'and neither have you.' She squeezed his hands for emphasis. 'Later today, someone will snipe on the army ... they'll return fire ... and when all the firing's stopped they'll discover a body. Nice and neat and good-bye to Mr Lee.'

'Thank you.'

Nuala shook her head. 'No, thank you. You saved my life today ...'

'I think he saved all our lives,' Jane said, coming up behind Patrick and resting her hands on his shoulders over the back of the chair, vaguely annoyed at the way Nuala was clutching his hands so familiarly. 'What was Lee going to do?' she asked.

The Madam's dark brown eyes flashed angrily. 'He bashed Jem on the head and locked him up, and then simply lay in wait for you. He amused himself by telling me what he was going to do to me when he was finished with you both. You,' she looked at Jane, 'were to be shot, but he was going to be a little more inventive with you and me, Patrick, before killing us.'

'He's was a sadist,' Jane said with a shudder, 'he almost beat one of Patrick's friends to death.'

Nuala smiled at Patrick. 'Your prompt action saved us all.'

'What are we going to tell Mrs Lundy?' Jane asked.

Nuala shrugged. 'The truth ... well, not all of the truth,' she amended. 'Lee couldn't find either of you, and was then killed in a firefight with the special branch or army or the IRA.' She stood up and looked down at them. 'I think I'll go and organize some breakfast – it's been a long day – and it's still only morning.'

When Nuala had swept from the room, Jane knelt on the floor before Patrick, her face on a level with his. 'What's going to happen to us now?' she asked softly.

It took a few moments for the question to sink in and then he shook his head slowly. 'I don't know. We'll have to wait and see ...'

'We can't stay here ...'

'Why not?' he wondered.

'Because it's a brothel.'

He smiled slightly, and reached out to touch her cheek. 'I grew up in this house.'

'What about America?'

He shook his head. 'I don't know ... I don't know anything. All I want to do now is to sleep. I suppose the trip is still on,' he added, seeing the disappointed look in her face.

'Come with me!' she said quickly. 'There's nothing here for you – there never was.'

Patrick leaned forward and cupped her small oval face in both hands. 'I came to Ireland to find my past, I haven't gone through all this just to give up now. All that's left for me is here.'

'And what about me?' she demanded fiercely.

He looked at her blankly.

'Do I not mean something to you?' she demanded.

It took a few moments for the question to sink in, and

186

even as he was thinking about it Jane knew the answer. 'I'm just the servant girl, eh?'

He started to shake his head, but she continued on. 'I had my uses and now you've no further use for me. I was your ticket away from your mother.'

He stared at her in astonishment. 'But you suggested I leave my mother ...' he began, but Jane had already pressed on.

'And I suppose I was a little fun on the way, a little light relief. And now you've no further use for me ...'

'Stop it – both of you. You sound like children.' Nuala stepped into the room and closed the door behind her. 'Breakfast will be a few moments. Now, you've both had a shock, and neither of you is in any position or condition to start making decisions or judgements. You'll get some rest, and in a few hours we will know what's happening in the city and with Jane.' The Madam had changed into a black heavy wool dress similar to a type that Patrick remembered his mother wearing. She was also wearing a shawl of dark wool fringed with red around her shoulders, and the overall effect was to make her look far older than her thirty years. 'I've had beds made up for you both; you're back in your old room, Patrick ...' she smiled quickly, 'I keep thinking I should be calling you Master Patrick.' She looked at Jane. 'You'll be sleeping in Miss Senga's room. You won't be disturbed.' There was a tap on the door and then one of the servants entered, pushing a laden trolley. 'And now some breakfast.'

Stepping into the room was indeed like stepping into his past. It seemed to be exactly as he had left it, on that cold Friday morning three years ago. The bed beneath the window, the books on the small bookcase his father – no, Dermot Corcoran – had made for him. On the small cabinet beside his bed the sheaf of drawing paper, the cup of pencils and charcoal. Beside the small wardrobe hung the huge double-handed crusaders sword his 'uncle' Mickey had picked up in one of the markets for a few bob. As a boy, he had imagined himself a knight wielding the sword, doing brave deeds – although at the time he could barely lift it.

'Nothing's been touched, nothing changed.'

He turned, startled. He hadn't realised Nuala had been standing behind him.

'I kept your room and your sister's exactly as you had left them, but I moved into your mother's room myself. When she left she never said whether she was coming back or not.' She walked around the room, stopping by the window to look down into the street below. The morning was dull and overcast and the bad light did much to hide the general air of shabbiness that now claimed the street. 'When Lee came here, I thought he was coming to prepare the way for your mother's return.'

'She'll never come back,' Patrick said quietly.

'Oh, I know that now. But that was the threat Lee used to get me to work for him. I'm sorry.'

Patrick opened the wardrobe and peered inside; his clothes – too small for him now – still hung inside. He wrinkled his nose at the smell of camphor and the sweet-sour smell of mothballs. 'You could have thrown these away.'

Nuala shrugged. 'I just never got around to it.'

'You can dispose of them now.'

'You're staying then,' she said slowly.

'I've come home.'

'Why?' she asked suddenly. 'What is there for you here?' she asked, echoing Jane's earlier question.

Patrick sat down on the edge of the bed. Suddenly he felt tired – bone tired – and even the effort of answering Nuala's question he found exhausting.

'There's nothing left for you here.'

'My past is here … my future too. I think.'

The Madam nodded. 'We'll talk later. Rest now; you've had a troubled time.' She ruffled his hair as she walked past and for a moment he thought she was going to kiss him – like a mother kissing a child before bed, but she continued to the door and pulled it closed behind her. He listened to her muted foosteps hurry down the corridor and then the door opened to her own bedroom – once his mother's – a little further down the corridor.

He undressed slowly, fumbling with the buttons, his fingers numb, wrestling with the collar stud and then, finally naked, he crawled into the bed, wincing at the chill of the sheets. He pulled the blankets up to his chin and stared at the ceiling. He followed the cracks and lines that radiated out from the gas bowl. As a boy he used to lie in bed imagining that they were roads leading to a magic castle, and each night he would take a different road, each one fraught with different dangers. He had never reached the magic castle – he had always fallen asleep beforehand.

New cracks and lines had been added to the map on the ceiling, new roads to follow. Patrick rubbed his eyes, exhaustion settling over him like a leaden blanket. When he closed his eyes he saw again – and again – the blood seeping through the door. His eyes snapped open, staring at the ceiling – and as he watched, blood began to well through the cracks, long scars opening, blood dripping onto the sheets, touching his face, his lips ...

'Patrick!'

He came awake with a strangled scream, pushing himself up in the bed, clawing at his face, catching and holding the hand that had brushed across his lips. 'Jane,' he gasped. He was sheened with sweat, his hair plastered to his skull, and he immediately began to shiver. Jane wrapped her arms around him, brushing strands of hair from his forehead. 'I heard you moaning,' she said softly.

'A dream ... nothing more than a dream,' he mumbled, raising his head and looking into her eyes. 'I'm alright now.'

Jane stood up and pulled off the heavy dressing gown Nuala had lent her. Beneath she was wearing a long cotton nightdress. She turned down the covers and slipped into bed beside him, catching her breath at the cold, clammy touch of his skin. She wrapped her arms around him, drawing him close to her, pulling his head down onto her breasts. His arms went around her waist, and in moments he was asleep again. Jane listened as his breathing grew deep and regular, and then she gently disengaged her arms. He moaned slightly and then settled again. She was getting out of bed when the door cracked open and Nuala looked in. There was no expression on her face when she saw Jane. For a moment the two women looked at one another and then Jane tucked the blankets in around Patrick and, picking up her dressing gown, padded softly to the door. 'He was having a nightmare ...' she explained.

Nuala nodded, her eyes hooded, and then turned and walked away. Jane followed her.

The Madam's bedroom was warm, a large coal and turf fire crackling in the centre of one wall. There was a large bed directly across from it, a small dressing table beside the bed and beneath one of the tall windows that looked down onto the street was an old sea chest. Between the two windows was a huge wardrobe in a wood that was so dark it was almost black, with a long speckled mirror set into the door. Two chairs on either side of the fire completed the room's furniture. Nuala took one chair and Jane immediately sat down facing her without an invitation.

'Have you made any decisions?' Nuala asked directly, looking into Jane's eyes.

'You want me to go,' Jane said abruptly. 'Why?'

'Have you any feelings for the boy?'

'He's not a boy,' Jane said with a quick smile.

Nuala nodded, but said nothing.

'I'm very fond of him ...' Jane said cautiously, wondering where the conversation was leading.

'Do you love him?'

Jane thought about it for a moment, and then said quietly, 'I don't know ... I'm not sure.'

'If you truly loved him, you'd be sure,' Nuala said

confidently, 'you wouldn't have to think about it.'

Jane looked into the fire and then glanced at Nuala. The firelight had softened the lines on the Madam's face. 'I felt sorry for him when I first knew him in London ... he was so much under his mother's thumb. When he ran away with me, I felt so protective, he was so innocent ... do you know, he had never even kissed a girl, until he kissed me.'

Nuala smiled vaguely but said nothing.

'Since he's been here, he's grown more ... confident ... more independent. It's as if the longer he remains away from his mother the more he matures.'

Nuala nodded. 'She was always a powerful domineering influence.'

'The old Patrick I knew ... the English Patrick ... would have never come in here to look for me. The old Patrick would never have used that gun.'

Nuala raised her head slightly, nodding back towards the room they had just left. 'Has he made any decisions yet?'

'I don't think he's any decision to make. He's not leaving. He wants to stay here, he wants to discover his father's true identity. I don't know why it's so important to him,' she confessed.

'He was seventeen when he watched his father go out to die. Many young men of seventeen fought and died then also; Patrick didn't ... his mother wouldn't allow him.' Nuala smiled tightly. 'I think he's searching for reasons ... reasons why his father – or rather, the man he believed to be his father – went out to kill and die, reasons why he wasn't allowed to join him.'

'Was Dermot Corcoran his father?' Jane asked, watching Nuala intently.

'I've always believed so.'

'That's not what I asked.'

'It's the only answer I have.'

'But would Katherine have any reason to lie to him?'

'If it suited her; she delighted in manipulating people ... and it was something she was very good at.'

191

There was silence between the two women for a while, both of them absorbed in their own thoughts, the gentle heat from the fire lulling them. Finally, Jane looked up and spoke, 'You asked if I loved him, well, I can't answer that. But I don't think he loves me.'

'You admitted yourself that you're the first girl he's ever kissed ... and yet I'll wager, he's not your first,' she added with a smile.

Their eyes locked briefly, and there was no need for Jane to reply.

'I don't think he's capable of making a decision yet about you ... about any girl. Too much has happened in too short a time. A couple of weeks ago, he was a cosseted mother's boy – today he's a murderer! Give him time. And space.'

'You're advising me to go?' Jane asked quietly.

Nuala glanced at the round-faced clock above the fire. It ticked so slowly, so regular, as to be almost silent. 'The train leaves in two hours. It will take you to Cork where you will board ship to New York.' She stood up and took a slim sheaf of papers off the mantlepiece. 'Here are tickets and letters of introduction to some of Michael Collins' people in New York. They will arrange someplace for you to stay, and a job.'

Jane looked at the tickets. Long rectangular pieces of almost plain paper – and yet they represented a whole new life.

Nuala saw the questions forming, and pressed on. 'You're a friend of Patrick's, and Patrick is Dermot Corcoran's son, and his reputation is revered here.' She saw down and placed the tickets and letters on the floor between them. 'The decision is yours. I'll not force you.'

'If I stay ...?' Jane wondered.

'We'll do our best for you here, find you a job and a place to stay also.'

'If it was your choice ...?' she asked Nuala.

'It's not my choice.'

'But if it was?' Jane persisted.

The Madam stared into the fire and smiled wryly. 'A few years ago, I had the opportunity of going to America. I didn't take it.' She glanced up at Jane, her eyes glittering with the firelight. 'I've regretted it ever since.'

Jane nodded, but said nothing.

'You can make something of yourself out there. The class barriers don't seem to matter so much. A servant may still marry her master there without too many questions, too many raised eyebrows; you know that's virtually impossible here.' She turned away from the fire and reached out to touch Jane on the knee. 'You have some chance of a future out there – you've none here.'

Jane reached down and picked up the papers from the blood-red carpet.

As Patrick was awakening in the late afternoon, the train Jane was on was just pulling into Cork station. She was carrying a borrowed suitcase filled with clothing borrowed from Nuala. In her pockets she had ten pounds and the tickets and the letters of introduction. She wondered briefly what Patrick would say when he learned about her disappearance, and then decided it didn't matter now.

Nuala told Patrick about Jane's decision as he finished a bowl of soup she had brought in to him. 'It was for the best,' she finished.

Patrick nodded. 'She has her life to lead. I'm pleased for her; I know she'll be successful,' he said, surprising her.

'I know this must be a shock for you, but it was for the best,' she repeated. 'Perhaps you'll meet again.'

Patrick looked up at her and smiled slightly. 'Now that's not very likely, is it?'

CHAPTER TWELVE

It snowed during the night and Patrick awoke early to find the room bright with light. He lay dozing in bed, pleasantly warm, the events of the past two days going back and forth in his head.

Yesterday – was it only yesterday – he had become a killer. And Lee was dead. And Jane was gone.

He felt a vague sense of loss at her departure ... and some slightly guilty sense of relief. He was a free agent now, free to do what he pleased. He was grateful to her – he always would be – but he wasn't sure what he would have done with her had she remained. Out of a sense of obligation he would have remained with her ... but that would have brought too many complications. It would have tied him down – and he didn't want that just now, not when he was beginning to enjoy his freedom.

But that problem had been solved now.

Throwing back the covers he swung his legs out of bed – just as the door opened and Nuala entered, carrying a laden tray. Patrick coloured and immediately pulled the covers up around himself.

Nuala put the tray down on the bedside locker and turned to pull back the curtains. 'I've seen naked men before,' she said conversationally, 'and I helped bathe you as a child,' she added with a smile.

'What time is it?' Patrick asked.

'A little after ten.' Nuala poured tea from a squat glazed pot. She handed one cup to Patrick, and poured milk for him while he held it. 'Do you still take sugar?'

'If you don't give it to me I won't be tempted.'

Nuala sat at the end of the bed and sipped her tea. 'I've written a letter to your mother, explaining what has occurred in the past few days, omitting certain facts of course,' she smiled. 'I'll also include the newspaper account of Lee's "shooting".'

'I didn't realize it had been in the papers.'

'This morning's,' Nuala said, ' "Roof-top sniper slain", – something along those lines. It doesn't name Lee of course, but the description should be enough for your mother.'

'Are you going to say anything about me ... and Jane?' he added quickly.

Nuala smiled over the rim of her cup. 'I was thinking of telling her half the truth. I'll tell her that Lee was certain that you were both booked on board the boat for America.'

'But what if she investigates ...?' Patrick protested, 'she'll find Jane ...'

'She'll be looking for two people travelling together. Jane is alone.'

'Will that work?'

Nuala shrugged. 'It might. We'll have to be circumspect for a while, however, just in case she sends someone else over to investigate.'

'She won't be very pleased at losing Lee – he was obviously very important in her organization.'

'Like everyone else in your mother's organization he is replaceable; perhaps that's why she tried so hard to hang on to you. She can buy most things ... but not family.' Nuala shrugged. 'Lee's death will be an inconvenience, nothing more I promise you.' She finished her tea quickly and stood up. 'There's some clothes in the wardrobe – I've borrowed them from the lads. Later today, we'll go out and buy you some new ones. Now, I think you'd better get up. You've a meeting with Collins at the Pillar at noon.'

Michael Collins was leaning up against the metal rail that surrounded Nelson's Pillar when Patrick spotted him. The big man was wrapped up in a heavy overcoat, the collar turned up, a black hat pulled down over his eyes.

Patrick stood on the corner of North Earl Street and watched him for a few moments, shaking his head at the man's audacity, and then he moved out of the side street and carefully crossed the wet, icy cobbles.

Collins stepped away from the Pillar as Patrick approached. 'You're on time,' he said by way of greeting. The bells of the pro-cathedral were tolling noon.

'I got your message,' he said softly, not looking at Collins, his eyes on the ruin of the GPO.

Michael Collins turned to look at the blackened shell of a building. 'They'll rebuild it soon, but it will always be a symbol,' he said, 'a tomb for all those who died fighting for the cause.'

Patrick nodded silently. The man he had believed to be his father had died in there. The building was a ruin; the windows gaped blindly, blackened and empty, the roof was gone, and the whole front of the building was pocked with bullet marks, and streaked black where fire had swept through the building. The snow that had fallen during the night, dusting it in white, merely served to emphasize its desolation.

'What must it have been like in there?' Patrick whispered.

Collins took his arm and steered him away from the building and its memories. 'Look to the future,' he said, 'not the past.'

They walked down the length of O'Connell Street. What had once been one of the most beautiful capitals of Europe now – even three years after the Rising – lay desolated and gutted. The fires that had swept down the street in the last days of the Rising had gouged the heart from the city. Some efforts had been made at rebuilding, but they looked lost and forlorn amidst the derelict buildings and only added to the air of desolation.

They turned left at O'Connell Bridge and headed up Bachelor's Walk. Patrick walked on the river side, his fingers trailing against the low wall. Close to O'Connell

Street, the buildings were snow-covered ruins, but the further up the quays they walked, evidence of the destruction gradually disappeared, allowing Patrick a graphic example of just how localized the Rising had been. They had walked in silence and then, as they were passing the Ha'penny Bridge, Patrick said urgently, 'We're being followed. Two men.'

Collins grinned. 'I know. And two more on the far side of the river. They've been with us since the Pillar.'

'Your men?'

'Mine. If they weren't, they wouldn't simply be following us – they'd be shooting at us.'

Wind gusted snowflakes into their faces and they ducked their heads, holding down their hats.

'Why did you want to see me – and why here?' Patrick demanded.

Collins grinned, his face suddenly youthful. 'I wanted to talk to you. Since you've come to Ireland, you've caused me no end of trouble, and yet I barely know you.'

Patrick said nothing.

'Nuala tells me you've decided to stay here,' Collins continued.

'This is my home.'

Michael Collins nodded. 'You've sacrificed a lot, I understand.'

'In return for freedom,' Patrick said quickly.

'Are any of us truly free?' Collin asked.

'I want to join you. I want to fight for a free Ireland.'

Collins glanced at him. 'What do you know about us? I mean really know about us?'

'Enough. My father fought with you, died for you.'

The big man nodded, but said nothing.

They walked in silence for a while and then Patrick said, 'You know Joseph Hyde …?'

'I know Joe.'

'He'll vouch for me, so will Tom Rooney and Dan Brady.'

'I'm not doubting your credentials, and both Tom

and Joe have spoken highly of you and your commitment to the cause – in London. But its all very well to support us with words – are you prepared to act with us?'

Patrick began to nod, but Collins laid his hand on his arm, and said quickly, 'Think about what I've just said. Are you prepared to act ... to follow orders which you might not agree with, to do things which you might otherwise find repugnant?'

'I owe it to my father's memory; I owe it to him to continue the work he began.'

Michael Collins nodded, but said nothing. Snow began to fall, a light dusting that clung to their overcoats, and gathered on the brim of their hats. Patrick shivered, and pulled the collar of his coat tighter around his throat. 'I'm sorry if I've caused you trouble ...'

Collin shrugged. 'Trouble I can handle.'

'But I'm a problem.'

'You are.'

'This is a cause I believe in,' Patrick said quietly.

'I'm not doubting that you are sincere – in fact I'm quite sure of it. Your pedigree is excellent. I only knew your father vaguely, but I know he was held in high esteem by the leaders of the Rising, and so I've no doubt that you are committed. I know you've left home, and I know the reasons why. I'm just wondering if you realize what you're getting into. You will have to commit yourself to fight a guerrilla war against a far superior force. You'll face death at all times, and betrayal at every turn, and you will be up against an enemy that will show you no mercy.' He glanced sidelong at Patrick. 'Do you understand what I'm saying to you?'

Patrick nodded. 'You're trying to frighten me.'

The big man grinned. 'No, I'm only trying to tell you the truth.' He looked over the wall into the greasy water. 'Once the authorities become aware of you, you'll become a wanted man, with a price on your head.

You'll go on the run then – and you'll only stop when you are dead or this war is over. And I think we're looking at a long war.'

'I have a duty ...' Patrick said, 'a duty to the memory of my father and the cause he supported and died for.'

Michael Collins nodded seriously. 'I can understand that.' He stopped and turned to face Patrick, reaching out to take and shake his hand. 'You'll be staying with Nuala?' he asked.

'It is my home.'

'Aye, well then. Someone will call for you later this week, and you'll begin training. You'll be on my staff.' And then the big man nodded once and turned left over Capel Street Bridge, heading towards Parliament Street. Patrick stood by the bridge watching him retreat into the swirling snow. The two men on the opposite side of the river caught up with him and then the two who had been following brushed past Patrick and strode across the bridge after him. Within minutes he and his guards were gone, leaving Patrick alone on the quayside. Glancing up and down the quay for traffic, Patrick hurried across the cobbles and headed off down Capel Street.

He didn't feel anything – there was no sense of elation, no excitement, no feeling of accomplishment. It was simply another achievement, and Patrick Lundy was well used to getting what he wanted. He had set out to join the movement in London, and he had done so; he had come to Dublin with the intention of fighting with Collins, and he had achieved that. Now all that remained for him to do was to discover his true father's identity.

And he would do that.

The man known as the Brigadier had operated the British Intelligence service in Ireland for more than twenty years now. A small, neat, dapper – seemingly ageless – man with a taste for fine clothes, cigars, imported tea and women, he had survived when so many others had not because of a simple, basic refusal to accept anything on its face value, and never to get personally involved. Other people did the dirty work, the Brigadier merely sorted, sifted and catalogued. He had warned the British Government of the 1916 uprising in Ireland months before it had actually happened, and had managed to pass on not only the dates, but the times, the rebels, strength and armaments and even the identities of the leaders. Very little of the information had been acted upon, but when the Rising had been crushed, he made sure it was remembered that the Brigadier had forewarned of the event. And while much of the information had come from Major John Lewis and his mysterious informant, Lewis was dead now and – unfortunately – unable to accept his share of the credit.

The Brigadier sat in his tiny office in Dublin Castle and looked up from the report he had finished reading, smiling wryly. Lewis, why had he remembered Lewis now? In his report he had listed Captain John Lewis as having been killed in action, a gallant soldier defending his country, but the Brigadier was one of the few people who actually knew that Lewis had been shot at very close range by a small calibre pistol in his house on Clonliffe Road.

The Brigadier smiled and tapped the report again. That's what had dredged Lewis' name up from his subconscious. A man had been shot and killed while sniping on British troops from a house in the Coombe in the heart of Dublin. And yet the coroner's report showed that the man had been shot at very close range right through the heart. He had also been shot with a .38 calibre bullet, but the Lee-Enfield which the troops carried were .30 calibre.

The small man rubbed his hands together quickly, and then ran his fingers through his iron-grey hair. He opened the report and prepared to read through it again. This was obviously more than a simple shooting.

Patrick Lundy and Nuala sat in the sitting room,

listening to the muted sounds of revelry coming up from the floor below. It was a little after eight and 'guests' were beginning to trickle into the house. It had been snowing on and off through the afternoon and towards evening had turned bitterly cold, and the streets were now sheathed in a covering of frozen snow and ice.

'There won't be many callers tonight,' Nuala said, crossing to the window to close the heavy drapes.

'Is your trade seasonal then?' Patrick asked.

Nuala returned to her seat by the fire and made a face. 'Summers are best, but a dry night, no matter what the season, is always busy. However, a night like this – well, we'll get few enough callers, and those who do call won't be in any hurry to leave.'

Patrick leaned over and added a log to the blazing fire. It caught and sparked, and then began hissing softly as the sap boiled. The room was pleasantly warm and they had taken their tea there beside the fire, easy in each other's company, the warmth of the fire soothing, the only sounds the muted noises of the house and the gentle whispering of the snow against the window panes. When the light from outside had faded completely they hadn't bothered to light a lamp, preferring instead the warm colours of the fire, and it was only the occasional gust of wind through the ill-fitting casement windows that had finally forced Nuala into closing the drapes.

'Do you want a light?'

Patrick shook his head, the movement vague in the darkness. 'There's no need.' He sat back into the chair and sighed audibly. 'This brings me back. I can clearly remember sitting curled up in this chair – just like this, with a blazing fire and no lights – listening to the noises from below, wondering what was happening, but knowing it would be useless to ask my mother, knowing she wouldn't answer me.'

'And you never guessed?' Nuala asked with a smile.

'I never knew. I had led a very sheltered life

remember. I never even knew that there were places like brothels. I was completely ignorant of the act of love between a man and a woman.'

'What a lovely quaint expression,' Nuala said.

Patrick shrugged, embarrassed. 'That's my ignorance again.'

'So in all the time you lived here – you never realized you were living over or in a brothel?' Nuala asked in disbelief.

Patrick smiled at her disbelieving expression. 'I had no terms of reference. I told you – I was unaware of what went on between a man and a woman, and I was equally unaware that places like this existed for the sale of that act.'

The Madam shook her head in amazement, still finding it difficult to comprehend that Patrick had never even suspected that he was living in a brothel. 'When did you begin to suspect.'

'Shortly after we moved to London.' He looked deep into the glowing embers of the fire and smiled. 'I began studying medicine and mixing with students of my own age. I'm sure they must have thought me an absolute idiot and unbearably stuffy … but I learned a lot from them.'

'Your mother continued in her old trade.'

'She did.'

'I take it that business was not run from the house, as it was here?'

Patrick shook his head. 'We had a house in Mayfair and across the green from us Lee ran the business in an equally luxurious house that seemed to cater to the upper classes.'

'Did you know that there are also houses in Manchester and Glasgow?' Nuala smiled at his reaction. 'And I suppose you don't know that while your mother ran this – the most exclusive brothel in Dublin – she also controlled the movement of most of the stolen goods in the city?' She laughed now at the stunned expression on his face; even in the firelight, he looked as if he had been struck with a length of wood. 'You were probably too young to remember, but when the Crown Jewels were stolen in 1907, rumour had it that your mother was supposed to have been the one who arranged the theft.'

Patrick shook his head. 'That can't be true …'

'Well, it's not, I happen to know that for a fact. But it shows the sort of reputation Madam Kitten had in Dublin at the time.'

'I never knew …'

'I occasionally adopt her disguise when I'm dealing with special customers, or a difficult client,' she continued, standing up and crossing to a long, ugly teak cabinet that had been there as long as Patrick could remember. She opened it and lifted out two glasses and a crystal decanter. The firelight took the decanter and struck brilliants from it, spattering Nuala's face with sparkles of white, turning the amber liquid within to a warm gold, speckling the room with refracted light. She poured two generous amounts into the widemouthed glasses and carried them back to the fire, handing one to Patrick.

'I don't drink alcohol …'

'Learn to,' she said. 'You'll need it, after wandering around town all day in this weather; I don't know what Collins was thinking of.'

Patrick took the glass and watched Nuala bring hers close to her face, breathing in the heady fumes. He copied her, bringing the glass close to his nose and taking a deep breath. The rich bouquet caught at the back of his throat, and his eyes immediately watered. He cautiously sipped the liquid; it seared his mouth and slid down into his stomach like liquid fire. 'That's horrific,' he gasped.

'It is the finest Napoleon brandy,' Nuala said with a smile. 'It's from the stock your mother left behind, so I've no qualms about giving you some.'

'You obviously knew a different woman to the one I did,' Patrick remarked.

'Obviously,' Nuala said drily.

'Tell me about her,' he said simply.

Nuala shrugged. 'There's little enough to tell. She was

a madam, a brothel keeper who learned her trade from the notorious Bella Cohen, the Whoremistress. She dealt in stolen goods, and ran a very lucrative sideline selling information.' She nodded at Patrick's incredulous expression. 'Aye, that's right, she bought and sold information to the highest bidder.' Nuala sipped her drink, watching Patrick over the rim of her glass. 'There are other, slightly less wholesome stories about her, but I think we'll leave them for another time perhaps.'

Patrick nodded numbly. His head was throbbing and although he noted to his surprise that he had finished the glass, he couldn't actually remember tasting any of the liquid. 'Tell me about Dermot Corcoran,' he said, pronouncing each word carefully. His tongue felt as if it had grown to twice its size.

'Your father was a gentleman, in every sense of the word,' Nuala said fondly.

'Was he like me?' Patrick asked quickly, 'do I resemble him?'

Nuala guessed what was coming and took her time before answering. 'It's difficult to say of course; it would have been easier to say before Collins had Eddie do a job on you.'

'I think you're evading the question.'

Nuala grinned. 'Well, you're your mother's son all right – sharp and direct.'

'Am I Dermot Corcoran's son?' Patrick demanded.

Nuala finished her brandy. 'You don't look like him,' she said eventually.

'That still doesn't answer my question,' Patrick snapped.

The Madam sighed. 'Your mother was pregnant when she first arrived in this house on Christmas Eve, 1898. Of course no one realized that until later … but I think maybe Madam Cohen knew. Certainly, she never put your mother to work, except that she was a sort of secretary or bookkeeper. Some people said she was related to the Whoremistress, but that just wasn't true. Your mother may have known Dermot Corcoran at that stage, but I don't know. Certainly, Senga your sister is Dermot's daughter; she was conceived on a holiday the two of them had in Galway just before they were married.'

'How do you know all this?' Patrick asked very quietly.

Nuala turned to look at him. 'My sister worked in this house before me.'

'I didn't know you had a sister.'

Nuala shrugged, her expression tightening. 'She worked under the Whoremistress; the house wasn't as well regulated as it was under your mother. A whore's working life was quite short. Pregnancy, disease and death were commonplace. My sister was unlucky, she caught ... well, it's one of the hazards of the game. It took her looks, her sight and finally, her sanity.'

'I'm sorry,' Patrick said gently.

'Yes ...' Nuala breathed. 'Yes ... well, she knew your mother, used to visit her quite regularly; she helped me get the job here,' she finished, her voice grown soft and distant.

They remained silent, each absorbed in their own thoughts while the fire burned low. The bitterness within Nuala flooded into her mouth, and she regretted the brandy. She had watched the disease that had eaten at her sister's body destroy her mind, turning her into something she barely recognized. She hadn't told Patrick how she had walked into her sister's room one morning to find she had sliced through her wrists, using a hat-pin to open her veins along the length of her arm; she hadn't told Patrick how glad she had been. She looked across at the young man. He was ... what was the word ... a catalyst ... someone who caused change. Since he had come to Dublin, he had shattered her usually placid existence, brought bloodshed and death into her house, forced her into contact with the IRA, and dredged up memories that she had thought long forgotten.

The firelight had turned his eyes to mirrors, and for a moment he looked inhuman, a statue of bronze, and then his eyes slowly closed, and two lines of glistening liquid traced their way down his cheeks. Without a word she went to him, holding him close while he sobbed.

Patrick slept fitfully that night. Although the room was pleasantly warm and the bed was piled high with blankets, he felt cold, chilled through and through. He was beginning to realize just how little he knew about his mother; the woman he had once loved was turning into a monster before his eyes.

What was she? Who was she?

Obviously the woman he had grown up with bore no resemblance to the woman all Dublin knew of as Madam Kitten. She had concealed the two parts of her life perfectly – and in the light of what he now knew, she was continuing her trade in London, still running her exclusive brothels, still dealing in stolen goods.

And he was still no closer to finding out just who his father had been. Certainly not Dermot Corcoran – but who? Had she walked the streets before she had joined the brothel, and was he no more than an accident – unfortunate, but neither unexpected nor uncommon? But Nuala had said that she had arrived on Christmas Eve, 1898 ... and his mother had only arrived in Ireland in May of the same year. So perhaps the answer lay in those seven months.

Before sleep finally claimed him, he vowed to find out.

CHAPTER THIRTEEN

'The man's name was Lee, Michael Lee, born London on or about September, 1884, to an English mother and an Oriental – presumably seafaring – father. We may assume that his mother was a common prostitute, and the boy would seem to have grown up on the docks. There are numerous arrests for petty crime, theft, robbery with violence ...' The army captain looked across the table at the Brigadier. 'Not a very pleasant man.'

The old man smiled thinly, and waved the man to continue. 'He worked for some years as a small-time pimp, in trouble too often with the law to be successful, and then, some three years ago, he disappeared off the streets, only to reappear a little later as a "businessman." Upon investigation, it was discovered that he was fronting a high-class brothel. We don't know who was backing him, but the very size of the operation suggests great wealth. Lee moved amongst the highest class of society and Scotland Yard suspected a very real fear of blackmail.' The army captain looked at the Brigadier. 'Mr Lee recently attended a court function as a guest.'

'Not bad for a wharf brat,' the Brigadier mumbled.

The army captain smiled, and then continued. 'It would also appear that he occasionally indulged his homosexual predilections, usually with sailors off the boats close to where he grew up.'

'An interesting character, this Mister Lee,' the Brigadier said, leaning back in his chair, 'And now I'm curious to discover how he came to be shot in Dublin.'

The young army captain pulled another page from his report. 'Upon receipt of your request, sir, we investigated any Irish angle, but discovered none. We also ran a check on his friends – of which he seemed to have had very few. There were numerous associates, all of them shady, some of them morally dubious, and I should mention that he was on nodding terms with several members of the nobility and at least two members of the highest echelons of the clergy.' The man closed the report and looked across at the major. 'I did discover one curious fact. I'm not sure whether it would have a bearing on your investigation …'

'Out with it man,' the Brigadier snapped.

'Yes, sir! Michael Lee frequently visited the house of a society hostess, a Mrs Katherine Lundy.'

The Brigadier sat forward. Somewhere at the back of his mind a bell began ringing. He felt the first stirrings of excitement, but when he spoke his voice was level. 'Why did this strike you as curious; you said he was on close terms with members of the aristocracy and clergy.'

'She was his only wealthy female associate; the rest were fallen women, and he visited her with a regularity that suggested a closer relationship …'

'Aaah …' The Brigadier sat back into the chair, with a smile.

'We pursued our investigations into this woman's background – and came up with nothing.'

'Nothing?' The Brigadier hissed.

'No, sir. She appeared in London in the summer of 1916, purchased one of the most elegant houses in Mayfair, and now lives there quietly with her two children and at least half a dozen servants.'

'Now that is interesting,' the Brigadier murmured.

The captain smiled slightly. 'I thought it strange enough to be worthy of mention.'

'You have done well; I will commend you in my report. You're returning to London?'

'On the nightboat.'

'Continue your investigations – but concentrate on this Mrs Lundy now. I expect to be kept fully informed.' The Brigadier pushed back his chair, indicating that the discussion was at an end. The captain stood and saluted and then marched from the room, leaving the old man to ponder the mystery of Mrs Katherine Lundy, a society hostess, who knew a petty criminal, and whose history went back no further than three years ago to 1916 …

Nineteen–sixteen …

The bell that had been ringing in the Brigadier's skull began tolling more insistently.

Patrick walked up one side of the road and down the other, slowing only when he passed the house. He had thought when he looked at it that he would feel something. But it was simply a house, a three-storied house on Clonliffe Road, on the outskirts of Dublin. When his mother had first come to Dublin, this was where she had gone into service, this was where she had worked for a little more than seven months before ending up in Bella Cohen's brothel. Why – and how? Had something happened in that house which had driven her out onto the streets and into the arms of the woman known as the Whoremistress? With a sigh, he turned and walked away.

Nuala was waiting for him in a car at the end of the road. She opened the door as he approached, and he climbed in without a word. The Madam tapped on the glass partition and Jem pulled away from the kerb. 'Did you find what you were looking for?' she asked.

'I'm not even sure what I was looking for,' he said with a wry smile. He turned to look through the small back window at the house. 'Perhaps if we went to her employers?' he wondered aloud, 'perhaps they would be able to help.'

Nuala smiled. 'Are they likely to remember a servant they employed for a few months more than twenty years ago?'

Patrick nodded reluctantly.

Nuala reached out and squeezed his shoulder. 'However, we'll try. I know someone – one of our customers,' he's a librarian, and I know he does some genealogical research, I'll ask him to do a little research for us.'

'Discreetly …' Patrick said quickly.

'He'll be discreet,' Nuala grinned, 'he'll be doing this as a favour to us … and we'll make sure his payment is in kind. And his kind of payment he'll not want advertised.' She saw his expression and stopped. His eyes had turned hard and his lips were drawn into a thin line. 'What's the matter?'

'Nothing,' he said, a voice sharper than he intended.

Nuala sighed. Sometimes she forgot that Patrick was a young man – a very immature young man. 'What's the matter?' she persisted.

He shook his head. 'It's just to hear you talk like that … to talk about men and women … about selling their bodies …'

His voice trailed off, but Nuala remained silent, forcing him to continue.

'I mean … where's the love in it?'

'There is none,' she said sharply. 'We're talking about a product, an item to be sold, like a coat or hat or glove, only this time it's a woman's body for a time, a few minutes, an hour, a night. There's no love in it, the women know that … and if the men who avail themselves of our services like to think of love, then they're bigger fools than they look.'

'You don't have a very high opinion of your customers.'

'Give me a reason why,' Nuala spat vehemently. 'I've been in this business a long time, and I've seen men of all walks of life, men of letters, men of the church, the nobility, the common people … I've seen men with manners, with style, with wealth and position … and yet when they're alone with a woman, they're all the same. A naked woman's body has the power to make all men equal.' She turned away and stared through the window, looking out at the dismal streets.

'If you hate the business so much, why do you continue in it?' Patrick asked, very gently.

'I've grown accustomed to it,' Nuala said bitterly, 'it's sucked me in, made me as much of a whore as the girls who work the houses or the streets. I've grown used to the money, the wealth, the position and the power. It's trapped me ... much as it must have trapped your mother. She was a young woman once, happy and innocent. This business destroyed her ... in the same way that it's destroying me.' She turned suddenly, her face pale, her eyes wide and dark in her head. 'Don't let it eat your soul too!'

The church bells were tolling six when the small, dark man came for Patrick. He tapped lightly – almost gently – on the door of the brothel and kept glancing up and down the street. When Jem opened the door, the big man suppressed a smile. A newcomer, he guessed.

'We're not open yet.'

'Tell Patrick Lundy that I'm here – he's expecting me.'

'I don't know who you're talking about,' Jem said firmly, looking up and down the street, checking for strangers, 'there's no-one here by that name.'

'Look,' the man sighed, 'I've no time for this. I know he's here. Just tell him that the Big Fellow's sent someone for him.'

Jem blinked at the mention of Collins' nick-name, and then, almost reluctantly, he stepped into the hallway. Jem indicated the open sitting-room door. 'If you'd care to wait inside ...' he suggested.

'I'll stay here,' the man said curtly. He had pulled off his hat and held it in one hand, while his other hand was invisible behind it. Jem had the distinct impression that the man was holding a small gun. He had turned to climb the stairs when Nuala appeared followed by Patrick.

'This gentleman is looking for a Mr Lundy, ma'am.'

Nuala stopped on the stairs and looked closely at the man. 'I don't think I know you,' she said loudly.

'You wouldn't.' There was enough of a self-righteous tone in his voice to annoy her.

'And who are you?'

'You don't need to know my name.'

'You can leave this house now …' Nuala began, her temper rising.

'Wait,' Patrick said, 'if you two have quite finished …?' He looked at the man. 'I believe you have a message for me?'

'Are you Patrick Lundy?'

'I am.'

'The Big Fellow sent me for you.'

'I'll get my coat and hat.' Patrick turned and raced back up the stairs, leaving Nuala glaring at the small man.

'You don't like this house?' Nuala demanded.

'I never said that.'

'You don't have to say anything.' She walked down the rest of the stairs until she was standing before the man. He was about her height, but her presence was intimidating. Jem smiled openly at the man's expression.

'Why don't you like this house?' she asked softly.

'I've nothing against this house,' the man said, and Nuala could tell by the tone of his voice that he was preparing to go on. 'But I'm not sure I approve of the business that goes on in this house.'

'Have you ever been in this house?' She didn't wait for him to answer but pressed on. 'Well then, how can you talk about what goes on when you don't know?'

'Houses like this won't survive in a Free Ireland. There's no place for them.'

'Aye, but there was a place for them when you were plotting revolution.'

'That's not true.'

'There were times when the Easter Rising was plotted and planned in this very house,' she snapped, and then her scowl changed as Patrick reappeared, buttoning up his coat, his hat and gloves in his hand. 'Will he be late?' she demanded, looking at the man.

'Are you his mother?' the man snapped.

'Come on,' Patrick said, pulling open the hall door, 'let's go before there's an argument.'

The small man glared at Nuala for one final moment and then stalked out after Patrick.

Nuala closed the door with a bang that echoed up and down the street.

'What are you doing living in a place like that?' the man demanded, falling into step beside Patrick.

'I've nowhere else to live.'

Patrick's answer seemed to catch him off-guard, and he remained silent for a few moments. Eventually he said, 'My name's Jimmy ...' Patrick thought he was going to add his surname, but he obviously thought better of it.

'Patrick ...'

They continued on in silence and walked down into Parnell Square at the top of O'Connell Street. They strolled past the Rotunda Lying-in Hospital, heading towards Capel Street.

'I don't suppose you want to tell me where we're going?' Patrick suggested.

'You're right, I don't.'

Patrick hid a smile. The man was still smarting from his encounter with Nuala and Patrick wondered if he was a member of the Legion of Mary, a staunchly Catholic group that had set up on the very edge of the brothel area of Monto with the intention of 'saving' the girls. And while many of them didn't want to be saved – the Legion had converted enough to make it worth their while staying in the area. He glanced at the man again – there were no outwards signs of any especial religious fervour, no crucifix, no pins in his lapels – but then, if he were a member of Collins' group, he would hardly wear anything that might attract attention to himself, Patrick reasoned.

'Are you a Catholic now?' the man asked, the question so appropriate that it startled him speechless for a moment.

'Well yes, I was baptised a Catholic ...'

'That's not what I asked,' the man said sharply.

Suddenly growing annoyed with the man's aggressive

213

manner, Patrick snapped. 'I answered the question you asked me.'

There was silence for a few moments, while they turned right into Capel Street.

'I'm sorry, I had no right ...' Jimmy began.

'You're right – you hadn't.'

The man nodded. 'Aye, well ... well, I'm sorry. I've been out of line, I suppose,' he admitted. 'It was just ... it was just having to go to that place ... I just couldn't understand how anyone would want to live in a house like that.' He glanced sidelong at Patrick. 'That's only an opinion, mind you,' he said quickly, 'I'm not condemning.'

Patrick smiled wanly. 'I was reared in that house. It's my home.'

The man nodded slowly, although Patrick could see that he didn't understand.

'My mother was the Madam,' he said patiently, 'she ran the house.' He smiled at Jimmy's horrified expression. 'But she was a good mother; my sister and I went to the best of schools, went to confession every Saturday night, Mass every Sunday. We never knew there was anything strange about the place, never saw the customers, and we considered all the girls as our aunts.' He looked at the man carefully. 'And although I know now that it was a brothel, there was a lot of love – genuine, real love – in that house, a lot of happiness ...'

'In the new Ireland ...' the man began, and then shook his head savagely. 'Well, we'll talk about that later. Here we are.' He glanced up and down the street before ducking into a half-opened door almost at the end of Capel Street where it ran into Bolton Street.

Immediately inside the door were two men; both were armed.

Jimmy muttered something in Irish and the men moved aside to allow them both to pass, and then resumed their positions in the shadows on either side of the door. Patrick followed Jimmy up a bare flight of stairs. There was another guard on the top of the stairs,

214

and a fourth outside the only closed door on the landing. He knocked once and then twice as Jimmy approached and the door immediately opened.

Jimmy stood aside and allowed Patrick to precede him. The young man stepped into the dark, smoky room and the door closed behind him, Jimmy remaining outside. There were six or seven men in the room – in the darkness it was difficult to determine the number ... and then Michal Collins stepped out of the shadows and clasped Patrick by the hand. 'Come, sit. Thank you for coming.'

'Thank you for asking me.'

Collins turned back to the room. 'This is Patrick,' he said quietly, 'he will be joining this unit. You know we thrive and survive on secrecy, and so I'll suffice it to say that Patrick's pedigree is impeccable; his father was a confident of Pearse and Plunkett and fought alongside us in '16. He was one of those who paid for their belief with their lives. His son wants to continue his work. I know you will all assist him in every way possible.' He looked back at Patrick and the young man stepped forward slightly, and squinted into the gloom.

'My father died for Ireland; I don't want to let his sacrifice be in vain.'

'Well said ...' someone murmured from the shadows.

'He seems very young,' another voice muttered from off to one side.

'And English,' a third voice added.

'Patrick is young, and he has lived in England,' Collins agreed easily, 'but you'll have to take my word that he has sacrificed a lot to be with us today.'

'Well that's good enough for me.'

And then Collins led Patrick around the room, introducing him to the shadowy figures, calling them only by their first names. Patrick got the impression that they were all reasonably young men – in their mid to late twenties or early thirties, most of them soft spoken, and in nearly every case he noticed that their hands were callused and hardened from manual labour of some kind.

215

Collins stopped before the last man in the room, a tall broad-shouldered giant. 'This is Gerard …' The giant's hand swallowed Patrick's. Michael Collins looked up at the tall bearded man. 'I want you to look after Patrick, Gerard; show him the ropes, teach him what he wants to know.' The big man grunted non-committally. 'He's a friend of mine,' Collins said gently.

'Aye, well then …'

Collins turned back to Patrick. 'Gerard will look after you, train you after a fashion. This group is part of a cell, and each cell only knows its own members. So even if one of us is captured, we won't lose everything. Now,' he rubbed his hands together briskly, 'and now I think to business …'

The next hour was spent discussing 'business'. Most of it was beyond Patrick, and seemed to be concerned with recruitment in the country, the scarcity of arms and ammunition and the constant harassment by the RIC and Special Branch G-Division. There was some political news, and then, just when Patrick was beginning to wonder what he had got himself into – after all, he hadn't come to Dublin to join some debating society – he suddenly realized that Collins was discussing the British Intelligence system in Dublin.

'I think we all know that the authorities have an extensive and reasonably successful intelligence service in Ireland. It has improved tremendously in the last few years, especially since the Rising, and I prophecy that it will soon be in a position to do us real and lasting harm.' There was silence while he caught his breath. 'Now, we have recently discovered that the British Intelligence Service in Ireland is run by an enigmatic gentleman known only as the Brigadier … but we think we may have discovered his true identity.' He looked around the silent room. 'The removal of such a man would greatly facilitate us …'

'So what did your secret organization discuss tonight eh?' Nuala walked into the kitchen as Patrick was

216

pouring himself a cup of tea.

He reached for a second cup and grinned. 'Not a lot; it was mainly boring political stuff, and then they went on to talk about someone called the Brigadier ...' He saw Nuala's expression harden, 'What's the matter?'

'What did they say about the Brigadier?' She sat down at the table across from him and reached for the tea.

Patrick shook his head slightly. 'They didn't know a lot about him. They suspect that he runs the British Intelligence Service in Ireland.' He stopped in surprise as she burst out laughing. 'What's so funny.'

'Patrick,' she said gently, 'the Brigadier has been in charge of British Intelligence in Ireland since about 1895.'

Patrick looked at her in astonishment.

'His real name,' she continued, 'is Richard Grennell. He's a man in his late fifties or early sixties – a very neat and tidy man.'

'But ... but how do you know this?' Patrick demanded, 'Collins discovered this man's identity after what sounded like months of work.'

'Perhaps he should have asked me first,' Nuala smiled. She stared into her half-empty cup, and suddenly sobered. 'The Brigadier was very friendly with Tilly Cusack – you remember Tilly?'

'Aunty Tilly ... of course,' Patrick said in surprise. She had been his mother's closest friend and his own god-mother. She had left Ireland in 1916 and now lived with her husband in Edinburgh, although he hadn't seen her for some time. He had the impression that there had been some sort of falling out between her and his mother; he had often wondered if it was because she had married an English army captain?

'Your aunt Tilly was the woman who introduced your mother to this house,' Nuala said slowly and carefully, her dark eyes on Patrick's face gauging his reaction. 'Tilly was a street-girl, dividing her time between the lucrative theatre circuit and this house. This was in the days when it was run by the notorious Bella Cohen. Anyway,' she shook her head slightly, 'this is beside the

217

point. Tilly was very friendly with a man known as Captain – later – Major John Lewis ...'

'My mother worked in the Lewis household!'

'It's the same man,' Nuala nodded. 'Well, another of Tilly's close friends was the man known as the Brigadier, Richard Grennell. He was Lewis's senior officer – although by this time Lewis had officially "left" the army and taken up a post in the General Post Office. Lewis was a spy, he ran the day to day operation from the Post Office, but Grennell was his boss ... that's how I know Grennell ran British Intelligence.' She sipped her tea and added, 'He's not a particularly nice man; he used Tilly to spy on Lewis – which was fine until Lewis found out about it.'

'What did he do?' Patrick muttered.

'Threatened her with his pistol, and then raped her.' She saw Patrick's surprised look and continued grimly. 'Yes, you can rape a whore!'

'I never said ...'

'You didn't have to.'

'Look ...' Patrick pushed his cup of cold tea aside, and stared hard at Nuala. 'I'm hearing this for the first time, remember ... you're shattering a lot of illusions.'

'I would have thought you knew.'

'No,' he breathed.

'Oh, Patrick,' she said, reaching out and placing her hand over his, 'the person to ask is your mother of course. She is the only one who can answer all your questions. So much happened in the years leading up to 1916, and then that year was just extraordinary ... and the final week.' She shook her head. 'The final week was ... it was terrifying. I don't know the half of what went on. I know your father went out to fight, and Mickey with him, and I know neither of them came back. I know your mother sent me out one morning towards the end of the week to discover what I could, and when I could find out nothing, she went out herself. But I don't think she went into town. When she left this house she turned to the

218

right, and that would have taken her away from the city centre. She came back a couple of hours later, pale-faced and shivering. She passed over the control of the house to me … and I was little more than a girl, with no real knowledge of running a place like this. The following morning she was gone. I got some letters from her, bits and pieces of information telling me how to run the house, or where various bits and pieces were kept. But there was never anything substantial from her, and no forwarding address. The next contact I had was when Lee arrived looking for you.'

Patrick frowned, attempting to catch onto something Nuala had said earlier. 'You said … you said that Tilly had brought my mother here in the first place. How did they meet …?'

The woman stood up. 'Let's talk upstairs; it's too cold down here, and we need some privacy for this.' Even as she was speaking the door opened and one of the girls walked in. She stopped in surprise, seeing Nuala and Patrick sitting at the bare table.

'What is it, Mary?'

'I was going to make some tea, Ma'am. For the vicar,' she added with a sly smile in Patrick's direction.

Nuala grinned. 'Make your tea, Mary. Mr Montgomery and I were just leaving anyway.' As they were walking up the carpeted stairs, the Madam jerked her head in the direction of the sitting room, where vague sounds of laughter were barely audible. 'The vicar likes his tea before he gets down to the serious business of sinning.'

'Sinning?' Patrick said with a grin.

' "To forgive sin, one must fully understand it," ' Nuala said in a falsetto imitation of a man's voice. 'So the vicar sins at least once a week, forgives himself and then preaches a fire and brimstone sermon on Sunday on the perils of fornication.' She opened the door to her room and walked in, leaving Patrick to close it behind him. 'Lock it,' she said, without turning around,

219

crossed to the fire, poking it to a blaze and then added three thick black sods of turf. A deep, damp woody odour suffused the room.

Surprised, he turned the key in the lock.

'Since Lee broke in, and very nearly changed all our futures, I've taken to locking it. I remember it was something your mother used to do.'

'I don't remember,' Patrick confessed.

'There's obviously a lot you don't remember.'

The young man grinned. 'No, it's just that there's an awful lot I don't know – it's as simple as that.'

Nuala sat in the high-backed winged leather chair that had once been Katherine Lundy's favourite and Patrick sat down facing her. 'Do you really want to know?' she asked quietly.

Patrick looked from the fire, his eyes amber and dead in his shadowed face. 'I need to know,' he said tightly.

CHAPTER FOURTEEN

'Did your mother ever tell you how she came to be madam of a brothel?' Nuala asked curiously.

Patrick smiled. 'We never knew it was a brothel – therefore, the question never arose.'

'I used to wonder how she explained it away,' Nuala said softly. 'Well,' she continued quickly, 'when she arrived here on Christmas Eve, 1898, she was already two months pregnant. Of course we didn't know that until later, until the 7th of July to be exact,' she said with a smile.

Patrick managed a wan grin; the 7th of July was his birthday. 'Would anyone have known she was pregnant?'

'I would imagine Madam Cohen knew – in fact, she would have had to have known. You see, a pregnant woman was never allowed into a flash house; there was some superstition about them being bad for business. When it became apparent that she was pregnant, that's when some of the girls began to think that she was one of the Whoremistress's relatives. And that impression was reinforced because Bella Cohen treated her so well. Katherine – your mother – never "worked" in the house, and I mean worked in the way the girls tonight are "working". My sister told me that there was a lot of jealousy when your mother first arrived, although I doubt if your mother was even aware of it – I'm sure it was never shown openly, certainly not with Bella Cohen around. Anyway, Katherine Lundy soon made herself indispensable to the Whoremistress, and gradually took over more and more of the day to day running of the house.'

'Go back a bit,' Patrick interrupted, 'back to when she first arrived. She was pregnant then?'

Nuala nodded. 'At least two months.'

'And had she … had she been working the streets?' he asked tightly, not looking at her.

'I don't think so.'

'Then how did she become pregnant?'

Nuala shrugged. 'I've no way of knowing.'

'Would anyone?'

'Tilly Cusack almost certainly would,' Nuala suggested.

'She arrived in this house on Christmas Eve,' Patrick persisted, vainly attempting to catch onto something he had picked up earlier.

'That's right.'

'Now, she had arrived in Dublin in May of that year. So that means in … in what, seven months, she has met someone, and known them well enough to become pregnant by them.'

'You don't have to know someone well to become pregnant by them,' Nuala said with a smile, 'but continue, I know what you mean.'

'Well, we know she knew Dermot Corcoran then … but she was quite insistent that Dermot was not my father.'

'There would have been a man or men in the house where she was in service.'

'Yes …'

'Why was she let go?' Nuala asked suddenly. 'What did she do that was bad enough to have her dismissed on Christmas Eve? All we know is that she was dismissed by the mistress of the house, because I used to wonder what type of woman would throw an eighteen year old girl out on the streets on Christmas Eve.'

'She was pregnant,' Patrick said doubtfully.

'But not obviously so. She could have stayed another two or three months at least … No, it was something else; something must have brought the situation to a head.'

222

'Maybe she told someone, and they told the master or mistress ...' Patrick suggested.

'That's hardly reason enough to be dismissed from service unless ... unless ...' Nuala took a deep breath and hurried on, pursuing the elusive thought. 'Katherine was thrown out of the house because of her pregnancy, by the mistress when she discovered it,' she said quickly, leaning forward. 'But, surely that's a job for the butler – he controls the servants after all ...'

Patrick nodded quickly. 'Aye, or the man of the house. He would be responsible for employing and ultimately dismissing the servants ...'

'Unless the child was his!'

'Unless the child was his,' Patrick whispered very slowly. 'Unless the child was his and his wife had just found out about it,' he said triumphantly.

Nuala had already stood up and crossed the room to the bookshelves. She squatted down and plucked out a very thick, squat red book from one of the lower shelves. 'Let's see what *Thom's Directory* tells us ...' Supporting the heavy book on one arm, she quickly leafed through the close-printed pages. She glanced up at Patrick. 'What was that address again?'

'College House, Clonliffe Road.'

Nuala's painted nail tapped the page, and when she looked up her eyes were sparkling. 'Major – formerly Captain – John Lewis!'

Patrick shook his head in bewilderment. 'Does that mean something?'

'Major Lewis was one of the most important and influential British officers in Ireland prior to the Easter Rising. His immediate superior would have been Richard Grennell, the Brigadier.'

'I still don't see ...' Patrick began, but Nuala waved him to silence.

'Major Lewis conducted a very personal campaign against this house and your mother for many years, once even going so far as to kidnap and torture your aunt, Tilly Cusack. No one ever knew why.' She tapped the book again. 'But I think we may have the beginnings of an answer here.'

'What happened to Lewis ...?' Patrick asked quietly, his voice distant, 'is he still alive?'

'I don't know. He's certainly not in the General Post Office where he formerly had an office – I know just about all the lads in the GPO.'

'Would anyone in Ireland know?'

Nuala smiled, 'The only man who would know would be the Brigadier.'

Patrick looked at her, his eyes wide and shocked. 'But the IRA are going to kill him!'

'When?' Nuala demanded.

'I don't know. Soon.'

'Do you have his address?'

'No ... but I might be able to find out.' He stopped. 'Why?'

'So you could get to him first.'

'He's hardly likely to answer any questions I put to him, now is he?'

Nuala grinned. 'It depends how you ask them, doesn't it.'

'I'll have to think about it.'

Nuala nodded but said nothing.

'Do you think I'm Lewis's son?'

'I don't know. All we're doing here is guessing without too many facts.'

'Would this Brigadier know?'

'I think he might.'

The clock on the mantelpiece chimed midnight, startling them both. Suddenly, Patrick yawned. 'I'm sorry, I'm exhausted; it's been a long day. I think I'll retire. I'll think further about what we've just discussed.'

Nuala nodded. Her eyes were on the fire, watching the tiny flames dance across the sods of turf. 'It'll be a while before I get to bed.'

'I can never remember my mother actually going to bed,' Patrick said with a smile, 'and I often wondered why she got up so late in the morning.'

'Well, now you know.'

Patrick stood up and leaned against the marble fireplace. 'I'll have to be up early in the morning. One of the boys is coming to collect me. Tomorrow I begin my training with the IRA.'

Nuala stood up and faced him. 'Is it what you want?'

He looked at her, surprised at the concern in her voice. 'It's what I want,' he said eventually.

Nuala looked straight into his eyes. 'Be careful. Too many lives have been lost in the struggle for independence already. Young lives wasted, young men on both sides, Irish and British.' She paused and added. 'I don't want yours to be amongst them.'

'I'm only starting my training,' he smiled, 'it's not as if I'm really involved.'

Nuala stepped up to him, and then surprised him by taking both his hands in hers. 'You are involved – only I don't think you realize just how deeply you're involved. In London it was all talk – here you'll have to prove yourself, you'll have to act. You'll have to kill.' Patrick started to shake his head, but Nuala pressed on. 'Yes, you're the type they like. Young, idealistic, committed. The first thing they'll teach you is how to use a gun.'

'No!' Patrick pulled away from her.

'Yes. Of course, you've already killed a man. You've proved you can do it – now they'll give you a reason for killing.'

As they walked down the wind-swept promenade, Gerard, the bearded giant Michael Collins had introduced Patrick to the previous evening, reached into his pocket and handed Patrick a small metal object. Patrick had accepted it before he realized he was holding a gun. 'This is a 1907 Savage Automatic Pocket Pistol,' the giant said casually. 'You will keep it with you at all times.'

Patrick looked at the small weapon before stuffing it into his pocket. Although it only weighed a few ounces, he felt as if it were dragging down the pocket of his overcoat.

'As you may be aware,' the tall red-haired man continued, turning up the collar of his coat, 'we have to take whatever weapons we can, so you'll find your colleagues will carry any number of small arms. It's recommended that you familiarize yourself with them in case you have to use them at any time.'

'Will that be necessary?' Patrick asked. 'I mean how often would we have to use them?'

Gerard looked at Patrick for a moment, and then shrugged. 'As often as necessary.'

They continued down the promenade in silence, heading towards the high cloud-wrapped hill that dominated the small seaside town.

Gerard had called for Patrick just before nine that morning and, following a stroll down to Amiens Street Station, they took the train to Bray, a popular seaside town on the southside of the city – popular during the summer months, but deserted during the winter. On the journey, Gerard had spoken to Patrick about the cause they both served, about the fight for a free and independent Ireland, a fight that had been going on for centuries, and which had come to a head in the Easter Rising of 1916, but a fight that was still continuing. Sinn Fein had recently won an important political victory in the 1918 elections, and was now constituted as Dail Eireann, the Irish Parliament. Michael Collins had been elected to the seat for South Cork, and when the first Dail had sat in the Mansion House, he had been appointed as Minister for Home Affairs.

'Now some want talk and some want action,' Gerard said intently, 'but it'll take us years of talk to give us a free Ireland. There are other methods …' he added with a gap-toothed grin.

The seaside town of Bray reminded Patrick of Bognor or Brighton – it had the same long stretch of grand houses facing the sea, the same raised promenade, with its ornate rail, and its bandstand and whitewashed seats. In summer it would look lovely, he guessed. But now, in the depths of winter, it was desolate. The wind coming in off the sea was chill and raw, flecked with slivers of ice.

'Could you have a picked a lonelier spot?' Patrick asked, his teeth beginning to chatter.

'It's quiet,' Gerard said, 'and no one's going to venture out to investigate us. We can see for miles,' he said looking around, 'and if anyone comes too close, well, we'll have a fair warning.'

The big man set off down the promenade, his head ducked into the wind, one hand on his hat. Patrick gritted his teeth and followed, taking small comfort from the fact that he wasn't on the seaward side and taking the full brunt of the icy wind. Gerard was so big he afforded the younger man some protection.

Over the booming and hissing of the sea on the stony beach, Gerard talked about the founding of the IRB, now the IRA, and Patrick hadn't the energy to tell him that he already knew the history of the organization – probably better than Gerard. The big man then went on to tell how the organization now operated, and in particular how Collins' special group and the other groups like it worked. Patrick was dismayed to discover that Gerard spoke too often about the removal of targets and 'obstacles'. That was when the big man had handed him the gun.

'This is a 1907 Savage Automatic Pocket Pistol.' He glanced sidelong at Patrick and continued slowly and deliberately. 'It is a .380 calibre or 9 millimeter automatic, with a nine shot magazine which is held in the handle. It weighs just 21 ounces, and is only 7 inches long. There is a safety catch to the left hand side and the magazine is released by another catch on the handle. It's a nice weapon,' he added with a smile, 'nice and easy to use. It'll strip down without tools and is smooth all over – so it won't catch in your clothes. And while I think of it,' he glanced at Patrick, 'don't be getting yourself any fancy holster, or shoulder job to hold the weapon. Keep it in your pocket, or tucked into your belt. If there's a search, you'll have the devil of a job disposing of a shoulder holster – whereas if it's in your pocket you can just drop the gun behind the nearest hedge or into the gutter.' He tapped his breast pocket. 'Now some of the lads use one of them German Mausers, the Broom-handle, but I prefer my Savage.'

They had now reached the end of the beach, and had passed the last house, and Gerard took the path that led up towards the hill. 'During the summer this is a great place for picnics or just a stroll. It's grand sport to climb to the top of Bray Head.'

'This isn't summer,' Patrick said through gritted teeth.

Now that they had moved off the promenade and away from the booming of the sea, it grew almost silent and the trees that covered the side of the hill cut most of the breeze. Tendrils of grey cloud snaked through the dark trees, cold and damp, smelling vaguely of salt and the sea. Gerard turned off the path and headed into the midst of the wood, Patrick struggling along behind, regretting that he hadn't brought his galoshes. The ground was soft underfoot, and within minutes his heavy brogues were letting in water.

Gerard stopped in the middle of a small clearing. 'Always a good spot,' he remarked, 'in summer the pefect place for a picnic, and in winter, perfect for a little target practice.'

'Shooting?' Patrick asked surprised. 'You cannot be serious.'

Gerard grinned. 'Who's going to come up here on a day like this then, eh? And even if they did hear the shots – and you have to be very close to hear them in the first place – then actually getting to this clearing, except along the path we came, is a long, slow and mucky job.' He crossed the clearing and set up some chunks of chopped wood on an old, rotted stump. He walked back towards Patrick, his own gun in his hand, 'And now I'll show you how to shoot. Who knows; it might even save your life some day …'

*

'... And then we spent the next hour shooting the bloody guns.' Patrick sneezed. 'You were right you know – the first thing they showed me was how to use a gun.'

Nuala resisted the temptation to say, 'I told you so.' Instead she tested the small copper bath of water in which Patrick was soaking his feet, and lifted the kettle off the fire and added more water to the bath.

'That's hot!' Patrick winced. He was sitting on a straight-backed chair in Nuala's room, wearing his pyjamas and dressing gown. His feet were soaking in a bath of hot water, and there was a glass of hot whiskey and honey on the table beside him. So far he had resisted the temptation to taste the concoction. 'Look, I'm all right,' he protested.

Nuala looked unconvinced. When he had arrived home a little less than an hour ago, she had taken one look at him and ordered him up to his room to change out of his sodden clothes. When he had wandered into her room a little later, he had found a hot footbath, warm towels and hot drinks laid out.

'You're like a mother hen,' he added with a smile.

'Let's see about that hair of yours.' She took up one of the heavy towels and, standing behind Patrick, began rubbing at his thin, fair hair. 'Having just saved you from your mother,' she said suddenly, 'I don't want to lose you to pneumonia.'

'Why?' Patrick said abruptly. 'Why, all I've done is cause you trouble since I came here. I would imagine you'd be quite pleased if I just walked away and you never saw me again.'

Nuala, who had been rubbing briskly at his hair, now stopped. When she started at his hair again, her movements were much more deliberate.

'When you came here first,' she said slowly, almost distantly, 'I resented you, and what you represented. You were a threat. And certainly I've sometimes found myself getting angry at how you disturbed my ordered life. But as I watched you, I discovered that you possessed many of the characteristics that so endeared me to Dermot Corcoran. He may not have been your natural father, but you've many of his traits. And you were loyal to your friends – and I suppose, having few friends, it's one thing I look for in a man. You have courage too – the courage to follow your convictions, the courage to act when the situation arises. And you saved my life.' Nuala put down the towel and came around to stand before Patrick. She reached out and cupped his chin with her right hand, and then she stopped and kissed him, her lips brushing across his. 'And I suddenly found that I didn't want you to leave,' she said very softly.

Shocked, Patrick simply looked at her. 'Why?' he asked eventually.

'Because ... because I'm very fond of you. I suppose, in time, I could come to love you.'

Patrick started to smile – until he realized that she was serious. 'Nuala ...' he began.

She pressed her fingers to his lips, silencing him. 'I don't expect you to say anything. There are too many years, too many experiences between us ... let's leave it at that. At least now you know how I feel.'

She was turning away when Patrick said, 'Do you know how I feel?'

Nuala turned to face him. 'What do you mean?'

'I mean you've told me what your own feelings are – and yet you never asked mine. Is it inconceivable that I should have feelings for you?'

'You hardly know me.'

He smiled shyly. 'You don't know me at all.'

'I knew you when you were growing up here ...'

'You knew me as a boy,' he said quickly.

Nuala nodded. 'What are you trying to say then?' she asked.

Patrick shrugged uncomfortably. 'I don't know. I've never known a woman before – except for Jane Bradley of course.'

Nuala smiled, but said nothing.

'I feel comfortable with you. I was never comfortable in her presence,' Patrick continued, 'maybe we started out on the wrong foot, but somehow I felt she was using me. I was wrong – I think,' he added.

'Did you sleep with her?' Nuala asked directly.

Patrick coloured – much to Nuala's amusement – and then said, 'I thought nice girls didn't ask questions like that.'

'Nice girls don't run brothels,' she smiled.

Patrick reached down and picked the towel up off the floor where Nuala had dropped it. He began to dry his wet feet, concentrating intently on his toes, not looking at the woman's face. 'We slept together,' he said eventually.

'Who initiated it?'

Patrick remained silent, so Nuala said, 'She did, didn't she?'

Patrick nodded.

'When you were in bed – were you comfortable with her?'

'I don't know what you mean?'

'What were you thinking of?' she persisted, watching Patrick intently.

The young man thought about it for a few moments, and then he looked up. 'I wasn't comfortable. Yes, it was … it was exhilarating, but … but I know what you mean. I kept thinking that this was a mechanical act, with little joy in it.'

Nuala nodded, a slight smile curling her lips. 'Exactly,' she whispered enigmatically, turning away.

Later, much later, when even the house was silent, and the only sounds were the gradual settling of the old boards, and the creaking of the rafters, Nuala slipped into Patrick's bed. He awoke suddenly, startled and disorientated, and the cry that had begun in the pit of his stomach, died in his throat when he felt the naked female – undoubtedly female – body beside him.

In the ghostly pre-dawn half-light, Nuala's teeth

231

flashed in a smile as her hands moved down his body. 'Shall we see if you're still comfortable in my presence. Let's see if there's any joy to be found between us …?'

Patrick reached out, touching her large breasts, his hands sliding around her back to pull her close, and then he kissed her, gently and passionately, surprising himself. When he had kissed Jane, it had always been a hurried, fumbled affair, and they had made love almost violently, and the kiss – usually nothing more than that first kiss – was simply a prelude to the act of copulation.

With Nuala it was different. Although their lovemaking began with a kiss, neither of them seemed inclined to break that kiss, and it continued for minutes while their hands explored their bodies.

And later, much later, as the icy windowpanes sparkled with the light of a new day, and their bodies had joined in that ultimate embrace, Patrick realized that for the first time he had truly made love to a woman – and knew its joy!

CHAPTER FIFTEEN

There would come a time when Patrick would look back on that period of his life and think of it almost as a dream. It was one of the few times in his life that he could remember being truly happy and contented. And it also fulfilled all his boyish fantasies.

He was living a dual – and secret – life. By day, he continued to work with Doctor Meredith, while at night, he continued his training with Gerard in the methods of the IRA and, when he came home in the early hours of the morning, he usually ended up sleeping with Nuala. He often maintained that despite the expensive education his mother had paid for, he learned more and experienced more in those few months. Whatever remained of his boyhood innocence was finally lost in those heady days and nights ... and he was an apt and willing pupil in his two roles. None of his companions in the IRA cell, with the exception of Michael Collins, were aware of his relationship with Nuala, and Collins never commented on it. Those who knew, that lived within the confines of the notorious Monto, preferred to keep their opinions to themselves: too many of them had come up from Dublin's squalid streets.

Patrick continued to act as Doctor Meredith's assistant, and his easy manner and youth soon assured him a steady stream of patients – usually female. His opinion of the small stout doctor changed too; although the man's casual attitude towards his patients sometimes infuriated Patrick, he had to admit that the man was a brilliant doctor and a superb surgeon.

Within the set up, Patrick demonstrated a certain proficiency in planning and organization, and assisted

Collins with the execution of a series of daring prison escapes of captured personnel. In April 1919, Michael Collins was made Minister of Finance. The Big Fellow was aware that the new post would eat into his already limited time, and so he asked Patrick to act as his contact with the Volunteers. It was a position Patrick proudly accepted – even though it placed him in far greater danger and his higher profile within the organization virtually ensured that he would end up on the police wanted lists. But by accepting he felt he had come very close to achieving what Dermot Corcoran had achieved before him.

Nuala tried to dissuade him from accepting the position; time was running out. The political situation had become much more unstable, with attacks on the police by the Volunteers happening far more frequently, and in return, G Division of the Dublin Metropolitan Police, the unit concerned with the detection of 'political crime', had stepped up their activities, determined to destroy Collins and his group.

The Brigadier stood at the window of his rooms overlooking Merrion Square, his hands deep in the pockets of his plush dressing gown. The slim dark cigar in his hand remained unlit.

In the bedroom behind him, the young woman dressed hurriedly and silently. She had known Richard for nearly three years now – what had started out as a casual acquaintance, had gradually slipped into something more comfortable. She now saw him perhaps once a month; in the beginning they had gone to the theatre and then to one of the better restaurants for a meal before finally ending up in bed together for a night of gentle – if uninspired – lovemaking. Lately however, the theatres and restaurants had stopped and their lovemaking had ceased to be anything more than a brief passionless tumble between the sheets. But she recognized the signs: he was becoming bored with her.

Tonight though, had been different; tonight he had

been rough with her, stripping her so hurriedly that he had torn some of her best clothing. When she had complained, he had snapped at her, saying he would pay – and she resented the implication. She was not a whore. Admittedly, he bought her nice presents, but she never took money when she slept with him. And when he had been unable to perform with her, she had gloated – unfortunately, he had seen the satisfied gleam in her eye, and had ordered her to leave.

Richard Grennell heard the front door slam, and winced. It was just after four in the morning, and the other residents in the house wouldn't be too pleased at being awoken at such an hour. He watched the young woman stride down Merrion Square, crossing to walk alongside the spiked rail that enclosed the small square park. It still lacked a few minutes to sunrise and the park exuded tendrils of mist and fog which quickly smothered the slight figure of the woman. He watched her go without the slightest trace of regret.

Turning away from the window he sat down at the rolltop bureau and pressed the catch which was disguised as part of the ornate beaded scrollwork. Rolling back the top to reveal the plush green leather writing pad and the numerous nooks and pigeon holes, he depressed another hidden stud and the main drawer clicked open. The Brigadier pulled out the score of thin onionskin pages, and read again the tiny ornate script which covered them.

Reading the report again, he suddenly realized that this was the reason he had been unable to perform with Eileen earlier. For one of the first times in his long and occasionally distinguished career, Brigadier Richard Grennell was afraid.

The Brigadier had been aware for some time now that the Irish Volunteers were, if not aware of his actual identity, then certainly aware of his existence. Recently a report had come into his possession in which the mysterious and elusive Michael Collins had stated that for their cause to succeed, it would be necessary to 'put out the eyes of the British Government in Ireland.' And if Collins intended to put out the 'eyes' – what would he do to the 'brain' that directed them? Brigadier Richard Grennell was that brain.

He had even gone so far as to apply for a transfer – which had been refused. His superiors in Whitehall considered his knowledge of the country and its people to be second to none, and it was felt that if he were to leave Ireland now, it would seriously jeopardise the British presence in the country, and undoubtedly delay the capture of Collins and the destruction of the IRA.

It was only a matter of time before the IRA found him. He opened a drawer of the bureau and took out a heavy American Browning pistol. He worked the slide, chambering a round, and then eased down the hammer on the loaded weapon. He left the heavy weapon on the desk beside him as he worked. There was a revolver in the bedside cabinet, and he carried a tiny pocket pistol – a Derringer – in his coat at all times. When the IRA came for him, they wouldn't catch him unawares, and he was going to ensure that he cost them dearly.

He worked through the reports he had brought home from Dublin Castle the previous night. Three detailed attempts to capture Collins; the Brigadier shook his head in frustration. What was the point in wasting all this time and effort when they didn't even know what he looked like? A big man, pleasant features, late twenties: what sort of description was that?

There was another report concerning Monto, the notorious red-light district. Several years ago when the authorities wanted to close down the whole area, the Brigadier had protested, arguing that while it existed it contained the problem within a recognizable, controllable area. His arguments had been accepted, and Monto had remained. But the Brigadier had other reasons for allowing Monto to continue; for years he had concentrated on infiltrating men – and women – into Monto, or buying informants there, and the twenty or so people he had working in the district and the houses

236

now provided an invaluable source of information on both the political and ordinary criminals.

He looked down a report which listed several high-ranking British officers who had taken to frequenting some of the plusher brothels. In ordinary circumstances, the Brigadier wouldn't have bothered putting a watch on the men, but these were not ordinary times.

He noted with a smile that Madam Kitten's old place, number eighty-two, was still popular. There was a new woman running it now since the Madam had disappeared. Idly he turned a page, referring to a list of names on the back of the report ... a Nuala Kelly or Kennedy, formerly a servant in the place. He noted that the unnamed writer of the report had also added that the present Madam was now keeping company with a young man, who was possibly a medical man, and possibly involved with the Volunteer movement. The Brigadier tapped the report with his pencil, and made a note on a pad – there was something there which might be profitably followed up. The young man's name was Patrick.

The final report was from London, and it contained the synopsis of the previous three months investigation into the woman known as Mrs Lundy. He skipped to the end to read the results and opinions of the investigating officers ...

'... and it would seem that Mrs Katherine Lundy is indeed involved in the procurement of women for immoral purposes ...

'... the clientele is drawn from the upper classes, and includes many members of the aristocracy ...

'... also owner or part owner of similar establishments in Manchester and Glasgow ...'

The Brigadier read on, reading the section devoted to personal history, looking for something, although he didn't really know what he was searching for.

'The woman occupies a fine house ... but no business is conducted on the premises. Trade is conducted in a

house almost directly opposite. Mrs Lundy's house ...'
the Brigadier skipped through the woman's history,
'servants ... two children, a son Patrick, of about
nineteen years, a medical student with strong Irish
sympathies, and a daughter Senga, still of school-going
age ... Patrick Lundy is no longer living at home, and all
investigations have failed to disclose his present
whereabouts ...

'One of Mrs Lundy's closest associates, Michael Lee,
the manager of her London house, was recently the
subject of a report from your office ...'

The Brigadier sat back suddenly. He pushed the
report away, and stared at the tooled green leather
beneath, now worn dark with years of use and abuse.
Almost afraid to think, he was prepared to allow the
disparate strands and ideas to form themselves; it was a
process with which he was familiar – it was his gift to be
able to take several strands from different sources and
weave them into a coherent whole. Taking up a pencil
he began to write on his notepad ...

'Michael Lee died in Dublin in suspicious circumstances ... Michael Lee was Katherine's closest associate,
and manager of her London house ...

'Patrick Lundy, Katherine's son, a medical student,
had disappeared ... the woman who ran Katherine's
brothel in Dublin had a new boyfriend, named Patrick,
also interested in medicine ...'

Coincidence?

The Brigadier didn't believe in coincidence. It was
time to take a much closer look at this young man.

Patrick put down his newspaper and poured himself
another cup of tea. Across the table, Nuala was going
through the post which had just arrived and, without
asking, he topped up her cup. He had picked up his
paper again and was about to return to it when he
noticed that she was watching him, a smile on her lips.

'What's so funny?' he asked gently. Whilst he
admitted that she was not a great beauty, he always

thought she looked her loveliest first thing in the morning, her hair uncombed, without make-up, her eyes wide and clear in her head: 'dishevelled and interesting,' was how he described her.

Nuala shrugged. 'I always promised myself I would never get married,' she said with a wry smile. 'I never wanted the responsibility of a husband and children ...'

He put down his paper waiting for her to continue. 'And ...' he persisted.

'And yet here I am, practically married to a man nearly thirteen years my junior!'

'I wouldn't say practically married,' Patrick protested.

'What would you say it is then? If you have breakfast, dinner, tea, and then supper with the same man every day for the past couple of months, then I think you'd consider yourself practically married.'

'You forgot the important bit?'

'What important bit?!'

Patrick grinned like a delighted schoolboy. 'Breakfast, dinner, tea, supper ... and bed.'

Nuala shook her head in disgust. 'Is that all you think about?'

'No,' he said quickly, 'I never think about it – except when I'm with you!'

'Get away with you!' Nuala turned back to her post. She picked up a letter and the smile faded from her face. She paled.

'What's the matter?' Patrick asked, coming to his feet.

Nuala tossed the letter across the table at him. Even before he had picked it up, he had recognized his mother's firm handwriting. 'It's addressed to you,' he said, looking at Nuala.

'Open it,' she commanded.

Patrick wiped a butterknife on his napkin and slit the top of the envelope. There were two sheets of Katherine Lundy's personal ivory coloured writing paper inside, covered on both sides with his mother's hand. As he pulled out the sheets, there was the faintest suggestion of lavender, and for a single moment, he felt he was back in London, with his mother at her bureau, writing goodness knows how many letters in the course of a day, with each page faintly tainted with the scent of lavender from the empty perfume bottle she used as a paperweight.

'Patrick?'

He looked up quickly, smiling sheepishly. 'Sorry – miles away,' he said.

Nuala nodded, watched him carefully as he quickly read down the page and then turned it over. She envied him the speed at which he read; her own reading was painfully slow, and she preferred to dictate her letters.

'It's addressed to you,' Patrick said eventually. 'My mother apologizes for the long delay in replying to your letter in January. She then goes on to thank you for all the assistance you rendered Michael Lee when he was in Dublin, and apologizes for any inconvenience he may have caused you with the authorities,' he looked up and grinned. 'It then goes on to explain that I – that is me, Patrick – had been lured away by an older woman, a servant girl ...'

'You seem easily lured by older women,' Nuala grinned.

'... and furthermore it seems that I am now in America, where she is currently pursuing her inquiries. Aaah, now here's an interesting piece,' he continued, quoting directly from the letter now, ' "in view of the Volunteers' connection with the Clann na Gael in America, I wonder if it would be possible for you to instigate inquiries with your contacts in Dublin to see if Patrick made any contact with them during his brief stay there. Bearing in mind his interest in the movement, I feel sure that he would have attempted to make contact if that were possible ..." ' He glanced across at Nuala. 'Clever woman, eh?'

'It's only a fool who underestimates her.'

He frowned as he continued. 'She then goes on to say that in view of the expanding market in London for quality, unspoilt – and unspoilt is underlined – produce, she wonders if you would be in a position to supply fresh goods on a regular basis, for a straightforward fee to be mutually agreed.' He looked at Nuala. 'What is she talking about?'

'Oh, but you can be so innocent sometimes. She's talking about flesh dear boy. About women. She wants me to procure young, fresh and unspoilt – by which she means virginal – girls for her London operation.'

'Which you won't!'

Nuala looked up in surprise. 'Why not?'

'You can't. It's … it's immoral,' he protested.

'Patrick, let me remind you that you are living in a brothel. You are already living on immoral earnings; in common terms you might be considered a pimp.' Shocked speechless, Patrick could only look at her, while she continued, picking her words carefully, realizing that this was one of the times when her experiences, expectations and background were so far removed from Patrick's as to be completely alien.

'Your mother's offer is a grand opportunity for some young girls to make their way in London society.'

'You cannot be serious!'

'I am. Your mother ran one of the finest houses in Dublin, and if her operation in London is anything similar – and I'm sure it's probably better – I would have absolutely no hesitation in sending her fine, healthy, attractive girls. When your mother has finished dressing and grooming them, you wouldn't even recognise them. Once they've worked for your mother for a few years, they should be in a position either to go into business for themselves, or else find themselves a suitable gentleman to keep them in the style to which they've become accustomed.'

'You are selling girls,' he snapped; Nuala's nonchalant attitude outraged him.

'It's a business,' Nuala said coldly, 'and you've lived with me for long enough now to realize that's the type of business I'm in. When you arrive home here every

241

evening, what do you see? You see a dozen attractive young women wandering around in their underwear, and if you walk the corridors of this house, you'll hear the sounds of passion coming from every room, and if you linger outside any of those doors for long enough, you'd hear an entirely different sound altogether – the sound of money changing hands. This is the oldest occupation in the world, and like it or not, you're stuck in it. You were born into it,' she finished abruptly.

'That doesn't mean I have to like it.'

'I'm not asking you to like it – I'm just asking you to get used to the idea. I'm just asking you not to get so moral with me when you stumble on some aspect of my job which you don't like.'

'I don't like any aspect of it,' Patrick said sullenly.

'Well, this is the only thing I can do,' she said coldly. 'Either this, or go on the streets. And at least this way I get to choose whom I sleep with.'

When the silence between them threatened to lengthen uncomfortably, Nuala said, 'Why does this bother you so much?'

Patrick shrugged. 'I don't know. I've thought about it often enough. But I can't help thinking of an eighteen or nineteen year old pregnant girl ending up in a house like this.'

'I don't understand.'

'It could have been different.'

The woman nodded. 'It could. That pregnant nineteen year old girl could have ended up working the streets … or in the river. You can't change the system.'

'My father … Dermot Corcoran tried.'

'Did he succeed?' Nuala asked, her voice unintentionally bitter. She pushed her chair back from the table and stood up. 'You cannot change human nature,' she said, turning and walking from the room.

Patrick sat at the table, finishing the last of the tea, the morning papers unread before him. Once again, he had been made aware of the many differences that existed between him and Nuala and the society that made them both. He thought he understood – albeit vaguely – the urge that had encouraged Dermot Corcoran to begin his campaign for the city's poor. Although he had only been a simple newspaper reporter, his stories about the privations of the poor had struck a chord with the wealthy and had set in motion a chain of events that had gradually brought about changes – changes which were still taking place.

Finishing the last of the cold tea, Patrick Lundy reached a decision.

Later that same day, Patrick asked Michael Collins to place him on the 'active duty' list. When the Big Fellow questioned Patrick's motives, all the young man would say was that he wanted to help bring about some changes.

CHAPTER SIXTEEN

'I was beginning to get worried.' Nuala stood in the door and watched Patrick strip off his grimy clothes. From the looks of them – and him – she guessed that he had slept rough for the past four days.

'You would have been informed if anything had happened to me,' Patrick said tiredly. 'But I'm sure you would have found out anyway from your own sources.'

The woman said nothing. He pulled off his undershirt and she noticed the long thin bruise just below his ribs, and there were other bruises around his shoulders. But she knew enough not to ask him what he had been doing. She stepped into the room and began to pick up the clothes he had dropped onto the floor; they smelt of stale sweat, leaf mould, rotten wood and damp. She took a quick look at his hands; the soft flesh of his palms looked harsh and red and the web of flesh between his thumb and forefinger was almost black, blood crusting just beneath the skin – and it wasn't with dirt. She immediately knew what he had been doing.

'You're serious about going on active service with the IRA then?'

Patrick looked at her, surprised.

'Unless I'm very much mistaken, you've spent the last four days training with them in the Wicklow Mountains.'

Patrick was too tired to argue, and could only shake his head in admiration. 'How did you know?'

'It doesn't take a genius to work it out.' She opened the wardrobe and pulled out his long dressing gown. 'Here, put this on before you catch your death ...' she smiled quickly, 'although if you haven't caught it already, you'll never catch it. Did you sleep indoors at any time over the weekend?'

'There was a barn on Saturday night,' Patrick said shrugging on the dressing gown, 'it wasn't very dry though.'

'I'll have a bath drawn in my room; the fire's lit, and you can soak for a while.'

He leaned over and kissed her quickly, conscious of his three day growth of beard. 'That would be heaven.'

The bath was large and deep, although Number Eighty-Two had been recently fitted out with proper bathrooms, some of the customers had a preference for the old-fashioned bath. Patrick sank into the hot water with a contented sigh, while Nuala sat back into the deep leather chair before the fire and watched him. He had fleshed out over the past few months – although it was by now obvious that he would always be lean, and the muscles and sinews were clearly visible beneath his now lightly tanned skin. The boy was becoming a man. She smiled, remembering the first time she had seen him naked, he had been as pale as a dead fish. He had kept his hair short, and it had turned a pale yellow white, which contrasted sharply with his thin, slightly-curved black eyebrows and long eyelashes.

Patrick opened his eyes – and found Nuala staring at him, her eyes pale amber points of light in the shadows. 'Penny for them,' he grinned. He suddenly bent forward deeply and ducked his head beneath the water. When he surfaced, he shook his head from side to side, spraying droplets of lukewarm water everywhere. He brushed the water from his face with both hands, and smiled at Nuala. 'Come on – penny for them.'

'What did you do over the weekend?' she asked, 'beside live like tramps and play with your guns.' Her hand appeared out of the darkness, pointing at his hands which were resting against the edge of the copper bath. 'You won't be able to use those tomorrow.'

Patrick brought his hands close to his face and grimaced at the bruising. He flexed his fingers experimentally, and then pressed on the bruised flesh. 'You're right. But I'm getting good,' he said, immediately sounding like a child with a new toy. 'I can put ten rounds – a full flip – into a target no bigger than an envelope at ten yards.'

'Is that good?' she asked innocently.

Patrick nodded. 'It's good.'

'What are you going to do when you're shooting at something other than envelopes?'

Patrick concentrated on his hands, ignoring the question.

'What's going to happen when you have to kill someone, Patrick?' she asked leaning forward, staring hard at him.

'I've already killed someone,' he said sullenly.

'I know that.'

'And if I'm ordered to kill someone, then I'm sure they'll deserve death.'

'Are you going to make that judgement?' she asked quickly.

'No, it will be made by people better qualified than I to make that decision.'

'Then you're a fool' Nuala spat. 'They'll make the decisions, you'll do the killing, and you'll be the one who'll be shot down or jailed for the crime while they remain free to destroy someone else's life.'

The venom in her voice surprised him, and while he was attempting to think of a suitable reply, she was gone, the door rattling in its frame as she slammed it hard enough to blow the foaming bubbles off the top of the water. He shivered in the chill draught. The young man shook his head. He wasn't sure what he was going to do about Nuala.

He knew she meant well, and she seemed to have his best interests at heart ... but just what did she mean to him? He grinned suddenly. He remembered thinking exactly the same about Jane. He stopped, surprised – he rarely thought of Jane now, indeed he rarely thought of anyone from his previous life. Except his sister. He felt guilty that he had made no effort to rescue his sister from his mother's clutches, but as Nuala had so rightly pointed out, he wouldn't have been able to bring her up properly. Far better to allow her to continue her education with her mother, and then rescue her, and this would also give him time to prepare a proper home for him.

And only occasionally he admitted to himself that it was an excuse, a selfish excuse – he was enjoying his present life too much, he was enjoying his freedom too much, to want it disturbed by anything or anyone.

Patrick sank deeper into the bath, allowing the now tepid waters to lap around his chin, and closed his eyes. What did Nuala mean to him, the same thought came back around again and again. She was a friend ... a lover ... a mother. The final analogy disturbed him, and his first impulse was to reject it, but he resisted the temptation and thought the idea through. Nuala was older than him, wiser in many respects, although he was far better educated and more intelligent. Her wisdom came from experience – and no money, no schooling could buy that. She was successful in her career – if that was the right word – and had both the power and the money to achieve whatever ambitions she had, except she didn't seem to have many ambitions. It was true she clucked after him like a mother hen, ensured he had fresh, clean clothes, and that he ate properly when he was home, and worried about him when he was late, and in this respect she wasn't so different from his mother.

There were two main differences however – she never pried too closely into where he had been, nor whom he had been with. His mother never allowed him that freedom. And of course, both women knew the answers anyway.

And he loved her. He didn't – couldn't – love Katherine Lundy.

Later that same night, when she slipped naked into his bed, he rolled around, his arms encircling her waist,

247

pulling her close. 'I love you,' he murmured sleepily.

Nuala said nothing. But she buried her head against his chest and wept silently.

Patrick awoke as the church bells were tolling noon. He automatically crossed himself, and then grinned foolishly; he had been brought up as a good Catholic, but good Catholics didn't have mistresses and live in brothels. He rolled over, reaching for Nuala, but the bed was empty – although it was still warm from the heat of her body. He sat up in bed as Nuala came into the room carrying a breakfast tray. She was wearing a sheer black lace night-dress that was translucent in the noonday sunlight, and he found that he could look at her almost naked body without passion. He felt sure that was significant – he just wasn't sure how significant or in what way.

Nuala sat down on the edge of the bed and poured tea from the small squat pot that had once been Dermot Corcoran's gift to Katherine Lundy. 'I'm going down to town today. Would you like to come with me …?'

'Well …'

'Unless you've something better to do?'

He shook his head. 'Nothing, I suppose. Doctor Meredith knows I'm back in town; I'll see him tomorrow for evening surgery. Yes, let's go to town. We'll have lunch somewhere nice … take a stroll through the Green.'

Nuala nodded happily. 'That would be nice. I'll have Jem bring the car around.'

'He can drop us in town, and we can arrange to meet him later.'

They ate their late breakfast in comfortable silence; despite their many arguments and disagreements, their arrangement was as comfortable as any settled marriage.

When he had finished his second cup of oversweet tea, Patrick threw back the covers and swung his legs out of bed. Nuala reached over and ran the tip of her finger along the bruise beneath his ribs. 'How did you come by that?'

Patrick smiled, rubbing at the dark line, and then winced as his bruised flesh protested. 'We were training with various weapons, pistols mostly, and some rifles. I was getting along fine until we came to the shotgun. I was shown how to load it, how to carry it, and it was explained to me how powerfully destructive it could be, and then I came to fire it. Unfortunately, no one told me about the two triggers – there are two triggers on the type of shotgun we were using, one for each barrel. The idea is that you pull one trigger and then the other ...'

Nuala started to smile, anticipating the climax.

'... of course, I pulled both triggers together.' He shook his head, remembering. 'Knocked me clean off my feet, and I fetched up against a root on the ground.' Still shaking his head, he reached under his pillow and took out a small black automatic pistol.

'Jesus!' Nuala breathed. 'You didn't sleep with that under there?' she demanded.

'I've got to get used to it – and so have you. Where I go, it goes.' He released the magazine and then worked the slide, deftly catching the round that had been in the chamber.

'You stupid bastard,' Nuala hissed, 'that was loaded.' Visions of the gun going off under the pillow flashed through her mind.

'Loaded, but not cocked.'

'Don't you ever do that again. You can sleep with it or you can sleep with me, but not with both.'

'Nuala ...' he began.

'I'm not joking,' she said quickly, her voice matching her stony expression. 'Now, I've put up with a lot, but I draw the line at sleeping with a gun under my pillow.'

Patrick grinned sheepishly. 'I suppose so.' He shoved the gun in the bedside cabinet.

She leaned over and kissed him quickly. 'Sometimes you're nothing more than a big kid.'

'That's why you love me,' he said impudently, pulling on his dressing gown which he had left on the back of the chair at the foot of the bed.

'God only knows why I love you,' Nuala called after him, and when she heard the bathroom door at the end of the corridor slam, she added quietly, 'I certainly don't.'

Patrick regretted bringing the pistol with him. Although it weighed less than two pounds he felt it was pulling his trousers down and he had to resist the temptation to keep hitching them up every few moments. However, Gerard had insisted that he should carry the weapon at all times, 'You never know when it'll come in handy. If there's a search then just lose it; drop it behind a hedge, in a bush, in a bin, and sure maybe we'll be able to go back for it later. And if it's found well then, small loss. So long as it's not found on you.'

Grafton Street was busy with people, the fine weather having brought the crowds into Dublin's most fashionable street. Unlike O'Connell Street, which had been devastated in the Rising, Grafton Street had escaped relatively unscathed – a few shattered windows, nothing more. And while O'Connell Street and the streets surrounding it were still struggling to re-establish their businesses, Grafton Street, and the smaller streets off it, were consolidating their hold on the market.

Nuala was content with watching the people strolling along the streets, while she window shopped. But she showed no inclination actually to venture inside and eventually, having walked up one side of the street and down the other, Patrick demanded to know why, since they had come out to shop, they had bought nothing.

'At these prices?' Nuala asked in astonishment. 'What I'm looking for now are ideas, I want to see what's new in the shops, what the wealthy are buying, what they are wearing.' She slipped her arm through his and moved him up Grafton Street, making towards St Stephen's Green. To the casual observer they might have seemed a slightly odd couple; although the age difference between them was noticeable, there wasn't enough of a difference for them to be mother and son – brother and sister or aunt and nephew perhaps.

'I can buy this stuff at much better prices anyway,' she added with a sly smile.

'How?' he asked naively, and then he realized what she was hinting at. 'Oh.'

'Yes, "oh",' she mimicked his disapproving tone.

'Do we have to?' Patrick asked stiffly.

'No, we don't. We can squander our profits buying everything at the retail price, while the other houses buy theirs cut-price. For goodness sake Patrick, we have to compete. Your mother taught us that lesson.'

They had neared the top of Grafton Street now. This part of the street was a little quieter than the lower reaches and directly across the road was the solitude of St Stephen's Green, a haven of calm in the bustle of the city. Nuala had stopped to look into a show window, while Patrick walked to the edge of the path, looking up and down the street. Traffic was heavy; principally carts and carriages, mostly bicycles and the odd motor car. In the distance a tram was swinging around from the left, to come down past the College of Surgeons.

He was just about to turn back for Nuala when a small pleasantly faced elderly gentleman approached. 'Patrick Lundy?' he said, looking at him quickly, a delighted smile on his face.

And even as Patrick acknowledged his name, he realized he had made a mistake.

The small hard barrel of a pistol was pressed into the base of his skull.

'We can shoot you,' the elderly gentleman continued, his voice and tone conversational, the accent educated and English, 'or you can come with us.'

'Just what is going on here ...?' he began.

'You're going to help us with our inquiries,' the man standing behind Patrick snapped. 'And in the meantime you can shut up.' A hand – large and callused – reached around, patting at his pockets. The man grunted in satisfaction when he felt the shape of the pistol. He tugged it from Patrick's belt. Seconds later, he said, 'Fully loaded.'

251

The elderly man smiled, but only his lips moved, his eyes remained cold and hard. 'Of course you will be able to explain how you came to be carrying a loaded pistol.'

'Who are you?' Patrick demanded, desperately playing for time, praying that Nuala would realize what was happening and not do anything stupid. The last thing he needed now was for her to be captured also. He saw the cream coloured hat she was wearing appear through the crowd, weaving towards him …

Patrick stamped down hard on the shin and foot of the man standing directly behind him, and then lunged backwards. He felt the back of his head connect with the man's face. The man screamed and the gun went off so close to Patrick's head that his hair was scorched by the blast. Patrick turned in time to see the man stagger backwards onto the road, blood streaming from his nose. Wild-eyed, he swung the pistol around for a second shot …

The tram only hit the man a glancing blow, but it was enough to cave in the back of his skull. He was dead before he hit the ground at Patrick's feet.

The elderly man jammed a pistol into Patrick's ribs. His teeth were bared in a feral grin. 'And now it's murder, boy.'

Michael Collins and two of his men were actually waiting for Nuala by the time she got back to the house, still shocked by what she had witnessed. She had been about to call out to Patrick when she had noticed the two men standing very close to him. She had heard the gunshot as she watched with horror as one of the men – at first she thought it might have been Patrick – staggered out onto the busy road, only to be thrown forward again by the blow from the tram. Police had arrived on the scene almost immediately, and Nuala had been horrifed to discover that Patrick was the object of their attentions. The dead man – there was no doubt that he was dead: the back of his head had been crushed – had been left on the street, two guns lying by his side. Nuala had pushed through the crowd, only to have her suspicions confirmed: one of the pistols was an army issue Webly, the other was Patrick's Savage.

As she hurried down the length of the Green, past the Shelbourne Hotel to where Jem would be waiting with the car, she tried to work out what had happened. Patrick had been accosted by two plainsclothes policemen – probably from G-Division – and there had been a struggle. In the struggle one of the men had gone onto the road, only to be hit by the tram. Of course the police had found Patrick's gun – that bloody gun – and now he was responsible for the death of a policeman – and they would make sure the charge was murder.

But why had they picked Patrick? He was very respectably dressed, and certainly not acting in any way that would draw attention to himself. Was it nothing more than chance, an extraordinary piece of bad luck ... or was there something else to it?

She spotted the car in the distance and picked up her pace.

Had they been watching him, perhaps? There had been two men she remembered, a tall, broad man who had gone onto the road – had Patrick pushed him? – and the smaller, elderly man ...

'The Brigadier,' Collins said decisively. 'It can only be the Brigadier. Now all we have to do is to work out what he wants with Patrick.' The big man was pacing up and down Nuala's sitting room, while his two companions stood silently before each of the windows, watching the street below. Collins suddenly stopped and knelt before Nuala who was curled up in her favourite chair before the fire, her eyes red-rimmed and bloodshot, but with no tears left now. She had cried them all out on the high-speed journey across the city into Summerhill. She had had every intention of contacting Collins, and had been shocked to find that he had arrived a few moments before she had. He already knew the story by then.

Collins took Nuala's hands in his. 'Now listen to me

for a moment. I want you to go through everything that you saw. Tell me exactly – word for word. It just doesn't work out, you see. Patrick just isn't high enough in the organization to warrant special treatment from the Brigadier. Now think!'

'You'll get him out, won't you?' Nuala pleaded.

'I'm certainly going to try.'

CHAPTER SEVENTEEN

The cells in Great Brunswick Street police station were below ground, cold and damp, and slightly echoing. Patrick stood against one wall, his hands deep in his pockets, listening to a low moaning come from one of the adjoining cells. He felt curiously unafraid: events had happened so fast that he felt almost apart from them. It was someone else who had been roughly bundled into the police van, someone else who had been hurried into the Police Offices, someone else who had been unceremoniously locked in a cell. He was seen to almost immediately and, although he had been arrested by uniformed officers, no charges had been brought, and once inside the station, plainclothes officers had dealt with him, and once all the details and a statement had been taken and signed, Patrick had been left alone in the cell.

For a long time nothing happened. He had no way of measuring time: all his belongings, as well as his belt, shoelaces and necktie had been removed, but he guessed it must have been close to three hours before footsteps sounded along the corridor outside and a key turned in the lock. A small man stepped inside and the door immediately closed behind him. Patrick heard the key turn in the lock. Although the cell was dimly lit, he immediately recognized the elderly man who had accosted him on the street.

'I set out to catch a sprat – instead I hooked a salmon.' The elderly man pulled over the room's single wooden chair and, after dusting the seat with his handkerchief, perched on the edge.

Patrick remained standing against the wall, his arms folded across his chest.

'All I wanted to do was to talk to you ...' he saw Patrick's ill-concealed expression of surprise, and hurried on, 'indeed, it's true. All I wanted was a little conversation about your past, your dear mother, and I thought we could have a few words about your present situation, your friends, that sort of thing ...' he finished vaguely.

Patrick remained silent.

'Instead, what do we find? We find a dangerous armed criminal, a member of an illegal organization, who brutally slays a police officer while resisting arrest.'

Patrick started forward – and the gun appeared in the elderly man's hand; it was a tiny double-barrelled Derringer, and the two barrels looked like eyes. The small man's expression didn't change. Patrick sank back against the wall, and the gun disappeared.

'Well, at least that's how the police will see it,' the man continued as if nothing had happened. 'And you know, I wouldn't be at all surprised if you were found to have some connection with the killing of Detective-Sergeant Smith on 30th July. And of course there's also the matter of the missing servant girl who came to Dublin with you back in January of this year; whatever happened to her?' He smiled humourlessly. 'Let's face it boy, you're way out of your depth on this one.'

'I don't know what you're talking about,' Patrick said quickly, his voice low and sullen. 'I don't know anything about the shooting of your detective.'

'Who said anything about a shooting?' the man said immediately.

Patrick floundered. He had indeed been aware of the plot to kill the detective. The man – whose nickname was The Dog – hated the Republican movement with a passion that amounted almost to a mania, and constantly harassed and hounded its members. His knowledge and tenacity made him a dangerous foe and, following several direct warnings, which he ignored, he was shot dead outside his home in Drumcondra. Patrick had nothing to do with the shooting, but he had delivered two of the warnings, one by letter which he had posted, and the second which he had delivered by hand. 'I read about it in the paper,' he said finally.

'Well, I'm sure you did. My name, by the way, is … well, shall we say I'm usually called the Brigadier, but you may call me sir.'

Patrick blinked. His suspicions had been confirmed.

'And you are Lundy, Patrick Montgomery Lundy, born Dublin, 7th July, 1899, recently turned twenty years old.' He looked at Patrick, his grey eyes like polished stones. 'This may take some time, you could sit down.'

'You have the chair,' Patrick said reasonably.

'There is the floor,' the Brigadier suggested without a flicker of amusement.

Patrick smiled and slid down to the floor, his knees drawn up to his chest, his arms wrapped around them. The feeling of unreality persisted – indeed strengthened. He knew what happened to people suspected of killing policemen, and he had been expecting the worst. The last thing he had expected was to end up sitting on the floor of a cold, damp cell, listening to an old man talk to him gently – almost civilly – although that civility did little to conceal the implicit threat.

The Brigadier pulled a long slim notebook from his pocket and tapped it against his smooth chin. 'For a twenty-year old you've certainly packed a wealth of experience into your short life. Born and raised in a brothel, educated privately and then in some of the best schools, dispatched to England in the care of a known prostitute named Tilly Cusack in the early days of the Easter Rising.' He looked down at Patrick and grinned. 'Resumed living in a brothel in Mayfair, while you took up your studies both in medicine and revolution, and then you returned to Dublin – in the company of a servant girl it says here, but I'm sure that's not true – where you returned to your old address. You are currently living in number eighty-two Lower Tyrone Street, and employed by Doctor Montague Meredith as an assistant, while continuing your association with the illegal Volunteers.' He put away the notebook which he hadn't once opened during his recital of Patrick's past. 'Is there anything you wish to disagree with?'

Patrick shook his head.

'Nothing? Then everything I've said is correct and true?'

'I didn't say that!'

'Well then correct me where I was wrong. We must keep the record straight.'

Patrick shook his head, resting his forehead on his knees. 'There's nothing I wish to say to you.'

'I think there's a lot you want to say to me, boy!' the Brigadier suddenly snapped.

Patrick looked up, startled by the man's change of tone.

'I'm the only one standing between you and the gallows.' He stood up suddenly, upsetting the chair. 'Think about that for a while, my boy. And when I return you had better be prepared to talk to me!'

Michael Collins leaned against Trinity College Wall, directly opposite the main entrance to the Great Brunswick Street Station, his right leg raised, right foot flat against the ancient stones. He was wearing a flat cap, pushed high on his head, and was dressed as a common labourer. There was an unopened newspaper tucked under his arm and an unlit cigarette between his lips. With the late afternoon sun washing the street in warm golds and bronze, he looked like any other labourer making his way homewards.

The police station's double doors flapped open and a man stepped out onto the broad flat steps. He patted a soft-brimmed hat onto his head and turned to his left, heading down Great Brunswick Street. Michael Collins waited a few moments, then set off in the same direction. The man took the first turning to the left, into Tara Street, and when Collins darted across the road and rounded the corner, he was in time to see the man heading towards the bridge.

The two men met on the bridge, both resting their forearms on the parapet, looking upriver towards O'Connell Bridge, looking into the sunset. The man's name was Joe Kavanagh, a detective with the infamous G-Division, and a close friend of Michael Collins.

The tall thin man, with his shock of black hair just visible beneath the brim of his hat, was extremely nervous. 'This is stupidity,' he snapped as Collins ambled up.

Michael Collins grinned, his broad face lighting up like a child. 'And who's going to check on two lads having a chat at the close of the day – and one of them a detective like yourself.'

'I don't know how you do it,' Kavanagh said tightly, 'I'm not even sure why you do it. But some day you're going to get yourself shot.'

'Some day,' Collins agreed. 'Did you get what I was looking for?'

Joe Kavanagh sighed. He was one of four spies Collins had actually working within the G-Division, and occasionally the Big Fellow made demands upon his men which bordered on the foolish. On one extraordinary occasion, he had actually entered the Great Brunswick Street Station at night and made his way through the classified files. Collins's request this time had been no less hazardous: he wanted the police file on Patrick Lundy.

'I got it,' Kavanagh said eventually. 'But don't even think of breaking this one out,' he added, knowing the way Collins's mind would be working. 'This is one of the Brigadier's specials; a young man early twenties, Patrick Montgomery Lundy, held on possession of a deadly weapon, resisting arrest and directly causing the death of a police officer during the ensuing struggle. Curiously, no charges have been proferred so far.'

Collins looked at him quickly. 'And what do you read into that?'

Kavanagh shrugged his thin shoulders. 'I don't know. But if the case against this young man is so open and shut, why delay charging him? Unless,' he added softly, a sudden thought having struck him, 'unless, the Brigadier intends to work him.'

Michael Collins laughed humourlessly. 'It's what I would do myself in the same circumstances,' he said, 'first threaten and abuse him, then show him the error of his ways, and then turn him against his former friends.'

'If this young man walks away, then I'd advise you to be very careful of him indeed.'

'I know. But I want him out of there before the Brigadier can get his claws into him.'

'Impossible.'

Collins shook his head stubbornly. 'He is one of our own; I'd do the same for you.'

'I know that. But he's in one of the underground cells, with a guard on the door and every door in between.'

'When is the guard changed?'

'He'll be changed ...' Kavanagh consulted his watch, '... soon.'

'Whom do we have inside?'

'Well ... Dave Neligan on duty ...'

'And who'll draw up the rota?' Collins demanded, an idea beginning to germinate.

'It'll be typed ... it'll probably be typed up by Ned Broy!' Ned Broy was one of Collins's most valuable men inside the Station; although only a clerk typist, his position allowed him access to all the confidential documents, and after a while it became almost a habit for him to prepare a copy of all the official documents passing across his desk for Collins.

'Go back now. Tell Ned I want Dave Neligan posted to watch that room. He's to contact me in the usual way if he's successful ...'

'And if he is?' Joe Kavanagh asked cautiously.

'If he is, we'll walk out with Patrick Lundy tonight!'

Just before eight o' clock, David Neligan took up position outside the door to the room holding the dangerous prisoner. Less than five minutes later he was presented with duly signed and authorized papers which allowed him to surrender the bemused prisoner into the custody of a detective from Dublin Castle. With Kavanagh gripping him tightly by one arm, and Michael Collins with an equally strong grip on the other, Patrick Lundy was marched through the building and out into a waiting carriage. He was halfway to Monto before he realized he was free.

The Brigadier crumpled up the sheet of paper and began again. This was now his sixth attempt to explain how the prisoner had escaped. He sat in his silk dressing gown, a tumbler of Irish whiskey on the desk before him, and began once again, his usually elegant script slightly untidy and ragged.

Richard Grennell was annoyed when he had arrived back at the cell a few minutes after eight to find the door unguarded, but his annoyance had turned to absolute outrage when he discovered that the prisoner was gone. But that rage had been as nothing when compared to his frenzy when he discovered that the prisoner had been 'officially' signed out, on documents that looked so genuine that he had called the Castle simply to ensure that Lundy hadn't actually been taken there. No one at the Castle knew what he was talking about. He couldn't blame the officer on the door – after all, the papers had looked genuine, and so the only person to blame was himself – he should have realized that Collins would break Lundy out. Only the reasons escaped him. Lundy was a small – a very small cog – in a much larger machine. Or was he? Did Lundy possess information that the Volunteers didn't want to fall into the hands of the authorities? Was it possible that he was actually privy to the workings of the inner circle, which Grennell was sure must exist within the group?

And he had had him within his grasp ... and allowed him to walk away.

Dipping his pen into the ink-well, he began the report again. Well, at least there were several lines of inquiry open to him, and questions would have to be asked – for example, where had the highly professional documentation come from which had ensured Lundy's release.

He began jotting quick notes to himself ... and then stopped. How close was Lundy to Collins? The Brigadier recognized Collins's hand in this daring and audacious plan, and why would Collins want to get involved unless Patrick Lundy was in possession of some information which might prove useful? But then why not kill him outright – why go to all the trouble and risk to snatch him?

And where was he now?

Following the discovery of his escape, a squad of armed detectives had descended on the house in Tyrone Street. Aside from a dozen whores preparing for the night's business, and three surly louts who ostensibly acted as waiters, the only other person in the house was the Madam, Nuala Kennedy. Her surprised, outraged and angered act did little to impress him. He was convinced that she knew where Patrick Lundy was, but although the house was searched from top to bottom there was no sign of the man and, as far as they could see, nothing had been removed from his room. Leaving two officers on duty outside the house, the Brigadier had returned to the station to make a preliminary report, before heading home.

'Brigadier Grennell?'

The voice at the door was accompanied by a quavering tapping. He thought he recognized the voice of the woman who lived below.

He crossed to the door of the sitting room and opened it – and the knurled end of a walking stick struck him hard in the stomach. He doubled over, retching, gasping for breath, and then he was dragged by the hair into the room and flung across a chair. He was roughly and efficiently searched, and the Derringer removed from his dressing gown pocket. The remainder of his arsenal was also discovered and confiscated.

The woman who had called out to him was also

herded into the room. It was indeed the woman from the floor below. She had answered a knock on her own door and had opened it – thinking it was the Brigadier – only to be taken prisoner by five men. She was then marched upstairs and forced to play her part in the deception.

While two men held him down with guns trained on him, two more systematically searched the room, dumping everything they considered to be of use into a doctor's black Gladstone bag, while the fifth man sat with the elderly lady, chatting quietly to her in a pleasant and courteous manner – while also holding a gun trained on the Brigadier.

There was noise and movement behind the Brigadier and he realized that another person had entered the room. 'Nearly done,' one of the men said, and a voice – a familiar voice – from behind him said, 'Sixty seconds remaining.' The man then walked around and squatted down before Richard Grennell, and smiled.

'I think it's time you and I had a little talk,' Patrick Lundy grinned. He rested the cold barrel of a pistol against the Brigadier's cheek and added coldly, 'And this time on my terms.'

CHAPTER EIGHTEEN

Nuala stood at the window, looking down onto the cobbled street below. It had begun to rain earlier that evening, and the streets were damp, the cobbles glistening, wreaths of mist coiled around the gas bowls. Although it was damp, it was almost unpleasantly hot – and Nuala guessed that they would have a thunderstorm before the night was out. Neither the heat nor the damp kept the customers away, but on nights like this – hot, sticky nights – trouble could flare very easily.

She pressed her fingers to her forehead, attempting to ease out the pressure that had built up there. She was in a foul humour, and she knew that someone was going to catch the sharp end of her tongue tonight.

Patrick had been freed – she could barely believe it – and Collins proved once again that his reputation for sheer audacity was well deserved. She had only learned of the escape when the Brigadier and his men had raided the house – well, it wasn't the first time it had been raided, nor would it be the last. But Patrick had been free nearly four hours now, and he still hadn't got in touch with her.

And that, more than anything else, accounted for her ill humour.

Of course the house was probably being watched; there was no one in the street below, but they had two newcomers in tonight, both young men, obviously military or ex-military, and neither in any hurry to leave.

She pressed her forehead against the cool glass and allowed the thought that had wormed its way insidiously into her consciousness to float to the surface: was Patrick worth all this trouble? Since his arrival back in January he had caused her nothing but trouble – oh not directly of course. But he had been responsible for bringing the house to the attention of the police – and for a brothel, that was tantamount to suicide. Oh, she paid her dues every month – all the houses did, and that ensured that the police didn't bother her in the normal course of events, but even her paid friends wouldn't be able to help her if she came to the attention of the men in G–Division.

And that begged the question: did she love Patrick Lundy enough to allow him to remain here with her? Could she afford to have him remain with her? It was basically a choice of futures: either she could continue in business or she could continue with Patrick.

But not both.

Patrick Lundy was now very firmly established on the wanted lists – and she could not afford to harbour a wanted fugitive. There really wasn't any choice. She turned away from the window and glanced at the clock over the fireplace – it was going on for eleven – where could he be?

Patrick was in the cellar of a safe house on Brunswick Street – less than a hundred yards from the Police Station. The only other occupant of the room was the Brigadier, Richard Grennell, and he had been bound hand and foot to a chair. Light came from an oil lantern which had been placed on the floor to one side of the room, and which decorated the walls with darting angular, irregular shadows.

'You know these men want to kill you,' Patrick said to the man, attempting to keep his voice as calm and reasonable as possible, although the elation at having been freed from prison and capturing his captor still hadn't worn off.

'Many men have wanted to kill me, some have even tried – but I'm still here,' the Brigadier said calmly.

Patrick had to admire the man's courage in the face of almost certain death.

'They've allowed me to have a few words with you before they talk to you.'

'I'm sure that was decent of them.'

'I just have one question for you: why did you take me prisoner today?'

The Brigadier looked at him for a few moments, and then he started to laugh. He was still dressed in his silk dressing gown over a pair of cream-coloured silk pyjamas, and he cut a ridiculous figure, but it obviously didn't bother him in the slightest.

'I've already answered that, boy. I simply wanted to talk to you about your mother, and why you had returned to Ireland.' He saw Patrick's disbelieving expression and continued with a cold smile. 'It is the truth, believe what you want. You were the one who was foolish enough to get caught with a gun on your person, you were the one who resisted arrest in the course of which that detective was fatally wounded.' He smiled. 'Well, that's how the authorities will see it anyway. I knew you were with the Volunteers, but I never figured you warranted the attention of the Big Fellow himself.'

'He was a friend of my father's,' Patrick said quickly, suddenly defensive.

Grennell snorted rudely. 'Not your father's – not your true father that is!'

'What do you mean?'

The Brigadier's eyes narrowed and then he nodded slightly, a ghost of a smile on his thin lips. 'So you really don't know? I suspected as much. Well my boy, since I'm probably the only one alive today – with the exception of your darling mother – who knows the true story of your birth and the name of your real father, I'm afraid this information is going to cost you.'

Patrick started to shake his head.

'And if your IRA friends kill me, then you'll never know.'

Patrick paced the small room, the lantern throwing unnatural shadows onto the damp walls. If what the Brigadier said was true – and he had no real reason to doubt it – then here was the very person he had come to Ireland to find. He stopped beside the lantern; even though it was midsummer, he felt suddenly chilled and was glad of its heat. He looked at the Brigadier; the light from below lent his face a slightly demonic cast, and he knew that this was a truly dangerous man – a survivor – a man would betray him at the earliest opportunity.

'How much do you know?' he asked eventually.

Grennell smiled. He knew he had him now. 'About what?' he asked, playing him along.

'About my father – my real father that is? Do you know his name?'

'I know it all, boy.'

Patrick crouched down to face Grennell at eye level. 'So you say. But in broad terms, tell me what you know – without naming names of course.'

The Brigadier smiled. 'I know your father's name – your true father that is, not Dermot Corcoran; I know how he met your mother, what he was, and more importantly, I can tell you about the part your mother played in the Easter Rising.'

Patrick frowned. 'She took no part ...'

The Brigadier shook his head. 'You were sent to England with Tilly Cusack a few days before the end, leaving your mother behind. I am in a position to tell you what she did – and why.'

'Is my father still alive?'

But the Brigadier just smiled and said nothing.

'And in return you want me to set you free?'

'No.'

Patrick looked at him in surprise.

'In return I want you to contact police headquarters and tell them where I am – as simple as that. You needn't be here when they arrive.'

'And what about later?'

The Brigadier shook his head. 'I don't understand.'

'You'll come after me.'

The man smiled. 'I'd be a liar if I made you any other promises.'

Patrick leaned back against the wall, considering. There were two men in the house; they were only rank and file and knew nothing that might be of any use to the authorities – well, nothing that they wouldn't already be aware of. But Collins was coming down in ... he glanced at his watch ... in about thirty minutes. There probably wasn't enough time for the Brigadier to tell his story and then for Patrick to go and contact the police ...

'Here's the deal,' he said suddenly. 'I'll contact the police for you – they should be here in minutes, you're actually in Brunswick Street. I'll meet you tomorrow at noon at the obelisk in Phoenix Park and you can tell me what you know. As simple as that. Do we have a deal?'

The Brigadier nodded.

'And come alone. If you betray me, I'll kill you.'

'You won't kill me,' Grennell smiled.

Patrick returned his smile. 'Well not until I've got what I want from you.'

Michael Collins and Joe Kavanagh were walking down Brunswick Street when the shabby house with the boarded up windows was raided by a large force of uniformed police and detectives. The street came alive with noise and confusion. Without a word the two men turned around and walked calmly away. As they passed the door to the police station, Joe Kavanagh calmly wished Collins a good night and went inside. When he had discovered what had happened he would leave word with the librarian in Capel Street library.

Michael Collins meanwhile walked around into D'Olier Street. There were two police officers standing outside the Junior Army and Navy Stores, the enormous department store, and he tipped his hat to them as he went past. They returned the salute and wished him a good evening, unaware that they had been within a few feet of the most wanted man in Ireland.

Collins continued across O'Connell Bridge and into the ruin of O'Connell Street. He walked along quickly, his head down, his hat pulled down over his eyes, his collar turned up against the drizzle, his hands in his pockets, looking like a clerk returning home from work. A single man out alone any evening was liable to be stopped and questioned by the police – although this night he had little enough to worry about; he was carrying no incriminating documents, although he was armed. He didn't even look at the ruin of the General Post Office as he went past – it had become an all too familiar sight for Dubliners over the past three years, and now only strangers and tourists stopped and stared. He turned right into North Earl Street, and then left into Marlborough Street, automatically making the sign of the cross as he passed the pro-cathedral on the left.

And now that he was off the main thoroughfare, his attitude and mannerisms changed. This was an area where the weak were preyed upon, and a clerk with his hands in his pockets would be sure to attract attention. Michael Collins now walked with his head up, his hands loose by his sides. Just before he turned to the right up into Tyrone Street, he became aware that he was being followed. As he turned the corner he stopped, blending back into the shadows. Moments later, two young men, with shabby clothing and too bright eyes hurried around the corner. They stopped not two feet away from him.

'Where'd he go?'

'Can't've gone far.'

Street-scum, Collins decided, looking for easy pickings. 'Can I help you, gentlemen?'

'Jaysus!'

Both men spun around, false, thin-lipped smiles appearing on their lips. 'Christ, but you scared the bejaysus out of us.' They squinted into the shadows to where the vague shape of a man was just visible. 'Ahem, could you spare a light, mister?' One of the youths, taller and thinner than his companion reached into his coat pocket to produce a crumpled packet of cigarettes – and a straight razor. The second youth also produced a razor; he took his time thumbing the razor out of the mother-of-pearl handle. Now both men were grinning, and their movements had become nervous, jittery.

'Now we'll be having your watch and your wallet, and maybe that coat too …'

'And your shoes, and anything else we take a fancy to.'

'And I suppose you'll want this too?' The gun came up out of the shadows, the double-click as the hammer was cocked seeming to echo up and down the street. The black barrel of the gun was barely inches away from the taller of the two. 'Drop the razors.' The blades clicked onto the street. 'Now, go away,' Collins hissed.

Ashen-faced, the two young men turned and ran down the street.

Collins watched them go, and then bent and scooped up the two razors. Easing down the hammer on the gun, he tucked it back into his belt, and then continued on up the street, heading towards number eighty-two.

The grand days of the brothels were nearly gone. Tyrone Street, once the very heart of the infamous Monto – the most notorious red-light district in Europe – had now turned into a row of shabby tenements. There was still the rough graduation as one went up the street, with the cheaper houses, the kips at the lower end, and the flash houses, the better-class houses at the other end. Despite the rain, the houses seemed to be busy, with all the windows alight, although there was less traffic than usual on the cobbled streets.

The door to number eighty-two was closed, but it opened immediately to Collins' solid knock. He stepped inside and brushed water from his coat. 'Madam in?' he asked, shrugging it off.

The man nodded upstairs and then turned away to place his coat on the stand behind the door. As Collins started up the stairs, the door to the sitting room opened and a young man with his arm draped around the shoulders of a hard-eyed smiling young woman stepped out into the hall. The two men's eyes met briefly, and then Collins continued on his way, his right hand trailing along the banister rail, his left touching the butt of his pistol. The man was army, and while his reasons for being here might be 'legitimate', Collins had survived far too long to take very much on trust or accident. But there was no shouts, no challenge, and he continued up to the top floor, where Nuala had her rooms.

She was waiting for him at the top of the stairs, and as he stepped onto the landing, both Jem and Patrick appeared. Both men were armed, Jem with his shotgun, Patrick with a pistol. They looked past the Big Fellow to see if there was anyone on the stairs behind him.

'There are two new faces in tonight,' Nuala explained.

Collins nodded. 'Army?'

She nodded, and then shrugged. 'It might be nothing ... but best not to take any chances,' she added, opening the door to the sitting room.

'Very wise.' He turned to Patrick. 'Everything all right?'

Patrick nodded quickly. 'Fine, fine.'

'Did the Brigadier tell you anything?'

'Nothing,' he said, walking past Collins, unwilling to meet his eyes. 'I'm sure he knows, but I didn't want to ask him too many questions, I thought it might excite his interest.'

Michael Collins nodded. He was about to follow Nuala and Patrick, when he suddenly remembered something. He turned to Jem and handed him the two razors. A quick look of understanding passed between the two men. 'Two young lads'll need a shave in the morning.'

'I'll see they get it,' the blond-haired man smiled humourlessly.

Nuala was pouring tea for Collins as he entered the sitting-room and closed the door, leaving Jem to watch

271

the landing, his sawn-off shot-gun cradled in his arm. Nuala glanced up at him. 'We'll have plenty of warning if the two downstairs decide to do anything.'

Collins nodded. 'Were you raided today?'

'Tonight, just before we opened for business.'

He accepted a cup of tea and sipped it cautiously, and was pleasantly surprised to find that it wasn't the usual tenement brew – which was usually put on to boil for breakfast and then kept going all through the day and on into the night, so that by the evening the tea was foul. But this was fine pale aromatic tea. 'China?' he asked.

Nuala nodded, pleased. 'China. I buy it from Becker Brothers, the tea importers in North Earl Street.'

'I know it.' He sipped his tea looking from Nuala to Patrick. He had the impression that he had come at an awkward time – there was an almost palpable tension between them, and he wondered if they had been arguing. 'I think you might be in for another raid,' he said quietly.

Both looked at him, surprised.

'The safe house in Brunswick Street was raided tonight – just before I got to it. I didn't stick around long enough to see what happened, but we can only assume that the Brigadier is now free and our lads captured. Joe will find out details and leave a message in the usual place.' The usual place was Capel Street Library. He turned back to Patrick. 'What time did you leave the house at?'

Patrick looked at Nuala. 'What time did I get here at … nine?'

'A little after. I remember winding the clock on the mantelpiece at nine.'

Patrick turned back to Collins. 'A little after nine then. Why?'

Collins shook his head. 'No reason. Was everything all right then?'

'Fine.'

'Anything suspicious. Anyone lurking around outside?'

'Not that I could see.'

Michael Collins finished his tea, and Nuala immediately offered him more. He hesitated a moment, and then accepted. 'Thank you, I will.' He added milk and sugar and drank deeply. 'I just want to know why the house was raided on this particular night. There's a possibility that it was being watched of course, and someone saw the Brigadier being brought in.'

'He was rolled up in a carpet,' Patrick said. 'I was there.'

'Any lights showing through the windows?'

'Painted black – and in any case the only light in the house was the lantern I lit when I was speaking to the Brigadier in the cellar.'

Collins grimaced. 'Well, maybe Joe will be able to shed some light on it.' He smiled at the unintended pun, Nuala joining him, realizing what he had just said, but Patrick didn't get the joke. He finished his tea and stood up. 'I wouldn't stay here tonight, Patrick. Just in case there's a raid,' he added.

Patrick nodded. 'Any ideas where I should go?'

The Big Fellow considered, and then said, 'Remember Eddie …?'

Patrick thought about it for a moment, and then said, 'The make-up lady?'

'Tap once, twice after a count of two and then once again. Ask her if she would mind putting you up for the night, and do a job on you in the morning. We'll have to change your appearance again, now that you're wanted for murder.' Making his way to the door, he looked at Nuala. 'I'll wish you a good night, and Patrick,' he added, 'if you are venturing out again tonight, please be careful.'

'I'm always careful,' Patrick said almost petulantly.

'Not careful enough,' Michael Collins said with a grin.

When he had gone, Nuala went to stand by the window looking down into the street below. 'So you've made your choice,' she said eventually, continuing where they had left off.

Patrick shrugged uncomfortably. 'I think circumstances have made it for me.'

'You still have the choice,' she said, turning away from the window. 'Leave the Volunteers, go away for a while and then come back and live with me when all the fuss has died down.'

Patrick shook his head.

'Why not?' she demanded.

'I don't know why not. I just can't. It's something I have to do.'

'So you're going to go on the run with the IRA? You're going to end up dead in a ditch somewhere,' she spat.

Patrick shrugged but said nothing.

Nuala turned away and stared out the window, not seeing the street below. 'I thought you cared for me?'

'I did. I do.'

'But you love your cause more than me.'

Patrick remained silent. He suddenly thought of his mother, and Dermot Corcoran on the morning he went out to fight with Pearse in the GPO. Did they have a conversation like this? Had she given Dermot a choice … the same choice Nuala was now giving him? Dermot Corcoran had chosen to go because it was a cause he truly believed in. Did he truly believe in the cause he was fighting for? Or was he doing this because for the first time in his life he was doing something that he wanted to do; this was his decision … right or wrong it was his decision.

'Make your choice, Patrick,' Nuala said fiercely. 'Which do you care for most?'

And suddenly Patrick found that there wasn't any choice to make.

CHAPTER NINETEEN

The Brigadier checked his watch a final time before slipping it back into his waistcoat pocket and walking away from the towering Wellington Monument that dominated Dublin's largest parkland, the Phoenix Park. He had been standing there since a few minutes to twelve, waiting for Patrick Lundy, and it now lacked five minutes to one. Obviously the boy had had second thoughts.

He was walking past a stand of trees towards the wrought iron gates when Patrick stepped out in front of him. 'Good afternoon, Brigadier.'

The Brigadier stopped. Both hands were in his pockets and there was a small revolver in his right hand pocket. He looked past Patrick, checking the trees on either side, and then he turned and looked behind him.

'I am alone.'

The Brigadier nodded, finally turning to look at Patrick. There were deep circles under his eyes and his hair was uncombed and the Brigadier got the impression that the young man had slept rough. 'You kept me waiting long enough,' he said testily. It was a brilliant summer's day and his face was sheened with sweat. The monument he had been standing beside stood out in the open with no cover or shade in any direction.

'On the contrary sir, I've been here since a little before eleven. I watched you arrive, and I've been watching you ever since.' He turned to the right. 'Let's walk.' He deliberately turned his back on the Brigadier and allowed the older man to catch up. They walked in silence across the grass towards the path.

'I was wondering if you'd come here,' Patrick said

finally, jerking his thumb back towards the Wellington Monument, 'or to the Phoenix.' He inclined his head in the direction of the tall Phoenix monument in the distance.

The Brigadier looked surprised. 'I didn't even think about it,' he confessed. 'This was the obvious choice.'

'An Irishman would have come to the Phoenix,' he said easily, not looking at the man. He was acutely aware of his surroundings, conscious that a trap could be sprung at any moment. If it was he was determined that the Brigadier would be amongst the casualties.

The brilliant August sunshine had brought the crowds out, and the park was filled with couples just strolling together, families picnicking on the grass, while children ran everywhere. Patrick noticed that the women's fashion this year tended to be bright crisp colours, and that more of the younger men were wearing pale coloured blazers and matching trousers. He felt curiously provincial and out of place in his simple black suit.

Patrick turned to the right, heading into the hollow that held the Zoological Gardens, now eighty-eight years old and one of the oldest in Europe. Patrick paid for them both, and they walked under the quaintly thatched entrance and turned to the left, heading down to the lake. Patrick took that path that led around the lake, following it to the left until he came to a shaded seat, which afforded them some measure of protection from the blistering sun, and a modicum of privacy. The gardens were crowded, and the cries and roars of the animals mingled with the buzz of conversation.

'You have a talent for subterfuge,' the Brigadier remarked, removing a silver cigarette case from his pocket. The sudden movement made Patrick's hand dart towards his belt, and the Brigadier smiled slightly, his suspicions confirmed. Flipping open the lid, he offered it to Patrick, who refused; taking one for himself, he deliberately tapped one of the long slim cream-coloured cigarettes against the case before continuing. 'If I wanted to arrange a clandestine meeting with someone I didn't trust, and whom I suspected might have brought along armed companions, I might have chosen a place like this myself. We are surrounded by people on all sides, we can see without being seen, and if there is any shooting, the crowd will panic and in the resultant confusion, you might be able to make your escape.'

Patrick nodded, keeping his face expressionless. He had been thinking along very much the same lines when he had decided to bring the Brigadier to the Zoological Gardens.

'Of course, bringing me here was a mistake.' The Brigadier paused to light his cigarette, and threw his head back to blow smoke skywards. He glanced at Patrick. 'Were there to be trouble, you would be trapped within these environs.'

'I never thought of that,' Patrick conceded.

Richard Grennell nodded. 'Still, you display a certain degree of natural cunning – obviously inherited from your father,' he added with a slight grin. 'I read somewhere that the talents of parents can be passed to their children.'

'Who was my father?' Patrick asked tightly, concentrating intently on the man. The park, the people, even the blistering August heat, barely intruded on his consciousness.

'Your father ...' the Brigadier turned to look out across the water. 'Where do we begin?' He glanced sidelong at Patrick and then hurried on when he saw his fixed expression. 'To understand your father, you must realize that he worked for me – indeed, he was my best man. I have run the British Intelligence Service in Ireland since the early 1890s, but I presume you know that ...?'

'I didn't realise you'd been in business for so long,' the young man remarked.

'Nearly thirty years,' he nodded. 'With your father's assistance, I built up one of the best intelligence networks in the British Empire. Dublin is the second capital in the Empire, the closest colony to home, and the most troublesome. The Irish race built our roads, our cities, and filled our armies ... caused us more trouble than any of our other colonies ... This country breeds revolution, do you know that? And because it's so close to home, it's the most dangerous ...'

'My father?' Patrick whispered.

'Your father ... your father was John Lewis, Captain and then later Major, John Lewis. He was the man responsible for supplying us with the actual date of the Easter Rising – unfortunately, the authorities on the mainland were not in a position to act upon that information at the time. Oh, don't look so surprised boy, we knew revolution was in the air ... all we needed was the date. Lewis gave us that date.' He shrugged, smiling wryly. 'And what happened? Because it was a bank holiday, there was no-one on the mainland who could decode the message Lewis sent.' He shrugged again. 'But no matter. Your father also supplied us with information about the rebels' arms and numbers, good information, valuable information, which we used to crush the Rising.'

'Where does my mother fit into all this?' Patrick wondered.

'Your mother was a servant girl in the Lewis household ...'

'College House on Clonliffe Road,' Patrick said, nodding quickly, pieces of the jigsaw falling into place.

'Just so.'

'Your mother became pregnant by Lewis – he always had an eye for the ladies – and when this was discovered by his wife, Anne Lewis, she was dismissed from the house.'

'On Christmas Eve, 1898.'

The Brigadier nodded. 'Well you cannot blame Anne. John Lewis treated her very shabbily, but she extracted a revenge of her own, I suppose.'

Patrick looked at him quizzically.

The Brigadier grinned. 'He was so caught up in the preparations for the Rising, that he paid her little heed. What he didn't know – until it was too late – was that she had gone out and joined the revoluntionaries. She was one of those killed in the College of Surgeons.'

'I'm only interested in my own family,' Patrick said quickly. He felt cold and chilled, and the blood pounding in his head was becoming almost painful.

'No one definitely knows what happened to your mother for the next few years. We know that she ended up in the company of the famous Whoremistress, Bella Cohen, and ended up working for her. And I don't mean working as you would normally understand the word in a brothel.' He finished his cigarette and tossed the butt into the water; its hissing attracted a curious duck. 'Your father then made her acquaintance again in 1907, when he was investigating the disappearance of the Irish Crown Jewels. We suspected, but could never prove, her involvement. She dealt in stolen goods, and there were whispers – unsubstantiated – that she had actually arranged the theft. It's not true of course, but it's the sort of thing she would have done. Your mother and father had some sort of fracas that year – I could never get all the details – and in the struggle she stabbed him ...' the Brigadier smiled tightly, 'effectively emasculating him as far as I can understand. That same year, your mother married Dermot Corcoran.' He lit another cigarette, his movements almost automatic. Although his gaze was fixed on the water, he obviously wasn't seeing it as he looked back into another time, another place.

'Your mother re-enters our story in 1916. We knew the Rising was imminent – all we needed was the date.' He turned to look at Patrick. 'Your mother supplied us with that date.'

Patrick started to shake his head, his eyes wide with horror, but the Brigadier pressed on. 'She had her reasons, and whatever else you might think about her, you have to admire her courage and her ruthlessness.

Her husband, Dermot Corcoran, was deeply involved in the Rising; he was privy to the council meetings, and aware of the plans at a very high level. But Katherine Lundy knew – as most right-thinking people knew – that the Rising stood no chance of success. She pleaded with him to forget the whole idea, but he refused. So, she conceived an extraordinary and desperate plan. She made contact with Lewis, and offered to sell him all the information she had on the Rising in return for a letter stating that Dermot Corcoran was a British spy; she hoped that when the Rising started – or finished – she could use this to spirit her husband away.'

Patrick listened with mounting horror. He wanted – desperately wanted – to disbelieve the story, but he recognized too many of the elements to dismiss it as a lie.

'Lewis gave her the paper,' the Brigadier continued softly, 'and it was useless, of course. Then Dermot Corcoran was killed in the Post Office.' He finished abruptly.

'There's more,' Patrick said immediately through gritted teeth.

'No,' the man said, almost gently. 'There's no more.'

'Lewis betrayed my mother – and you're telling me she let it go at that? She's not the type. What happened?' he demanded fiercely.

'I don't know what happened,' the Brigadier said firmly, 'but I'll tell you what I think happened.'

The young man nodded. His head was pounding and his throat felt as if it had been seared by something red hot. There was a sour feeling in his stomach, and he felt he was going to vomit.

'Katherine Lundy went to see John Lewis in the house on Clonliffe Road. There was no one else living there at the time, but we do have one witness – a neighbour – who saw a woman who fits your mother's description arriving at the house, receiving no answer at the front door and then going around to the back door – and in the light of what we discovered, that is significant.

'Your father, John Lewis was there, and there would seem to have followed some sort of discussion – an amicable discussion too, since we discovered two empty cups of tea. However, at some stage an argument developed …'

'And …?' Patrick pressed when the Brigadier seemed disinclined to continue.

'And we found Major John Lewis on the kitchen floor, with a kitchen knife still clutched in his hand. He had been shot twice from very close range with a small-calibre pistol.'

Patrick surged to his feet and took a few steps away from the seat. 'She didn't do it,' he shouted, 'she didn't do it.' There were tears on his face as he surged blindly towards the exit. 'She didn't do it,' he muttered to himself. But he knew she had.

Jem discovered Patrick slumped at the kitchen table. His hand was curled around the butt of a pistol, and there were bread crumbs scattered around him. Jem turned around and went to find Nuala. He knew that the two had argued the night before – and he had thought that was the last they'd seen of Master Patrick. And good riddance too. He had nothing against the boy – but he was simply trouble and, like some sort of strange magnet, seem to attract trouble wherever he went. Jem had known people like that in his career in the navy; curiously though, they rarely ended up in trouble themselves, merely caused it to those around them.

Patrick awoke as Nuala hurried into the room, the gun coming up, pointing at her … and then Jem brushed past her and simply took the gun from his trembling fingers. He pulled out the magazine, and worked the slide on the weapon to ensure it was empty, before dropping the gun into Patrick's left coat pocket and the magazine into his right. He turned around to the sink to fill the kettle with water.

Nuala sat down in the chair facing Patrick, resting her hands flat on the polished wood of the table … lacing her fingers together. She was shocked by his appearance. There was straw in his hair, and she noticed that he was wearing exactly the same clothes he had been wearing the previous day. His expression was haggard, and the circles under his eyes were deep and dark. But the look in his eyes frightened her – it was the haunted terrified look of a trapped animal.

'What brings you back?' she asked simply, keeping her voice neutral.

'I … I had nowhere else to go,' he said slowly, and then fell silent.

'Where've you been?'

He shrugged. 'Around.'

Frowning, Nuala asked, 'Where did you go last night, when you left here?'

'A walk. I walked for a while.'

'Did you go to the place where Collins told you to, the make-up lady?'

He shook his head.

'Why not?'

He shrugged again. 'Didn't get around to it. I'll go later.'

Jem placed two cups of tea on the table before them. Standing behind Patrick he looked at Nuala and silently pointed to the door: do you want me to leave?

She shook her head almost imperceptibly. She looked at Patrick. 'Drink your tea,' she said firmly. Obediently, he picked up the tea and, cupping it in both hands, began to sip the hot, sweet liquid. 'Do you want to tell me what happened?'

Patrick continued drinking the tea, seemingly intent on it.

'Has there been an accident, a shooting? Patrick, what's happened?' she demanded, looking desperately at Jem.

'I met the Brigadier,' he said finally, his voice sounding numb and distant.

Nuala looked from Patrick to Jem and then back to Patrick. 'Go on.'

'He told me about my mother … and my father. My father,' he said, picking the words carefully, sounding them. 'My father, Major John Lewis …' he continued, unaware of her shocked expression. 'And he told me how my mother betrayed the Easter Rising to the British, how she sold them all the information she had in return for some sort of useless pardon for Dermot Corcoran. And he told me how she had shot John Lewis … my father …' His voice, which had risen to a shriek, now dissolved into sobs.

She left him to cry for a while, simply watching him, allowing him to exorcise the demon that was now eating at his soul. He had come to Ireland to discover the truth about his past; perhaps he should have guessed that the truth would not be to his liking.

When the sobbing had eased, Nuala came around the table and, standing behind Patrick, wrapped her arms around him. Resting her head atop his, she murmured, 'We'll sort something out, don't worry, we'll sort something out. Now come on,' she eased him to his feet, 'let's get you to bed, we can discuss this later, when you've rested.'

Between them, Nuala and Jem helped Patrick upstairs into his bedroom. He moved like a sleepwalker, seemingly unaware of his surroundings, locked within some inner world, attempting to come to terms with a past that was not what he had imagined it, trying to come to terms with a murdered father, and a mother who had betrayed all he held important, trying to come to terms with the fact that his mother had shot his father.

While Jem brought some hot water, Nuala undressed him and laid him out naked on the bed. When the big man had brought the basin of hot water, some soap and a towel, Nuala washed him down, and then dressed him in his night-shirt. Finally, she tucked him into bed and kissed him on the forehead. She pulled the curtains and was leaving the room, when the voice came from the bed, 'What's going to happen to me?' He sounded like a lost child.

'I don't know, Patrick,' she said truthfully, 'you sleep awhile, I'll see if I can sort something out.' She remained standing by the door, waited for him to say something else, but when there was nothing, she turned and left the room.

In the small bedroom, Patrick stared at the cracks on the ceiling and wished – desperately – that he was a small boy once again ... when life was simple, when he could trust and love his parents. When he eventually drifted off to sleep, his dreams were troubled.

Jem was waiting for Nuala in the sitting room, a large Scotch and ice in his hand. She took it from him gratefully and sank into the leather chair before the unlit fire. 'What are we going to do, Jem?' she asked, suddenly feeling exhausted. She was almost afraid to think too long on what Patrick had just told them – it would invite too many questions, questions which she could not – or would not – want answered at this time.

Jem sank into the chair directly opposite. He perched on the edge of his seat, his legs splayed, his elbows resting on his knees. He stared at Nuala with his disconcertingly bright blue eyes. In his accented voice he asked her simply, 'What do you want to do?'

She looked at him.

'The choice is yours. Give up the boy – either to Collins or the authorities, or shield him, or send him away.'

'Why would Collins want him?' she wondered.

'He never explained how he came to meet with the Brigadier this morning. Such a meeting would hardly occur by chance.'

She nodded slowly, another piece of the jigsaw falling into place. 'So, Patrick did a deal with the Brigadier last night, information about his past ... in return for ... what, contacting the station ...?'

'Something like that.'

Nuala shook her head slowly, disbelievingly. 'Patrick

contacted the station, told them where he was, and the Brigadier agreed to tell Patrick the story of his parents.'

'Is the story true?' Jem asked.

Nuala nodded. 'Some of it I knew, and what was new fitted in with the rest. I'm left with no choice but to believe it.'

'No wonder the boy is distressed,' Jem said, not unsympathetically.

'You have a hard heart, Jem,' Nuala said fondly. 'It must be your German blood.'

'I have no feelings for the boy,' Jem said neutrally.

'What will happen if we turn him over to Collins?' she asked.

Jem shrugged. 'That's hard to say. The Big Fellow is tough, but fair. He might be prepared to take into account the exceptional circumstances in Patrick's case. And if his father was such an important figure in the movement, then that might help also.'

'Or he might have him shot?' she concluded.

Jem nodded. 'He might.'

Nuala finished her drink quickly, but held on to the empty glass, turning the stem around in her fingers, admiring the faceted glass. 'So, if we turn him over to the authorities, he'll hang for the "murder" of that detective, and if we turn him over to Collins there's a fifty-fifty chance that he'll be shot for betraying them, and costing them one of their most valuable prisoners, and two men.'

'When I worked the brothels in Berlin,' Jem said suddenly, surprising her, because he rarely spoke of his early years in Berlin's red-light district, 'there was a case where the son of one of the Madams fought an illegal duel in which his opponent was killed. The authorities wanted him, and the dead boy's father wanted him. The boy's mother simply sent him to a military academy in the south. What is that proverb: out of sight, out of mind ...'

Nuala nodded decisively. 'That's what we'll do then. We'll send him abroad – America, I think. Will you arrange the documentation?'

He nodded.

'I'll sort out tickets and luggage. We'll let him rest up for a day or two …' There was a knock on the door and she paused. 'Yes.'

The door opened and one of the servants entered.

'Yes, what is it Mary?'

The maid dropped a quick curtsey. 'Begging your pardon Ma'am, but there's a Mister Collins to see you.'

CHAPTER TWENTY

Michael Collins strode briskly into the room, his hat in his hands, his coat thrown over his arm. 'We may have a problem,' he said abruptly.

Nuala and Jem both came to their feet when the Big Fellow entered; they could almost feel the raw energy the man exuded.

'What's wrong?' Nuala demanded, hoping that the tone of her voice was in keeping with how she was supposed to sound.

'Have you seen Patrick?'

'I thought he was going to spend the night at one of your houses,' Nuala said, not answering the question.

'That was the general plan, but when I called for him today, he hadn't shown up, and Eddie knew nothing about it.' He looked hard at Nuala. 'You've no idea where he is?' he insisted.

The Madam found she couldn't hold his almost accusing gaze and she dropped her eyes. 'We ... we had a discussion about the Volunteers and Patrick's involvement with them last night,' she said quietly. 'Well, discussion is the wrong wrong. We fought about it, and I gave him a choice: he could remain here with me or he could go and fight with you.' She looked at Collins, a thin smile playing about her lips. 'You won.'

Collins nodded shortly, as if he had expected nothing different. 'He's a good lad. But now he's missing.' He tapped his hat against his leg in frustration. 'All I have to do now is to try and find out where he is. I've got men scouring the city for him. I've checked with the lads at Brunswick Street Station, but he hadn't been picked up.'

'Any word on the Brigadier?' Jem asked.

'Oh, he's safe and sound, back home with an armed guard watching over him. Joe Kavanagh discovered that someone 'phoned the station last night, giving his location; a male voice with an accent, maybe northern or Scottish. That's all we know. But if I find out who it was ...' He left the sentence trailing; he didn't need to finish it.

'What happens now?' Nuala asked.

Collins shrugged. 'We go on looking for Patrick – sooner or later we'll find him.' He frowned slightly. 'I have a feeling that the Brigadier's hand is in here somewhere.' He smiled slightly. 'I've a good mind to pay him another visit ...'

'So soon ... you wouldn't dare?' Jem said quickly.

Michael Collins winked. 'They wouldn't be expecting another attack so soon; I think we might walk away with him very easily indeed.' He shrugged. 'Well, we'll see. I'll wish you both good day then. If – by any chance – Patrick returns here, have him wait and then get a message to me.' He nodded again. 'A good day to you both.'

Jem crossed to the window and then waited until he saw Collins' burly form stride resolutely down the street. He glanced back over his shoulder at Nuala. 'You know if he lifts the Brigadier again – and I've no doubt but that he means to do it – then the jig is up. You heard Collins – he's not going to be in any mood to deal lightly with the man who betrayed him.'

Nuala nodded. 'I know,' she sighed. She suddenly looked a lot older than her two and thirty years. She smiled at Jem. 'Yesterday evening when he walked out, I was glad that he had gone; I'd come to the conclusion that he was more trouble than he was worth. But I didn't sleep last night for worrying where he was, what he was doing. And I missed him. I missed him,' she repeated, almost as if she were admitting it to herself for the first time. Then her lips tightened and curved into a humourless smile. 'But that doesn't blind me to his faults and failings. Now he's back, and suddenly we're in trouble again. Oh Jem, what have I got myself into? What am I going to do?'

'You don't have many choices.'

'No, I don't,' she agreed, 'and I don't like to have these decisions forced upon me.'

'What sort of decisions?'

'Whether we're going to save his life or not.'

'I thought we were going to send him away,' the big German smiled slightly.

'And if the Big Fellow finds out about Patrick? When he's finished with us, he'll go after Patrick, and you know he'll not rest until he has doled out some justice, and the Volunteers have contacts all over the world – especially in America.'

Jem nodded. The Volunteers received massive donations of cash from their friends in the United States. 'So what do we do?' Jem asked.

'The only danger we have is if Collins speaks to Grennell. So, we make sure the Big Fellow never gets a chance to talk to the Brigadier.'

'How?' Jem asked quietly.

'With a little help from you.'

There was a gentle tap on the door and the Brigadier looked up as the young police officer stepped in. 'Begging your pardon sir, but there's a lady to see you.'

Grennell turned away from the pile of correspondence on his desk. This was the material the Volunteers had taken the day before; when the police had raided the house in Brunswick Street, they had also been lucky enough to discover everything he'd lost, so at the end of the day his abduction had turned out to have been an interesting lesson in the methods of the IRA.

'I've no wish to be disturbed.'

'Yes sir. I told her that sir, but she said to say her name is Eileen …'

'Aaah. That's fine then. Where is she now?'

'At the main door.'

'Let her come up.'

'Very good sir.' There were now three guards on the house. One at the main door downstairs, another on the stairwell, and a third directly outside his door.

He returned to his correspondence and a few moments later he heard the door crack opening followed by the swish of heavy cloth. 'I'll be with you in a moment m'dear,' he said without turning around.

A car horn blared in the street below, followed by a screech of brakes, and then another horn blew. The Brigadier stood up to look out the window, parting the curtains slightly. A motor car had gone out of control, striking two other cars before careening across the road, mounting the footpath and smashing into the railings surrounding the park. A man jumped from the car and ran screaming down the street and, moments later, the car exploded in a ball of orange flame. Two of the large window panes beside Grennell cracked, the sound like twigs snapping.

The Brigadier turned around, an amused smile on his lips – just as Nuala fired off both barrels of the sawn-off shotgun. The weapon had been wrapped in a blanket and tied up inside a hessian sack, leaving only the triggers exposed. The explosion, although muffled by the padding, reverberated around the room, and the blast lifted the small man off his feet, sending him crashing down behind the table, scattering its contents across the room. He was dead before the final sheet of paper drifted onto his body.

Nuala tucked the weapon beneath her skirt and casually walked from the room. There was no guard outside the door – they had been drawn to the commotion in the street – and so she locked the door and stuck the key in her purse.

Nearly two hours passed before the Brigadier's body was discovered.

It was late in the evening before Patrick awoke. He lay in bed, not moving, not thinking, looking at the shadows on the wall. There was still the faintest glow of sunshine close to the ceiling, and the room felt hot and stuffy and drifting up from below he could hear the muted chatter of the girls, and guessed that it must be close to eight, just before opening time.

He sat up almost reluctantly – and found Nuala sitting at the end of the bed.

She put down the newspaper she had been reading, and carefully took off the wire-framed spectacles she had recently taken to wearing. She looked closely at Patrick, noting for the first time how much he had changed since he had arrived six months ago. The cosmetic changes Eddie had made then had long since gone, and although his face still looked young and unlined, the innocent expression was gone, and there was a certain weariness in the eyes, a degree of caution, as if the world had dealt him too many blows and all he expected were more.

'How do you feel?'

He shrugged. 'Fine.'

There was silence between them, and then they both started to speak together.

'Are you hungry …?'

'I'll have to go …'

They both smiled and Nuala began. 'I'll get you something to eat.'

'Thanks, but I don't think I've the time. Collins will be looking for me.' He threw back the covers and swung his legs out of bed.

'He's already been here,' Nuala said quietly.

Patrick stopped and looked at her.

'Earlier today; he was worried because you hadn't gone to the safe house.'

'I'll have to contact him …'

'You'll get dressed and then come down to the sitting room where we can talk.'

'I've no time …' he began.

'Make time,' Nuala said firmly. She stood up and walked to the door, and stopped with her hand on the handle. 'And this time you'd better listen to me – your life … and mine too, may depend on it.'

Nuala was pouring tea when Patrick walked into the sitting room. He was wearing the suit he had originally come to Ireland in, his hair was damp and he had shaved. Nuala smiled; when he had first started living with her, he had taken similar care with his appearance, although lately, he had often arrived to the breakfast table unshaved and his hair uncombed. Perhaps it signified something in their relationship – she didn't know.

'Eat something,' she said.

'I'm not hungry,' Patrick said quietly, although when he did sit to the table, he found he was ravenous and then remembered that it had been nearly twenty-four hours since his last meal.

Nuala sipped her tea and watched him for a few moments. 'Now, listen to me Patrick,' she said quietly, 'listen very carefully.'

Patrick looked up at her, surprised at the seriousness in her voice.

'I know the deal you did with the Brigadier,' Nuala stated flatly. Patrick stopped eating, but she pressed on, 'And if I could work that out, well then it wouldn't take much for Collins to work it out either. And if he ever found out that you had betrayed him ... well, you know the penalty for traitors.'

Patrick had put down his food; he had lost whatever appetite he had left. He simply watched her, wondering where all this was leading.

'Collins called here today, looking for you. Naturally, I didn't tell him you were asleep upstairs,' she smiled. 'But he did express the opinion that he suspected that the Brigadier was involved in your mysterious disappearance which, I suppose in a way, he was. He was talking of going after the Brigadier again. He thought it would be easy enough to abduct him a second time since it would be the last thing the authorities would expect.' She saw the look of alarm in Patrick's eyes and pressed on. 'And you know of course if they did capture the Brigadier, this time they would make sure he didn't get away.'

Patrick finished his cold tea, desperately trying to assimilate what he had just learned, wondering how he was going to work his way around it.

Nuala let him sweat for awhile, before adding, 'And that's why I shot him.'

Patrick dropped the cup in shock, the fine china shattering against the saucer, breaking them both. 'That was hand-painted Spode,' she said, distracted.

Patrick ignored her. 'What did you say?' he whispered.

Nuala came around the table and began to gather up the broken crockery. Patrick grabbed her wrists, forcing her to her knees beside him. 'What happened!'

Nuala shook her hands free. 'I shot him! I took Jem's shotgun and shot him ... for your sake. Because I love you,' she added bitterly.

Stunned, Patrick sank back into the chair. Nuala rose to her feet, massaging her wrists. 'You've nothing to fear from him now. You can go to Collins ...'

'Why?' Patrick interrupted her.

Nuala looked down at him. 'I told you,' she said shortly.

'You risked everything to protect me?'

'There was a little self-interest,' she smiled, 'but yes, it was done to protect you.'

'Why?' he persisted.

Nuala pulled around a chair and sat facing Patrick, her knees almost touching his. She reached out and held his hands while she spoke.

'I love you. However hard you may find that to believe, I love you. And knowing that we cannot be together, knowing that you love your cause more than you love me, doesn't mean that I love you any less. I am now thirty-two years old, well past the age where women are married, and my occupation isn't the type that tends to lead to many offers of marriage. Oh aye, I know most of the great Madams are always called Mrs, but it's more an honorary title than a real one. I'd grown used to the idea of spinsterhood ... and then you arrived. And you were innocent and naive and trusting, and I think I fell in love with you almost immediately. But you were nineteen, and I twelve years your senior ... and twelve years is a lifetime.

'And then suddenly you were sharing my home and my bed, and I don't think I was ever happier.

'Until you grew up.

'You had your cause, and I should have guessed that it would mean more to you than some old woman, with a poor education and not much to look at.

'So you've made your decision – and I'll not try to hold you back, you've got your life to lead.' Nuala took a deep breath, steadying her voice, which had started to tremble. 'So I killed the Brigadier because he was a threat to you; I killed him because I loved you. Because I still love you.'

Patrick leaned forward and kissed her gently on the lips. 'Nuala ...' he began.

She pressed her finger tips to his lips. 'No, let's leave it at this ... with no lies, no promises. You've given me something, you made me feel young again ... and I like to think I gave you something in return.' She stood up suddenly. 'Let's leave it at that. You know you can always come back here. It's your home; if you're ever in trouble, you can always come back to us.'

'I'll try not to abuse that privilege.'

Nuala crossed to the fireplace and took down an envelope on the mantelpiece. She returned to the table and gently placed it beside the shattered crockery. 'There's a hundred and twenty pounds in there – that's all I could raise in cash, but it's enough to get yourself a start.'

He started to shake his head. 'I can't.'

'Pay me back when you can,' she said firmly.

'How can I thank you?' Patrick asked softly.

'By trying to stay alive. When these troubles have run their course and Ireland's future has been settled in one direction or the other, people will remember who did what. And what you see as being the right and proper thing to do now, mightn't be viewed in the same way then. But listen to me,' she suddenly laughed, attempting to take the sting from her words, 'I'm the last one to give advice.'

Patrick stood and took her in his arms then he kissed her, holding her close. It was a chaste embrace, and for the first time, Patrick realized what he might be giving up. Dermot Corcoran had walked away from his own mother in circumstances which must have been very similar; he had ended up dead, and she a drunken tyrant. 'I'll never forget you,' he said fervently.

'You'll forget me,' she said confidently, 'maybe not today nor tomorrow, but someday you'll meet someone more your own age, someone more suited, and then you'll forget me.'

'I won't,' he said firmly. He stepped back from Nuala, holding her at arms' length. 'I know I've brought you nothing but trouble, but it was all unintentional, and I am grateful, truly grateful for all that you've done for me.' He faltered, unsure what to say.

Nuala turned away and busied herself with the pieces of the broken cup and saucer. Finally, with nothing more to say, he left the room and walked down the corridor to his own room. He filled a small bag with a few clothes and threw his coat over his arm. He checked the sitting room on his way back down the corridor, but it was empty. At the end of the stairs he met Jem. The German looked at him impassively, and then Patrick stuck out his hand. 'Thank you,' he said quickly, surprising the man.

Jem nodded.

'You'll take care of her for me,' Patrick asked, inclining his head upwards.

The big man nodded again.

'You'll do a better job of that than me I'm sure,' Patrick said quickly, unable to keep the bitterness from his voice, and then turned to the hall door. Jem opened it and looked out into the street before allowing Patrick out; satisfied, he stepped back. And as Patrick walked down the steps, he called out, 'Be careful.'

Patrick nodded, without turning back. When the door closed behind him, it had a vaguely ominous, curiously final air to it.

CHAPTER TWENTY-ONE

When the door to number six Harcourt Street opened and the familiar bulky figure of Collins bustled down the steps, Patrick Lundy pushed away from the railings of the house opposite and darted across the road, taking care to cross at an angle that would bring him in ahead of Collins.

The Big Fellow saw him coming and, if he was surprised, he showed no sign. He nodded amicably to the younger man as Patrick fell into step beside him and together they walked in the direction of St Stephen's Green.

'I need to talk,' Patrick said quietly.

Without looking at him, Collins nodded. 'I've been looking for you.'

'I know. Nuala told me.'

'I was beginning to get worried about you. I've got men out all over town looking for you. I thought the Brigadier might have caught up with you.'

'No ... I ... I know it was wrong of me not to go to Eddies's ...'

'Not only wrong but stupid,' Collin snapped. 'If you're going to work with me, you'll learn to do as I say when I say it.'

'I'm sorry ... I had some bad news,' Patrick said quietly.

'Oh?' Collins glanced at him.

Patrick nodded towards the Green. 'Let's find a seat inside; we can talk there.'

'If you wish.'

The two men crossed the bottom of Harcourt Street and then waited until the traffic had eased before darting across the road and into the Green by one of the small side gates.

It was like walking into another world. It was still and silent and although summer still lingered in the air, the trees were beginning to turn for autumn and the paths were covered with a crackling green gold carpet.

As Collins and Patrick walked through the park, the Big Fellow remarked that all Dublin was here – from the nannies pushing their charges around in perambulators, to the ragged children from the slums running barefooted on the grass.

'We were often taken here as children,' Patrick remarked, 'this was our back garden.'

'Did you ever come here alone?'

Patrick shook his head. 'We were always accompanied. Even as we grew older, someone always came with us.'

'You were never truly free then,' Collins remarked, watching a gang of street urchins run screaming through the trees. They were all barefoot, in ragged clothing, and yet they were all smiling; happy for the moment.

'The first time I experienced true freedom was earlier this year when I left home.'

'When you came searching for answers to your past …?'

Patrick nodded. 'Yes … unfortunately.'

'I take it you've found them.'

'I got the answers yesterday.'

They walked on in silence for a few moments, and then Collins said, 'I take it they weren't what you wanted.'

Patrick laughed humourlessly. 'You could say that.'

Collins took a turn to the left that would bring them around by the lake. He pointed to an empty seat and both men moved over and sat down on it. It was situated close to the water's edge, partially shaded by some bushes, and yet it afforded them a clear view in all directions.

'The Brigadier met with an accident,' Collins said conversationally.

'Oh,' Patrick said, suddenly discovering that his throat was completely dry. 'What sort of accident?'

'Shotgun at very close range. Both barrels.'

'Oh,' Patrick said again, waiting for Collins to continue, wondering if the big man could hear the pounding of his heart. 'Did we get him?'

Collins shook his head. 'Not ours. Perhaps his murky past caught up with him.'

Patrick suppressed a smile. In a way the Brigadier's past – in the shape of Patrick Lundy – had caught up with him.

'However, it also looks like we've got an informer in our midst.'

'Why? ... Because someone betrayed the Brigadier's location to the police,' Patrick answered his own question. 'Do you know who?'

'Not yet. I don't think he's highly placed though.'

'Why not?'

'He could have betrayed us at any time in the past, and there have been other occasions when the authorities might have caught some or all of us together.'

'I would have thought rescuing the Brigadier would be considered quite a coup.'

Michael Collins leaned forward and winked. 'Ah, it is, I suppose, but you know, I doubt if we'd have broken him. He was – for all his faults – a true professional,' he said with grudging admiration. He suddenly waved the thought aside with a quick movement of his hands. 'But tell me your story,' he said quickly.

'My story's got to do with betrayal,' Patrick said suddenly, not looking at Collins, his eyes on a group of children playing on the opposite side of the lake. 'What would you do to someone who had betrayed a great number of men, bringing them to almost certain death?'

'If that person was still alive, well then there would be a trial ... and execution.'

'But if there were a reason ... a very good reason for that act of betrayal.'

Collins shrugged. 'I don't know. Without knowing the circumstances, it's very difficult to say.' He turned to look at Patrick, noting the tense set of his jaw, the tension in his whole body. 'But I don't suppose you're going to tell me the circumstances, are you? This has something to do with your family, hasn't it?' he added shrewdly. 'How did you finally discover it?'

Still avoiding Collins' eye, Patrick launched into the story he had prepared while waiting for the Big Fellow to come down from his office in Harcourt Street. 'I finally managed to track down a retired whore who used to work for my mother. When your time on the streets or in the houses is over, most whores drift into moneylending – usually, but not always, to other whores – or they drift into the costume business, supplying dresses to the younger girls. That's what this woman had done until fairly recently, although she'd retired since about 1915. You know my mother ran one of the most exclusive brothels in Dublin?' Patrick asked.

'Only by hearsay,' Collins said drily.

Patrick grinned. 'Aye, well. She did, and that's the reason she was so close to this woman. I gather there were other connections, and I suspect the woman dealt in stolen goods – I know my mother certainly did. Anyway, this woman knew all about my family background; she knew about my mother, how she came to Ireland, and how she became involved with the Rising.'

'I thought your mother wasn't involved in the Rising?' Collins said quickly. 'Your father certainly played a part, but not Katherine Lundy ...'

'Listen. In 1898, my mother became pregnant by a man named Captain John Lewis, whom she later discovered was involved with the British Intelligence Service in Ireland. And later, when Dermot Corcoran, the man she later married became involved with the Volunteers, she feared for his safety, so she contacted

Lewis again, and offered to sell him whatever details she could glean about the Rising, in return for a pardon for Dermot. Dermot Corcoran, needless to say, knew nothing of this.

'Lewis agreed and gave her a sheet of paper – which she later discovered to be absolutely useless – and she passed on to him the date of the Rising, the landing of Casement's guns, various troop movements and dispositions.

'And then Dermot was killed in the GPO.

'So she killed Lewis. She took a gun around to his house on Clonliffe Road, and shot him twice.' Patrick's voice which had become more and more strained during the telling of the story, suddenly cracked. 'And I am John Lewis's son.'

There was a long silence after Patrick had finished. Collins's gaze was fixed straight ahead, absorbing and evaluating the startling revelations, and then he suddenly stood up. Looking down on Patrick, he said, 'And what has this to do with you?'

Patrick looked at him in astonishment. 'Don't you see? My mother betrayed the Rising to my father, who was a senior officer of the British Intelligence Service in Ireland.'

The Big Fellow frowned. 'I don't see what this had to do with you.'

'But how can you trust me?' Patrick demanded fiercely. 'How can you possibly trust me, knowing that?'

Collins smiled wistfully. 'I learned a long time ago to judge a man's character as I find it, not by his parents or his station or by the amount of money he possesses. What you've told me – while it is astonishing – doesn't alter my feelings towards you. Unless of course you would rather resign ...'

'No ... no,' Patrick said quickly. 'I don't want to. But there is something I want to do ... something I have to do.'

Collins looked at him.

Patrick stood up to face Collins. 'I want to go on active service. I have a debt to all those men who died because of the information my mother passed over. I owe them something ... and I owe it to myself. My father may have been John Lewis, but I think I'm more Dermot Corcoran's son.'

'You are that,' Michael Collins grinned, and then he sobered. 'You don't have to do this ...'

'I do ... I feel I do.'

'As you wish then.' He walked away from the seat, Patrick following him. 'I am creating a special Squad within my Intelligence Unit,' Collins said slowly, 'it will be accountable only to me, take orders only from me. It will do whatever I think necessary to further our cause ... and it will carry out those tasks without question. There will be killing involved,' he added softly.

'I realize that.'

'If you're interested, there's a place in it for you. You'll be paid four pounds, ten shillings a week, and I'll see you're treated well. If you do join up, it'll mean you will have no further contact with Nuala or the house in Tyrone Street under any circumstances. For this unit to operate and survive, it must do so in absolute secrecy. For generations, Irish societies and organizations have been bedevilled with informers and, as we saw only yesterday, our own organization is not immune, so you'll work with the other members of your unit, eat and drink with them, even sleep with them when your unit is on call.'

'You can count on me.'

'I already have. Now, I'll introduce you to the other members of your unit later. We'll meet in Vaughan's Hotel on Parnell Square at eight tonight.'

Michael Collins was walking away when Patrick asked: 'What will happen to my mother?'

Collins stopped and looked back at him. 'She committed a crime ...'

'Please ...'

'What do you want me to say, Patrick?' he snapped. 'Do you want me to tell you that nothing will happen to her, that she'll go unpunished. Although from what you've told me, perhaps a higher authority is already punishing her.'

'Will you order her execution?'

'At the moment, I've other things on my mind – she'll keep,' he smiled. 'We'll discuss it later. At the moment, we've got to plan our campaign against the authorities. If we're going to have any success against them, we're going to have to put out the eyes of the British. The first task of the new special unit, the Squad, will be to eradicate all British spies and informers.'

'All of them?'

'All of them.'

When Patrick Lundy arrived in Ireland in late January, 1919, he had been a boy. His experiences with Jane Bradley and later with Nuala Kennedy were to be his first introductions to the adult world.

In the months that followed, while the guerrilla war in the countryside intensified, Patrick Lundy went on active service as a member of Collins's Squad in Dublin and the suburbs. In those violent and bloody months he lost much of his humanity.

On the 12th of September, 1919, Patrick Lundy killed his first man – a detective constable – without a second thought. Detective Constable Hoey had just walked out of police headquarters in Great Brunswick Street, and rounded the corner into Townsend Street when Patrick, who had been lounging outside Tara Street Fire Station, along with two others from his squad, walked up to him and emptied the contents of his Savage automatic pistol into the man's back. Although he had been terrified before the shooting – terrified from the moment the Big Fellow had ordered him 'to take care of the man', when the moment of the shooting actually arrived, he had felt a deep calm come over him. By doing this he was in some way expiating his mother's guilt. He had pulled the trigger without a qualm. When he had shot Michael Lee – what seemed like a lifetime ago now – he had reviewed the killing again and again for weeks afterwards; the Townsend Street killing never cost him a thought.

He was part of the group which carried out a campaign of terror against known British informers, warning them of the inadvisability of continuing to work for the authorities. His ruthlessness set him apart from the others, and even within the organization, men learned to steer well clear of the man they had nick-named 'The German,' because of his blond Teutonic looks. Patrick's appearance had been altered by Eddie to such a degree that he felt himself that he could stand in front of his mother and not be recognized by her. His hair had been cut close to his scalp, so that it stood bristling on his head and then both hair and eyebrows had been bleached white. After several weeks on the run, he had acquired a gaunt, slightly haggard appearance – although he ate well, and slept equally well – and he had adopted the nervous habit of rubbing his chin with the forefinger of his left hand, the sound rasping and irritating.

He was part of the group which shot down Detective Sergeant Barton on 30th November. Patrick did not actually pull the trigger, but he was the man who stopped and engaged the detective in conversation, while the two other members of his unit opened fire on the man. As he fell to the ground dying, Patrick had calmly turned and walked away.

Patrick had few friends within the organization; Collins being his closest associate, but Collins was now on every wanted list, and Patrick saw less and less of him. With nothing else for him in Ireland, the Cause soon came to mean everything. He was obsessed with eradicating his mother's sin, and he felt that so long as he continued to carry out his duties, then Collins wouldn't order her assassination. Men had been killed for betraying just one man, but she had betrayed an entire revolution. She had been judged and found guilty, and the punishment was death – and the only thing keeping her from receiving her just punishment was his performance.

He had no contact with Nuala, and while she attempted to keep track of him through her contacts within the organization, no one there knew of anyone who vaguely resembled Patrick Lundy, and although she was aware of the 'German's' activities, she never made the connection between the two.

Christmas of that year was a sombre one. The violence that had swept through the country over the past few months had brought much bitterness in its wake, and there were few families who had not lost either a relative or friend and there were many empty places around the tables for Christmas dinner.

Nuala celebrated quietly with Jem; they ate and drank too much and afterwards they made love for the first time since Patrick Lundy had usurped Jem's place in Nuala's bed. It was not that she loved the bouncer, she was simply lonely, and as he moved atop her body, she closed her eyes and wondered where Patrick was now; she wondered if he was still alive.

Patrick Lundy was very much alive, and working not a mile away from Monto. He was standing in the foyer of the Hibernian Hotel on Dawson Street with one of Collins' Intelligence Officers. The two men were chatting quietly together, and Patrick was carrying a brightly wrapped parcel under his arm. The hotel was brightly decorated and an enormous Christmas tree dominated one corner of the foyer, and from the lounge drifted the sounds of too many people ushering in the Christmas spirit early. Every time the door opened, both men looked up and then their heads dipped back down again. When a slight, sallow-skinned young man appeared the Intelligence Officer simply said, 'That's him,' and then walked away, heading into the lounge. He needed a drink to settle his stomach. His part was done.

Patrick walked outside onto the bitterly cold street and waited for the young man to appear. He was calm and composed, as he always was when he was working, his mind fixed on the job in hand, nothing else intruding into his single-minded determination. He waited patiently for over an hour before the sallow-skinned man appeared, pushing his way through the revolving doors of the hotel and hurrying down the steps. He immediately turned to the left, heading down Dawson Street. Patrick hurried to catch up with him, and when he was alongside the man, said, 'Excuse me ...?'

The young man turned to look at him, a smile beginning to appear on his lips. 'Yes ... can I help ...?'

'Happy Christmas ... informer!' Patrick pushed the barrels of the shotgun through the brightly coloured Christmas paper and shot the man at point-blank range. Without a backward glance he turned to the left and calmly walked down South Anne Street, heading for Grafton Street.

The church bells were tolling ten.

CHAPTER TWENTY-TWO

It was, Nuala reflected, one of the coldest days she could remember. She sat close to the small fire, a blanket around her knees, a book resting unread on the arm of the table.

The house was silent, the bitter weather having severely curtailed business. Trade had been down by more than fifty per cent over the Christmas period, and while, traditionally, the houses did less business over the holiday season – a lot of her clients found that their consciences began to bother them about this time – this year had been disastrous. And the unstable political situation hadn't helped. The city was tense, liable to erupt in sudden violence, and the presence of the police almost oppressive, and that too discouraged ordinary people from walking the cold, hard streets.

Christmas Day and New Year's Day, 1920, had fallen on a Thursday, which meant that business tonight – Friday, the second of January – should have been getting back to normal. Whatever pangs of conscience and New Year's resolutions her clients would have had or made, would be due to be forgotten about now. At least that's how it had been every other year ...

But not this year ...

Nuala glanced at the clock: it was close to ten and there hadn't been one person in. Nuala watched the grey ash appear over the fire. If business didn't improve, she would have to let some of the girls go – and she hated the very thought of it; in the house they had some protection both from the customers and the police, but on the streets they had none. Here at least there were certain standards of cleanliness and hygiene maintained, prices were fixed, and the girls had the advantage of having Jem and the other male servants around. Nuala herself dealt with the police, which lent the girls a certain anonymity, and at least allowed them to walk the streets unmolested by the officers of the law. It was a popular fallacy that the police took their payment in kind – in all her years in the trade, Nuala had only known one officer who preferred to receive his payment with one of the girls every week, rather than in hard cash.

Well, if there wasn't going to be any business tonight, she might as well prepare for bed, catch up on her sleep – although she'd been doing a lot of catching up in the last week or so. She was actually banking down the fire when there was a tap on the door and Jem entered. She knew immediately that something was wrong.

'We've got a visitor,' he said briefly. 'You'd better come with me.'

Nuala followed him down into the kitchen and there – crouched in the seat he'd last occupied nearly six months ago – was Patrick Lundy. Thinner, gaunter, his eyes deep sunk, his hair no more than a fuzz atop his head, the beginnings of a beard on his chin. It sounded almost a paradox – but although he looked virtually unrecognizable, she still recognized him. Something twisted inside her, something deep in the pit of her stomach and high in her chest.

When he looked up at her, she was suddenly terrified by the look in his eyes – it was like looking into the face of a beast.

'What brings you back?' she said finally, her voice little more than a whisper, the pounding of her heart making it difficult for her to catch her breath.

Patrick moved stiffly in the seat and lifted his left hand onto the table, palm upwards. It was covered in blood.

'Patrick …' Nuala said urgently, and Jem just managed to catch him before he hit the floor.

'He's very lucky,' Doctor Montague Meredith said, stepping out of the room and facing Nuala and Michael Collins. 'The first bullet struck him from behind, entering just below his right bottom rib, striking it at an angle, and exiting almost directly above his navel. The second passed between two ribs, nicked the bottom of his lung, thereby collapsing it, and then exited straight out through the front of his chest – also passing between two ribs. If it had struck either of the sets of ribs, it might have been deflected up into the chest cavity or downwards into his stomach or any of the larger body organs.'

Nuala turned away so the two men wouldn't see the tears on her face, and walked down the corridor, leaving them to follow her.

Collins asked the question she was afraid to ask. 'Will he live?'

'He's lost a lot of blood,' the small stout doctor said cautiously, 'but undoubtedly his medical training saved him. He did his best to stop the flow of blood … Yes, I think he'll live.'

Supper had been prepared and set out on the sideboard while the doctor had attended to Patrick, and Nuala began filling two plates.

'You should not have gone to any trouble on our account …' the Big Fellow began.

Nuala shook her head. 'It was no trouble. Thank you for coming. Thank you both.'

'You're lucky your man found me first time,' Michael Collins said to Nuala, 'it was only coincidence that I knew where the good doctor was plying his trade this night.'

Nuala poured herself a cup of tea and went to sit by the fire, which had been re-lit and now blazed up the chimney. 'Where did he find you – Vaughan's Hotel?'

Collins sat down in the seat directly across from her, a plate piled high with cold meats perched precariously on his knee. 'The same.'

The doctor sat on one of the high-backed chairs against the wall beside the sideboard, picking at the food with his fork. 'I was around the corner in Hill Street tending to one of our lads who had suffered at the hands of the police.'

'How is he?' Collins asked immediately looking across at the doctor, concern on his broad face.

'Bruised and battered. He's a couple of cracked ribs, a cracked cheekbone and his nose is broken. He'll mend.'

'Does he know who did it?'

The doctor nodded. 'They were uniformed and their numbers are engraved on his memory.'

Collins nodded grimly. 'We'll attend to them later.' He attacked his meat with particular intentness, and then looked across at Nuala. 'Would you be prepared to keep Patrick here – at least until he mends? I know it's an imposition on you – but at the moment, we really have no other place to go. I'm sure you're aware of the situation we're in at the moment.'

Nuala nodded. The conflict between the authorities and the IRA had turned into almost open warfare in the streets. 'I'll keep him … I don't suppose I've any choice.'

'Oh, you have a choice,' Collins said immediately. 'If you say no, then we'll find someplace else for him … one of our houses in the suburbs or even the country. But I'm sure he wouldn't get the same care as you'd give him,' he added persuasively.

'I'll keep him … you know I'll keep him.' She looked intently at Collins. 'Have you any idea who did this?'

The Big Fellow glanced at the doctor, and Nuala felt sure she had missed something. She turned to look at the doctor. 'Do you know who shot him?'

'It is being investigated at the moment,' Collins said quickly, 'we'll let you know what happens.' He wiped his mouth with a napkin and stood up. 'And now we really must go. We don't want to draw any undue attention to this house at the moment, eh?'

Nuala came slowly to her feet, wondering why the sudden hurry to leave the warmth and food – unless there was a reason.

'The doctor will call to check on Patrick every day – and he will leave an address where he can be contacted at any time in case of emergencies.' Although he had made it sound like a simple statement, Nuala recognized the command in his voice.

The doctor also came to his feet – much more reluctantly than the Big Fellow. 'He'll sleep for a while, and I've left some morphine for the pain. Make sure he doesn't get too much of it.'

'I understand.'

Both men hurried from the room and Nuala followed them out onto the landing and then stood at the top of the stairs listening to them make their way downstairs. She heard Jem wish them a good night and then the hall door opened and closed again almost immediately. She shivered in the wind that had gusted up the stairs, and then turned away to stand outside the door to Patrick's room, her hand on the handle. She was almost afraid to open the door; what would she do if she found him dead? Although she hadn't seen him in months, it was only now, now that he had stepped back into her life, that she realized that she still loved him.

Jem came up the stairs and stood behind her, not touching her, aware that she was troubled by something. 'What's wrong?'

She shook her head. She wasn't sure herself what was amiss – just the vague feeling that perhaps Collins hadn't been as open with her as he should. She respected the need for secrecy, but she was sheltering one of his men – he owed her the courtesy of telling her the truth.

'Do you still have contacts within the Volunteers?' she asked suddenly.

'Some,' he said cautiously. 'They've become a lot more secretive in the past year or so,' he added, knowing what Nuala was going to ask, 'but I'll see what I can find out.' He leaned forward and kissed the nape of her neck … and she froze. Jem stepped away, nodding slightly, his suspicions confirmed, and then he turned and headed down the stairs without another word.

Nuala opened the door and stepped into Patrick's room. It felt hot and close and the air was tainted with the metallic odour of blood overlain with the sharper, harsher taint of ether. Patrick lay still and unmoving in the centre of the bed. He looked almost transparent against the white sheets, and she had to strain to see the rise and fall of his chest. She crossed to the bed and pulled the sheets up to his chin, and then clasped his hands under the blanket. They felt as cool and as fragile as a child's, although there were now pads of hard flesh at the base and the tips of his fingers. She smiled fondly remembering the first time she had felt his hands – she had marvelled then how any man's hands could be so soft. His hands had lost that softness, much as he had lost a lot of his gentleness. Another victim of the Rising. She looked at the lines on his face, the furrows on his brows, and the crease marks along his cheeks and wondered what troubles had etched themselves into his face.

And she wondered what he'd been doing over the past six months ...

Doctor Meredith returned around noon the following day. Under Nuala's watchful eye, he changed the dressing and then injected Patrick with an ampoule of morphine. He worked quickly and efficiently, but seemed unusually nervous, and at first Nuala thought he might have been followed.

When she suggested that he could leave by the back door, he gratefully accepted, and only then did she guess that the man was embarrassed to be seen in a known brothel in broad daylight. After all what would his patients say – mind you, she smiled, if any of his patients were in a position to be able to report on the doctor's whereabouts, they certainly weren't likely to go spreading it abroad ... explaining what they had been doing in the same neighbourhood might just prove to be a little too difficult.

Shaking her head in amusement, Nuala went back to Patrick's bedside, where she had spent the night, her hand clasped in his. He was still sleeping, his restlessness of the last few hours eased by the morphine the Doctor had injected. Brushing strands of hair from his eyes she sat down beside him and slipped his damp hand into hers. For the moment, she was content.

Nuala nodded off around three in the afternoon. She awoke with a start some hours later to discover that night had fallen, and from below she could hear the faint sounds of merriment. At least there were some customers in tonight. She went to move – and then discovered that Patrick's fingers had tightened on her hand, and even as she watched, his breathing grew ragged and suddenly his eyes opened. The pupils were large, the eyes terrified, his face twisted into a tight angry mask, and then his terrifying expression faded and something like a smile twisted his lips. He tried to speak, but he couldn't form the words.

Nuala pressed her fingertips to his lips. 'Sssh. Say nothing. You've been wounded. You're back home. Everything is going to be all right.'

Patrick's eyes fluttered and closed – and then snapped open again. His fingers clawed at the flesh of her hand, tearing the skin, grinding the bones together, and his mouth opened in a gasp of pain.

'Jem … Jem!' Nuala shouted.

The door crashed open as the German appeared almost immediately, a short leather strap almost lost in his hands. He disengaged Patrick's fingers carefully and then pressed both his hands to the sheets.

'The morphine,' he said quietly to Nuala, 'he is in pain.'

Nuala's fingers felt stiff and bruised where Patrick had squeezed them, and she could barely wrench the drawer open and pull out the long black case the doctor had left. Snapping open the catch, she lifted out the hypodermic, and then, desperately attempting to follow Meredith's instructions, she filled it from the purple coloured bottle he had left. Holding the needle straight up in the air, she carefully depressed the plunger, watching the clear liquid squirt upwards.

Jem meanwhile had pushed up Patrick's pyjama jacket, exposing his arm, already puckered with punctures from where Meredith had previously injected him.

'I can't,' Nuala said suddenly. She looked at Jem. 'I can't.'

The big man grimaced. 'I will do it. But you must talk to him. Tell him I'm going to give him relief from the pain. He mustn't struggle. If the needle breaks in his arm, it could kill him.'

Nuala knelt by the side of the bed and cradled Patrick's head in her arms. Placing her mouth close to his ear, she began to whisper to him, crooning to him like a mother to a child, promising relief from the pain that even now consumed his body.

Jem wound a length of cloth around Patrick's arm, bringing the veins up and then checked the needle again. Lying the needle almost flat against his arm, he pressed it into the flesh, piercing the skin, and then slowly eased the plunger home ...

The result was almost immediate.

With a hissing sigh, Patrick relaxed, and Nuala felt him go limp in her arms. His eyes closed easily and his face, which had been locked into a rigid mask, smoothed out.

'He'll sleep now,' Jem said shortly, wiping a tiny spot of blood from Patrick's arm. 'I suggest you do the same.'

Nuala looked up from her position beside the bed. 'I want to be here when he awakens.'

Jem lifted the empty needle into the air. 'He won't be waking for awhile. And you can do nothing for him now except watch him sleep. Come on.' He reached down and Nuala almost reluctantly took his hand and rose to her feet. 'Get some rest. I'll have some tea brought up to you soon. In the meantime, I'll clean this.'

Nuala looked at the needle with its darkened, bloodstained tip. 'Thank you. And thank you for injecting him. I just couldn't ...'

The German shrugged. 'Some people can't. But it

never cost me any bother.' He turned away before Nuala could ask any more questions about her servant's enigmatic past. She knew surprisingly little about him, although he had been with her now since late 1916; he had worked in the brothels in Berlin, and Paris; had sailed aboard ships both legitimate and otherwise, and had spent some time in South Africa, and when they had first made love he had showed her the 'tricks' he had learned from the women of Peking. She didn't love him, although she felt comfortable and safe in his presence, and she guessed he didn't love her. Perhaps that was why they got on so well together.

Jem brought her in a tray of tea about half an hour later. She was sitting up in bed, a heavy woollen shawl one of the girls had brought back from the West of Ireland thrown over her shoulders, a newspaper spread out on the coverlet before her.

Jem sat down on the edge of the bed, poured two cups of tea, and passed hers across. They drank in silence for a few moments, and then Nuala asked, 'Are we busy?'

Jem shrugged. 'Four tourists in. They're talking about an orgy with all the girls involved, but they've had a bit to drink, and I doubt if they can get up to anything in their condition.'

Nuala looked at him closely, wondering if he was making a joke, and then deciding that the slip had been accidental.

'They wanted to know if there was a special bargain rate for orgies,' Jem continued seriously. Without smiling, he added, 'They wanted to know if they paid for all the girls and they didn't get around to some, would they get a refund.'

Nuala sipped her tea. 'What did you say?'

'I told them that this was like a fruit market; they paid for all the fruit they took, and whether they ate it or not was not our concern.' He smiled briefly, showing his strong teeth.

'I don't think I've heard that expression before,' she

smiled. 'There are other versions, but that is the polite one.'

'Jem – what are we going to do about Patrick?' Nuala asked suddenly.

'I've a feeling we've had this conversation before,' the German grinned.

'You know what I mean!' Nuala snapped, more forcibly than she intended. 'I'm sorry,' she said immediately, 'it's just ...'

'You're tired,' Jem nodded. 'I know.' He poured another cup of tea for himself; Nuala shook her head when he lifted the pot in her direction. 'We can do nothing for the moment,' he said finally, 'the man is wounded, and cannot easily be moved. When he recovers, I would imagine he will go back on active service with his unit, and our problem will be solved.'

'Have you managed to make any contact with your friends in the organization?'

Jem shook his head. 'Some, but I haven't heard anything about the shooting yet,' he lied. Jem had heard enough rumours to be able to put two and two together. He had a very good idea who had shot Patrick Lundy – and why. 'All the talk now is about some advertisements that have appeared in the English newspapers looking for auxiliary policemen to work in Ireland.'

'Will they get anyone?' Nuala wondered.

Jem shrugged. 'There's a lot of unemployed army boys,' he suggested.

'Ah well,' she passed her empty cup across to Jem and threw back the shawl, sliding down beneath the covers, 'I don't suppose they'll cause us any trouble.'

Jem leaned over and kissed her forehead. 'No, I suppose not.'

They were both wrong.

CHAPTER TWENTY-THREE

First there was the, ragged searing, consuming pain ... and then the pleasure ... ice-cold, silk–smooth pleasure ... and with the pleasure came the dreams ... the dreams were an escape, an escape from the dreariness, the pain, the loneliness and the fear ... in the dreams there was peace and contentment.

Like a child that has learned to associate crying with attention, Patrick Lundy had learned to associate the pain with pleasure, and at some deep unconsious level he realized that if he cried out then there would come the pleasure and the dreams.

The young man opened his mouth and screamed ...

Nuala closed the door behind her and crossed the room to sit before the fire, facing Patrick, who was bundled up in a blanket huddled before the fire. In the past six weeks he had lost a lot of weight, his skin had pulled taut over his bones, giving his face a vaguely skull–like appearance, his eyes had sunk back into his head and were black rimmed, feverishly bright against the ivory colour of his skin. She looked at him for a few moments, and then asked, 'How do feel?'

Patrick nodded, and then attempted a smile. 'Better ... much better.'

'The doctor tells me your collapsed lung has re-inflated ...'

Patrick nodded. 'I can breathe now. It hurts a little ... that's all.'

'Is there any pain?' she asked carefully, watching him closely.

'Some ... a little, but I can cope with it. The nights are the worst for some reason.'

Nuala nodded. 'Jem tells me you had a bad night last night.'

Patrick tried to grin, but only his lips twisted, turning it into a grimace. 'Everything ached together. Maybe I overdid it yesterday.'

She nodded. 'But you managed to get some sleep?'

'Jem gave me an injection.'

The woman nodded slightly. She was becoming concerned with the amount of morphine Patrick seemed to require to ease his pain. 'And how are things today? Is there any pain?'

Patrick started to shake his head and then seemingly changed his mind. 'Some ... a little.'

Nuala nodded. She stood up and tucked the blanket in around him, adjusting the pillows behind his back. 'Is there anything you want?' she asked. He shook his head and she settled back into the chair.

The silence between them grew; neither seemed inclined to break it. Patrick was too wrapped up in his pain; the burning in his lungs and at the base of his stomach was bearable at the moment, but soon that pain would intensify until it felt as if his whole body was on fire. But the drugs would help that. It had become something of a game ... a tantalizing game: to see how long he could last before screaming out for the drug. And then the pleasure would be all the more intense because it had been delayed and anticipated. He was startled and almost annoyed when Nuala spoke again, breaking into his reverie.

'Do you want to talk to me, to tell me what happened?'

It took a few moments for him to realize that she was talking to him, and when he looked at her, his eyes were distant, clouded.

Nuala leaned forward. 'What happened, Patrick? What happened to you?'

He shrugged and then winced as stitches pulled. 'I got careless.'

'That's not what I meant and you know it.'

'I was on duty and I was shot,' he said stubbornly. He could cry out now, scream out his pain and hunger and then wait for the blessed relief.

Something in his expression betrayed him, and Nuala's face closed, her eyes hardening. 'You owe it to me,' she snapped. 'I need to know.'

'I owe you …?' Patrick whispered, 'what do I owe you for?'

'When you were wounded, where did you run, where did you come to? And who took you in,' she pressed on, 'who took you in and cared for you, whose fire are you sitting before now, whose food have you been eating, who has paid for the medicines for you? All I'm asking in return is an explanation.'

'He's a killer,' Jem said suddenly, stepping into the room, carrying a tea tray, 'he started out as part of Collins' Special squad who specialized in removing British spies in Ireland. But then something happened and Patrick here started out on something of a personal vendetta, removing those he saw as a threat … police, army officers, ordinary men and women whose only crime was to collaborate with the "enemy".' Without looking at either Patrick or Nuala, Jem spread the cutlery on the small side table, and laid out the plates. 'His nickname in the organization is the German, would you believe,' Jem smiled tightly, 'because of his appearance.' He glanced in Patrick's direction; the nickname wouldn't hold true now; Patrick's hair had grown and regained its former colour, and the rough growth of beard on his face gave him a shabby appearance. He looked like a man approaching fifty. 'Mister Lundy killed people, Nuala, usually from close range, with a small automatic pistol or a shotgun. He has done so callously, apparently without regret and certainly without question. Even within the organization he fights for he is loathed by the ordinary rank and file.'

Jem was about to continue, but Nuala held up her hand. 'Is this true?' she whispered, her eyes fixed on Patrick's face.

Patrick stared at Jem for a few moments before turning back to Nuala. 'I have killed people,' he admitted.

'Can you remember how many?' Jem asked quickly.

'I didn't keep count!' Patrick snapped and then winced.

'He's shot down policemen in the streets, administered beatings, punishment shootings, threatened and terrorized. I never met his mother ... but from what I've heard of her, she'd have been well proud of her son.'

'So would his father,' Nuala murmured, standing up and crossing to the window; suddenly she didn't want to be close to the stranger she thought she knew. She turned away from the window and looked at him. 'Tell me it isn't true.'

Patrick looked at her defiantly. 'It's true.'

'Why?'

'I did what I was told.'

'Without question?' she demanded. 'But Jem said you went on some sort of rampage ...'

'Yes, it's true in the beginning I did what I was told to do, but then I did what I had to do!' he suddenly blazed. 'I had my reasons.'

Jem went to stand beside Nuala. 'And you think you love him?' he asked contemptuously. 'You don't even know him.'

Patrick's head came up and he looked curiously at Nuala.

She shook her head. 'I don't love him,' she said quickly, but even to Patrick's ears it lacked conviction.

'He's a murderer, Nuala, and he's the worst kind – he doesn't kill for money or gain, he doesn't even kill for love – he kills because he feels it is right. He has made himself a god with the power of life and death.'

'I never killed anyone who didn't deserve death,' Patrick said defiantly.

'And what are you: a judge, jury ... and executioner?' Patrick started to shake his head, but the German continued on, his voice low and hard, his German

320

accent more pronounced now. 'Do you know what this great hero did in the cause of Irish freedom? On Christmas Eve he shot a man in Dawson Street ... I'm sure he'll say it was an order, but no one sanctioned this killing. This man was married, with a two year old daughter, and his wife was pregnant with a second child, due in April of this year. Now how about that for a Christmas present for the woman? She lost her baby,' he added, 'another casualty to your cause.'

'I don't see ...' Patrick said through gritted teeth.

'But the dead man had friends ... and even his enemies were sickened by the brutal killing. And on the second of last month they caught up with Mister Lundy here. And do you know something – they were IRA. The dead man was IRA. You shot one of your own men – and you were shot by your own people!'

Patrick opened his mouth and screamed with the pain and anguish.

Jem's hand abruptly clamped around his throat, choking him, cutting off his air. 'Don't scream,' he said evenly. When he stepped back from the chair, there were livid finger marks across Patrick's throat. Tears gathered in his eyes, but remained there, unshed. 'You've become a mad dog – even your own people don't want you,' the German hissed. He suddenly turned on his heel and strode from the room, leaving Patrick and Nuala alone.

'Nuala ...?' Patrick began, but she turned her back on him, looking down into the street below. 'Nuala ... I didn't know ... you've got to believe me, I didn't know he was one of our own ... I wouldn't ...'

'Would it have made any difference to you if you had known?'

'I was told he was an informer ...'

'Do you believe everything you're told?' she blazed, rounding on him. 'Do you think it excused you. Do you sleep easy with your conscience?'

'It never bothered me,' he mumbled.

'Well think about it then,' she hissed. 'Think about the

man you killed on Christmas Eve, think about his wife and child waking up on Christmas Day with the Christmas present you'd given them, think about the woman losing her child because of you. Think about that, Patrick Lundy!' She stalked from the room, not looking at him.

'Nuala,' Patrick whispered, 'the pain ... I need something ...' He heard her door slam further down the corridor.

Patrick Lundy sat before the dying fire, staring deep into the flames. He was aware of a sickness deep in his stomach, and he knew if he concentrated too long on it, he would vomit. His throat felt raw – scorched almost – and he felt as if his head were about to explode. He almost expected to feel his wounds rip open, and his blood spurt out in time to the pounding. He was also aware of the pain of his healing wounds – it was bearable at the moment, but it was accompanied by the hunger, the terrible, gnawing hunger that could only be soothed by the needle. He deliberately turned his thoughts from the needle and tried to concentrate on some of the things he'd have to sort out ... had he really been shot by his own people ... and why ... and? But the pain was too much; it was a fiery blanket smothering him and he knew that without the pain he would be able to think more clearly.

Patrick Lundy came slowly to his feet, the blanket sliding off his shoulders. Although it was warm in the room, and he was wearing a heavy woollen dressing gown over his pyjamas, he felt suddenly chilled. Shivering, he attempted to retrieve the blanket, but his stomach wounds prevented him from bending. With his right arm pressed tightly across his stomach, crouched over like an old man, he inched his way across the room, moving towards the table Jem had laid out for tea. Although he was shivering with the chill, sweat popped out on his forehead and began to trickle down his face and he could feel moisture under his arms and down his back. It was perhaps a dozen steps to the table – but he considered it a major victory when he reached it. From the table to the door another eight steps, and when he had reached that far he had to stop, resting his head against the door frame, attempting to control his breathing, unwilling to strain his tender lungs. He was covered in a fine sheen of sweat – and chilled right through to the bone. Even his teeth were chattering. Every bone in his body ached now, and the pain across his stomach was a tight close-fitting band. He had to dry his hand on his dressing gown before he could turn the handle of the door and manoeuvre his way out into the corridor, but once he had achieved that it was surprisingly easy to make his way – pressed tight against the wall – down the corridor to his room.

The needle was in its case in the top drawer of the chest of drawers. Alongside it was the bottle of clear liquid, a morphine solution, Doctor Meredith had left. Stuffing the bottle into his pocket and holding the black box containing the needle, he lurched across to the bed and then collapsed onto it. He lay on the bed for perhaps five minutes attempting to catch his breath and regain control of his hands which had now started to tremble almost uncontrollably.

It took him two attemps to prise the lid off the bottle and another two attempts to fill the syringe. He wasn't sure what dosage he was on, but from his medical days he estimated ... how much? He stopped abruptly. How much? What dosage was he on, what strength was the solution in the bottle? To have come so far and to be thwarted now ... he daren't risk it; an overdose would kill him.

And then the hunger rose up and consumed him ...

Patrick half-filled the syringe and hoped it was enough. With trembling fingers he injected himself in the back of the hand, and then pulled himself up onto the bed to await the needle's results. It came moments later, and suddenly all the pain, and the questions vanished. The world was a much simpler place, and as he drifted off to sleep, he solved all his problems, and Nuala's ...

'He injected himself,' Jem said, 'we called you as soon as we discovered what had happened.'

'How much has he taken?'

Jem lifted the bottle. 'I've been marking it,' he tapped the bottle with his blunt fingernail. 'There's his regular dose, and that's what's missing ...'

'That's nearly twice his usual dosage.'

Jem nodded, but said nothing.

'How long has he been asleep?'

'Four, five hours ... something like that.'

The doctor checked Patrick's heart rate again. It was shallow and rapid. He glanced at Jem and shrugged; both men knew there was nothing they could do now – except to wait for the drug to run through Patrick's system. 'Let's hope he makes it,' the doctor muttered, glancing sidelong at the German, 'Collins won't like it if he doesn't survive.'

Jem glanced at him, but said nothing.

Whatever reaction Michael Collins had been expecting he certainly hadn't expected the verbal attack Nuala launched the moment he arrived. He sat quietly, listening to her rage at him, wondering briefly at her sources of information: whatever they were, they were very good and he resolved to make a definite effort to plug that source as soon as he got back to his office. Finally, when she had run out of steam and invective, he began to speak, his strong dark eyes holding hers, his voice calm, measured, confident. 'I didn't make Patrick Lundy a killer,' he said evenly, 'he placed himself in that role, and yes I used it, I'll not deny that. Like most medical men he makes an excellent killer – for he is able to view the human body dispassionately. It is also true that he undertook several very hazardous operations for us in the past few months. He is considered one of our best operatives.'

'And ...?' Nuala asked tightly.

Collins shrugged, a quick movement of his hands and shoulders. 'He took it upon himself to carry out some unauthorized operations.'

'He killed people,' Nuala stated flatly.

Collins nodded.

'Did you authorize those killings?'

'I did not.'

'So he was a renegade?'

'Yes, well you could say that.'

'Well, why didn't you take care of him yourselves? Why did you allow him to run amok the way he did?'

'Our own security system beat us,' he confessed. 'We just didn't know where he was from one day to the next. We were catching up with him – following the trail of bodies – when the Christmas shooting took place.'

'What happened?' Nuala demanded.

'It was an accident,' Collins continued simply, 'a tragic accident. Somewhere down along the line, Patrick learned that we suspected this young man of being an informer ... Patrick didn't wait for any evidence.'

'And was he?'

'What?'

'Was he an informer?'

'We'll never know now. The young man was a member of one of our cells; the other members were of course unaware of the suspicions surrounding him, and so they assumed that he had been killed by the authorities. Because of his ... ahem, his marital status and the timing of the killing, feelings ran high, and by a series of coincidences and good – or bad, as the case may be – luck, they stumbled on Patrick's identity. They concluded that he was a British spy – and his accent helped there – and so they tracked him down, ambushed him, and shot him.'

'So he was shot by his own men.'

Collins smiled a little sadly. 'A victim of our own secrecy, I'm afraid.'

Nuala leaned forward and for a moment Michael Collins thought she was going to strike out at him. 'Did you know the dead man's wife was pregnant?' she whispered.

Collins shook his head. 'I knew afterwards,' he said quietly. They stared at each other for a few moments, and then Collins said, 'Does Patrick know?'

'He knows. I thought it best to tell him.'

The Big Fellow nodded his head slightly. 'Perhaps it would have been better to allow him to regain his full health,' he suggested.

Nuala said nothing.

'The doctor tells me his progress is mixed – physically, he seems to be healing well, although he apparently complains of great pain.'

She nodded.

'The doctor is worried that he has become overly fond of the morphine – would you agree?'

Nuala raised her eyes and looked at Collins. 'He is an addict,' she said simply.

'Aaah,' Collins breathed, his face registering distaste, and Nuala instinctively knew that this strong, proud man would have little time for the weaknesses of others.

'You took a boy, a simple boy,' she continued, her voice filled with hate, 'you turned him into a killer, a murderer, and now that he's a morphine addict because of you, you've no further use for him.'

Collins stood up suddenly. 'Patrick Lundy has been temporarily retired from active service – that's all. When he's well again, he can resume his old place in the Squad.' He nodded to her and strode across to the door.

'And that's it?' Nuala asked incredulously, 'you're just going to walk out and leave him like that? Surely, you'll see him before you go?'

For a single moment, Nuala thought he was going to say no, but then he nodded his head. 'I'll see him,' he said quietly.

Michael Collins stepped into the room, and closed the door behind him, and then stood with his back against the wood looking at the vague shape on the bed. The room was in semi-darkness, and smelt warm and close, the odours of sweat and medication predominating. 'The Patrick Lundy I knew wouldn't have allowed me to walk straight into his room like that,' he said loudly into the dimness.

Patrick stirred at the sound of the voice and turned over in the bed to look at the Big Fellow. He attempted to smile, but his muscles wouldn't obey him, and it turned into a scowl.

'How do you feel?' Collins asked.

Patrick thought about it for a few moments, and then nodded. 'Fine … I feel … fine.'

'Is there any pain?'

Even from across the room he could see Patrick's expression change. 'Oh yes, there's pain. But it's getting better,' he said hurriedly.

Collins walked over to the bed and looked down at Patrick. From the doctor he knew that the wounds were healed and, aside from a little bruising, there were no ill effects. 'When will you be getting back to us Patrick, we need you.'

Patrick nodded. 'Soon I think.' He nodded more vigorously. 'Soon.'

Collins sat down on the end of the bed, and Patrick eased himself into a sitting position. 'The authorities have been advertising in England for new recruits for the police force over here. My sources tell me they're choosing mainly unemployed ex-army.'

Patrick thought about it. 'Experienced men,' he said at last, his tongue moistening his lips.

Collins nodded. 'Aye, and they could be here within the month – certainly by the end of March at the latest.'

Patrick nodded. 'Yes … I should be back by then … certainly by then.'

Collins temper suddenly flared. 'You have a week. If you're not back by then, don't bother. I want men committed to the cause, not to some bottle or needle.'

'No … it's just the pain,' Patrick said, his eyes filling with tears.

'Within the week,' Collins said, surging to his feet. The door rattled on its hinges as he left and even Patrick could hear him clump his way downstairs. He waited to hear the front door close, but when he heard nothing, he knew the Big Fellow had left by the back door.

The door to his room opened quietly and a tall blond-haired figure stepped inside.

Patrick started, and then relaxed. 'I thought ... he'd come back.'

'How's the pain?'

Patrick nodded. 'It's ... all right.'

The point of the needle glistened in the wan light. 'Then you don't need this?'

Patrick looked at the needle for a few moments and then slowly rolled up his sleeve. 'Thank ... thank you ...' he gasped and the drug coursed through his system. He looked at the figure with blurring eyes. 'You're a good friend ...' he murmured.

Jem wiped the blood from Patrick's arm and rolled down his sleeve, before leaving the room.

CHAPTER TWENTY-FOUR

On March 26th, 1920, eight hundred of the newly enrolled 'special constables' arrived in Ireland. Because of a shortage of uniforms, the men wore the dark green police cap and uniform, and the khaki army trousers, and they quickly became known by the name which was to spread terror throughout Ireland – the Black and Tans.

And with the arrival of the Black and Tans the war with the flying columns of the Volunteers took on a new and bloody phase.

There were times when he frightened her, times when he terrified her. When she had first known him, he had been a quiet gentle individual, and then when he had fought with Collins' Squad, he had obviously been a ruthless killer, and so she imagined that the real Patrick Lundy must lie somewhere in between. But now she only saw the extremes.

Patrick had recovered from his wounds – his physical wounds. The healing had taken a long time, and the man who emerged looked considerably older than the wounded man who had lain down on the bed. He had lost nearly four stone in weight and now weighed little more than six stones, skeletal and gaunt, and his skin had assumed a pasty yellowish tinge. His hair had grown and he hadn't shaved in months – although Jem occasionally trimmed his beard – and he looked like a man in his fifties or sixties. He complained of pain all the time – a residual ache from his wounds, pains and stiffness in his joints, constant headaches. He rarely ate, because of the cramps he suffered, and the only relief he got was with the drug.

Jem administered the morphine for Patrick when the pain became more than he could bear. He had tried to do it himself at first, but only succeeded in puncturing his flesh and failing to find a vein. When Nuala became alarmed at the quantity of the drug Patrick was taking, Jem had assured her that he had watered down the dosage, so that Patrick was actually getting far less now than he imagined. It wasn't much, but it gave her some solace.

Unfortunately Jem was lying.

The tall German was determined that Patrick Lundy was going to succumb to his morphine addiction. He had examined the problem posed by the wounded man carefully and decided that it would be far better for everyone concerned if Patrick simply didn't wake up one morning. But it had to look like an accident.

He had been able to sympathize with him to some extent when Patrick had first arrived in Ireland, for he had run away from home when he was a lad. His father had been a Junker, who had served with distinction in the German colonies in Africa before retiring to his homeland in the beautiful Black Forest. He had fully expected his son to follow him into the military, and the argument that had followed Jem's refusal to take up the service had been extraordinarily vehement. So the young man – barely into his teens at that stage – had run away. He had ended up in Berlin and through chance had drifted into a life of petty crime, before finally ending up working in a male brothel in the red light district, where his clear good looks and youth made him popular with the men and women alike. It was an easy, enjoyable life, and he was already beginning to make plans for his retirement when the brothel was raided. In the furore that followed, one of the police officers fell to his death from a third storey window; a dozen people had been implicated in the crime, but when the police had finally finished rounding up all the suspects only Jem was missing. Wanted now for a crime he hadn't committed, he had fled to Hamburg, and then took the first available ship which was bound – ironically – for the German colonies on the African continent. His seafaring days had made him strong, and taught him self-reliance, and had first introduced him to people of Patrick Lundy's type – weak-willed, ineffectual – and while not especially dangerous to themselves, destructive to those around them.

When the man had arrived wounded, he had felt sorry for him – he knew the kiss of a knife blade and the stinging fire of a bullet, and so had no compunction about giving him the morphine. But when he saw how easily the man had become addicted to the narcotic, his sympathy had turned to disgust, and when he saw Nuala's obvious concern, his disgust had turned to hatred.

Jem loved Nuala in a strange, gentle way. His was not a great passionate love, but rather a gentle affection that ran far deeper and was far more abiding than any passion. They had slept together less than two dozen times in the years they had known one another, and had made love less than half that number; he had been quite content merely to lie beside her, holding her while she slept, and it was an easy arrangement that suited them both.

And then Patrick Lundy had arrived.

At first Jem didn't mind the attention Nuala lavished on Patrick – after all he was nothing more than a boy, and she would have no interest in him. Later, when he discovered that they were sleeping together, he controlled himself and said and did nothing – it was an affair that would soon burn itself out, and he felt his patience and restraint had been justified when Patrick had left to go on active service with the IRA.

With Patrick out of the way, Jem had been careful to devote more time to Nuala and they had started sleeping together on a regular basis, and it was reaching the stage where he was beginning to believe that Nuala's feelings towards him were deepening into something like love – when Patrick Lundy had returned.

And gradually everything had changed.

Nuala lost interest in him as she devoted more and more time to caring for Lundy. When he had recovered from his physical wounds, she had taken him to her bed again – although Jem knew the drug would have rendered him almost completely impotent.

And Jem became the employee once again – a trusted, valued employee – but still an employee. What friendship there had been between them was gone now, another victim of Lundy's return. Making the decision to kill him therefore was all the easier. And Lundy himself had provided the means – all Jem had to do was to increase the dosage of morphine. If the drug itself didn't kill him, then an overdose could be easily arranged.

Nuala was standing before the window looking down into the cobbled street below when Jem arrived. Although the door was half opened, he tapped before stepping into the room and pushing the door closed behind him. Patrick was asleep in the chair before the fire, snoring slightly. He slept a lot these days, usually waking early in the morning when the effects of the drug wore off. There were a few minutes of lucidity in which he would make plans for the future, and then the craving would return and with the craving the hunger, and then all thoughts of the future would be swept away and he would only think of the drug … the drug … and the pleasure.

'You wanted me?' Jem asked quietly, looking from Patrick to Nuala. He rarely saw Patrick during the hours of daylight, and he was almost shocked to see how ill and old he looked. Another month, maybe six weeks perhaps, he thought suppressing a smile …

Nuala turned from the window. She too had aged in the past few months – or perhaps it was just that she didn't bother to take as much care of herself as she used to. At one stage she tinted her hair with a foul-smelling henna concoction which she bought in the chemist's on

O'Connell Street, but she hadn't done that for a while and now her tightly curled chestnut hair was sprinkled with long strands of silver. She no longer wore her glasses as assiduously as she had and there were frown marks on her forehead and lines at the corners of her eyes from squinting. Jem also noticed that the dress she was wearing – the same simple dress of white and yellow cotton she had been wearing yesterday – was sprinkled with smuts from the fire. The old Nuala would never have worn the same dress on two consecutive days.

'I'm going to let some of the girls go,' she said quickly, crossing to sit in her customary chair before the fire. She folded her hands in her lap and Jem noticed that her nails – her once long, fine nails – were ragged.

The German pulled a chair away from the table and carried it over beside Nuala. 'Why?' he asked simply.

Nuala shook her head, and Jem saw the tears sparkling in her eyes. 'I've no choice,' she said quietly. 'When was the last time we had a full house?'

He nodded; the present restrictions imposed by the Black and Tans had ensured that few honest people were willing to venture out onto the streets at night. It had been too long since Number Eighty-Two had experienced a full house. He was personally convinced that the days of the grand brothels were over – given another year or two they would vanish completely.

Nuala lifted a pile of bills from the floor beside her and passed them over to him. 'I've paid as many of these as I can, but the others …'

Jem ran through the bills. The top four were from a chemist, and were for tincture of morphine. 'Well, this is an unnecessary expense for a start.'

'It's necessary,' she said shortly, 'as necessary as the bills for the drink and the food and the doctor's bills. They all have to be paid, as do the girls – and we just don't have the money.'

'Who are you going to let go?'

Nuala shook her head quickly. 'I haven't decided yet.

I suppose we'll start with those who aren't really popular ...'

'The specialists?' Jem shook his head. 'They may not appeal to all the customers, but those who do look for their special services, pay well.'

Nuala rounded on him. 'I don't want to get rid of any of them – but I've no choice. If you can see any other way, then tell me, I'll be only too glad to take it.'

Jem allowed his eyes to fall to the bills on the floor and then he looked up at Nuala. 'We'll just have to cut down on certain things; won't we?'

Patrick usually awoke around six, feeling tired – even though he had just slept through most of the day – and slightly headachy. And Jem was invariably on hand to relieve the pain.

Occasionally – like today – he awoke with no pain, just a vague numbness, a feeling of disassociation, and he was able to lie content in his bed. On days like this, he was even able to make ambiguous plans for the future; perhaps he could rejoin his unit, perhaps he could return to England, perhaps ...

But that life, the life in England with his mother and sister, cosseted, enclosed, seemed like a dream, or a half-remembered novel, and more recently, his days on the road with the Squad, the murders, the beatings, that too seemed like the activity of another person.

The door opened and Jem stepped into the room; in his hand was the cloth-covered plate that Patrick had come to associate with pleasure. No words passed between them as Jem sat down on the edge of the bed and began to fill the hypodermic from the small blue bottle. Patrick was already rolling up his sleeve when Nuala walked in. The tableau remained unbroken for at least a minute and then Nuala pointed to the needle in Jem's hand. 'Tell me what you're doing,' she said softly, her voice sounding strained, almost forced.

The German looked at her in surprise. He lifted the

needle and the bottle of morphine slightly, allowing her to see them properly. 'You know what I'm doing.'

'Tell me,' she whispered.

Jem looked from Patrick back to Nuala. 'I'm giving Patrick his medication.'

'How much?'

He shook his head in puzzlement.

'How much are you giving him?' she suddenly screamed. She flung something across the room, and Jem instinctively ducked – until he realised it was nothing but paper. One fluttered to the floor by his feet and he lifted it, reading the title. He frowned. 'It's a bill from the chemist's for morphine ...' he said, looking up – and then he stopped.

Nuala was pointing a tiny silver pistol at him. Holding it in both hands she pulled back the hammers on the Derringer.

'Jem ...?' Patrick asked, frowning, desperately attempting to sort out what was going on. 'Jem?'

The German ignored him. He was concentrating intently on Nuala and the gun in her hand. He had seen the weapon before – a small double-barrelled silver Derringer with mother-of-pearl handles – it had been a gift from Dermot Corcoran to his wife, and it was the same weapon she had used to kill John Lewis. To the best of his knowledge Nuala had never fired the weapon, and he wasn't even sure if it was loaded.

'Nuala?' he asked.

'Tell me what's going on Jem,' she said, her voice level again, the gun now held rock steady in both hands straight out in front of her.

'I don't know what you mean,' he said slowly, playing for time. He knew she couldn't maintain that straight-armed stance for too long without tiring.

'I talked to Doctor Meredith,' Nuala said tightly. 'I spoke to him about Patrick's morphine addiction. And I spoke to him about the amount of morphine Patrick was taking, and how often.'

Jem shook his head. 'I don't know what you mean,'

he said carefully, not looking at her face, watching only the gun, which was beginning to waver in her hands.

'He was able to tell me about some recent research which had been done into the soldiers who had come back from the war. He looked at the amounts of morphine Patrick was taking – and he discovered that at the rate his addiction increased, he should have kept taking greater and greater doses and overdosed a long time ago.' She stopped and added softly. 'Unless some-one had been carefully regulating his dosage, maintaining it at a high – but not lethal – level.'

Jem started to rise from the bed and the gun came up in Nuala's hand. It was now pointing at his face, and her grip was as solid and as hard as the look on her face.

'Why?' she asked simply.

The German looked at her for a while and then simply shrugged. 'I love you. I envied the attention you were paying him. When he became addicted to the drug I thought you would become disgusted with him, have nothing more to do with him.'

Nuala lowered the gun. 'Jem, I love him – despite his faults I love him. You were … you were a friend, and we had some good times together, but I never loved you.'

Jem nodded. He looked at the needle in his hands turning it around and around. It was more than half-full – enough to keep Patrick under for twenty-four hours at least – although a lethal dose to anyone else. Ignoring Nuala he filled the hypodermic all the way.

'Jem …?' Nuala asked.

'If he hadn't turned up,' the German asked, his voice strained, his clipped accent pronounced. 'If he hadn't turned up, what would have happened then?'

'I don't know. Who knows what would have happened?'

'And if he had died while on service with the IRA, what would have happened then? Would anything have happened between us?'

She shrugged, wondering where the questions were leading.

'And if he was to die now!' Jem lunged across the bed, and grabbed Patrick by the hair, pulling him forward and across his knees, so that he was lying on his back, looking towards the ceiling, his throat stretched taut, with the point of the needle resting in the soft flesh beneath the chin. When the German looked back at Nuala his face was implacable, his accent harsh and guttural. 'What use is he to you?' he spat. 'He's an addict, a weak, spineless addict, who killed when it was easy to do so, who shot unarmed and defenceless men and considered himself a soldier. What use is he to you?'

'You made him the addict,' Nuala whispered.

He shook his head. 'People like him are born addicts; weak, cowards ... All I did was bring it to the surface.'

'You made him the addict,' Nuala whispered again.

'For your sake!'

'For my sake?' she asked incredulously.

'The boy is trouble. He's been nothing but trouble since the moment he arrived. He brought Katherine Lundy back into your life, he brought police with him, he brought death. Believe me,' he said fervently, 'I'm doing you a favour.'

He lifted the needle away from Patrick's throat and moved it to the carotid artery.

And Nuala shot him.

In the confines of the room, the noise was incredible. She had pulled the trigger all the way back, firing off both barrels together. The first shot took him high in the head, the short .22 bullet lifting him up and away from Patrick, the second shot punching him high in the chest, driving him back off the bed.

Patrick staggered to his feet. When Jem had released him he had fallen headfirst to the floor. He was dazed and confused, not quite able to comprehend what had happened. He looked at Nuala, at the smoking gun in her hand and then turned to look for Jem ... and then he stopped. The wall behind his bed was sprayed with blood ... a bright red flower-like design. It was a pretty design. He looked at it in wonder for a few seconds before something else caught his attention. On the floor by his feet, something sparkled and glittered. He crouched down to look at it – and discovered it was the remains of the bottle of morphine, and the metal syringe lay embedded into the carpet, its needle bent and twisted out of shape.

Patrick knelt in the broken glass and touched the damp pool of morphine with his fingertips, and then he brought his fingers to his lips …

Nuala hit him across the face, the force of the blow knocking him onto the ground alongside Jem. 'You stupid bastard!' Her voice was a cold hiss. She kicked him in the pit of the stomach with her small pointed shoe. 'You stupid bastard!' She was still kicking him when the servants arrived and dragged her off moments later.

CHAPTER TWENTY-FIVE

There were times in the months that followed when Patrick would have killed Nuala himself. If he closed his eyes he could see his hands around her throat, tightening, squeezing the life from her ... and all for the drug.

He had screamed himself hoarse, battering himself against the door and walls – until he had been gagged and tied down to his bed, with a guard at the end of his bed to watch over him.

The first three weeks had been the hardest. Doctor Meredith had visited him daily, and then Collins had started visiting again, when he had learned how Jem had been slowly killing Patrick with the drug. When he had first arrived, he had found it hard to believe that the dishevelled and ill-kempt old man was Patrick Lundy. The man tied to the bed looked closer to sixty than the twenty-one years he was.

He wrinkled his nose at the smell in the room, a mixture of sweat, urine and faeces, and then looked at Nuala. 'Who's looking after him?'

'I am,' she said immediately. Nuala looked tired; sleep was something to which she was rapidly becoming a stranger. Patrick, although restless during the day, seemed to come alive during the hours of darkness. And in the quiet, dead hours of night, he would toss and turn, moaning aloud like a man in great pain. Sometimes she would remove the gag and listen to him. His talk was confused, rambling, a mixture of child-talk, mingled with obscenities, oaths, threats, promises ... and her name. Nuala often heard her name in his ramblings, and it gave her hope.

'How is he now?' Collins asked.

Nuala looked at the sleeping man and smiled fondly. 'He's getting better,' she said loudly, almost as if she were forcing herself to believe it.

'And the German?' he wondered.

'That's been taken care of,' she said quietly, not looking at him.

The Big Fellow nodded. 'We could have helped.'

'I'm quite capable of taking care of my own problems,' Nuala said quickly.

Collins nodded again, but said nothing.

'Perhaps you could come and see him,' Nuala suggested quickly. 'He often talks about you ...'

'You know things are difficult now,' Collins said gently, 'but I'll try, you know I will.'

'I know.' She was going to add that perhaps if he had kept calling in the beginning none of this would have happened. Surely he would have been able to see what was happening, what Jem was doing to Patrick? But if she hadn't been able to see what was happening under her nose, what chance had Collins?

'Take care of him,' the Big Fellow added, looking at the bundle on the bed. 'For his sake ... for your sake.'

The weeks that followed were indeed difficult ones for Nuala, although once Patrick had got over the initial soul-destroying craving for the drug, it became a little easier. Initially, his stomach wouldn't hold the food she spoon-fed him and she went back to simple basic recipes the like of which would be fed a child. She washed him, trimmed his hair and shaved his beard, and as time passed, he became more and more lucid, although still physically weak. With nothing else to do, they talked for hours, rediscovering the elements which had drawn them together in the first place, and gradually Nuala came to understand what had driven Patrick to go on active service and join Collins' Squad. It made his earlier actions a little easier to comprehend, a little easier to forgive. She began to speak too about herself, about growing up in abject poverty just outside Wicklow

340

town to the south of Dublin. Her parents – then little more than teenagers themselves – had survived the Great Famine that had devastated the country in the 1840s by adopting the Protestant faith in return for soup and bread, and although all the children, including herself, the last born, had been brought up as Protestants, her mother had also instructed them in the Catholic tradition. However, because they were ostensibly Protestant, the four Kennedy girls were able to secure positions as maids in Dublin. Her two elder sisters were now married with families of their own, although she hadn't seen them in years, and her older sister had died insane from syphilis. When she had started to speak of her elder sister, and her pain became apparent, Patrick had reached out and took her hand, squeezing it gently. 'There's no need,' he said quietly, 'you've already told me.'

She was sitting on the edge of the bed and she moved closer into his arms. He held her tight as the light gradually faded, dipping the room into shadow. They both dozed off and awoke with a start some time later as the noise from below seeped up through the floorboards.

No words passed between them, but they both knew that their relationship had changed, had solidified into something stranger, something far more mature and enduring than their previous tenuous liaison. Without being asked, but by mutual consent, Patrick moved into Nuala's bed that night.

It had taken nearly six months for Patrick Lundy to fully 'recover' from his wounds. His memory of those months would always be sketchy, having assumed an almost dream-like aura.

In July, 1920, Patrick Lundy began to put his life back in order.

In July, 1920, a new group arrived in Ireland to supplement the Black and Tans. These were the Auxiliary Division of the Royal Irish Constabulary, soon to be popularly known as the Auxies. They were drawn from the unemployed officer class, unlike the Tans whose men were mainly from the ranks. All the men held the rank of Police Sergeant, and they were paid one pound a day – ten shillings more than the Tans – and this, coupled with the fact that they were officially part of a Corps d'Elite, created deep and dangerous divisions between the two groups.

The Auxiliaries were a much more dangerous group than the Tans; under the mistaken illusion that they were up against a huge army of highly armed rebels, they fought with a viciousness and tenacity that initially surprised the IRA. They soon realized that the Auxies were a force to be reckoned with, and accordingly changed their tactics.

Patrick Lundy walked past the Shelbourne Hotel alongside Michael Collins. It was Sunday, the 25th July, and the day was hot and heavy, the sun shining from a pale blue sky, and not a breath of a wind. The city was quiet, the good weather having enticed most people out to the sea. Across the road, two young men strolled alongside the railings surrounding St Stephen's Green, while behind Patrick and Collins another two walked, matching them pace for pace.

'I hope they are yours,' Patrick said, glancing into the polished glass of the Shelbourne Hotel, catching the reflections of the two across the road.

'Well, I'm glad to see you're still sharp,' the Big Fellow said with a broad smile, 'but you can relax, they're mine. There's twelve of them assigned to watch over me,' he said, sounding almost embarrassed. 'They're called the Twelve Apostles.'

'Do I know them?'

Collins shook his head. 'It's unlikely. There's a lot of new faces with us now, Patrick. Too many perhaps,' he added ominously. They turned left before Merrion Row, and walked up the east side of the Green, the fine Georgian doors looking pale and blistered in the sunshine. 'I'd like you to come back, Patrick.'

342

Patrick stopped, looking at Michael Collins in surprise. 'Me?'

Collins, who had walked on, stopped and turned back to Patrick. 'Why not?'

Patrick strode up to stand beside him. 'But I thought after ...'

Collins slapped him on the back, staggering him. 'You were one of my best men, Patrick. If I'd a hundred like you, I would have won this damned war. What happened to you was ... well, it was unfortunate. You'd been working hard – too hard – and your mind snapped ... battle fatigue I think it's called. Shell shock or something like that.'

Patrick's gaunt face broke into a broad smile. 'So I'm forgiven?'

'If anyone needs forgiveness, then it's me. I should have been more understanding; I should have stood by you.'

Patrick looked away, embarrassed. One of Collins's great qualities was his ability to admit a mistake.

'What we need now, Patrick, is someone like you.'

'I'm sure you've plenty of young men with you.'

'I have. And damn few that I can trust. That's where you come in. I know you, I can trust you; you can act on your own initiative, you can be ruthless when the need arises, cautious when necessary – and you've a good solid English accent.'

'What do you want me to do?'

'I want you to vet the newcomers. We've been infiltrated by the British. The authorities have become more and more organized over the past few months. They've hurt us time and again – aye, and we've hurt them too. But now they're beginning to get a little too close. I've concocted a two-fold plan. In its first stage, it will remove those spies within our organization, and in the second stage, we'll remove all the spies in Dublin.'

'All of them?' Patrick asked in a whisper, suddenly cold now, even though the day was hot and airless.

'All of them,' Collins said with a hard smile. 'I've said

before I would put out the eyes of the British in Ireland, and by God, this time I'm going to do it.' He looked at Patrick and grinned. 'Well, will you do it, will you join us again?'

Patrick hesitated, and Collins' eyebrows rose in a silent question. 'I want to discuss it with Nuala,' he said eventually. 'I feel I owe it to her, after all she's done for me.'

Collins nodded. 'Of course.' They had reached Earlsfort Terrace, and now turned to the right, heading down the south side of the Green, half way to completing their circuit. 'She's a good woman, Patrick. Not many would have stood by you.'

'I know that,' Patrick said softly. 'But you know she's little enough time for the organization.'

'I think you might be surprised,' Michael Collins said … and then the smile froze his face. 'Are you armed?' he asked casually.

Without taking his eyes off Collins' face, Patrick shook his head. 'No, are you?'

'Unusually, no.'

The two men who stepped out into their path were dressed in the dark green – almost black – of the Royal Irish Constabulary but both men were wearing the beret of the Auxiliaries, and while one wore a .45 Service Webly slung low on his hip, his companion had his pistol tucked into his belt.

'Nice day for a stroll, gents.' The accent was umistakably London English.

'Hot too,' his companion added, stepping away from the speaker, his hand on the butt of his pistol.

'You must be sweltering in those togs, mate.' Patrick played up his English accent.

Both men visibly relaxed hearing the English accent. 'On holiday, mate?' one asked.

'No such luck, bloody work. Just saying to me mate here, trust us to have to work on a day like this.'

The Auxiliaries nodded sympathetically. 'What sort of work is that, mate?'

Patrick dabbed at his forehead with a handkerchief. He could see Collins' four bodyguards moving in, their hands beneath their coats. Another few seconds and there was going to be firefight. He looked at Collins and grinned. 'Me and Mike is booksellers.'

'Go on!'

'God's truth,' Patrick said quickly, 'we work for Webbs on Charing Cross Road.'

''I know it well,' the younger, more talkative Auxiliary said quickly. 'How's Joe?'

'He's coming along. Still a bit stiff you know, and the bad weather gives him the odd ache or two.'

The man pushed back his beret and frowned. 'If I ever caught the bastard who worked him over about a year back ...' he let the sentence hang, but the three men nodded sympathetically.

Michael Collins deliberately looked at his watch. 'We best be going ...' he said, looking at Patrick.

Patrick nodded. 'We better. We've got to see a chap who's selling his library. You chaps any interest in eighteenth century religious books?'

Both men laughed. 'Not me, mate.'

Patrick raised his hand in salute. 'Good luck now.' He dabbed at his face as they walked past. The four body-guards faded back out of sight, their hands appearing.

Collins gave a short whistle. 'Well, you haven't lost your nerve, I'll say that for you.'

'That was close enough,' Patrick said quickly, reaction beginning to set in, a cold shivering beginning in the pit of his stomach. 'I thought the jig was up when he mentioned Joe Hyde's name.'

'It might have been a bit awkward,' Collins agreed.

'It could have been more than that. We could have ended up stuck in the middle of a gunfight.'

Collins shook his head. 'No. These boys are good shots – the best – they'd have taken those two down on the first try.'

'I'm glad we didn't have to put it to the test,' Patrick said fervently.

The two men had stopped at the corner of Harcourt Street. 'I've a few things to get in the office. Will you come up?'

Patrick shook his head. 'No thanks. I think I'll take a leisurely stroll home, I've got some things to sort out in my own mind, and then I want to talk to Nuala. But I want to have my own case settled in my mind before speaking to her.'

'I understand.'

Patrick grinned. 'I only wish you did. You've always had a vision of what you wanted, and you've set out to achieve it.'

'We don't always get what we set out to achieve,' Michael Collins said quietly, 'but it's the trying that matters.'

'Will you ever achieve true independence for Ireland?' Patrick asked curiously.

'Yes,' Collins said, turning away, and there was no hesitation, no doubt in his voice.

Patrick walked down along the west side of St Stephen's Green, his head bent, deep in thought. This was really his first long walk alone in the city since ... since his accident. Nuala had insisted that his addiction was directly related to his accident and hence should be considered as one and the same thing. The only reason she had allowed him out today on his own, he knew, was because she knew he was meeting Collins, and would be safe with him. He smiled at the irony – safe with the most wanted man in the British Isles.

Patrick looked up as he passed the College of Surgeons. He could still see the impressions where the bullets had struck the stonework during the Rising. He wished he could have fought alongside them then; it was a much simpler war – or so he believed. There was none of this subterfuge – at least not in the final week. Then, the enemy were clearly defined, one side against the other. Not like now, when the talk was of killing spies, when seemingly ordinary men and women might be the enemy. He turned down Grafton Street, still lost in thought. Was he going to go back on active service again – never knowing where his next meal was coming from, never knowing where he was going to sleep, becoming some sort of killing machine, obeying orders, 'This man is a spy, this man is an informer,' and dealing with them accordingly? Did killing these ordinary people, whose only crime was to earn themselves a few shillings, actually change the course of the struggle? Suddenly, the face of the man he had shot on Christmas Eve popped into his head. Usually Patrick Lundy was never able to remember the faces of the men he had shot. This one he couldn't forget. Even during his addiction – when the drug had smothered the pain and brought the dreams – that had been the face that had haunted him. That man had left a young widow and daughter. What were their feelings towards the IRA now, whose side did they support at this stage? And had that death advanced the struggle any further? It was a question he didn't need to answer.

A sudden thought struck him, and he laughed aloud, startling an elderly couple who were standing in front of Wests the Jewellers.

What was he turning into – a revolutionary with a conscience. What was that phrase – all's fair in love and war. Well this was war, wasn't it? Not a nice clear war with each side wearing different uniforms fought in some muddy field. This was a war none the less, a war, fought on the streets, by ordinary men and women for a cause they believed in. So all he had to do was to decide whether he still believed in the cause. His father – or at least the man he had believed to be his father – had fought for it, died for it, his mother had betrayed it. Where would he stand, with his father or his mother?

Patrick stood alongside the mirror, looking at Nuala, who was dressing. She had had something done to her hair, had it cut and shaped around her face, that had stripped years off her age, and he began to get a glimpse of what she must have looked like when she was

eighteen. Her body was still that of a young woman –
though perhaps her breasts were a little too big, and
beginning to sag, and her stomach a little too rounded –
only her eyes betrayed her and they were old, old. 'I'm
thinking of going back on active service again,' Patrick
said cautiously, unsure of her reaction.

Nuala nodded, without looking away from the
mirror; she was applying a deep red colour to her lips
with a brush.

'I wish you wouldn't use that colour,' Patrick said
quickly, 'it's so ... cheap.'

She nodded with a quick smile. 'I know. It makes me
look like a tart!'

He came around and knelt on the floor in front of her,
and then pulled her close, pressing his lips to her
freshly-applied lipstick, smearing it, ignoring her moan
of protest. He could feel the warmth of her skin through
the thin material of her shift, feel her breasts against his
chest. And then – abruptly – he pulled back. They were
both panting.

'What was that for?' she demanded.

'Does there have to be a reason?'

Nuala shrugged. She looked in the mirror and made a
disgusted face; her lipstick was smeared down her chin
and across one cheek. 'You want something,' she said
flatly.

'No ...'

'Yes,' she contradicted him. 'You're after something.'
She glanced up from her reflection in the glass. 'Yes,
you're after something. Now, come on. Out with it.'

'You should have been my mother,' Patrick
grumbled.

'I'm nearly old enough to be your mother.'

Taking a deep breath, Patrick spoke so quickly that all
the words ran together. 'I'm-thinking-of-going-back-
on-service-with-the-IRA.'

'I heard you the first time,' she straightened up.
Staring at Patrick, she asked, 'And why are you telling
me?'

'I wanted to talk to you first, before I made the final decision.'

'Surely you've already made up your mind?'

Patrick shrugged. 'I've made a decision – of sorts.'

'And …?'

'Well, look. Answer me two questions. Should I go back on service with Collins? And will you marry me?'

CHAPTER TWENTY-SIX

On Wednesday, August 18th, 1920, Patrick Lundy and Nuala Kennedy were married at number forty-three, Kildare Street, at the diocesan registry offices.

Patrick barely made it to the registry office in time; he had just returned from Cork where Terence Mac-Sweeney, the Lord Mayor of Cork and most of the Cork Number One and Two Brigades had been captured in a raid on Cork City Hall. Patrick had been sent down to Cork with orders from Collins to rout out the traitor who had undoubtedly betrayed the meeting and deal accordingly with him, and also to look into the possibilities of freeing MacSweeney.

As an outsider – and regarded with something approaching awe by the local IRA – Patrick found it almost pathetically easy to establish the identity of the traitor, by the simple method of examining the roll call for the previous meetings and comparing them with the last ill-fated meeting. The meeting on the 12th had been unusual, being one of the few occasions when most of the members of the two brigades would be present, as well as officers from the Irish Republic Brotherhood and representatives of the proscribed government, Dail Eireann. Only two men hadn't attended the City Hall that night; one had been wounded in a raid on an army barracks three days previously and was unable to walk, and the second man ...

Patrick, with two locals, visited the man in his shabby one-room apartment on the banks of the Lee. They knocked on the door, and softly identified themselves.

And from within a single shot rang out.

When Patrick kicked the door in, they found the man lying on the straw pallet that served as his bed. There was a packed suitcase by his feet, and fifty pounds in new notes scattered all across the floor. The man had put a gun to his mouth and pulled the trigger.

A search of the man's belongings revealed a cigarette package with a name scrawled on it in pencil. The name was that of a local publican with known British sympathies. Patrick simply walked into the bar at just before closing time on Tuesday night, ordered a pint and when the publican brought it to him, put his hand in his pocket, pulled out a gun and shot the man three times at point-blank range. He then turned on his heel and walked out of the silent room without a backward glance. Less than twenty minutes later, he was on the road back to Dublin, dozing peacefully in the back of a lorry hauling vegetables to the Dublin market.

Patrick arrived in Dublin shortly after dawn, and then spent a couple of hours with Eddie in her rooms in Fownes Street. There he washed and she shaved him, trimming his hair at the same time, and at ten thirty he set out to walk to Kildare Street, where he was married at eleven o'clock. If Nuala thought anything about the gun she felt in his breast pocket when she leaned over to kiss him, she said nothing.

Buswells' Hotel, in Molesworth Street, around the corner from the registry office in Kildare Street, was quiet at this time of day, and Patrick and Nuala had the circular dining room to themselves. They ordered breakfast, and were surprised when, a few moments later, two glasses of sparkling wine arrived, 'with the management's compliments.'

'How did they know?' Nuala whispered

Patrick shrugged and grinned. 'I suppose when they get two well-dressed people in here first thing in the morning ...' he lifted his left hand, 'with bright new rings on their fingers, then it's a sure enough guess.' He looked at Nuala. 'Are you sure this is the way you wanted it?'

She nodded quickly. 'We've not much religion between us, you and I, and I couldn't see myself walking down the aisle in white, now could I?'

'With your girls on one side in all their finery, and my lot on the other, decked out in their guns and bullets,' Patrick added quickly.

Nuala laughed. 'Oh Patrick, I am happy.' She reached out with her gloved hand and rested it on his. 'I love you,' she said simply.

'I love you too,' he said truthfully, 'perhaps more than you'll ever know. I don't think I'll ever be able to thank you for what you did for me. You saved my life, my sanity ...'

She squeezed his fingers. 'I should be thanking you,' she said sincerely.

'For what?' he asked, surprised.

'For giving me a new lease of life. You've made me feel ten years younger.'

'I don't think I've ever seen you looking so well,' he said, looking at her closely. Nuala was wearing the minimum of make-up – and he rarely saw her without make-up – just a touch of colour on her cheeks and lips, and she looked a lot younger than her thirty-three years. She was wearing a simple Worth suit of burnt-orange wool, trimmed with beaver fur at neck, wrist and waist over a ribbed silk blouse. Her dress ended just above her ankles, revealing mustard coloured stockings that matched her gloves, and her hat was also of beaver fur. The style was now going out of fashion, she knew, but the simplicity of the outfit suited her years, and tended to disguise her fuller figure.

'Where did you get the suit?' she asked.

'One of the boys runs a gentleman's outfitters,' Patrick said, straightening his cravat. 'What do you think?'

'You should wear a suit more often,' she smiled. He was wearing a simple charcoal grey three-piece suit with a faint black line running through the cloth, and a trilby. He had never worn a hat before, and she thought it lent him an air of authority and presence.

'Well, Mrs Lundy, what shall we do today?'

Nuala grinned wickedly. 'What would your mother say if she knew you'd gone and married without even telling her?'

'Forget her,' Patrick said quickly.

'So, she's not the only Mrs Lundy now.'

'She's no right to the name either,' Patrick remarked, sipping the wine, blinking as bubbles exploded against his face. 'Her married name is Corcoran, although I noticed that all her papers are made out in the name of Lundy.'

'What name appears on your birth certificate?'

'Patrick Montgomery Lundy,' he said, speaking to Nuala, but watching two men who had appeared at the door of the hotel, and were speaking to one of the waiters. 'But my sister's is made out in the name of Senga Corcoran Lundy. Now sit very still,' he continued, his voice even, the smile still fixed to his lips.

Nuala's fingers tightened on his hand. 'What's wrong?'

'Maybe nothing,' he said lightly, not believing it himself. He hadn't been on the road for such a long time without being able to spot plainclothes police. He looked at the faces, but didn't recognize them, but then he'd been out of touch for so long.

The two men looked across at Patrick and Nuala, and began to make their way through the tables towards them. One had his hand in his pocket, and the second man was unbuttoning his coat when Patrick suddenly stood up, the gun in his hand. He pointed it at the man with his hand in his pocket. 'Yes, gentlemen?'

The two men stopped and looked at one another.

'You – take your hands out of your pockets. Both of you keep your hands where I can see them.'

'I think there's some mistake ...' the smaller of the two men began. His accent was unmistakably educated British.

Without taking his eyes off the men, Patrick held out his hand to Nuala. 'Come around behind me love.

Don't walk in front of me,' he warned as Nuala came slowly to her feet. 'Do you want to tell me who you are?' he asked, looking at each man in turn. He had guessed from the accent that they were either Auxies, or some of the paid spies and informers that were drifting into Dublin from all parts of the British Empire, looking for employment in the security services.

'Look mate, go easy with that gun. I think there's been some sort of mix-up here ...'

And then the maid walked into the room. She screamed and dropped the plates onto the tiled floor. Both men dived to the floor, guns appearing in their hands as they went down. Patrick fired twice at the nearest man, hitting him both times. The second man dived behind a table, which he dragged down to cover himself, firing as he went. Bullets spatted around Patrick as he calmly fired at the circular wooden table, thankful that he was carrying the heavier .45 calibre automatic, rather than his usual .32. The bullets punched through the wood, and the man surged to his feet, blood on his chest, an amazed look on his face. Patrick took aim and calmly shot him through the head.

'Let's get out of here!' He turned back for Nuala, expecting to find her crouched behind him. Instead, she was standing pressed up against the wall at his back, her hands at her breast. 'Jesus, love, you should have got down, they might have hit ...' he began, and then he noticed the glazed look on her face, and the bright redness on her lips. 'Nuala?' He reached for her as she moved away from the wall.

There was a long smear of blood on the wall behind her.

Patrick gently eased her hands away from her chest ... and blood welled from the wound just below her breastbone.

'Oh, Jesus ...'

Blood trickled from Nuala's lips as she attempted a smile. 'I didn't think you were a religious man ...'

Wrapping his arm around her waist, he eased her

away from the wall and half-carrying, half-supporting her, he moved towards the exit. His foot kicked a gun lying on the floor and he stooped to lift it, stuffing his own half-empty weapon into his pocket. There was no sign of the hotel staff, and the foyer and desk were empty. Pushing open the doors he staggered down the steps and out onto Molesworth Street.

A car had just stopped outside to allow a young couple to alight. They were both well dressed and Patrick immediately – instinctively – knew from the way they looked at one another, the way they moved, the way they held their hands, that they had just been married. The girl screamed as Patrick staggered up with Nuala, the front of her blouse now sodden with bright blood. Patrick waved the gun at them. 'Go away.' And then he turned his attention to the driver of the car. 'Now you can drive, or I can drive, it's your choice …'

'Where do you want to go …?'

'A doctor's, a hospital … anywhere.'

'I reckon Mercer's Hospital just off the Green's the nearest.'

'I don't care – just do it.'

Patrick knelt in the back of the car, cradling Nuala's head in his arm. He pressed his hand to the hole in her chest, attempting to staunch the flow of blood, but knew it was useless. He could feel her blood pulse against the palm of his hand, feel it seep through his trousers from the corresponding hole in her back. His mind was racing desperately, attempting to recall whatever shreds of medical knowledge he still remembered, but found that he could recall nothing. He was whispering to her, simple, repetitive things, nonsense words, snatches of songs, children's rhymes, desperately attempting to keep her conscious until they reached the hospital. He knew if she lapsed into unconsciousness, then he had lost her … and he couldn't conceive of that. Not yet, not so soon. Not so soon….

'Where's the hospital?' he screamed, the sound tearing at the back of his throat.

'Nearly there, nearly there …'

'Come on Nuala, we're nearly there, nearly there … it's not so bad … I've been shot too … it hurts doesn't it … I know it hurts, but don't think about the pain, concentrate on something else, that's a good trick, think of something else … anything … where do you want to go for your honeymoon … I was thinking maybe Paris … Paris would be nice … maybe we could stop off in London and introduce you to my mother … what a shock she'd get eh … Oh Nuala I love you, I love you … don't die on me … please God, don't let her die on me …'

Nuala's lips moved, bloody saliva bubbling on her lips, and Patrick moved his ear closer to her mouth to catch her words. For a moment all he could hear was the sound of her breath – wet and reeking of the copper stench of blood – and then, faint, a mere ghost of a whisper, 'I love you Patrick Lundy.'

The car lurched to a halt, and the door was wrenched open. 'We're here.'

But it was too late.

The police arrived at the hospital less than half a minute after Michael Collins arrived. Collins had found Patrick slumped against a wall on the ground floor, his head back against the cold tiles, his face a rigid mask of pain. There was blood on his coat, shirt, face and hands, but none of it seemed to be his. The big man squatted down beside Patrick. 'We can talk later. Let's get out of here now before the police arrive.'

Patrick allowed himself to be hauled to his feet and, with Collins's left arm around his shoulders, allowed him to lead him from the hospital out into the street.

Two men, one in plain clothes, another wearing the uniform of the Dublin Metropolitan Police stepped up in front of them. 'Patrick Lundy …?' The plainsclothes man put the question, looking from Patrick to Collins and then back to Patrick. 'There's a few questions we'd like to ask you concerning the death of two officers in Buswell's Hotel …'

'I don't think this gentleman is in any state to answer questions at the moment,' Michael Collins said evenly.

The DMP man produced his baton and rested it squarely against Collins chest. 'And just who might you be, eh?'

Collins looked the man in the face and smiled, and the policeman stopped suddenly. 'You don't want to know who I am. Now look around you,' he advised, 'and keep your hands in full view at all times.'

The DMP man looked around, and spotted the four hard-faced young men moving in. They all had their hands in their pockets, and one was wearing a long overcoat, which obviously had had the pocket linings removed, for stubby barrels of a sawn-off shotgun were just visible.

'Walk away,' Collins suggested.

The two men looked at one another and then they both turned around and walked away, deciding that another turn around the block wouldn't do them any harm.

Patrick roused himself from his stupor as he was being bundled into a car. 'Nuala …?'

'It's being taken care of,' Collins said reassuringly.

Patrick nodded, frowning. There was something else he wanted to ask … but for the life of him he couldn't remember.

The house was empty. No, he corrected himself, the house only felt empty. Downstairs, at least twelve girls were plying their trade and half that number of servants, both male and female, were also working. But for Patrick Lundy, the house was empty. With Nuala gone, the life had gone out of it.

Patrick's memories – vague and distressing, disturbingly like a morphine dream – were of Doctor Meredith bending over him, while Michael Collins hovered in the background. And then there had been a series of bumpy journeys, usually at night, and usually hidden in or under something. He had spent the last two days living with a couple of IRA sympathisers in the tiny seaside village of Skerries, twenty-two miles beyond Dublin, where at least he was safe from the flurry of police activity that followed the shooting of the two plainclothes detectives. Finally the message had arrived from Collins, calling him back to Dublin, and he had come down on the first train, arriving in the city centre a little after nine the previous day.

Patrick's next ordeal had been to return to number eighty-two. He had been fine until he had reached the door and then, when he had to walk into the sitting room and face the girls, the tears had come – from him and from them. And running through his and their grief was the single thread – he was responsible. He knew it and so did they; no one said anything, but they all thought it.

Collins arrived the next day. Patrick was finishing breakfast, reading through the morning paper, when the door opened and the Big Fellow stepped into the room – to find himself facing Patrick's gun.

Patrick's hand was trembling as he lowered his arm, letting down the hammer. 'I'm sorry. I'm jumpy. You shouldn't have been allowed in like that,' he said, suddenly growing angry, 'I might have killed you.'

'Don't let it worry you,' Collins said soothingly, moving into the seat across from Patrick. 'You're too good a shot for anything like that to happen.'

'Not good enough,' Patrick said bitterly, the expression on his face hardening to a mask of hate. 'If I'd been faster, I'd have got those two bastards before they'd a chance to fire.'

'Patrick, it's a miracle you walked away at all.'

'I was talking to Nuala,' he continued as if he hadn't heard Collins, 'and I saw them come in. And then they came into the dining room, and I knew – I just knew – that they were going to come over to us, but I had to be careful you know, just in case. I mean I wouldn't want to shoot one of our own men, and I thought they might possibly be messengers from you. But they looked like

358

police; they smelt like police. I should have trusted my instincts. I pulled a gun on them, and I knew for certain then that they were police. We would have walked out ... we nearly did, but some stupid bitch appeared, and dropped a tray, and they both dropped to the ground, guns in their hands. I got one immediately – the one with his hand in his pocket as we were trained, and the other only managed to get off two or three shots before I got him too. I thought everything was alright ... I was sure he had missed ...' his voice trailed away, and he added softly, 'but he hadn't.'

'We've a traitor, Patrick,' Michael Collins explained patiently, 'someone in the organization and someone high up. Now there have been numerous attempts to infiltrate us in the past few months, and we managed to foil all of them, or so we thought. Obviously we've missed one.' He broke off a piece of toast and began to chew it methodically. 'And they know your identity, Patrick. You've gone on the most wanted list, alongside me.'

'I want that traitor, Mick,' Patrick said desperately.

'He's yours – just get rid of him.'

But Patrick shook his head. 'Not just him. All of them. By the time I've finished there won't be a spy left in Dublin.'

CHAPTER TWENTY-SEVEN

Nuala Kennedy Lundy was buried a week later on Wednesday, the 25th August, 1920. The delay was caused by the autopsy, and the coroner's court, which was a brief, perfunctory affair, in which the coroner found that Mrs Lundy had met her death by misadventure, and returned a verdict of murder by person or persons unknown. The coroner deplored the fact that Mrs Lundy was the wife of a known IRA man and commented that here was the wasteful death of yet another innocent in this senseless war. The sitting of the coroner's court lasted thirty minutes and, murder being commonplace in Dublin that year, received no notices in the papers.

Patrick didn't attend his wife's funeral on Collins's advice. Most of the whores of Monto turned out for the funeral. Nuala's reputation was better than her predecessor's, and her house still maintained its excellent reputation for taking care not only of its customers, but also of its girls. With his usual audacity, the Big Fellow attended both the church and the graveyard, and reported back to Patrick that the priest saying the funeral mass seemed somewhat put out to find himself facing a church filled almost entirely with young women, dressed in a variety of fashions – not all of them suitable to the occasion.

'Was there anyone else there?' Patrick asked quietly. He was standing with his hands behind his back, staring out into the night.

Michael Collins stood behind the young man watching him carefully. Collins prided himself on the fact that he knew men, could judge them with an almost uncanny accuracy: it was one of the reasons his intelligence network was so successful – he always picked the right man for the job. And yet Patrick had fooled him once before; he had never thought that Patrick Lundy would make the cold-blooded operative he had, and he had never imagined he would have succumbed to the drug so easily. And now? Now, he seemed to be taking his wife's death remarkably calmly … but Collins was all too well aware that often the rage that lurked beneath the calm could erupt without warning. He had seen it happen too often before, and Patrick had cracked once before, gone berserk … what was to stop it happening again?

Patrick turned from the window, his eyebrows raised in a question. 'Well, were there?'

'Pardon? I'm sorry, Patrick, I was miles away.'

Patrick nodded understandingly. 'I asked were there any uninvited guests there?'

Collins smiled. 'A couple of men from G-Division certainly, including a couple of our own … and one or two I didn't recognize, new faces, hard faces, harder eyes. Professionals.' He frowned slightly. 'This is a situation we will have to sort out fairly quickly. The authorities are reorganizing their intelligence network, and have been doing so for the past few months. There doesn't seem to be any particular order or method to this new arrangement, and that of course makes it difficult for our men on the inside to get any handle on it.'

'Just get me the names,' Patrick said firmly, 'and I'll take care of it.'

Collins nodded. 'I was thinking of a somewhat more formal operation,' he said slowly, 'certainly there are one or two men that need dealing with immediately, but I think a concerted effort might have even greater effect.'

'Take out the network on a single day?' Patrick suggested.

'Exactly.'

Patrick smiled. 'It might indeed.'

'It will need very careful planning,' Collins said softly, watching him closely.

Patrick nodded. 'Let me think about it. I'll come back to you in a day or two with some suggestions.'

The clock struck eleven and both men stood up simultaneously. 'I must away,' Collins said quickly, 'I'll see you tomorrow perhaps?'

Patrick nodded. He reached for Collins's coat and held it while Michael slid his arms into the sleeves. 'Be careful ...?' he suggested.

Collins grinned. 'I'm always careful.'

Both men turned as sounds of a commotion below drifted up the stairs. There were voices raised in anger, mainly female, with a Dublin accent predominating. Patrick reached for the heavy blackthorn stick he kept beside the fire and was walking to the door when he realized the disturbance had ceased. He turned back to the fire, and shrugged. 'It happens ...' he began, when the door crashed open.

Both Patrick and Michael Collins had guns in their hands before the door had stopped moving ... and Katherine Lundy stepped into the room.

The woman strode past the two men, ignoring them both and made her way to the fire. Standing with her back to the fire she removed her gloves, her hard eyes riveted to Patrick's face. Tossing her gloves onto the side table, she said, 'So ...' and sat down.

Michael Collins lowered his pistol, eased back the hammer and tucked it back into his belt. He rested his hand on Patrick's gun and gently eased it down. 'Who are you?' he demanded, his accent thickening with his sudden anger.

The woman's eyes flickered in his direction and then they came back to rest on Patrick. 'Ask him,' she said tightly.

Collins looked at Patrick, his eyebrows raised in a silent question. Patrick's face was a rigid mask, completely expressionless, matching his eyes, which were dead in his head. 'This is my mother,' Patrick said in a voice barely above a whisper. 'This is Katherine Lundy.'

Collins nodded – his suspicions confirmed – and turned to look at the woman with renewed interest. What he saw didn't impress him. Katherine Lundy was a plump, rather plain woman, who could have been aged anywhere between forty and sixty. Her face, which had once been pretty perhaps, was now lost in rolls of fat, her eyes deep sunk behind high cheekbones, purple-coloured bags beneath her eyes. She was overly made up, her lips too scarlet, her teeth a pale yellow colour, and there was a sprinkling of shattered veins across her cheeks which her make-up failed to hide. She was wearing an ankle-length coat of some dark fur which was totally inappropriate to the season, and the hat perched on her head was at least one size too small. He found it hard to reconcile this frumpy woman with the harridan that Patrick had once described.

'Hello Patrick,' Katherine said softly, her voice completely devoid of all emotion, 'I thought you were in America by now. I had quite given up on you.'

'What do you want?' Patrick asked brusquely. The gun was still in his hands, although now it was pointing at the floor.

'I've ordered tea. At least some of the staff still recognize me,' she continued, ignoring his question. She looked around the room, an expression of distaste on her face. 'How shabby this has all become.'

'What are you doing here?' Patrick demanded, his voice growing louder.

'Remember whom you're speaking to,' Katherine snapped.

For a moment, Patrick felt cowed, and then suddenly the gun came up and he was holding it in both hands, pointing it at her head.

Her gaze flickered to the weapon, and then moved away. 'You haven't the nerve,' she said without hesitation. She looked away, and continued speaking. 'I was always surprised that you chose medicine as a career when you couldn't stand the sight of blood. I think you'd sooner shoot yourself than shoot me,' she smiled humourlessly.

'I've discovered that it's very easy to kill,' Patrick whispered. He thumbed back the hammer on the heavy pistol. 'I could kill you now,' he continued. He glanced over his shoulder at Collins. 'This is the woman who betrayed the Rising to the British in 'sixteen. This is the woman who sold out her husband and the men who fought with him, who betrayed his cause, and if the Rising failed for any particular reason – then this is one of those reasons. Perhaps she is the reason.' He turned back to his mother. 'I've killed people for less, much less. I've killed people for talking to the enemy, for selling them goods, for even being suspected of dealing with them. And so why shouldn't I kill you?'

'Because I'm your mother,' Katherine snapped, looking from Patrick to Collins, wondering at the second man's identity, wondering what was his connection with her son.

'Somehow that doesn't mean that much to me,' Patrick said, his voice beginning to tremble.

Collins stepped in front of Patrick, and gently took the gun from his hand. 'Not now, not here,' he said looking directly into Patrick's troubled eyes. He eased down the hammer on the pistol and then dropped the gun on the table.

'You seem to have some sort of control over him – and just who might you be, may I ask?'

Collins turned and favoured Katherine with a broad smile. 'Madam? I am Michael Collins.'

Katherine nodded. She was of course aware of the name, although like many people, she had never actually seen the Big Fellow. 'So, you're Collins,' she said appraisingly, committing his description to memory. 'The most wanted man in Ireland. There is a handsome reward – what is it now, ten thousand pounds – for information leading to your capture.'

Collins smiled. 'But you'll not collect it, madam.'

The two stared at one another for a few moments and then finally, Madam Lundy looked away.

A knock on the door broke the uneasy silence that had fallen. Collins stepped back and opened the door, and then stood to one side while one of the girls carried in a tray with the fine silver tea service that was actually reserved for special guests. Another maid followed, carrying a second tray with fine china.

'Aaah, tea.' Katherine looked from Patrick to Collins. 'I only anticipated two ... but you are welcome to join us Mr Collins.'

'I think not, but thank you. Patrick ...?' he left the question hanging.

Patrick shook his head quickly. 'I'll be alright.'

'And sure why shouldn't he be?' Katherine asked quickly. 'What harm can come to him here with his own mother?'

Collins strode over to Katherine and stooped down until his face was barely inches from hers. 'Don't push him, madam.'

'Are you threatening me?'

Collins smiled, but it was completely without humour. 'It is not a threat madam, merely a friendly warning.' He straightened before she could say anything else. 'I'll see you in the morning,' he said to Patrick, as he walked past. 'Be careful. Do nothing foolish,' he added softly. Aloud he added, 'I'll see my own way out.'

Katherine waited until she heard the front door slam, and then she poured the tea, milking both cups, adding two spoonfuls of sugar to Patrick's. He took the cup without a word and sat down in the easy chair facing her.

They drank their tea in silence, like two casual acquaintances who have exhausted their fund of topics of trivial conversation.

Finally, Patrick broke the silence. 'How is Senga?'

Katherine nodded. 'She's fine.'

'I miss her.'

There was a pause and then Katherine said, 'I notice you didn't miss me.'

Patrick smiled at his mother. 'I don't.'

Katherine sat back into the chair, both hands wrapped around the cup, watching Patrick closely. 'You've changed,' she said finally. When Patrick remained silent, she continued. 'You've ... matured.'

'I've grown up in the past year and a half,' he said softly.

'I thought you'd gone to America,' Katherine admitted, trying to draw him into conversation.

'I know. You were meant to think that.'

Katherine turned the teacup around in her hands, controlling her temper with difficulty. The old Patrick would never have spoken to her in such an impertinent manner. 'I was so worried about you, I sent Mr Lee to look for you ...'

'You sent Mr Lee to bring me back any way he could. You also sent Mr Lee over here with instructions to kill Jane, to make an example of her. Instead, he was the one made an example of.'

Katherine's usually impassive face twisted in anger, and then just as quickly, the mask returned. She attempted to bait Patrick into some sort of revelation. 'I always thought there was something suspicious about his death. For the first week or so, he sent me almost daily reports on his progress ... and then suddenly he ends up shot by the police for something stupid.'

'He was an evil man, he deserved death.'

'You're twenty-one years of age, boy, you're not in a position to judge who is deserving of death.'

'Are you? How old are you now ... forty ... forty-one. Can you make that decision now? How old were you when you made the decision to send several hundred men to their deaths, eh? Thirty-five, thirty-six. What age do you have to be before you can start making life and death decisions?'

Katherine leaned forward suddenly, startling Patrick, but she was only reaching for the teapot to pour herself another cup of tea. 'You've been busy while you've been over here, I see,' she said quietly.

'You'll never realize just how busy,' Patrick said grimly. 'And yes, I looked into your background. And I found it fascinating ... and revolting.'

'You weren't there,' Katherine said, suddenly defensive. 'Whatever decisions I made, I made for our good, the good of the family.'

'And what about the husband you betrayed? What about his colleagues, his friends?'

'My first loyalty was always to my family. Unfortunately, my husband's was to his cause first, and his family second. I hope you're not going to make the same mistake.'

'I don't think my father made any mistakes, did he?' Patrick asked bitterly. 'I don't think Captain John Lewis betrayed his cause.'

'Lewis betrayed me!' Katherine suddenly shouted, and then, sobering, she added, 'he betrayed himself. And he paid the price for his betrayal.'

'And what price was that?'

Then it was Katherine's turn to smile maliciously. 'I shot him.' Watching Patrick's face intently, she added, 'He was a cruel man, a killer, who had murdered several people by his own hand, and sent countless others to their deaths. You may have been the fruit of his loins, but you were always my son.'

But Patrick shook his head savagely. 'No, I am truly John Lewis's son.'

'You don't know what you're talking about!' Katherine snapped.

'No mother – you don't know what you're talking about. You don't know what I've done in the past eighteen months. Do you know what happened to Mr Lee for example?' he hissed. Patrick smiled, baring his teeth like an animal. 'I shot Mr Lee ... in this very room in fact.'

Katherine started to shake her head, but Patrick pressed on. 'How do you think I got to be so close to

367

Michael Collins in such a short time, eh? Oh, being Dermot Corcoran's son helped, but that wasn't enough. I had to prove myself. And do you know how I did that mother; do you know how I proved myself, how I earned my manhood?' Patrick's face had twisted into an ugly mask. 'I became a killer.'

Katherine surged to her feet. 'Stop it. Stop it right now.' Her hands were shaking and she clasped them together in front of her. 'I suppose you're trying to impress me, to show me how grown up you've become ...'

Patrick threw back his head and laughed.

Katherine took a step backwards, obscurely frightened now. And as Patrick's laughter spiralled upwards into hysteria, she suddenly realized that he wasn't lying. She squeezed her eyes shut, pressing her hands to her ears, for the first time in years feeling vulnerable, and terribly frightened. Events were slipping out of her control ...

The laughter stopped.

Katherine opened her eyes to find Patrick standing before her, calm and composed, a slight quizzical smile on his thin lips, his head tilted to one side, and in that single moment, he reminded her irresistibly of John Lewis. And she realized then that he was capable of killing, in the same way that his father had been capable of killing ...

'Go back to England, Mother,' Patrick said quietly, his voice barely above a whisper. 'Go back to your brothels and your whores. Go back.' He took a step closer to her and she flinched. 'But leave my sister out of it ... leave her out of all this. If she goes into the life, I will kill you.' Suddenly the revolver was in his hand, his arm straight out in front of him, the heavy barrel inches from her face. 'I will kill you,' he promised. 'Go back to England, Mother, and send her away. Send her to the continent where she can finish her schooling, untainted, uncontaminated by you and your kind.'

'You are Lewis's son,' Katherine said bitterly, beginning to regain her composure, and in that moment, she also realized that she would have to deal with him as she had dealt with Lewis.

'I am. I admit it. And you will do as I say. Now you can do it willingly, or I can kill you and, as your heir, I will then be in a position to do it instead. It's a simple choice really.'

Katherine nodded. 'I don't really have any choice, do I?'

'You don't.'

'I'll do as you say.'

'You will,' he nodded. 'While I live, you'll do as I say.'

Katherine Lundy suppressed a smile. Her son had put it beautifully, capturing her own thoughts. 'While he lived.' Well, that mightn't be too long.

CHAPTER TWENTY-EIGHT

As September rolled into October, the war became more and more bitter, with atrocities being committed on both sides. The Director of Intelligence for the Crown was Sir Ormonde Winter, a career soldier who had experience and the ability to organize a professional intelligence network, and soon the IRA found themselves under pressure from all sides. A new breed of agent was being used against them – petty criminals, mercenaries, and soldiers of fortune – willing to risk their lives for the lucrative rewards offered. The IRA retaliated, and informers were ruthlessly shot. At night, during the hours of curfew, the empty streets echoed to the sounds of the lorries and armoured cars, and then doors would slam and glass break, and perhaps a shot or two ring out. And then silence.

In October, a new and disturbing element crept into the raids – silence. Special operatives of the British Intelligence service carried out their raids in complete silence, using heavy silencers to muffle the reports of their guns. The authorities had realized that if they destroyed the IRA network in Dublin then the countryside cells would fall apart and, without Collins' brilliant leadership, disintegrate completely.

Men were now trained in London and dispatched to Ireland under a number of covers and aliases, and they in turn sent their information back to London, the authorities having finally recognized that Dublin Castle was no longer safe. Also operating in Dublin at this time were the Intelligence Units of the Army, the Royal Irish Constabulary, G-Division of the Dublin Metropolitan Police and the Igoe Gang – police officers from the country stations drafted into Dublin to watch for IRA operatives from the country visiting headquarters in Dublin.

And in October, 1920, the Cairo Gang arrived in Dublin; their sole purpose to destroy Collins's organization.

Collins came close to capture in October, and two of the IRA's top men in the south, the two men who had organized the Soloheadbeg raid, Sean Tracy and Dan Breen, came close to capture in a Dublin suburb. Breen was wounded and barely escaped with his life.

Patrick Lundy survived two assassination attempts in late September. Although he had no evidence to the contrary, he suspected his mother of orchestrating the event. Suddenly the police, army, Auxiliaries and Tans began paying the house in Tyrone Street a lot of attention. It was raided four times in one week and, eventually, through his contacts within the police, Patrick learned that information coming from London was directly associating the house with the IRA gangs, and named Patrick Lundy directly.

In the middle of November, both Patrick Lundy and Michael Collins came to two decisions. Both were to do with killing.

'I think you should reconsider,' Collins said coldly.

'Give me a reason,' Patrick said, his voice equally chill.

'She is your mother,' Collins said, pushing away from the iron rail that surrounded Nelson's Column in the centre of O'Connell Street.

Patrick hurried after him, while across the street, two hard-eyed men moved out of the shadows of Clery's windows to follow the two men. Neither Patrick nor Michael Collins paid them any heed – they knew there were another two on the other side of the street. All four men were armed, and would fight to the death to protect their leader, Michael Collins.

Collins strode down the centre of O'Connell Street – or Sackville Street – as it still was officially called. A chill wind was sweeping down the broad street, flecked with ice and the promise of rain. Although it was a little after three in the afternoon, it was almost dark and the night promised to be bitterly cold.

'Give me a reason,' Patrick demanded, catching up with the Big Fellow. 'If it was any other spy or informer ...'

Collins stopped and rounded on Patrick, his face hard, his eyes flat, like stones. 'Yes,' he whispered, 'if it was any other spy or informer, but it's not. It's your mother. You want me to order your mother executed.'

'No,' Patrick shook his head slightly. 'I don't want you to order my mother's execution. If it is to be done, I'll do it myself.'

Collins shook his head and walked away, head tucked into his collar against the wind, hat brim pulled down over his eyes.

'She knows us ... she knows you and me,' Patrick called after him.

'Give me proof of her guilt,' Collins snapped. 'Real solid proof; not your type which is nothing more than hearsay and speculation.'

'What about the sudden activity since she left here; how close have the authorities come to you ... and to me? How many times has number eighty-two been raided in the past month alone. There is a permanent watch being kept on us; the house is plagued with spies, both without and within ... I know that certainly two of the girls and one of the male servants is in the pay of the British.'

'So, what do you want to do – kill them?'

Patrick shook his head. 'No, not yet anyway. At least this way we know the faces; next time we might not be so lucky.'

They had now reached O'Connell Bridge and both men stopped, turning against the wind whipping up river, holding onto their hats. 'Don't worry,' Collins said, preparing to depart, 'you'll have someone to kill soon enough.'

'What do you mean?'

Collins smiled grimly. 'We're going to put out the eyes of the British in Dublin.'

Patrick remained silent, waiting, knowing there was more.

Collins turned to look back up the broad street, still bearing the scars of the abortive Rising. Much of the street was still covered with hoardings and scaffolding, and it would be years before the evidence of the Rising had been completely wiped away. 'Go and see Cathal Brugha, the Minister of Defence. He has files on thirty-five British agents operating in Dublin. Some he's not sure of, and if there's any shred of doubt, then leave it to one side. We can watch those and act later if necessary. But there's twelve or fifteen definite spies in the group. I want these particular ones removed from the game. Take care of it.'

'When?' Patrick asked.

'In four days time, on Sunday, 21st November.' Michael Collins turned and smiled briefly at Patrick and then, his head ducked against the wind, walked across the bridge, towards Westmorland Street. He turned to the right, heading up Aston's Quay. It was Patrick Lundy's last meeting with the Big Fellow.

The following days were spent in frenzied preparations for the operation on Sunday. Patrick was surprised to find that planning for the operation had been under-way for some weeks now, and that the IRA were well aware of the identities, locations and habits of the spies.

Patrick's part in the unfolding drama was relatively simple. His task was to vet the men for the job, and assign them to their tasks. He spent most of Friday interviewing the men; aside from the dozen or so men who would actually do the killing, backups were needed. Where possible, one man would do the shooting, while at least one and possibly two companions would accompany him to act as guards or backup if something went wrong. Another man would wait in the street.

Arms and ammunition were the next priority.

Although most of the IRA still preferred the German Parrabellum pistols or Mausers, Patrick insisted on the more reliable revolvers for the actual shooting, and where a group of three was entering a house, at least one would be carrying a sawn-off shotgun.

Large scale street plans were secured, and the houses of the marked men – the 'particular ones' as they were nick-named – were picked out, and all the possible escape routes plotted.

When everything was in readiness, Patrick reported to Cathal Brugha, and he in turn passed the message on to Collins. And the word came back that the operation was to go ahead. They would kill on Sunday.

Patrick awoke early Sunday morning – although he wasn't really sure if he had slept at all during the night. He had moved away from number eighty-two for the night. The house was becoming too hot for comfort and the police and military presence had made it such that business was practically at a standstill. He had already spoken to the girls, suggesting that if they wished to go back on the streets, or move to other houses then he had no objections. Only one left.

Patrick had spent the night in one of the IRA's safe houses on the corner of Amiens Street, directly across from the station, about ten minutes walk from Gloucester Street. He didn't want to get caught at this late stage in the game; the police had been particularly vigilant of late, and one of the reasons Patrick had quit number Eighty-Two for the night was because two of the key figures in his plan – MacKee and Clancy – had been captured by the Auxiliaries shortly after two that morning. A cyclist had brought the news to Patrick just as he was preparing to turn in for the night. He had immediately dressed and, ignoring the curfew, made his way through the silent streets towards the nearest safe house.

He lifted his watch from his jacket pocket and looked

at the face, which was faintly illuminated in the wan morning light. A few minutes off six. Time enough.

He was dressing when he heard the noise below. Patrick froze. The house was deserted, and only used by the IRA in times of emergency. His gun was under his pillow and the sound of the hammer being cocked sounded unnaturally loud in the bare room. On stockinged feet he crept to the door and, with one hand, carefully turned the handle and peered out onto the bare landing. It was deserted, dust motes circling lazily in the dawn sunlight shafting in through the grimy windows.

He was moving down the stairs, heart pounding, when he heard the noise again. It was the sound of someone tapping gently on the hall door.

Patrick ducked into the sitting room, and peered out through the dirty tattered curtains into the street. A battered black bicycle was leaning against the rail, and it was the bicycle more than the messenger that Patrick recognized: it looked like the bike Paul Flynn – one of the servants from the brothel – rode. He padded back out into the hall and, placing his ear to the door, said quietly, 'Who's there?'

'Paul, sir, I've a message.'

'Shove it through the letter box.'

'Yessir. But I've to wait in case there's a reply.' A small brown envelope appeared in the letterbox, bearing the crown of the Royal Mail. It was a telegram. Patrick squatted on the floor – out of the line of fire – and carefully slit the envelope. The thin sheet of paper inside contained just fourteen words.

'Arrive Dublin on morning mailboat. Arrive City at nine. Meet at station please. Senga.'

'When did this arrive?' he demanded through the closed door.

'Less than ten minutes ago, sir. One of the lads at the house opened it in case it was something important.' There was a pause and then the young man added, 'I hope that's alright, sir.'

'That's fine, Paul,' Patrick said automatically. He

crumpled the paper in frustration; he had an appointment that morning, an appointment he didn't want to miss. Gritting his teeth in frustration, he closed his eyes and concentrated ... and then jumped when the young man on the other side of the door said, 'Will there be a reply, sir?'

'No reply, Paul,' Patrick said numbly. 'Go back to the house and wait for me.' He wasn't sure if there was a reply he could make. He was supposed to be killing a man at nine.

When he heard the bike clatter away from the rail, Patrick dashed upstairs and began to dress hurriedly. He had no guarantees that young Paul Flynn hadn't been followed from the brothel, but one of the reasons he had survived so long – one of the lessons Collins and experience had taught him – was to trust his instincts. Less than five minutes later, Patrick Lundy walked away from the house.

The killings were to begin at nine – no sooner, no later; they were planned to occur almost simultaneously all across Dublin, and in one fell swoop, wipe out most of the British Intelligence Agents in Dublin. Secrecy and timing were essential.

Patrick Lundy stood outside the door of Number Twenty-Two Lower Mount Street and looked up at the upper storey windows. His target was up there – Lieutenant Angliss, whose real name happened to be McMahon – and his colleague, Lieutenant Peel. Both men were experienced intelligence operatives, and Angliss had seen service all across Europe and most recently in Russia as an agent for the Crown. He had been drafted to Dublin, along with the rest of the specialists, to destroy the IRA network.

Patrick glanced at his watch ... a little off seven. Both men had another two hours to live. He moved his arm, feeling the weight of the pistol in the waistband of his trousers. This man deserved death – he was one of the prime targets this day and also the most dangerous – and yet, because there were two men in the house, Patrick knew he stood no chance of killing one without raising the alarm.

And Senga was coming in at nine.

His life seemed to be made up of choices between his family and his cause. His mother's life – aye, and his father's too – seemed to have been governed by the same choices: family or country.

He glanced at his watch again – seven o'clock on the button – and then put it away. He had reached his decision.

The front door of the house was closed, and all the windows had their curtains pulled. Patrick took the key from his pocket and looked at it for a moment, and then resolutely strode across the street.

With the exception of a few tenements, Lower Mount Street was mainly a commercial street, and especially quiet at this early hour and because it was a Sunday. The only signs of life came from the large nursing home next door to the lodging house. Patrick held his breath as he fitted the key into the lock and turned, praying the door wouldn't be bolted, that the key would work. It did.

The house was almost completely silent, only the maid shuffling about upstairs. His rubber-soled boots making no sound on the carpeting, Patrick moved quickly upstairs, the long, double-edged knife in his left hand glinting a dull orange in the soft interior light.

There were two rooms on the first floor, and both were occupied by British agents, Angliss/McMahon – and Peel. With a tiny shrug, Patrick stepped up to the door on the right hand side, closest the stairs, and tried the handle. It was locked. Walking across the corridor, he tried the second door, and this time the door opened.

The bed was situated to the left of the door, up against the windows that looked down into the street below, and on the bed, a dark-skinned, dark-haired man snored softly, both hands outside the coverlet, a copy of the previous day's *Mail* lying across the bed. Patrick crossed to the bed and gently pulled down the covers, and then, placing the point of his knife against the man's bare chest, he took out his pistol and rested it against his upper lip. Pressing the cold barrel against the man's lips, he thumbed back the hammer. In the silence of the room, the click sounded like a stick breaking. The man's eyes snapped open. They were cold and grey, the colour and texture of stone.

'Who are you?' Patrick whispered.

The man started to shake his head and the foresight on the barrel of the gun bit into the soft flesh of his nose.

'Who are you?' Patrick demanded again, 'your name. What is your name?'

'Angliss ... Lieutenant Angliss,' the man said calmly.

'You were warned to leave Dublin,' Patrick said with a hint of a smile. 'You decided not to accept our invitation. Now may God have mercy on your soul.'

The man's eyes flared as Patrick leaned down with all his weight, driving the knife up between his ribs, sundering his heart. He died without a sound.

Patrick Lundy stood up, and then calmly drew the covers across the bloody wound in the man's chest, and then he closed his accusing eyes. Surveying the room, but finding nothing astray, he left the room, closing the door and turning the key he had found on the inside of the lock. He dropped the key in his pocket, he moved quickly down the stairs, letting himself out the hall door into the street. He stood on the step for a moment, looking up and down the street. But it was still and silent, as it had been three minutes earlier when he had entered the house. Straightening his tie, he set off down Mount Street, looking for a tram that would take him to Dun Laoghaire.

Two hours later, when the IRA raided the house on Lower Mount Street, they burst into Angliss' room and pumped five shots into his 'sleeping' form. Peel, alerted by the shots, piled furniture against his door, and then crouched against the wall while the IRA fired through the door, the heavy bullets ripping through the room.

They were actually on the point of breaking their way in when a passing Auxiliary patrol happened upon the scene. The confrontation that followed was the only resistance the IRA found that morning.

Eleven British officers engaged in spying on the IRA were killed that morning, four were wounded and survived. Two Auxiliaries were shot in the engagement in Mount Street, and an officer of the Veterinary Corps was accidentally shot in the Gresham Hotel. One IRA man was wounded and captured.

Rumour and speculation doubled and redoubled the numbers killed, until it was firmly believed that fifty officers had been slaughtered, and the entire British Secret Service in Dublin wiped out. In retaliation the Black and Tans mounted a machine gun on a railway bridge overlooking the All-Ireland Football Match in Croke Park. Another group climbed onto the wall and formed a line looking down into the stadium. At a little after three o'clock, they opened fire into the crowd, killing men, women and children, spectators and players alike. Fourteen people died, and sixty-two people were seriously wounded.

The newspapers christened it Bloody Sunday.

Standing on the quayside, Patrick pulled his watch from his pocket and checked the time against the bells tolling behind him in the wealthy suburb. Nine o'clock. The teams would be starting their grisly work now ... starting and finishing it without him.

As the first of the people began to appear off the boat, Patrick forgot all about the IRA mission underway in the city. He pushed forward, eagerly scanning the crowd, wondering if he would recognize his sister ... after all it had been nearly two years. She would be thirteen now, and quite the young lady too, he was sure. Quite the young English lady if his mother had had her way.

Twenty minutes later the crowd had gone, and there was still no sign of Senga. Puzzled, he made his way towards the gangplank where one of the ships officers was still standing.

'Excuse me ...?'

The man turned to look at him. 'Can I help you, sir?'

'I was expecting my sister off the boat ... and I was just wondering if she could be still on board.'

The man lifted a thick red-bound notebook. 'I've checked everyone off the passenger manifest sir, and everyone had disembarked.'

A cold knot settled into Patrick's stomach. 'Was there a Senga Lundy aboard would you know. A young girl, twelve or thirteen, striking black hair?'

Even as his blunt finger was tracing its way down the list, the man was shaking his head. 'I think I would remember sir ...' When he looked up, Patrick was gone.

Every instinct was screaming at him to leave. He tried to rationalize it: it might have been a mistake. Senga might have got the date wrong, might have missed the boat, might have ...

But Patrick didn't think so. His every instinct, the same instinct that had kept him alive over the past months, told him that something was very, very wrong.

The boat train was pulling out of the station, steam and white-smoke swirling around the building. Patrick swore bitterly, and was turning towards the open end of the station when he spotted the three men making their way towards him. Patrick dropped to one knee, the heavy .45 revolver in his right hand, his elbow braced on his knee. Why hadn't he brought the automatic – he could have used the extra rounds now.

The three figures scattered, and Patrick knew then that these were professionals. Army, Auxiliary, Police, or hired guns, he wondered.

He dropped flat to the ground and began to roll, stopping only when he came up against the wall. As he came to his feet the last of the smoke from the departing engine was dissipating, and as he lunged for the door to the office, the first shots spattered into the tiled wall on his left. The ornate tiles shattered, spraying him with slivers of ceramic, and then a second gun opened up, chewing into the wood of the door by his hand. As he shouldered his way into the room, he realized that there were two different calibre guns firing at him, a .45 and possibly a .32. And that meant either Auxiliaries – who could use their own weapons – or hired thugs.

Patrick pointed his gun at the dumbfounded clerk at the desk and raced to the window. Without looking at the man, he asked, 'Any other way out of here?'

'No, sir.'

'Lock the door,' he ordered, 'and then find someplace to hide.'

'Yes, sir.'

While the terrified clerk turned the key in the lock, Patrick picked up a table and threw it through the meshed glass window. The sound was deafening, and Patrick knew he had only seconds before one of the three – if that's all there were – made their way around to this side of the building.

Ahead of him was the boat.

Patrick had covered half of the hundred yards separating him from the boat before the first of the gunmen appeared around the side of the clerk's office. The first shot struck sparks from the cobbles by Patrick's feet, the second buzzed by his head. Without looking around, Patrick fired, and heard glass shatter behind him. There were some cases piled high on the wharf and Patrick changed course for them. He had almost reached the boxes when a sudden burst of gunfire ripped one of the boxes apart. Tommy gun, he breathed, one of the American Thomson sub-machine guns. Hired guns, professional killers, he realized.

He covered the remainder of the distance between himself and the boxes in a long flying leap that carried him across the top of the boxes and down in a bone-jarring heap on the other side. Another burst of machine gun fire shredded the top of the crates, showering him in splinters and sparks.

Lying flat on the ground, he peered around the edge

of the boxes – in time to see two of the gunmen make a run towards him, while the machine gunner remained by the office to cover them.

Patrick's first shot took the first man in the centre of the chest, the force of the blow flipping him over, directly into the path of the second man. The second gunman went down hard on the cobbles – only to rise again almost immediately ... just as the machine gunner let loose again. The burst almost decapitated him. Surprised, the machine gunner stopped firing and Patrick immediately opened fire on him, holding the bucking pistol on target. He wasn't sure if he had got the man, but he disappeared and the firing stopped. Patrick took a few minutes to reload before he stood up.

'So it is true what they say about you!'

Patrick wheeled, the gun coming up. There was a figure standing at the top of the ramp, a woman dressed all in black, her face covered by a thin black veil. Patrick didn't need to be told her identity.

'When you told me you were a killer, I confess I didn't believe you ... and then later when my own sources confirmed it, I found it difficult to believe: my own son a killer. A cold-blooded, ruthless, merciless killer.'

'I'm John Lewis's son remember,' Patrick said tightly, not looking at his mother, watching the suddenly empty station and wharf. Where had everyone gone? But of course, the last couple of years had taught Dubliners the advisability of disappearing when the firing began.

'Yes, you are the Captain's boy,' Katherine said, the bitterness thick in her voice. 'I thought I had bred it out of you but I was obviously mistaken.'

'It must be something in the blood,' Patrick said turning back to look up at his mother. 'What brings you here anyway?'

'You got my message ..?' she asked.

Patrick nodded. So it had been a trap ... and that also meant ...

'The gunmen ... they were yours?' he asked in amazement.

'Employees. Good men too.'

'You brought three men over from London for the sole purpose of killing me, your own son!'

'No Patrick,' Katherine's voice had dropped to a chilling whisper. 'I brought four!'

He felt the pain before he heard the sound of the shot. And then he was on the ground, something having sledgehammered him in the back, his gun clattering away across the cobbles. Instinct drove him then, tumbling, rolling, ignoring the ice and fire in his back and lung. Shots struck sparks from the cobbles by his face. He was aware of the figure in black, like some icon of death staring down at him, faceless, menacing and ultimately terrifying. There was another hammer blow against his left arm, the blow actually lifting him off the ground, rolling him over.

And then he sailed into space.

In the last seconds before the darkness claimed him, he realized he had rolled over the edge of the pier ...

Katherine Lundy stood on the gangplank of the mailboat and watched the bubbles rising from the spot where Patrick had gone in. He had been hit at least twice, she was sure of that, and no one would have been able to survive a drop like that.

When the water had resumed its customary oily swell, she turned away, satisfied.

CHAPTER TWENTY-NINE

London, November 1920

The maniacal laughter echoed down the corridor, bringing Senga Lundy suddenly, terrifyingly, awake. She started up in bed, heart pounding, briefly wondering whether it had been part of her dreams ... or ...

The laughter – higher, wilder – came again, and the young girl clutched the sheets up to her chin. She had recognized the sound now, and realized where it was coming from, but that didn't ease her nervousness. Her mother must have returned at some time during the night. Senga wondered briefly whether she had been drinking or whether she was simply having a bad dream. Not that she cared. It had been a long time since Senga Lundy had cared about her mother.

Restless now and knowing from experience that sleep would be a long time coming, Senga slid from the warm sheets and padded across to the window to stare out into the night. The streets, still shining damp after a recent shower, reflected back the street lights. They were silent and deserted, and no lights shone in the houses that surrounded the park. She looked into the sky, attempting to gauge the time, but there was no sign of light on the horizon, and the sky was clouded over with neither moon nor stars showing. The night felt late, however, it possessed that curious still quality that she associated with the middle hours of morning. She could always go out onto the landing and look down into the hall below at the tall grandfather clock, but the thought of wandering around the house frightened her in some vague way and she didn't want to chance meeting her mother, especially if she had been drinking.

Leaning her elbows on the window-ledge, Senga mused that the last two years had seen a dramatic change come over her mother. Although she seemed to be drinking less, her temper had deteriorated, and she seemed infused with a gnawing bitterness. From the staff who had been in employment when Patrick had left in January 1919, only one remained, and that was Mrs James, the cook, and her connection with her mother seemed to go back quite far. But few servants would stand for Katherine's abuse and, of course, nowadays, the servants were not as they had been; she had often heard her mother complain that the Great War had destroyed many, many things, including the manners of the working classes. Some day Senga was going to remind her that she came from a working class background herself. She seemed to be suffering from fits of depression and often she didn't speak to Senga or any of the servants for days, keeping to her rooms, not even receiving visits from her business managers. When she did venture out of her room, her humours were unpredictable and violent, and she had on occasion struck Senga without the slightest provocation.

Now the girl avoided her whenever she could.

Looking into the darkened night, she wondered what her mother was dreaming about, wondering what would make a callous hard-hearted bitch like that cry out in fear and terror ...

There was the nightmare – always the nightmare.

In her dream, she saw the knife coming towards her face. It was moving slowly, so slowly. In her dream she lifted her right hand and stretched out her arm, the tiny pistol almost lost in the palm of her hand, pointed it at the man who had once been her lover – and pulled the trigger, flame spitting towards his face ...

Only now the face was not that of John Lewis, but rather Dermot Corcoran, her husband ... and Patrick, her son. The three faces melted into one, like some grotesque mask, until she was unable to distinguish one from the other.

She saw the bullet strike home, and the man spun away, John's and Dermot's and Patrick's face spinning past her eyes one by one. He crashed to the floor, blood on his shirt, the red ichor obscuring his face.

And he rose again.

And this time he was completely soaked through, and she could smell the filthy water, saw it drip from his hair, sludge and debris encrusted onto his shirt, and now the face was that of her son. Her dead son. The one she had had killed.

Katherine screamed, and the scream awoke her. She sat bolt upright in her bed, shivering. She was covered in an icy sweat that made her night-dress cling to her skin, and the sheets felt damp beneath her body. Her mouth was dry, and her throat felt raw and torn from the shriek. There was a decanter of water by her bed, and although the water tasted flat and brackish, she drank three glasses in quick succession. The water did little to ease her throat and only added a stomach ache to her discomforts.

She slid out of the bed and pulled off the sheets, tossing them into a bundle behind the door. She drew another set of sheets from the linen box at the end of her bed and flung them across the mattress, smoothing them out as best she could with her hands, and then she pulled off her damp night-dress and dropped it atop the damp sheets. Naked, she slid between the sheets – gasping at their chill – and attempted to go back to sleep. She turned the clock on her bedside table: a little after three, the dead hours, when even the whores in the brothels slept, and when the street girls retired for the night, all business done. Katherine lay back on the pillow and tried to compose herself for sleep, but the image of the face – the triple mask – kept coming back to haunt her. Surely only those with a guilty conscience were haunted ... and if the truth were told she wasn't sure if she felt guilty because of Patrick's death.

She had hired four of the best killers London and the provinces had to offer and brought them to Dublin with the intention of at least frightening her son – terrifying him more like – into submission and if he wasn't prepared to submit then …

The men had been given instructions that they weren't to fire unless fired upon first, and she had also warned them of Patrick's reputation, which she had been inclined to doubt in any case.

But it turned out that his reputation had been more than deserved. She had discovered that three dead men later. Four, if she counted him, although his body hadn't surfaced when he had rolled off the pier and splashed into the waves.

But he had deserved it. He had betrayed her – like all the men in her life, he had betrayed her.

Dermot Corcoran had had his cause, and had put that first, and had paid the price for his devotion to that cause. John Lewis had also paid the bitter price of his betrayal, and now Patrick … well, he too had paid the price. She had given him his chances, but he had left her, spurned her after all she had done for him, he had threatened her, mocked her … and she couldn't let that go unpunished, now could she?

Well, bad blood would show through, and Lewis's blood ran in his veins, but at least Senga was Dermot Corcoran's child, and untainted. She wasn't going to lose Senga. The child was hers, and she had learned from her mistakes with Patrick. She had been too easy with him, too lenient; she had allowed him the freedom which had enabled him to become contaminated by his IRB associates. Well, that wouldn't happen with Senga. She would be thirteen next April, and quite the young lady, and as such she would have a young lady's education, complete with finishing school. Katherine was determined that Senga would marry a title, and for that she needed the education. It would be quite a step wouldn't it, for the daughter of a servant, and a whoremistress to marry into a titled family? The woman smiled delightedly at the thought. She had enough clients from the nobility to recognise their many faults, but she also realized that there were few disadvantages to being one of the upper class. Class had its advantages, and she was determined that her daughter would have access to them.

But first the education.

Senga dutifully kissed her mother on the cheek as she came into the dining room later that morning. 'It's so nice to see you back,' the girl lied convincingly, 'I wasn't expecting you.'

'I told you I wouldn't be away long,' Katherine said, pouring tea for her daughter.

Senga nodded, brushing strands of her thick dark hair off her face. Her mother said many things, few of which were true, and many times she said she would be gone for a day or two, only to end up being away for a week or more.

'I concluded my business quicker than I anticipated,' Katherine continued, staring intently at Senga, almost looking through her with the intensity of her gaze.

The young girl thought her mother looked tired ... and old. There was an unhealthy pallor to her skin, a tightness across the cheeks, and there were deep bags beneath her eyes. She looked as if she hadn't slept all night.

'You look tired,' she said carefully.

'I am a little,' Katherine confessed, 'I was late arriving back.'

'You should try and rest, Mother, you're doing far too much.'

'Somebody has to,' Katherine attempted a smile, but it did nothing more than curl her lips. 'I'll try and rest a little later, dear.'

Senga nodded, concentrating on the slightly salted porridge her mother insisted she eat during the winter months.

Katherine began to sort through the letters that had

arrived in the last two days, dividing them as usual into those which demanded to be read immediately and those which could wait. 'How is the new governess?' she asked.

Senga shrugged.

'And what is that supposed to mean?'

'She's fine ... I suppose.'

'You suppose?' Katherine asked sharply.

Senga put down her spoon. 'Her French isn't very good; my German is better than hers, she cannot draw, cannot sing, plays piano badly, and she hasn't advanced beyond simple arithmetic.'

Katherine sighed and shook her head. 'Well, she'll have to go.'

Senga nodded. She hadn't mentioned that the new governess – who had been there just over two weeks – was seeing a gentleman. She was keeping that in reserve, just in case her mother changed her mind and was thinking of allowing the woman to stay.

Katherine put down the post and looked closely at her daughter. It was very easy to see herself in the serious looking young girl with the lustrous thick black hair. But she hadn't had Senga's advantages when she was growing up; her education had been minimal, and she had been thrown out of her home when she had turned eighteen – virtually sold into slavery – for her wage, which she never saw in any case. She hadn't seen a proper pair of shoes until she was fifteen, when she was starting her first job in a tea shop. Senga had how many ... twelve, fifteen, eighteen, pairs of shoes?

'How would you like to go to Switzerland?' she asked suddenly.

'Switzerland ...?' Senga stopped with a spoonful of the lumpy porridge half way to her mouth.

Katherine took off her thin wire-framed spectacles and began to polish them with the corner of her napkin. 'I want you to have the education I never had. I've always done my best to give you everything you wanted.'

389

Senga mechanically ate the porridge, wondering where this was all leading.

'You know I have always stressed the importance of education. This world is changing, changing at a terrifying pace. Twenty, even ten years ago, it wasn't quite so crucial for a young woman to have an education, but those days have gone. The war changed things Senga; whether it's changed them for good or ill I don't know, but you will have to live with those changes. Women took the place of men during the war, on the fields and in the factories; they experienced a freedom they never had before – and they're not going to give up so easily. There will be a place for women in society now, a place they've never had before, a place in industry and commerce, in politics. And those with education will have all the advantages.'

Senga nodded automatically. She had heard similar tirades before and they had never amounted to anything.

'Now you've done well with your tutors, but I think it's time we took your education a step further. I have decided to send you to Switzerland.'

Senga stopped eating.

'There is a college there, run by a woman of my acquaintance. It specializes in "finishing" the education of young ladies.' Ignoring Senga's horrified expression, Katherine continued. 'I wrote to Madam Royer some time ago requesting a place in her college, and she replied just before I left for ... just before I left,' she amended.

'I don't want to go,' Senga said quietly.

'However, I don't see the point in sending you now,' Katherine continued, ignoring her daughter's protest. 'The present term is almost over and the Christmas holidays will soon be upon us. So, I have decided that you will be joining the college with the new term in January.'

'I don't want to go,' Senga said more forcefully.

Katherine stopped. 'I have decided.'

'I don't want to go.'

'This is not open for discussion, the decision is made.'

Senga's face twisted in a mask of rage and for a single moment, Katherine was uncannily reminded of Patrick. 'I'll not go. I'll run away – like Patrick!'

'I told you never to mention his name in this house again,' Katherine whispered, suddenly ashen-faced.

'You drove him away – and now you're going to do the same to me!'

Katherine's fist came down hard enough on the table to make every piece of crockery rattle. 'How dare you speak to me like that! You'll remember just whom you're talking to. Now this decision is made, and you are going. You're a little young it is true, but you're advanced for your age, if need be you can stay on another year. You'll thank me for this later on.'

'I won't,' Senga said sullenly.

'And you'll keep a civil tongue in your head,' Katherine snapped. 'Now, I'm sure you have something to do.'

'My breakfast …' Senga began.

'I'm sure you have something to do – now!'

Senga fled from the room, tears sparkling unshed in her eyes. She wouldn't give her mother the satisfaction of seeing her weep.

Without passing her daughter a second thought, Katherine picked up the first letter from the pile and began to read.

How will Patrick find me?

Senga stood at the window staring out over the park, with the same thought running around and around in her head. How would Patrick find her? And then the thought struck her; was this some scheme of her mother's to keep them apart. Had she somehow learned that Patrick was returning for her – he had said he would – and now she was going to ensure that when he arrived, Senga would be gone. And she was sure her mother wasn't about to tell him where she'd sent her.

The more she thought about it, the more convinced she became ... and the more determined she was to best her.

Not a day went by that she didn't think of her brother. Although he hadn't made contact with her in two years, she knew instinctively that her mother was doing her best to ensure they were kept apart. She didn't blame him for leaving; he had done what he had to do, he had made the right decision at the time – the right decision for both of them. He had told her he would come back for her – and she believed him. It was only a matter of time.

Patrick was in Ireland, she was convinced of that. She had heard something ages ago – more than a year certainly – that he had gone to America with the servant girl, Jane, but she was sure that wasn't true. That was about the time Mr Lee had disappeared. Senga knew he had gone to Ireland on some errand for her mother; and he had never returned. Senga liked to think that Patrick had something to do with that. She had no idea what was going on in Ireland; her mother still refused even to mention the country in the house, and Senga wasn't allowed access to newspapers. But just supposing ... just supposing, Patrick had managed to make his fortune over there. And just supposing her mother had discovered that and found out that Patrick was going to come back for her ... and suddenly there was this mad rush to get her off to Switzerland ...

Except there wasn't any mad rush. She had a month and more to go before she left for the continent. The fantasy collapsed, and Senga once more found herself looking out across the sad-looking park, the trees stripped of all foliage, the ground muddy, puddles sitting on the gravelled path. Leaning her head against the cool glass, she wondered if there was any way she could get a message to Patrick ... or ... or leave a message for him!

The thought hit her so suddenly, she felt breathless, and she remained absolutely still, allowing it to drift and settle in her own mind like some piece of flotsam. Deliberately not thinking of her idea she crossed to the fire and sat down before it, staring deeply into the glowing embers, and then carefully, almost delicately, she examined her idea, piece by piece, attempting to work it out.

There was no way she could get out of being sent to Switzerland. So, all she could do would be to leave a message for Patrick, and it would have to be left somewhere he would be sure to call when he returned to London, and the obvious place, indeed the only place, was with Joseph Hyde in the bookshop on Charing Cross Road. She had never met the man but Patrick had spoken of him often enough, and from the little she knew, she guessed that had been Patrick's contact with the Irish groups in London. So all she needed to do now was to get a message to Joseph … but that was probably easier said than done. She wasn't allowed out of the house on her own, and there would be no cause for her to go to a bookshop down on the Charing Cross Road; that would be a job for one of the servants. If her mother ever got to hear of it …

Unless …

Senga stared at the coals, a germ of an idea insinuating itself into her head.

The kitchen was warm, rich with the smell of Christmas baking, and it had an atmosphere thick enough to cut and slice. Dustmotes of flour hung on the still air, and as she moved deeper and deeper into the newly tiled kitchen, different smells assailed the young girl's nostrils, depending on which cupboard she was passing at the time.

Mrs Anna James was alone in the kitchen. Standing before the long wooden table, with her sleeves pushed up to her elbows, she was kneading dough with a single-minded determination that fascinated the girl. She was humming softly to herself – an air that Senga didn't recognize, but which she thought sounded vaguely Irish. Senga Lundy knew little about the cook; she came from Liverpool – although she had no distinctive accent – was of indeterminate age, her red hair now streaked with silver and was anywhere from mid-forties to mid-sixties. She was one of the few people capable of standing up to Katherine Lundy. There was some other connection with her mother – Senga suspected that it went back to Katherine's days in Dublin, but she wasn't sure what.

She tapped on the frame of the door and stepped into the room.

The cook turned, automatically drying her hands on her apron. 'Why Miss Senga, now what brings you down here eh?'

'The smells, Mrs James,' Senga said, sitting on the edge of one of the hard kitchen chairs. 'Have you done all the Christmas baking?'

The cook returned to kneading the dough. 'Sure most of that was done weeks ago; these are just a few bits and pieces. If you hang on a few minutes, there'll be some tarts fresh out of the oven, and if you say nothing upstairs, you may have one.'

'That would be lovely,' Senga nodded.

Mrs James nodded in turn. 'Aye, and while you're eating it, you can tell me what brought you down here in the first place.'

Senga stared at her, open-mouthed.

'Oh, don't look so surprised. You come in here looking as if you're about to burst with something, and you expect me to think everything is alright.'

'I need your help,' Senga said in a rush. 'Mother is sending me off to Switzerland in the New Year to school and if I go I will have no way of getting a message to Patrick but I thought of a way and all I need....'

'Slow down, slow down,' the cook smiled. She wiped her hands again and went to sit in the chair beside Senga. 'Now, start at the beginning and start slowly. What's this about your mother sending you to Switzerland?'

The girl nodded, tears suddenly sparkling in her eyes.

'It's true. She told me earlier that she's sending me to some sort of finishing school in Switzerland for a year or two or more.'

Mrs James nodded sympathetically.

Senga lowered her voice conspiratorially. 'But I think she may be doing it simply as a way of getting me out of the country, because I think Patrick may be coming back. Now, there's no way I can get out of going, but I can leave a message telling him where I've gone if he does return.'

The cook nodded again.

'But the only place I can think of leaving a message is with Joseph Hyde who works in the bookshop on the Charing Cross Road ...' she began to falter beneath the cook's hard stare. 'And I wondered if you would be good enough to deliver it for me. Please. I cannot do it myself.'

Mrs James nodded. 'Of course I'll do it. You write out the message and give it to me and I'll pass it on. Don't you worry about it in the slightest.'

'Thank you ... thank you, Mrs James.'

A few minutes later, when Senga had gone, trailing crumbs in her wake, Anna James made herself a cup of tea and sat at the table, her large hands wrapped around the cup. Katherine had lost her son, she mused, and the way she was going about raising her daughter, she was going to lose her too. The girl had been confined for too long – and sending her to school was not a good idea. Once she discovered the freedom of being away from her mother – even if it was at school – she wouldn't be back.

And Katherine had no one to blame only herself.

CHAPTER THIRTY

It was different.

Different from anything she had ever experienced. It was terrifying and Senga hated it; she had been there for less than a week now, and she wished herself anywhere else in the world – even back with her mother.

The school had no formal name; everyone referred to it as the Chateau, and perhaps it had at one time been a chateau – now it was 'a school for young women of quality' – at least that was what Madame Royer, the director, had said in her opening speech to the three new girls. However, all that remained of the original building was the stone shell. The interior had been gutted and refitted with small partitioned rooms, and the large bedrooms on the first and second floors had been cut up to such an extent that eight girls now shared a room that had once been intended for one. The bedrooms were tiny, each one holding a hard bed, a small cheap wardrobe, an equally cheap dressing table and a chair. Only some of the rooms had access to the windows. The spartan decor was intended to encourage 'self-reliance.'

It was, Senga reflected, little more than a prison. She stood at the window of her room – she was one of the lucky ones – and looked down over the Lac de Neuchatel, and reflected that it was a very clever prison. It was situated in one of the loveliest places she had ever seen, with purple, snow-capped mountains looking down onto deep green forests surrounding a lake that was so blue it looked as if it had been painted. But that same beauty was also part of the prison. The Chateau was about four miles from the nearest town of Neuchatel, four miles along a virtually non-existent road – which was under thick-packed snow and ice for five or six months of the year in any case, and now for example, in the depths of winter, the school was virtually cut off. So, to effect an escape one would need …

Senga smiled at her reflection in the glass. Here she was, less than a month in the place, and she was thinking of escaping, of running away. She had nowhere to run to, no place to go. Shaking her head, she sat back at her dressing table, pushing away the letter to her mother, which the girls were supposed to write home every Sunday. Senga had dutifully handed an envelope to her form-mistress every Sunday evening for the past three weeks, but the envelopes had contained nothing more than a blank piece of paper. She had had no contact with her mother since she had first arrived in Switzerland on the 10th of January, on the final stage of an exhausting journey that had taken her from the docks in London, to the coast of France, then by train to Paris, train again onto Basel, from Basel to Berne and finally by car from Berne to Neuchatel.

When she had walked away from her mother on the docks, she hadn't looked back, she hadn't said good-bye, and when she had walked up the steps to the deck of the ship, she had gone straight to her cabin. It gave her some small comfort that her mother would be waiting on the freezing docks looking for her. But she also knew that if she had paused or turned back, then the anger and frustration that had been building up inside her since before Christmas would have exploded into tears and bitter recriminations … and she didn't want to give her mother that satisfaction.

Martha, her governess had accompanied Senga across Europe. A tall thin, dour woman, who spoke rarely, but who watched the girl intently. Knowing her every move was being watched, and would no doubt be reported, Senga didn't give the woman the satisfaction of seeing her weeping, and was careful to act as if nothing untoward was happening. But at dead of night, when the cabin lights had been turned off, with her face buried in a pillow, the tears came freely, bitterly.

Martha had finally left her at the station at Berne, passing her into the care of a small, round-faced man wearing the grey uniform of a chauffeur, who had been waiting beneath the clock tower. The woman handed over Senga's bags, and an envelope, said a prim good-bye to Senga, turned and walked away.

The man looked at Senga in surprise. 'A nice lady,' he said, in perfect, unaccented English.

Senga nodded.

'The car is outside,' he continued. 'My name is Stoltz. I am the chauffeur and general handyman around the Chateau. And you are …' He turned his head to read the tag on her valise. 'Senga Lundy … from London. Ah, you are English.'

'Irish,' Senga said abruptly. 'I was born in Dublin, Ireland.'

The man nodded. 'Well, I think you will find it very different here. This is neither Dublin nor London. It is quiet.'

'And cold,' Senga said. She was frozen through and her teeth were beginning to chatter.

'We will hurry. This way. I have some blankets in the car.'

Senga followed Stoltz through the surprisingly busy station, marvelling at its tidiness, and its curious air of timelessness that clung to it. It seemed almost too perfect, too 'correct' to have ever been used for anything so mundane as a train station. She guessed the station probably hadn't changed much in the last fifty years. And the streets of Basle too had that curious air of timelessness about them. The main thoroughfares reminded her in some strange way of Dublin; the streets cobbled and comfortably crowded, the buildings a curious mixture of styles, but with little modern architecture intruding into the picture. The people too reminded her of the Irish. There seemed to be little urgency in what they did; they seemed to have a purpose, but obviously speed was not a consideration.

The car was parked at the roadside. Senga wasn't sure what type of car it was, but it was long and sleek and black, and so highly polished that she could see her reflection clearly in it. There were also two girls of about her own age in the back.

Stoltz opened the door and allowed Senga to climb in. 'Now, the journey to Neuchatel will not be tiresome for you, you will have company,' he said, looking at each girl in turn. 'This young lady is Miss Senga Lundy, from Dublin and lately from London.' He indicated the short, stout, dark girl on the right, 'This is Mademoiselle Therese Theroux, who is joining us today, and this is Miss Victoria Edderidge, who is also from London.' The English girl was tall and thin, her pale hair just visible beneath the brim of her hood. She attempted a smile at Senga, but she was so cold, it didn't advance above her lips. 'Now sit, sit please.' The two girls moved over on the leather seats, and Senga sat down beside the English girl. Stoltz produced a heavy rug which he tucked in around her. 'The car will warm when we are driving,' he promised.

It had warmed up during the drive ... and that had been the last time she had felt warm. Senga suddenly shivered. Heating in the Chateau was kept to a minimum; Madame Royer maintaining that excessive heat made for weaker tissues and softer bones, and made the girls sleepy and unable to focus their full attention on their classes. Senga found it to be quite the contrary; she was so cold she couldn't concentrate on her classes, sometimes her fingers were too numb even to hold a pen. Nights were the worst. During the day, with the sun shining from skies that were almost painfully blue, there was at least some pretence at heat, but at night, with the wind whistling down off the mountains, ice-flecked, razor sharp, it became too cold to sleep. Then she would draw her knees up to her chest and pull her night-dress down over them, curling herself into a tight foetal ball, and she would think of a fire ... a roaring log and coal fire, sparks spiralling high into the chimney, the air redolent with the odours of pitch and wood, the coal hissing and crackling, the wood snapping. And then she would imagine herself sitting before the fire, basking in its warmth, the heat spreading through her, soaking into her taut muscles, her stiff bones, making her drowsy …

By then she had usually grown so cold that her fingers and toes were actually tingling as the circulation was cut off, and the semblance of heat was enough to allow her to drop off into an uneasy doze. Usually.

Senga hadn't made any friends in the school yet. It seemed Madame Royer deliberately pursued a policy of forcing her girls to be independent and self-sufficient, and with this in mind, discouraged associations or friendships of any sort. The school timetable was designed to keep the girls busy from rising to sleep. They were awakened at six, and breakfast was at six-thirty sharp. Classes began at seven-thirty with a series of gruelling physical exercises which Senga had at first hated, but which she quickly grew to enjoy as her muscles became accustomed to them. If the weather was clear the exercises were held out of doors in the bitterly cold raw dawn air; otherwise, they were held in a huge hallway. Classes proper began at nine, and continued until one, when there was a thirty minute break for lunch. From one-thirty until five in the afternoon, there were classes, and tea was served promptly at five-thirty. Following tea, the girls were expected to retire to their rooms to complete their daily study tasks and exercises. Lights went out promptly at nine.

Although she had been in it less than a month, Senga was gradually coming to the conclusion that this school catered – obviously – to the daughters of the wealthy and monied class, but it also seemed to specialize in girls who had been sent away to keep them out of trouble. School for scandalmakers.

From the little she had overheard – especially at the lunch or tea tables, where the girls were willing to risk punishment for breaking the rule of silence – all the girls would have normally been considered difficult, or had proved to have been, in one way or another, embarrassments to their families. And suddenly it made a lot more sense why her mother had sent her here in the first place. Not only was she receiving a good education – even Senga had to admit that the standard of schooling was excellent – but she was also out of the way, safe, unapproachable, and unable to cause any trouble. She hoped it was costing her mother a small fortune!

The only free day was Sunday. The school was multi-denominational, principally English and Continental Protestant, with few Catholics. Although Katherine had never encouraged her children to be church-goers, Senga had been brought up as a Catholic, and so, when she was asked her religion, she had said Roman Catholic almost without thinking. Twelve girls attended the Roman Catholic Sunday morning service; the only one Senga recognized was the small, stout French girl, Therese, whom she had met in the car from Berne. Following Sunday service, the girls were expected to study until the lunch gong sounded at twelve-thirty, and then from one-thirty, when dinner was over until five-thirty, their time was their own. This was one of the very rare times the girls could actually get to meet one another, but even then part of the time was taken up with the compulsory letter home.

Senga looked at the wristwatch which had been a Christmas present from her mother. She hadn't wanted to take it – indeed, she hadn't worn it until the day she was leaving – but it looked too beautiful to leave behind, and it was so useful. She touched the tiny gold face with the index finger of her right hand, tracing the ornate tracery around the watch face, round and round, almost as if she were winding back the weeks.

She wasn't going to forget her last Christmas in a hurry. She had missed her brother throughout the year; especially on the 7th July, which was his twenty-first birthday. Throughout the day, her thoughts had been with him, wondering where he was, what he was doing. She wondered if he was celebrating his own birthday – somehow she doubted it.

And then, when Christmas had turned around again, her thoughts had turned towards the brother she hadn't seen since January, 1919. She wondered if she would still recognize him now after all this time ... it was hard to imagine her brother as the father of a child. And she wondered where he was ... and how he was.

If there was any justice in the world – and if there was any forgiveness in her mother's heart – he would be home for Christmas. Unfortunately, there was neither.

Her mother ran her usual circle of parties and social gatherings over the Christmas Season. Surprisingly, Senga was ordered to remain in her room during the parties, and she later realized that this was to avoid any awkward questions concerning Patrick's disappearance. It gave Senga some small satisfaction to know that Patrick and herself were causing their mother if not embarrassment, then certainly inconvenience.

Senga had noticed one change however from the previous years; the parties lacked the sparkle, the elan, of the preceding years. Katherine Lundy's soirées had become one of the main events on the London social scene. They were mentioned in the gossip columns, and the weekly magazines, and Senga possessed a thick scrapbook of cuttings devoted to the activities of the 'genteel Mrs Lundy, and her incomparable contribution to the glittering social scene.' Reading through them Senga often found it difficult to believe that the reporters were writing about her mother; certainly, she didn't recognize her in the pictures they painted.

This year, however, no notices appeared lauding the season's premier party – and Senga noticed that Katherine herself seemed to have lost interest in the events. Previously, she had been involved at every stage of the planning and organization of the huge events, which invariably began months in advance. Now, it seemed, she was prepared to allow her endless supply of business managers to sort out the details, and she contented herself with simply making an appearance.

And she had been drunk on Christmas Day.

Senga had awoken early on Christmas Eve to the sound of crying. She had sat bolt upright in the bed, her heart pounding so painfully, she was sure it was going to burst. For a moment, she didn't know what had happened, and then she realized that the weeping which she had at first taken to belong to her dream, was real. Turning her head from side to side, she realized the sound was coming from her mother's room down the corridor.

The sound was so bitter, so plaintive and melancholy, that she couldn't ignore it. Throwing back the covers she slid out of bed and reached for her dressing gown which hung over her chair. Her feet found her slippers, and she padded silently towards the door. She silently opened her bedroom door a crack and looked out onto the darkened landing. Although the crying had sunk down to a muffled heart-rending sobbing, she could still hear the sounds, and one would have had to have a heart of stone to ignore them.

The landing was cold, with chill air wafting up from the hall below, and she suddenly shivered. She was tempted to turn back, but something moved her on down the corridor towards her mother's room. The sound was clearer now. Although it had sunk even lower, it was piteous, and Senga felt tears start to her own eyes in sympathy. She had actually raised her hand to rap on the door when something stopped her. Instead, her fingers curled around the handle, turning it slightly to the right. Unexpectedly, it opened.

Katherine Lundy's room was hot and smelt stale, but surprisingly there was no smell of drink in the air. Senga ducked her head into the room, her mother's name forming on her lips ... and then she stopped.

The vague grey lights from the street illuminated Katherine's bed, and Senga could make out her mother's face quite clearly, and the girl blinked in surprise – her mother was crying in her sleep. Stepping into the room, Senga looked at her in astonishment, wondering what sort of nightmare could reduce her to this state. Shaking her head, she backed up to the door and slipped out onto the landing. Holding her breath, she closed the door behind her, and then scampered down the corridor to her own room and her still-warm bed. She had never mentioned it, although she had heard her mother crying in her sleep on three subsequent occasions. In a vague, formless way, it terrified her.

The sound of crying brought her back to the present.

Senga looked up, the images in her mind's eyes dissipating ... and then she realized it was the English girl, Victoria, crying in the next room. The walls were so thin that every sound carried.

Victoria Edderidge had cried almost continuously since she had arrived at the school. Senga had tried to make conversation with the girl, but she was so withdrawn that she simply ignored her – and indeed, any of the others who had made an effort. After a while, people simply stopped trying. But the crying reminded Senga of those nights when she had sat up in bed, her arms wrapped around herself, listening to her mother sobbing in her sleep, silently begging her to stop, desperately wishing she knew the cause of her despair. She still felt vaguely guilty because she hadn't been able to help then, but perhaps she would be able to do something this time.

Picking up the empty envelope, Senga opened the door to her room and peered out into the corridor. At this time of day it was deserted; most of the girls were in their rooms writing home, she supposed. She tapped gently on the next door, listening intently. When there was no reply, she tried again, and this time hesitant footsteps approached the door.

Victoria's face was sheet-pale, her eyes red-rimmed and deep-sunk into her head. Strands of her pale blonde hair stuck to the side of her face. She looked at Senga, her eyes blank and uncomprehending.

'Is ... is everything alright?' Senga asked.

Victoria nodded brusquely, and began to close the door. Senga put her hand on the wood and pushed inwards, surprising the girl. She stepped backwards, her mouth opening into an 'O' of surprise. Senga took the opportunity to step into the room and shut the door behind her. Victoria backed away from the other girl until her legs touched the edge of her bed and she sat down abruptly.

The room was identical to Senga's, containing the same furniture in the same positions, and no attempt had been made to personalize it. Senga pulled over the chair and sat down into it, smoothing her pale blue pinafore across her legs. The two girls looked at one another for a few moments, and then they both began to speak together.

'Just what do you think ...'

'Do you want to tell me ...'

They stopped and Senga took the opportunity to continue. 'Do you want to tell me what has upset you so?' she asked gently, watching the other girl intently.

'It's none of your business,' Victoria snapped.

Senga shrugged. 'The walls here are paper thin. Every time you cry, I can hear it in my room. It keeps me awake, it worries me ...' she paused and then added, 'and I suppose I don't like to see someone else so unhappy.'

'Someone else?' The English girl looked up in surprise. 'Who else is unhappy here?'

'Me,' Senga said simply.

'You don't know what unhappiness is!' Victoria murmured, dropping her gaze.

'I think I know,' Senga said softly. 'I think unhappiness is being sent here so as to be out of the way, so that your own brother will not be able to find you, so that you will no longer be an inconvenience to your mother. I think that's what unhappiness is!' she finished with sudden fierceness.

Victoria was looking at her in surprise. 'Is that true?'

'It's true.'

The English girl turned her hands over and over in her lap. 'I was sent here because my father remarried, and wanted me out of the way while he and his new wife "became acquainted with one another." '

Senga nodded sympathetically.

'My brother and sister are both married, with children of their own, some of them about my own age. I'm sure they would have taken me in. No,' she said viciously, 'his new wife just wanted me out of the way. She was afraid I would come between her and my father.'

'What was she like, this new wife?' Senga asked quietly, careful to keep the conversation moving now that she had the girl talking.

'Younger than my mother ... oh, I don't know. But she'd be somewhere around my sister's age. About twenty-five.'

'Is she pretty?'

Victoria shrugged, a quick, dismissive movement of her shoulders. 'In a vacant, coarse sort of way, I suppose she is. I think she's the sort of woman most men find attractive.'

'Whose idea was it to send you here, do you think?'

'Hers I'm sure. Father had often spoken about sending me to a school, but I'm sure he meant in England. Now that I'm out of the way, she'll have everything her own way.' She looked darkly at Senga. 'You'll see the wills change, the children being cut off one by one, the various holdings sold up to pay for her extravagances. You wait, you'll see,' she added ominously.

Senga nodded, surprised by the girl's outburst. Obviously, this had been building up for a long time, waiting for someone to unlock the gates. She also had a very good idea what type of books the English girl read.

'And you ... why are you here?' Victoria asked suddenly.

'I told you. My mother sent me here to keep me out of the way. You see, there was some trouble with my older brother – he had joined a group she didn't approve of – and he ran away. But he always said he would come back for me. I think mother got rid of me because she must have learned that he was about to return.'

'How long has he been gone?' Victoria asked, interested now.

'Since January, 1919.'

'And where is he now, do you know?'

'I believe he's in Ireland. I know that's where he originally went, and I don't think he would have moved on,' she said slowly.

'But that's a terrible place. Full of shootings and killings.'

Senga was about to protest, but nodded. 'It is now. But I know a different Ireland. I know a peaceful, beautiful country, with friendly, honest people.'

Victoria smiled. 'You sound as if you've lived there.'

'I was born there!'

The English girl looked at her in astonishment. 'Why, so was I.'

Senga blinked. 'When?'

'Tuesday, the fifth of May, 1908.'

'I don't believe it! I was born on Tuesday, the twenty-eight of April, 1908,' she squealed. 'I'm a week older than you exactly.'

'Where were you born?' Victoria asked, grinning now, leaning forward, her elbows on her knees.

'In the Rotunda Lying-In Hospital.'

Victoria was nodding happily. 'Yes, so was I. I don't remember any of Dublin though,' she continued. 'We left there when I was about a year old. My father was in the diplomatic services.'

'My father was one of the most famous newspaper reporters in Dublin,' Senga said proudly, and then she continued more soberly, 'he died in the 1916 Rising.'

'Oh ... I am sorry.' Victoria's eyes returned to her hands, her fingers beginning to twist and twine. 'My mother just ... died. I woke up one morning and father told me that she had passed on in her sleep ...'

As the afternoon wore on into evening, the two girls reminisced, swapped memories, and talked about themselves and their families. Although their backgrounds and circumstances were very different, they had much in common: they were both intensely private people, slow to make friends, comfortable in their own company, and they had both been sent away by mothers – in Victoria's case, a step-mother – who had no time for them.

And as the evening drifted into night, they came to a conclusion. It slipped so easily into conversation, and they both accepted it, and yet it remained unstated until it was nearly time for them to part.

With the coming of the spring thaw, they were going to run away together.

Victoria would make her way to London, and Senga Lundy was going back to Ireland.

CHAPTER THIRTY-ONE

On Senga's thirteenth birthday, 28th April 1921, and exactly a week before Victoria Edderidge's birthday, the two girls walked away from the Chateau after lunch. They were both carrying small bundles which contained a change of clothing, and as much money as they had managed to save since they had hatched their plan on that Sunday back in February. Between them, they possessed four pounds in sterling and twenty French francs. They knew they would probably have to steal or beg to reach the coast, and they were both quite willing to do so.

They saw it as a grand adventure ... 'a desperate bid for freedom against all the odds', was how Victoria had described it to Senga one Sunday afternoon in early April when the two girls had been finalizing the plans. Senga had simply reached across and picked up the book Victoria was currently reading, *Escape to Love*.

'This isn't some sort of fairy tale,' she had said carefully, unwilling to upset her friend.

'I know that,' Victoria said indignantly.

The dark-haired Irish girl nodded carefully. She touched the book carefully with the tips of her fingers. 'So we're not really making a "desperate bid for freedom against all the odds," we're simply running away from school.'

The 28th of April was a Thursday, which meant that the afternoons were given over to a regimen of sports and physical exercises. The weather was dry now, though still bitterly cold and, weather permitting, the classes would be held in the grand courtyard behind the house, with Madame Royer herself leading the girls in a series of stretching movements, designed to improve posture, balance and deportment.

Both Senga and Victoria had reported to the infirmary the previous morning, complaining of stomach cramps, and a general feeling of nausea, and had been excused the exercise class by Madame Suskind, the Nurse, after a lecture of hygiene and general cleanliness during their monthly 'trial,' as she called it.

Their plans at this stage were loose.

They had spent many nights whispering together in either Senga or Victoria's bed, beneath the covers, planning what they would do, where they would go, and how they would get there, once they managed to escape the cloying confines of the school. They intended to travel south and west to Geneva, and then across to Lyon in France. From Lyon, they would make their way northwards to Dijon, and thence to Paris. From Paris, it should be a fairly simple matter of making their way either to England or Ireland. They had both deliberately closed their minds to the general practicalities of travelling half-way across Europe on four pounds sterling and twenty French francs.

That was the plan in its broadest terms, and neither of them was prepared to look too deeply at its flaws. But it was all dependent on getting away from the school, and to have any chance of achieving that they needed to be excused the exercise class. They intended to use the few hours' grace before their absence had been discovered to make good their escape.

They counted their success at the infirmary a good omen.

At a little after two o'clock, Madame Royer's rather harsh French accent began to drift over the silent grounds, exhorting the girls to 'lift ... lift ... lift ... turn ... turn ... turn ...'

It was the signal for the two girls to go.

They had left their bundles of clothing in the bushes close to the gates earlier that day, and now it was simply a matter of walking out of their rooms, along the short corridor, down the long, polished stairs, across the gleaming wooden floor and out of the open door onto the steps. Then, looking neither left nor right, their heads bent as if deep in conversation – although they were both too frightened and nervous to speak – they walked slowly away from the school.

The temptation to run was almost irresistible, the temptation to turn and look back almost equally so, but Senga, who was the stronger-willed of the two, maintained a vice-like grip on her friend's arm.

It was the longest walk of their lives.

At the gates they pulled the bundles of clothing from the bushes and now, out of sight of the house, they quickened their pace. Once outside the grounds they were in the most danger; it was forbidden for pupils to wander beyond the confines of the Chateau unless accompanied by an older girl or one of the teachers. The road leading up to the Chateau was relatively unused, and therein lay both its blessing and its bane. It was unlikely that they would meet anyone on the road, but if they did, that person would certainly have some connection to the school. And yet they both knew that they had little choice but to stick to the road; leaving the road – even in spring or summer – was tantamount to suicide. It was very easy to become lost in the mountains, and every new girl was told the story of the girl who decided to run away from school, but who had never turned up at home. Her body, frozen solid, was discovered in the spring thaw.

Both Senga and Victoria knew they had at least three hours before their absence was discovered, and even then it was unlikely that anyone would suspect that they had run away. They had been careful to leave almost everything behind, and the clothing they had taken with them were things which they didn't usually wear, and which, hopefully, they wouldn't be recognized in. They had thought about one of them travelling as a boy, but since neither of them had been able to secure any boy's clothing, this had fallen through.

They walked steadily for an hour, chatting quietly, excitedly together, knowing that every step took them further and further away from the school. They also knew that every step they took meant that it was now harder and harder for them to retrace their steps and return to the school. So no matter what they did, the die was cast.

They walked the second hour in silence, their feet beginning to complain, tiredness and the vague pangs of hunger making them irritable. They hadn't eaten since breakfast, since Madame Royer would not allow her girls to dine before exercises. And, since they had been keeping to the side roads and back lanes, determined to avoid any of the villages or towns that were still reasonably close to the school, they couldn't even stop at any of the village patisseries to buy food.

Darkness came early to the mountains, the sun dipping behind the snow-covered slopes, plunging the valleys into shadow, leaving only the higher slopes washed with colour. Shortly before five o'clock, following a brilliant sunset that had left both girls almost breathless with its beauty, twilight washed over the mountains in a grey, gritty veil. Without the vague warmth of the sun, the air immediately assumed a harder, sharper, chillier edge.

The sudden drop in temperature caught them both unawares, and they both knew that herein lay their first major challenge – they would have to survive a night on the road. All the horror stories they had been told about people freezing to death on the mountains came back to them now.

'I'm frightened.' Victoria's teeth were chattering so much that Senga could barely make out what she was saying.

'I'm cold and frightened,' she said, attempting to sound more cheerful than she felt.

They trudged on through the darkness. The sky was clear, the heavens littered with stars, and, although no moon illuminated their way, there was enough light from the snow-covered fields for them to see their way.

'We could go back,' Victoria suggested eventually.

Senga nodded, but said nothing.

'Will we?' the English girl persisted.

'We've come too far,' Senga said eventually. 'We wouldn't get back until morning – if we got back that is,' she added balefully. 'No,' she shook her head decisively, 'we'll find shelter for the night, and then press on in the morning.'

'Where?' Victoria demanded desperately.

Senga stopped, looking all around in the curious off-white light. They had been following a narrow winding track that paralleled one of the roads that led up from the valley. A narrow band of stunted trees and bushes screened the track from the road. Senga crossed to the opposite side of the track and parted the bushes. Looking back over her shoulder, she pointed across the fields. 'There!'

Victoria squinted into the darkness, but her eyesight was poor in daytime and at night she was virtually blind. All she could see was the whiteness of the fields, bracketed on either side by tall dark shadows which she took to be trees.

'There's a farm,' Senga explained.

'But we can't ...'

'I know that,' the older girl said patiently, 'but we'll spend the night in the barn, and be gone before morning.'

'Are you sure?' Victoria asked doubtfully.

'Have you an alternative?'

It took them nearly an hour to make their way across the fields. The snow was thigh deep off the road, and soon both girls were sodden through. Senga was becoming more and more alarmed as they pressed on and the buildings she had glimpsed from the distance seemed no nearer. She had lost all feelings in her toes and was now simply moving her feet forward mechanically. She knew the dangers though – it would be very easy to slip, twist an ankle or break a foot – and there was also the danger of frostbite, but she wasn't sure what the symptoms of that were. She was also worried about Victoria. The English girl was visibly flagging, holding tightly – painfully – onto Senga's hand, allowing her to haul her along. Her eyes were half closed and she was breathing heavily through her mouth, her breath pluming whitely on the night air, freezing onto her chin in a thin patina of ice. They had to reach shelter soon.

From the moment they had entered the Chateau as pupils, they had been warned of the dangers of wandering far from the school. Senga had originally thought the warnings nothing more than a ruse designed to keep the girls within the walls – another of the many devices, some subtle, others less so, which made them virtual prisoners. Now, she was beginning to realize that there was obviously some measure of truth in them.

So this was it – their grand adventure ended after only a day. And then what? Assuming they were found – and that wasn't entirely likely – what would happen to them? Expulsion, disgrace? Somehow, she thought that would be the least of their worries. If they weren't found tonight, there was a good chance they were going to die.

She had just decided she would leave Victoria – probably in the shade of that tree up ahead – and head off to the farm to get help, when the field abruptly ended and they found they were back on a road again. Beyond a sagging stone wall lay the farmhouse and outbuildings.

The two girls hugged one another and now, with renewed hope, they staggered up the track – the ruts frozen solid – which led towards the farm.

As they neared the house, they fell into single file now, keeping in to the edge of the track, moving as quietly as possible between the crackling pools of ice, trying to still their harsh breathing.

The farm was typical of the region, wood and stone, with a deeply sloping roof, designed to carry away the

414

snow. The heavy shutters had been drawn across the windows, but the girls could see chinks of light in one of the upper windows, and as they watched a shadow passed before it. They stopped – and somewhere close by a dog began to bark, startling them both.

Without a word, they fled across the open courtyard, heading towards the barn. A door suddenly opened shafting a long rectangle of light out across the courtyard, and a voice called out in guttural German. The dog fell silent until the voice called out again, and then he began again, his snarling savage and terrifying.

The barn was to the side of the farm, a long deep wooden building, redolent of cows and straw. It immediately felt warmer inside the building, the air temperature a few degrees higher than outside and without the cutting wind. It smelt dry and faintly musty, the odour of animals and old dung giving it an almost comforting atmosphere.

The dog's barking had now become almost frantic, and Senga urged Victoria up the rickety ladder to the higher shelves where the straw was stored. The English girl's legs were so stiff that they could barely make it up the rungs of the ladder, and Senga had to guide her feet as she climbed behind her. They suddenly realized the dog had stopped barking ... and then they heard heavy footsteps approaching, a man's voice muttering angrily.

Senga had barely pulled her feet through the opening when the doors were flung open and orange light danced across the walls. Heavy footsteps clumped into the barn. She parted the straw and peered down through the loose-fitting floorboards. There was a large bulky man standing below her. He had a long shotgun in one hand, the stock resting against his hip, while he held up an oil lantern with his left hand. A wiry black and white dog wound its way through his legs and raced to the bottom of the steps, and began barking furiously.

The farmer walked to the foot of the ladder and held up the light; the straw turned gold and bronze in the warm light, but the shadows deepened. The big man kicked the ladder in frustration cascading straw and dirt down on top of him. He swore and stepped back.

'Come down,' he snapped. He spoke German with a curiously flat accent. In the few months the girls had been at the Chateau, they had been intensively tutored in French, German and Italian, and knew enough to follow what he was saying.

Placing the lantern on the ground, he thumbed back the hammers on the shotgun. 'Come down or I shoot.'

Senga glanced back over her shoulder at Victoria, wondering what to do. The English girl had crawled behind a bale of hay and was staring intently at her, her eyes wide in alarm. Senga would find no assistance there.

And then the man fired upwards into the roof. In the confines of the barn the noise was deafening, and a bale of straw about four feet in front of Senga exploded upwards in a haze of straw and dust. He fired again.

Both girls screamed as the floor beneath them gave way.

'You must forgive him; he is a foolish man.'

The woman was tiny – smaller than Senga, and pretty in an almost startling way. She spoke English fluently, though with a pronounced French accent.

Senga wrapped her hands around the mug of steaming broth and nodded. She was still too cold, too frightened, to trust herself to speak, and every muscle in her body ached from where she had fallen from the loft into the straw below. She glanced sidelong at Victoria; she too seemed dazed and sipped her broth automatically, seemingly unaware of where she was.

'He was as frightened as you, I must tell you. He went out expecting thieves ... and lo, two girls fall from the heavens.' The woman leaned forward, lowering her voice conspiratorially. 'And he is mad because he shot a great hole in the roof of the barn, and now the snow will come in.' She shrugged expressively. 'But he is like that, it is his German blood; they have a temper – like us

416

French, but different – and they think first and then act.'
She sat back on one of the plain wooden kitchen chairs.
'So, he hears the dog barking, and he thinks – I think
too – that the thieves have come again, for we have lost
eggs and sometimes hens recently. I think perhaps it is
the poor from the village, for the winter has been hard,
and spring is late this year. But no matter. He grabs his
gun. "I will have them," he says and rushes out into the
night. And then I hear the shots and the screams, and I
think, "Mother of God, but he has shot someone" ...
and then he appears with you two, and him looking like
a ghost, and you two looking like the ghosts he has just
seen.'

'I'm sorry ...' Senga began.

The woman shrugged again. 'So is he. So am I.' She
straightened up. 'I am Maria Leiber, and of course, you
have met my husband Ernst.'

Senga said nothing.

The small woman looked at her with a curious
expression on her small, heart-shaped face. She touched
her lips with the tip of her little finger, and then she
smiled. 'Every term, at least one, but sometimes two
girls run away from the Chateau; they don't get far and
are usually returned a day or two later. Most of them
wait until the summer months when the weather is
more clement.'

Senga turned to look at the woman, her face
expressionless. 'Will we be returned to the Chateau?'
The unstated question was clear.

Maria Leiber shrugged. 'I will not betray you – nor
will Ernst. Why, I remember running away from my
own school once. I would have been around your age
too – what are you now, fifteen?'

Before Senga could reply, the door opened and Ernst
Leiber stamped into the room, accompanied by a flurry
of swirling snow. Looking at him, Senga wondered
what Maria could ever have seen in this rotund, bald,
red-faced man. He looked from Senga to Victoria, his
eyes finally returning to rest on the older girl. 'Lucky

417

you found shelter,' he said in simple French overlain with a strong German accent, 'a storm's come in fast, with snow and ice. You would not have survived in the open this night.' He turned to his wife, and spoke rapidly to her in thickly accented French, too fast for Senga to catch even the meaning of the sentence. But whatever it had been, Maria's reaction was a swift, '*Non!*'

'If we have caused a problem ...' Senga began, but Maria waved her silent. She ushered her husband out of the kitchen into a second, smaller darker room that was illuminated only by a glowing log fire. He clumped into the room, and moments later, the warm glow of an oil lamp brightened the wooden beams.

'Now, we will prepare beds, for you must rest, you must be exhausted, and in the morning we can talk and decide what must be done.'

'I hope we haven't caused any problems,' Senga began again.

But the woman shook her head and smiled tightly. 'There is no problem. We took in a traveller once, and he stole from us ... a few things ... of no great worth, but my husband has been wary of strangers since then.'

Senga nodded, but she didn't believe that was the real reason for the sharp exchange of words between the Leibers.

'Now, come, come with me, this way.'

Senga helped Victoria to her feet and half-carried her through the door into a second room off the kitchen. This turned out to be a small bedroom, which smelt strongly of spices and herbs. When Maria lit the gas bowl, Senga saw that the beams and rafters were festooned with drying bunches of grasses and long strings of herbs. Against one wooden wall was the bed, a rectangular box-like construction of polished wood, with a deep mattress set into the box. There were no blankets on the bed, but the woman opened an ornately carved wooden box at the foot of the bed and began pulling out thick blankets and fresh-smelling sheets.

'There is no fire in this room,' Maria explained, making up the bed, 'but it is never cold.' She reached out and touched a panel of stone that ran from floor to ceiling in the centre of the wall nearest the bed. 'This is the back of the chimney in the sitting room,' she explained, 'and so this is one of the cosiest rooms in the whole house.'

'Thank you,' Senga said, easing Victoria onto the bed. The younger girl was asleep on her feet, moving like an automaton.

'She will be well again with a few hours sleep,' Maria explained, seeing Senga's look of concern.

'Thank you,' Senga said again, and suddenly a wave of exhaustion swept over her, draining the blood from her face, leaving her ashen. She sat down on the bed with a thump.

'You too will need sleep,' Maria said kindly.

Senga sat and watched while the woman pulled off Victoria's clothes, folding them into a neat pile on a chair by the side of the bed. She pulled a long night-shirt from the box and worked it over Victoria's head. Then she gently tilted the girl over onto her side, and pulled the night-shirt down before pulling the covers up to her chin. Victoria curled into a tight foetal ball and immediately her breathing regulated and she slipped into a deep sleep.

Senga had been undressing herself, but was so tired that she allowed the woman to remove the last remnants of her clothes, and could only raise her head as the striped nightshirt was pulled over her own head. She slipped off the bed, standing to allow the night-shift to drop down past her knees, and then she sank back down onto the bed.

'Sleep now. Rest,' Maria said as she drew the blankets up around her.

'You won't betray us?' Senga asked urgently.

Maria Leiber shook her head. 'I won't. And I'll make sure no one else does,' she added enigmatically.

Senga Lundy was too tired to ask her what she meant.

419

CHAPTER THIRTY-TWO

The following morning Victoria was burning up. Senga had awoken to find herself damp with the heat from the girl's body, the long night-shirt sticking to her skin. She attempted to rouse her, but with no success, the girl simply rolled over in the bed, eyelids fluttering. Her teeth were chattering as if she were freezing, although her cheeks and forehead were almost too hot to touch, and her hair was plastered to her forehead and across her cheeks.

Frightened now, Senga darted out into the kitchen – just as Maria Leiber turned away from the stove with two steaming bowls of what looked like porridge. The smile faded from her lips when she saw Senga's expression.

'Something is wrong?'

'It's Victoria. She's not well ... I don't know.'

Maria followed Senga back into the small warm bedroom, and then clucked in dismay at Victoria's bright red cheeks. She pressed the back of her hands against her face, brushing them across her forehead, and then pulled down the covers to feel her chest and back. 'She has caught a chill,' she said decisively, 'she cannot be moved.'

'But we've got to be pressing on ...' Senga protested.

'Why?' the woman asked surprisingly.

'Because ... because ...' Senga began, and then realized she didn't have a single reason why they had to hurry on. 'The Chateau will be looking for us,' she finished lamely.

'They will be looking along the roads, at the stations and in the towns and villages. Two foreign girls travelling alone will be easy enough to find. But they won't be searching so close to home. No,' she shook her head with a stiff finality, 'you will rest here – you have no choice –

until Victoria is well again, and then you can continue on your journey. Perhaps by then people will have stopped looking for you.'

Senga nodded. She hated the thought of having their plans dashed so close to the school – they had made their escape, and yet they were still trapped. But they had been lucky so far, she had to admit; if they hadn't found the barn last night, they would have died in the fields, and supposing they had survived the bitter night, how would she have coped with Victoria's illness? How much worse would it have been ... or would she have awoken to find the English girl dead beside her? No – all things considered – luck had been with them so far. It had also been the greatest of good fortunes that they had stumbled on this farm, where at least they had been given a civil welcome.

'Is it dangerous?' she asked eventually, looking at Victoria's glowing cheeks, listening to her harsh breathing.

Maria shrugged her shoulders in a typically French fashion. 'If it is not cared for, then yes, it could turn into pneumonia, or the coughing sickness, but I would not worry. She is young and healthy, and she is warm and in bed, and that is the best place for her. Now ... help me to change the sheets and her nightdress; we must keep her cool and dry.'

'How long will it take for her to get well again?'

'A week ... ten days. The fever must run its course. Some people are strong and shake it off quickly, others ...' she let the sentence hang. They both knew that Victoria wasn't strong.

'I'm sorry,' Senga began.

'What for?' Maria asked quickly. 'This cannot be helped. You were sent here, and it is our duty to help you in your hour of need.'

'Thank you. God will thank you.'

Maria looked at her quickly. 'You are a Catholic?' she asked cautiously.

'I was brought up in Ireland,' Senga said with a smile.

421

'I was raised in a Catholic home,' ... though not a Christian one, she added silently.

Maria ushered her out into the kitchen, and pulled the door closed behind her. 'We will let her rest.' She manoeuvred Senga into one of the high-backed wooden kitchen chairs and then ladled more porridge into a carved wooden bowl. 'Eat.'

The girl looked at the glutinous substance, carefully prodding it with her spoon. It both looked and smelt disgusting. 'I'm not ...'

'One ill is bad. Two ill is impossible,' Maria said sharply. 'It is made of goats' milk. Now eat, and then we will have to decide what to do with you.' She poured herself a smaller bowl of the porridge and sat opposite Senga and ate the gruel without any real enthusiasm. 'Do you want to tell me why you were running away from the Chateau?' she asked.

Senga shrugged. It was only when she had started to eat that she realized how hungry she was and the porridge didn't taste half as bad as it looked. 'The school is ... like a prison,' she looked at Maria, wondering if she understood. The woman nodded, encouraging her to go on. 'We felt we were trapped. Everyone there had been sent away by parents who either didn't care or didn't want to have their daughters around to inconvenience them. It wasn't a bad school,' she added quickly, 'just claustrophobic. A lot of the younger girls talked about running away, but few of them had any place to run to. But Victoria and I had. Victoria has an older brother and sister, and she is sure that one of them will take her in. And I have a brother in Ireland. He will look after me.'

'But your mother ...?' Maria asked.

'She doesn't care for me. She drove my brother out, and now I'm not even allowed to mention his name in the house. I'm sure she sent me here because she was afraid he was coming back to London to take me away with him.'

'So you are both running away, one to London, and you to Ireland?'

Senga nodded.

'It is a long way ... and you have brought little with you. What are you going to live on?'

'We have some money,' Senga said quickly, and then shrugged, 'well, not a lot really, but enough to take us to Paris. And once we are in Paris, we thought it might be possible to get a job as artists' models, or something like that to make a little money. When we have saved a bit, we will continue on home.'

'I was an artist's model once,' Maria said, almost shyly, 'a long time ago, before the war.'

Senga looked at her closely, attempting to guess her age, and found it was impossible. She had the type of fine bone structure that would keep her young looking long into her declining years. Her skin was perfect, completely flawless, pale even here where cheeks tended to redden and lips crack in the cold and wind. 'You must have been very young,' she said eventually.

'I would have been around your own age,' Maria said with a smile, 'about fifteen or sixteen or so.'

Senga hid a smile and didn't bother to correct the woman's impression of her age. 'Did you enjoy it?' she asked.

Maria Leiber tilted her head from side to side, considering. 'Sometimes, yes, sometimes no. There were good times, and bad times, as there are in all things. During the summer when the weather was good, and there were artists aplenty in Paris, well then I was never short of work, but during the winter ...' she shrugged again. 'It is difficult to pose naked in some chill studio.'

Senga felt colour rise to her cheeks and lowered her head to her breakfast. 'Did you often pose nude?'

Maria nodded. 'I had a very fine body,' she said with a hint of pride in her voice, 'many artists painted it.'

'I don't think I could ever do that,' Senga said feelingly, 'I mean, stand naked while some strange men looked at me.'

'Most of them were simply looking at an object, whether it was a human body, a still life, a spray of flowers, the pattern of light on the water. It was simply something to be captured on paper or canvas. They never looked on you as a person ... well, most of them didn't,' she added with a sly smile.

'Most of them ...?' Senga asked.

'Oh, there were one or two who did more than look and paint,' she said with a laugh. 'But come now, enough of this. We have to decide what's to be done with you.' She reached for Senga's bowl and carried it over to the sink. The girl followed her. 'Now Ernst and I spoke about it last night; you see we weren't expecting you to travel on today anyway, not with the storms further down the valley. We decided that you two could be Ernst's nieces from Berlin – he has family there – and we thought that might help account for your strange accents. Although yours is good,' she said quickly.

'Your husband is German?' Senga asked.

'His family are from Berlin, although he has lived away from them for some time now. It was difficult during the war,' she said suddenly, 'being German or having a German name was difficult ...' She let the sentence hang, leaving Senga to wonder what difficulties the couple had experienced during the Great War. 'But that is all over now.' She nodded quickly, as if to convince herself of the truth. 'Now Ernst is a good man,' she continued, scrubbing vigorously at the remains of the porridge in the bowl, 'but he has a temper sometimes, and sometimes acts rashly ...'

Senga took the bowl from the woman and dried it thoroughly, wondering what she was leading up to.

'He has his ways, and he is bitter since the war. He had many friends in the valley until the war came ... and then of course, it was not wise to be seen with a German, and they ignored him, passed him by in the street. It has made him bitter. Sometimes he drinks,' she finished desperately, a little breathlessly.

Senga reached out and touched the woman's arm lightly. 'My mother drinks. I know what to do then,' she said softly.

Maria nodded quickly, blinking back tears. 'Stay out

of his way. When he is drunk he does … things … things he later regrets, but when the drink has hold of him …'

'We'll stay out of his way, I promise.'

'You are a good girl, Senga.' Maria ran her fingers through the girl's hair and then leaned forward to kiss her quickly on both cheeks. 'Now, see to your friend.'

Senga spent the remainder of the day sitting by Victoria's bed, holding a cold compress to her forehead, warm and snug in the small room, dozing contentedly. Occasionally Maria would peer into the room to check on Victoria, and late into the afternoon, she appeared to light a small ornate oil lamp that hung down from the rafters. The sickly-sweet smell of oil suffused the room. Maria returned moments later with two bowls of steaming milk, and they sat silently together, hands wrapped around the bowls, watching Victoria's rapid, shallow breathing.

Eventually Senga broke the silence. She finished the last of her milk and said, 'What will happen if she does not get well?'

Maria Leiber didn't look at her, and the girl immediately knew that the woman had considered the possibility. 'There are two things we might do,' she said eventually. 'We can get the doctor – but that would mean betraying you both, or we can accidentally "find" this young girl in a nearby field.'

Senga nodded. 'And what about me?' she asked.

'You would have to remain in hiding for some time until we were sure we weren't being watched, and then later you could continue on alone.'

Senga Lundy nodded. 'There is a third possibility,' she said quietly.

Maria looked at her but said nothing.

'We could go back to the school.'

The woman nodded. 'You could. Do you want to?'

'No.'

'Then don't. Make no decisions for the next few days – see how your friend progresses. If she is no better then

425

there is a hard choice for you to make. But if she is on the mend, then there is no decision to be made.'

Senga nodded. 'Thank you,' she said eventually.

Maria shook her head. 'It is nothing. I wish I had your courage.'

Senga looked at her in surprise. 'What courage?'

But the woman simply shook her head and said nothing. She took the empty bowl from Senga's hands and left the room, leaving the girl to ponder her words.

Senga must have dozed in the heat of the room. She awoke a little while later with a start to hear low angry voices in the next room which threatened to escalate into shouts. Ernst Leiber was speaking rapidly, the German words unintelligible to her, but the meaning was plain, especially when she heard him repeatedly use the words, 'girls,' and 'Chateau'. Maria's voice was lower, and she seemed to be pleading.

Senga stood up and crept to the door, placing her face against the warm wood. She was tempted to open it, but she daren't lest they hear her. Ernst was talking rapidly now, and she wondered if he was drunk, but his speech wasn't slurred, and he sounded more angry than intoxicated. The Irish girl knew without any shadow of a doubt that they were arguing about Victoria and herself, and she felt guilty that she had brought this down upon them, Maria particularly.

But they had had a choice: they could have taken them in – or left them to die in the bitter night. They had made their choice, and now they were forced to live with it; the German couple were stuck with their two unwanted guests, and the two girls were once again trapped. Now the Leibers had two choices: they could continue to shelter them, or they could turn them in. The girls too had decisions to make: remain where they were until Victoria's condition improved, continue on … or they could give themselves up. She smiled at the thought; she was beginning to think like a criminal, and yet all she had done was to run away from school.

The voices in the other room grew louder, and then

Ernst spat out something, which sounded like a curse, and moments later, the front door closed violently enough to rattle the panes in the windows. Senga heard a chair being moved, and quickly darted back over beside the bed, dropping into her chair and resting her head on her folded arms. The door opened seconds later and in the silence that followed, Maria said gently, 'If you are not awake, Senga, you must be deaf.'

Senga looked up sheepishly. 'I'm awake.'

Maria attempted a smile. In the half-light, it looked more like a grimace. 'I thought you might be. Did our shouting disturb you?' The girl started to shake her head when the French woman pressed on. 'I am sorry, but Ernst is excitable – and it is supposed to be us French who are excitable.'

She turned away and Senga followed her out into the kitchen. Most of the lamps had burned down, and the room was bathed in the warm glow from the fire and the butter-coloured light from a single oil lamp which took the edges off everything. Soft shadows curled in the corners. 'We have brought you trouble,' she said quietly, looking intently at Maria.

The woman seemed to be considering and then she nodded. 'Ernst is afraid the townspeople will discover who you are – what you are – and he is afraid that it will go badly for us if they do.'

'Could it? Go badly, I mean?'

Maria shrugged. 'Ernst is frantic – he is imagining plots and scenes that would only appear in bad paper-covered books. He thinks the townspeople or the authorities might say that we had kidnapped two English girls. It is nonsense I know, but certainly if they were to discover two English girls living in a German household questions would be asked, and perhaps the townspeople would ask their questions and then act before we could give them answers.'

'Where is Ernst now?'

'Gone out. He didn't say where he was going, but there is a drinking club in the village; I think he will

427

probably end up there.' She saw the sudden flash of alarm that widened the girl's eyes and smiled reassuringly. 'If he has gone there we are safe enough. He will drink himself insensible, and he will arrive home in the morning in the back of a cart, or I will have to go down before milking to help carry him home. He will be foul tempered tomorrow,' she added ominously.

'I'll stay out of his way,' the girl said, turning to stare into the fire, looking deep into its heart.

'Is there any improvement with Victoria; has her temperature subsided?'

'Not that I could see.'

'Well then, you must not sleep with her tonight; we don't want you getting a chill. Since Ernst won't be home, you can sleep in my bed.'

Senga turned around quickly. 'But he might come back.'

'I doubt it,' Maria said, the bitterness evident in her voice, 'but in any case I will bolt the doors. He will not be able to come in without waking me.'

'I seem to be causing you nothing but distress ...' Senga began, but Maria shook her head quickly. 'This distress I would have suffered had you been here or not. I love my husband,' she continued quickly, 'but he has faults. Every man has faults, and sometimes loving a man means ignoring or accepting his faults.'

The girl laughed, 'And how do men love women?'

Maria laughed, something like genuine humour in her laughter. 'Women allow men to love them. Men are like children or small animals,' she continued, 'and you must treat them accordingly, reward them when they do well, punish them when they fail.'

Senga shook her head. 'That won't work!'

The woman leaned forward and tapped her knee. 'It does. A woman may have any man she desires – if she desires him badly enough. But a man may not have any woman he desires no matter how badly he wants her.'

'That doesn't make sense.'

'In years to come it will. It is called power. And

428

women have power over men. It is the first great lesson of womanhood.' She stood up. 'Come, you can help me lock up.'

Senga followed Maria around the house, surprised to find that it was larger than she had first suspected. It was built on two floors, although the size of the top floor was deceptive because the slope of the roof lent all the rooms an irregular shape. The windows were shuttered and then locked, and then the heavy curtains were drawn across to cut the draught. All the doors were closed, and Maria explained that they usually slept downstairs in the winter and on into early spring to conserve heat.

The Leibers' bedroom was at the back of the house. It was warm and close, with heavy curtains across the windows, and the remains of a fire glowing in the grate. The room was very simply decorated and the polished wooden walls and floor had been softened by tapestries and rugs whose intricacy took Senga's breath away.

'Did you do that?'

Maria nodded, but said nothing.

'They're beautiful. They're so … so …' She knelt on the floor to examine one of the rugs, an ornate design of soft reds and blacks. Senga suddenly realized what the pattern represented and looked up in amazement. 'It reminds me of the pattern of coals in a fire …'

Maria nodded, pleased. 'That's what it is. I was lying in bed one evening, watching the flames on the coals and I suddenly realized it would make a fine design. You know,' she added, 'I made that nearly three years ago, and Ernst hasn't noticed it yet, much less worked out the design.'

'You're very talented.'

Maria touched the design carefully, her fingers tracing the outline of the shimmering design. 'I learned in Paris. My mother was a lacemaker,' she said suddenly, 'so I was brought up making lace and weaving a little, but always in the traditional patterns and styles. And then when I went to Paris to model, and I saw the new schools of art, I suddenly realized that there was so much else I could do

429

with shapes and colours and textures. So, using the skills I had learned as a child, I tried tapestry. Whenever I was short of money back then, I could always sell one of my tapestries for a few sous. It was something to fall back on.' She crossed to the large bed and pulled back the curtains and pulled out two long-handled warming-pans from under the blankets and carried them out into the kitchen. Senga heard her look in on Victoria, and moments later the small woman reappeared in the doorway. 'She's fine,' she said, 'she seems to be breathing more easily. Now quickly, to bed before you freeze.'

Maria Leiber undressed quickly and efficiently, and completely unselfconsciously, standing naked before Senga while she pulled on her heavy night-dress. The girl wasn't so comfortable in her nakedness, and turned her back on Maria while she undid her blouse, and lifted the heavy slip over her head. She quickly pulled on her night-dress while Maria was pulling back the blankets and not looking in her direction. With her night-dress covering her, she was able to pull down her grey twill 'rational' knickers.

'What are they?' Maria asked, watching Senga fold her clothes on the chair beside the bed.

Senga lifted the knickers in her right hand, a touch of colour on her cheeks. 'Knickers ... school knickers.'

'But they are horrid!' Maria said, something like astonishment in her voice.

'They are a bit.'

Maria reached for them and Senga reluctantly handed them across. The woman rubbed the cloth between her fingers. 'They are so coarse.'

'They are lined with cotton, but they are very uncomfortable.'

'Well then, you must not wear them. I have some French knickers; they are silk and comfortable. You must have them.'

'But ...'

'But what ...?'

'I couldn't.'

'And why not? I would like to give them to you as a gift. No-one should have to wear these.' She bundled the heavy twill knickers in her hand and tossed them across the room. 'These are for a child. When you wear silk you will be a woman!'

Senga blushed as she slid beneath the warm sheets. 'You are very kind,' she murmured.

Maria leaned over and kissed her forehead. 'Now sleep. And we must hope Victoria will be well in the morning.'

'And if she isn't?' Senga asked, snuggling down beneath the sheets.

Maria moved down beside her, her face inches away from the girl's. She wrapped an arm around her shoulder. The contact vaguely disturbed Senga, but she was reluctant to move in case she offended the woman. After all, she was French and the French were more demonstrative than either the Irish or the British.

'If Victoria isn't well or is worse, then we must find her a doctor, or …' the woman said slowly.

'Or?'

'Perhaps it would be better if she returned to the school.'

'I'll go back with her,' Senga said quickly.

Maria looked at her in astonishment. 'But why; if you do that, then all of this has been for nothing – even Victoria's illness will have been for nothing. No,' she shook her head firmly, 'if we decide that the English girl has to go back to the school, you must go on. You owe it to her; you owe it to yourself. Now, sleep, and let us see what the morning brings.' She kissed Senga firmly on the lips and then, before she could react, had rolled over with her back to Senga. The girl looked at her for a few moments, still feeling the pressure of the woman's lips against hers, and then she too rolled over.

But sleep was a long time coming. Something about Maria Leiber disturbed her, and she couldn't decide what. But whatever happened tomorrow – if Victoria had to go back to the school – she too would leave the house, either to continue on her journey or to go back to the school and admit defeat. But she certainly wasn't going to stay in this house on her own.

CHAPTER THIRTY-THREE

'Missing?'

Katherine Lundy repeated the word slowly and carefully, looking at the two elderly women standing in front of her as if she couldn't comprehend what they were saying.

The Misses Roper were the British representatives of the Chateau School, and although they had arranged schooling for the daughters of many of the nobility and on occasion royalty, and had grown comfortable in their presence, there was something about this Mrs Lundy which they found unsettling.

'As I have already said, Mrs Lundy, she would seem to have run off with another girl ...' Elizabeth Roper began again.

'It happens every year,' Charlotte, her younger sister, added with an attempt at a smile.

'Why?' Katherine Lundy sat back into the leather chair and steepled her fingers before her face. She had made no effort to offer the women seats, nor had she offered them any refreshment.

The sisters looked at one another for a moment and then Elizabeth Roper launched into the explanation they usually used on these occasions. It was a speech which they had perfected over the years and which usually served them well.

'This is a difficult time for young girls, Mrs Lundy, as I am sure you will be all too aware. They are poised on the verge of womanhood, and the child and the woman within the girl's body often encourage her to do strange and curious things. Girls are emotionally wrought at this time of their lives, and sensations are heightened. I

433

would suggest that homesickness might be the cause. Perhaps she grew lonely, and in her mind this grew to enormous proportions, and so one day she simply walked out, intending to return home to you ...'

'Where is she now?' Katherine asked bluntly.

The long silence that followed was broken by Charlotte Roper. 'We do not know, Mrs Lundy.'

'You do not know where she is, and yet you are sure she has run away. Could she not have been abducted?'

'By whom?' the older woman asked, aghast at the thought.

'I am a woman of some considerable means,' Katherine said tightly, 'it is not beyond the bounds of possibility that someone could have kidnapped her.'

The two women were at a loss for words for some moments, then Charlotte Roper suggested tentatively, 'But there are wealthier girls in the school, Mrs Lundy, and no letter or note demanding money has been received ...'

Katherine bowed her head at the suggestion that there were students from wealthier parents at the school. Somehow she very much doubted it. However, she wasn't going to admit that to these two women. Lifting her head and glaring at the two women, she asked, 'Was my daughter experiencing any sort of difficulties at the school then?'

'Oh none, none at all Mrs Lundy,' both women said together.

'Was my daughter under pressure of any sort? Was she being bullied?' Katherine's voice had grown harsh.

'I can assure you that nothing of the sort goes on at the Chateau,' Charlotte Roper said quickly, blinking shortsightedly at Katherine. A nervous tick began at the corner of her mouth. She was all too aware of Madame Royer's reputation for strictness, and Miss Roper had occasionally suspected that the Frenchwoman was often too strict with her charges. She was beginning to wonder did this hard-eyed, bitter-mouthed woman know something she shouldn't. You could never tell how parents were going to react; some were better than others. But this one was particularly bad.

'Some reason drove my daughter from your school.'

'Madame Royer spoke to her friends and companions, and they could shed no light on the mystery.'

'In my experience children only run away from unhappiness,' Katherine said bluntly. 'If I find my daughter was unhappy at your school for any reason; if I find she was bullied, or picked on by other pupils or teachers, I promise you I will not rest until the Chateau is closed down and its staff – and that includes you both – are behind bars!'

Both women blinked in surprise. Whatever they had been expecting to hear, it certainly hadn't been this, and the venom in the woman's voice made them realize that this was no idle threat.

'Now get out of my sight. I want daily – and I mean daily – reports on your progress, or otherwise. And if my daughter is not returned safe and unharmed to me, then you will hear from me. I'm sure you don't want that ...' She left the barely veiled threat hanging in the air.

'Madame ...' Charlotte Roper began, but the door opened and one of the servants appeared, summoned by some unseen bell.

'The Misses Roper are leaving, Margaret; kindly show them to the door.' Without another word Katherine turned away and picked up the letter she had been reading when the women had arrived, studiously ignoring the two women as they were ushered towards the door. However, when she heard the front door close behind them, she allowed the page to fall to the floor, and then, leaning her head back against the soft leather, she closed her eyes, squeezing them tightly. For a single moment a different Katherine Lundy showed through the mask of her face, an older, sadder, very vulnerable woman, a hint of the woman who might have been had time and circumstances dictated differently. Katherine Lundy truly loved her daughter. She had loved both her children – loved them with a passion and an intensity that was almost frightening. They were hers and hers alone – in a way she regarded them almost as possessions. They were a tangible link with a past she bitterly regretted having lost, and she was determined that they would not repeat the mistakes she had made. That was why Patrick's defection had hurt her so deeply – truly he had been John Lewis's son, only Lewis had had the capacity to hurt her so deeply. But he was gone now, and when she did think of him – which was often – she preferred to remember the eager young boy, and then the medical student. She created a little fantasy in which he would arrive home one day, his college books under his arm ... that the door would open and he would ...

But that would never happen. Patrick was dead, lying at the bottom of Kingston Harbour, beyond her reach. Even in death he had cheated her, rather like his father and her husband – neither of them had graves either, neither of them possessed a marker, a place she could visit, a place for her to leave her grief.

And now Senga was missing.

Katherine Lundy had been brought up a Catholic although it had been many years now since she had practised her religion. For form's sake she still attended the local Catholic church – and she made sure she was seen riding out every Sunday morning in her sombre 'widow's weeds' as the bells tolled calling the faithful to Mass. If she had kept to her religion, she wondered would events have worked out differently? She supposed if she was of a religious frame of mind, she would be beginning to wonder if this was God's way of punishing her, if He was extracting some sort of revenge because she had betrayed her religion and gone to the opposite extreme and lived off immoral and illegal earnings?

But she had lost her faith and such questions didn't arise ... except in the grey hours of morning, when sleep wouldn't come, and the woman who had been

436

Katherine Lundy, the simple ill-educated servant, reappeared briefly, subjugating the avaricious, scheming whoremistress she had become.

The fire snapped, startling her ...

With a self-confidence born of too many years making and abiding by her own decisions, Katherine thrust the doubts to the back of her mind and when she sat forward, her face had hardened into its accustomed mask.

Senga had run away from the Chateau for reasons which were obviously important enough in her childish imagination. No – not childish, Senga was as the Roper sisters had said, 'on the verge of womanhood,' so the reasons must have been important. Katherine would discover those reasons later – even if it meant razing the school to the ground in the process.

But first she had to find her.

Katherine pressed the bell built into the arm of the chair and Margaret the maid appeared almost immediately.

'Ma'am?'

'In the bottom of the bookcase, lying on its side, is a large red-covered book, called an imperial Atlas. Would you bring it in to me please?'

'Yes, Ma'am.'

When the maid struggled in a few moments later with the huge atlas, Katherine instructed her to place it on the small occasional table and push the table over to her chair. She dismissed the maid with an order to bring some tea and then, with paper and pen, began to work out her daughter's probable route.

Senga was a sensible girl; if she was running away, it would not have been a spur of the moment thing – the Misses Roper had said that she had taken clothing and money, and had reported herself ill that day, and that, apparently, was one of the reasons her absence had not been discovered until late in the day. Undoubtedly, Senga had known about that and used the school curriculum to her advantage and that confirmed that a certain amount of planning had gone into the escapade.

Katherine turned the Atlas' newspaper sized pages, looking for Switzerland. Where would she go, she wondered ... north into Germany, to Berlin ... or west to France and Paris, or possibly south to Italy and Rome ... No, she dismissed Rome, as being too far away, and she dismissed Germany, because Senga had not wanted to learn German and had resisted the language, but France now, France was a different proposition altogether. She spoke French, and had often said she wanted to visit Paris. And from Paris to London on the boat-train was a relatively short journey.

Katherine tapped the paper with her pen. She needed to know certain things ... She began to prepare a list, and high on the agenda was a comprehensive weather report starting on the day Senga had walked away from the school. The movements of two young girls, without proper transport and clothing, were going to be very much dictated by the Swiss weather. It would also be very useful to know how much money they had between them; not much, she guessed, because the Chateau was so isolated, there was little point in sending over money, because they had no place to spend it. She needed someone on the spot, she decided. She would probably send Martha Tilke to Switzerland to find out what she could. She had been Senga's last governess before Katherine had sent her to the school, and had accompanied her to Switzerland, and she had also taught at the Chateau.

Katherine had some contacts in the Parisian Underworld which might be useful; a pretty young foreign girl in Paris shouldn't be too difficult to find ... especially with the reward she'd offer. Now, she would also have to speak to the French and Swiss police ...

It was a little more than an hour later when Katherine finally put down her pen, and gathered up the pages of notes she had prepared. She was confident now that, with a little care, she should be able to find her daughter. No matter where Senga was, she would bring her home.

The clock on the mantelpiece chimed four, startling her, breaking in to her reverie. Katherine sighed and stood up, smoothing down her long emerald green dress, wondering what Senga was doing right now ...

Senga stood at the door to the Leiber farm and watched the horse-drawn wagon disappear around the bend in the road. Just before it passed out of sight, Maria Leiber turned around and waved back at her; Senga dutifully returned the wave, waiting until they were gone, and then she closed the heavy door behind her, dropping the bar across it and turning the large key in the lock. She had been a week in the house now, and for the first time in that week she felt safe.

And alone.

The young girl felt tears sting her eyes when she thought of Victoria. Her fever hadn't broken; indeed, it had seemed to get worse, and so, finally, Ernst and Maria Leiber had decided that there was nothing else they could do but bring Victoria back to the school. They were going to say that they had found her in their barn, delirious and feverish and only later, when she had started to rant and rave in English, did they realize that she must be from the school. They also hoped to claim some of the reward that had been offered for information leading to the safe return of the two missing girls.

It had been a strange, sometimes frightening week for Senga. She had spent most of the day with Victoria, sitting by her side, keeping her cool, forcing droplets of water through her cracked and swollen lips, whispering softly to her, calming her when the feverish dreams grew so frightening that she cried aloud and shouted in alarm.

But at night Senga slept with Maria Leiber.

Ernst Leiber drank every night, usually arriving home with the dawn barely in time to milk the cows, and then collapsing into the bed immediately afterwards, to arise around noon in a foul and sullen mood.

Throughout the whole week, he had exchanged barely two dozen words with the girl.

Senga didn't particularly like sleeping with the woman. She found her overly friendly, and she didn't like the way she watched her undress, nor the way the Frenchwoman seemed to deliberately flaunt her nudity while watching her beneath hooded eyes. And once, Senga had awoken from a disturbing dream to find that the woman had thrown one arm around her, her hand resting against her breasts, her fingers brushing her nipple through the cloth. She had gently manoeuvred her way away from the woman's embrace without awakening her. The movement might have been accidental, but Senga was slowly coming around to the conclusion that it was not. Then there had been the gifts of underwear Maria had given her; silk knickers, shifts, camisoles, stockings. And of course, Maria had insisted that she see her wear them, to judge the size ... the colour ...

Senga dressed quickly, taking some of Maria Leiber's heavier clothing and stuffing it into an old cloth bag. The woman had been so free with other items of her clothing, Senga didn't think she would mind giving these. Almost as an afterthought, she stuffed the underwear into the side of the bag. She then picked through the cupboards, pulling out some bread and cheese, cured meat and biscuits; she was determined she wasn't going to approach another farmhouse until it was absolutely necessary. Finally, she took a pair of Maria's boots and tried them on. They were a size too big, but she pulled on a second pair of socks – also Maria's – and then unhooked her heavy woollen coat from its peg by the door. There was a pair of gloves in the pocket, which she pulled on and then, with a final look around the warm kitchen, she heaved her bag onto her shoulder and stepped out into the crisp morning air. For good measure she locked the door with the key before dropping it into the rain barrel by the door. If it delayed the Leibers for a little while then it would be useful. Later, when she got to Ireland, she decided, she would write to Maria Leiber and pay for everything she had taken, but that was for the future.

'They claim they found her wandering on the road, two days before they brought her back to the school,' Martha Tilke said slowly, folding her notes and placing it alongside her cup and saucer.

Katherine looked at the governess over the rim of her teacup. 'I think I detect some disbelief in your voice.'

The woman tilted her head to one side. Her broad, rather square face was expressionless, her pale blue eyes half closed. She had just returned from her daily visit to the Misses Roper's Academy for the Education of Gentlewomen where telegrams from the Chateau arrived every day at noon. It had now been just over a week since Senga and Victoria had disappeared.

'Why did they keep her for two days before bringing her to the school?' Katherine asked.

'I asked the same question; they claim she was too ill to travel.'

'It is reasonable.'

Martha Tilke nodded. 'It is. But Madame, the Leiber's farm is no more than four miles from the Chateau ...'

Katherine put her cup down quickly and sat forward. 'I see. In three or four days travelling they should have managed a greater distance.'

'I would have said so. Unless, of course, Miss Edde-ridge was too ill to travel and they hid out in the barn for a day or two.'

'But why weren't they discovered?' Katherine whispered. 'No,' she shook her head firmly, 'something is awry here.' She stood up and crossed to the long low glass-fronted cabinet that stood beneath the windows. With a tiny key from an inner pocket she opened a door set discreetly into the side of the cabinet and pulled out a sheaf of papers. Standing beside the cabinet she began sorting through them quickly. 'These are the weather reports from France, Switzerland, Northern Italy and

Southern Germany for the past few days. I have also detailed weather reports from the area in and around the Chateau.'

'How ever did you get them?' the governess asked, astonished.

Katherine smiled secretively. 'Friends in low places,' she murmured. She lifted a sheet and looked at it for a moment, before turning around to face the woman. 'The night the girls ran away there was a storm, not a bad one, but enough I would think to force them to seek shelter.' She glanced up at Martha Tilke. 'This Leiber farm, is it isolated?'

'Reasonably so.'

'So it is not unreasonable to assume they found shelter in this farm for the night ... and then perhaps stayed on for another day or two until the hue and cry died down.'

The woman nodded.

'But perhaps this English girl, Victoria Edderidge, fell ill, perhaps she was even too ill to be moved, perhaps that is why they stayed at the farm. So ill in fact that there was nothing else for the Leibers to do but to bring her back to the Chateau.'

The governess nodded. She was amazed at the extraordinary change that had come over the woman while she had been reasoning from the information she had to hand. Her thinking was incisive, and her attention to detail – as evidenced by the weather reports and the conclusions she had drawn from them – was quite extraordinary. Martha Tilke had once thought that Mrs Lundy was nothing more than *nouveau riche*, someone who had married money, but now she suddenly realized that there was more to the woman than met the eye.

'Go to these people, these Leibers. Talk to them, pay them, threaten them, do whatever you think is necessary, but find out if my daughter stayed with them, and if she did, I want to know everything; I want to know what they talked about, what she ate. Perhaps we will be lucky and discover that she's still there, but I

442

doubt that. I think she's moved on. If she has, find out when she left, and if they have any clue as to her destination.'

'They may refuse to talk. And I may not be able to buy their information, what do I do then?'

'Send me a telegram; I will arrange the rest.'

'When do you want me to go, madam.'

'On the next train. I want my daughter back.'

The governess nodded quickly. She stood up and left the room to make her travelling arrangements, leaving Katherine alone with her notes, her sheets of paper, her reports. Katherine looked at the drinks cabinet. She needed a drink now, something to ease the burning deep inside her, but she knew the drink would dull her senses and she needed to remain alert. She slowly and deliberately turned away. She wanted her daughter back; she was going to have her back ... and nothing was going to stand in her way. Nothing and no-one. Senga was all she had left.

So far she had been lucky.

In the three days since leaving the Leibers' house she had managed to find shelter in barns and sheds on two occasions and last night she had sheltered in a ruined shepherd's hut that stank of sheep droppings and something long dead. When she had come upon it at twilight, she had thought the house was an old ruin, but with the morning light she decided that it was of much more recent origin. A war relic perhaps?

However, it didn't look like she was going to find shelter so easily tonight. And whereas on the previous nights the weather had been reasonably kind, tonight a chill wind was coming in from the north, carrying sleet and a touch of ice with it. She wasn't cold yet, but she would be. And she was hungry.

She had been aware she was approaching a town since the early part of the afternoon. Traffic on the road had grown heavier, and the sharp clean air had become tainted with the bitter woodiness of smoke and the faintly sourer smell of human refuse. Senga was all too aware of the dangers of using the towns and villages she passed, but she had little choice now. She needed to buy some food and, more importantly, she needed to find out how far she was from Paris. She had passed several smaller villages in the previous few days, but she had decided that a stranger would be more easily noticed in a village, than in a slightly larger town. But, whatever way she looked at it – it was a risk.

There was a bridge on the outskirts of the town, small and humpbacked, which carried the road over a fast-moving torrent that gurgled over the stones. Senga stepped off the road, and slipped down the embankment in a clatter of stones and mud to crawl under the bridge. Well, if she didn't find shelter for the night, this might do. Then, kneeling on the ledge beneath the bridge, she bent out over the water and attempted to wash some of the grime from her hands and face. She gasped when she touched the water – it was icy, cold enough to numb her fingers, and its touch on her cheeks and forehead left the skin tingling. Finally, she pulled the tin cup she had taken from the Leibers' from her bag and half-filled it with water, and was just bringing it to her lips …

'I wouldn't drink the water!'

The voice boomed beneath the bridge, almost upsetting her into the torrent with fright, the heavily-accented French barely comprehensible, but the warning was clear enough.

A shape moved on the other side of the river, vague and indistinct in the shadows beneath the bridge. 'Occasionally, the farmers and peasants upstream allow their animals to wander across the stream that feeds this river, and they foul it with their wastes.' Senga attempted to identify the speaker, but the acoustics rendered it both sexless and ageless. 'You might be lucky and the water might not actually kill you, but it might make you feel as if it had.'

Shading her eyes against the glare Senga made her way back out into the late afternoon sunlight.

444

There was a man standing on the opposite side of the river. He was young, pleasant looking and surprisingly well-dressed. There was an amused smile on his rather thin face.

'You are a camper ... a tourist ...?' he asked, tilting his head slightly to look at her.

Senga schooled her face to an impassive mask, nodding quickly. 'I am English,' she said, deliberately adopting a barbarous accent, using only the simplest French, not wishing to betray her grasp of the language. 'I am walking the French countryside.'

'A tourist,' the young man said, 'and so early in the year. And one so pretty,' he added with a quick smile.

Senga pretended she hadn't heard him.

'You are thirsty?'

She nodded.

He slipped his hands into the pockets of his expensive suit. Senga couldn't tell what it was, but it was beautifully cut, and in the latest style, broad-shouldered, slim waisted, with baggy trousers, and deep turn-ups.

'There are some good hotels in the town,' he said slowly and carefully, choosing simple words to allow her to understand them.

'I lost much of my money on the road,' Senga said quietly, 'I think it was stolen in one of the inns.'

He nodded sympathetically, 'Some of these country places will abuse the unwary traveller.'

There was a pause while they looked at one another. Senga wondered what he must be thinking of her. She wasn't exactly dirty, but she felt grubby, and she knew her uncombed hair and dirt streaked face and hands, and her stained clothing didn't create the best impression.

Finally the young man spoke. 'You are travelling far?'

'To Paris.'

His pencil thin eyebrows rose in surprise. 'A long way.'

'I have friends there,' she said quickly. 'I can borrow some money from them to continue back to England.'

There was another pause, which was broken by an icy gust of wind. The young man shivered. 'I am going a little ways along the road to Paris,' he said softly. 'If you would care for a lift …?'

Senga shook her head quickly. 'No, no I'm afraid I could not.'

'Why?' he asked.

His direct question took her by surprise. She took a moment before answering and then said, 'It would not be proper.'

He shrugged. 'In England it would not be proper perhaps, but this is France.'

Senga firmly shook her head. 'I could not, but thank you for your offer, it is kind of you.'

'As you wish.' He turned to climb back up the embankment. 'Are you sure there is nothing I can do for you?'

Senga started to shake her head, but changed her mind. 'One thing, if you would …'

He stood waiting.

'Could you point me in the direction for Paris?'

CHAPTER THIRTY-FOUR

The bread was warm, soft and tasted like nothing she had ever tasted before. She had to school herself to take only small bites and chew them thoroughly before swallowing. When she had first bought the long loaf, she had torn it in half and gobbled most of that in one go – and suffered for the next hour with violent racking hiccups which left her stomach feeling sore and bruised. She had been more cautious with the second half.

Senga had decided not to stay in the town. It was far smaller than she had first imagined, and her appearance – and the fact that she was a young girl travelling alone – attracted far too much attention for her liking. So she had contented herself with buying the long French loaves from the patisserie, and some spiced sausage and making herself a simple sandwich which she ate as she walked along the road. With the edge taken off her hunger she was free to concentrate on the more immediate problem of where she was going to spend the night. The wind that had blown up in the late afternoon had strengthened and was now beginning to gust strongly, bringing with it flurries of ice-tipped rain, and the temperature had fallen quite dramatically.

She kept to the main road – she made better time that way – her head ducked into the wind, the collar of her soiled woollen coat turned up, a scarf wrapped around her throat and up to her ears. She bitterly regretted not bringing a hat. Nibbling at the bread and sausage, she trudged on.

She knew she was just about reaching the point where she could no longer turn back. Theoretically, she could still turn around and go back to the Chateau, which was about a week's travel behind her, or it would be a simple matter to walk up to the nearest gendarme and give herself up. But she wouldn't – she couldn't. She owed it to herself; she owed it to Victoria. If she simply handed herself over to the police, it made a mockery of all their planning and all that they had gone through. No, she wasn't going to give herself up, nor was she going to be caught – not if she could help it. She smiled at the idea; she was beginning to think like a criminal. But she had done nothing wrong; she had run away from school, and that was no crime. Was it?

Senga shook her head savagely. There was nothing wrong with what she had done. Perhaps it had been a mistake ... she smiled ruefully, she was sure it was a mistake, but it wasn't a crime. However, she had been brought up to be completely, unquestioningly obedient and she was conditioned to think of every transgression almost as a crime, a mortal sin. Well, all her life she had done what she was told, carried out her mother's wishes and done her bidding, even when she knew the woman was wrong. She had seen her brother forced into a position where he had had no alternative but to leave, and she had then been forbidden even to mention his name in the house. And that was wrong: she knew that was wrong. And when she did think of her brother, on those many occasions when she had sat down to write him a letter, she had felt guilty because she knew she was going against her mother's wishes, and her mother's word was law, and so she had never actually sent him a letter. With her mother controlling her every move, she had grown up believing that she was dependent on other people, that she was a simple girl, unable to act on her own initiative. Well the last few days had proved how wrong that was. She had been away from the Chateau for nearly two weeks now, and while she had been with the Leibers for one week, she had still managed to survive on her own for nearly a week. And that was quite some accomplishment.

Although a still, small voice deep within her kept whispering that it was the next few weeks that would count. She had enough money for another week or ten days at the most, and when that ran out she couldn't buy food – what would she do then? But that was the future, and she was more concerned about the present … where was she going to shelter tonight? Glancing up into the lowering skies, she guessed she had very little time left before the storm broke.

Martha Tilke sat back into the chair and awaited Katherine's reaction. She had just returned from her mission to Switzerland and had come straight from the station to present her report to Madame Lundy. She was expecting some sort of comment from the woman, but when she did speak, it was not with the compliment that she had been expecting.

'And this is it?'

Martha Tilke looked up in surprise.

Katherine Lundy's face was like stone. 'Is this all you have to say to me?' Her voice, which had been under control, now crept higher. 'What have you been doing for the past ten days, eh? I discovered as much from here,' she snapped. She suddenly flung the woman's report back in her face. 'How dare you waste my time and insult my intelligence with this … this … this …'

'Madame …'

Paper settled over the room. 'I know what day Senga left the Chateau. I know the direction she went. I know where she spent the week … I have even seen the police reports on the Leibers. But what I wanted to do was to find out where she was. Where she was going.'

'Paris,' Martha Tilke blurted.

'What?'

'Paris,' the small woman said quickly, glad to have stopped the woman in her stride. 'Maria Leiber said that Senga had told her that the two girls were going to make their way towards Paris. The trail ends with the Leibers. First, they claimed they had found the English girl in their barn, but when I paid them, they admitted they had sheltered both girls for over a week, and it was

449

only Miss Edderidge's illness which forced them to take her back to the Chateau. When they returned to the farm about two hours later, Miss Senga was gone. She had taken some clothes, a little food …'

'And they have no idea where she went?' Katherine asked softly.

'None. Maria Leiber said they had talked about Paris together, but that was just talk, and I don't know if we can read too much into it.'

Katherine nodded.

'I'm sorry there's not more,' the woman said eventually.

'It's enough,' Katherine said very quietly, 'you did your best.'

The sharp-faced woman looked at her closely. 'Is there anything else you would like me to do?'

Katherine looked at her blankly for a few moments, and then nodded. 'Yes, you can accompany me to Paris. We leave on the morning tide.' She rose quickly to her feet, all traces of her anger now forgotten. 'I have friends in Paris,' she said slowly, 'perhaps they'll be able to help.' She said it in a tone that suggested that there would be no question but that they would help. She strode to the window, and stood looking out across the small park, plot and counterplot running through her brain. Behind her, suddenly realizing that the interview was at an end, Martha Tilke stood up and silently made her way from the room. Katherine never even heard her go.

Rain spattered on the glass before her face, startling her. She blinked quickly, and wondered where her daughter was, wondered what she was doing now … what sort of weather she was experiencing.

A portion of the wall had been crushed at some time in the past, and some of the stones were still blackened, but at least the portion which remained standing afforded her some shelter from the wind and sleeting rain that was now whipping in from the north.

Senga had trudged on through the afternoon, persisting even when the rain had started to come down – speckled droplets at first and then in a solid heavy ice-tipped shower that had left her soaked through and chilled to the bone. Finally, however, she had been forced to seek shelter out of the rain and wind, and had huddled down behind the first wall she came to.

Senga Lundy was cold and chilled; and this wasn't the sharp, almost exhilarating cold of the Swiss mountains, this was a wet, bone-numbing chill, that promised nothing but illness. Already she felt slightly dizzy, and there was a raw burning at the back of her throat, and she wanted nothing more than a warm, dry bed to lie down in. She felt she could sleep for a week.

An hour later, it was still raining, and the light had faded to a dull grey gloom that was slipping imperceptibly into full night. The rain had worsened, and Senga had sat numbly watching the ground before her turn into a thick glutinous muddy mass. For the first time since leaving the Chateau she began to feel frightened, really frightened. Even on the first night, when they had been trapped in the snow, she hadn't felt so terrified as she felt now; perhaps it was because she had been clean and dry, and hunger pangs hadn't been gnawing at her stomach. It had still been a great adventure then; they had still been full of optimism then. But no longer. She attempted to smile at her present predicament – cold, wet and hungry – but failed miserably. She finished the last of the bread – like everything else it was wet – and then held out her hand to the large cold raindrops and rubbed her wet fingers to her face. The sting of the cold water helped rouse her, and it was only with a supreme effort that she staggered to her feet, and settled her knapsack on her back. And then, with head ducked into the wind, she pressed on, more miserable now than she had ever been at any time in her life.

Time became meaningless. The grey twilight seemed to linger for an eternity – grey sky, grey clouds, grey light – and she used the wan twilight to press on. But when night finally fell, plunging the entire countryside into complete darkness, she was forced to stop. She sank down onto a time-worn milestone and buried her head in her hands. It was still raining, though not so heavily, but the cold had now intensified to a bitter, bone-numbing chill, that had her trembling so badly she felt as if she was going to vomit her simple meal.

There was every possibility that she was going to die on this road.

She spotted the lights long before she saw the car or heard the sound of the engine. They lanced through the countryside darkness in an almost solid arc, and the rain created a gauzy halo around them that intensified their light, until it looked as if a solid ball of light were approaching, twisting its way down the country lane.

Senga was past caring: it could be her mother in the car for all she knew; it might even be the police, but she knew that she needed to get in out of this weather and dry off – quickly.

Almost automatically she stood and made her way to the side of the road. She could hear the sound of the engine now, it was smooth and throaty – and she recognized it as belonging to a powerful car and not some peasant's truck. Blinking hard against the misty rain, she saw the lights dip, disappear briefly only to reappear up ahead of her, blindingly painful in their intensity after the total darkness of the surrounding countryside. She was waving furiously as the car appeared directly in front of her, its broad tyres hissing furiously on the damp ground. Perhaps because she was so tired she failed to realize that she was standing so far out on the road, and certainly it was because her reactions were dulled by the cold and rain, that it was only at the last moments that she realized that the car showed no sign of slowing down. She jumped, desperately throwing herself to one side, not quite believing what was happening. There was pain – a brief searing across the back of her legs – and she remembered hitting the ground hard and then rolling, the soft muck cushioning her fall, sliding in a water-filled ditch. The water was chill and bitter and she opened her mouth to scream. And then the warmth washed over her like a blanket and the darkness was equally welcoming ...

There were voices – dim voices, distantly heard, echoing – and there were faces too, but they were less distinct, and mingled uncomfortably, disconcertingly, with her dreams, until fact and fantasy were indistinguishable. There was pain too, she was aware of that, but it was vague, almost remote.

Mostly there were the dreams.

There were faces in her dreams – people she knew, strangers, friends, girls at the school, teachers, people she had encountered along the road.

And her mother. Always her mother.

There was a man's face in her dreams, a stranger's face and yet she felt she knew it, had seen it before. At first she thought it was her brother's face – because she was aware at some deep, unconscious level that she hadn't encountered him in her dreams yet – but this wasn't her brother's face, she was sure of that. There were times when it became quite intrusive. It was a thin face, a sharp face, with deep brown eyes over a sharp nose and thin lips. She was reminded of a knife blade ...

When she finally awoke the face was still there.

'The man under the bridge,' she said almost in wonder, suddenly realizing that the man looking down at her was one and the same with the person who had warned her off drinking the water.

'Indeed,' he nodded with a quick smile, and then bowed deeply, 'Jean-Michel Hugo at your service.'

Senga sat up quickly in the bed ... and then stopped, heart pounding, abruptly taking stock of her circumstances and surroundings. She was in a bed in what looked like an hotel bedroom – cheap furnishings and aged wallpaper – and beneath the faded sheets, she was naked. She clutched the sheets up to her chin, and pushed herself back up in the bed until her bare flesh touched the cool wood of the headboard.

'What has happened?' she demanded tightly, her eyes locked onto the young man's face.

Jean-Michel Hugo hooked his foot around the room's only chair and dragged it across the room to the side of the bed. He sat into the chair and carefully crossed his legs at the knee, adjusting the line of his suit trousers to ensure they wouldn't crease. He opened his mouth to speak, when Senga blurted, 'How long have I been here?'

'A week,' the man said softly. 'No,' he immediately added, 'this is the eighth day.'

'But that's ...' she began.

He bent to pick a newspaper off the floor and handed it to her. When she refused to touch it, he allowed it to fall to the sheets. It was *Le Monde* for Friday, the 20th of May. 'That is today's paper.'

'What happened?' Senga asked numbly.

The young man shrugged. 'There was an accident. We were on the road, when suddenly you appeared out of the night, arms waving. My driver just about managed to miss hitting you, but the edge of the running board caught you across the back of the legs, and you fell into a water-filled ditch. Damned near drowned too. You're alright,' he added hurriedly, seeing the expression that flashed behind her eyes. 'You were unconscious for about eight hours, and then, just when it seemed you would be well again, you contracted an illness, fever and chills.' He paused and then asked, 'How do you feel now?'

Senga hesitated before answering. She felt stiff and sore ... and hungry. 'I think I would like something to eat.'

The young man smiled. 'Always a good sign; a sign that you will be well soon. I will have some broth sent up to you.'

'Where am I?'

Jean Hugo smiled. 'This was the first hotel we met on the road after picking you up. Luckily it was one of ours.'

Senga looked at him in surprise. 'What do you mean – one of ours?'

'My father and his father before him built the family fortune on small hotels and roadside inns. We have forty or so scattered all across southern France, with larger hotels in places like Marseille, Lyon and Paris. I have spent the last month touring the south of France looking for suitable locations for new premises.'

Senga nodded disinterestedly. All she wanted now were her clothes, her belongings, a little money and ... 'Does anyone know I'm here?' she asked suddenly.

The young man shook his head. 'We took the liberty of examining your belongings, mademoiselle, but we could find nothing with your name or address – so there was no one we could contact on your behalf. But of course if you would care to give me an address, I will wire immediately ...'

'No ... no. There is no need,' Senga said quickly. 'I am unhurt,' she said carefully, choosing her words, wishing her command of the Frech language was more fluent. 'I am unhurt and there is no need to alarm my mother.' She saw Hugo's puzzled expression and attempted a smile. 'I had trouble enough getting her permission to come away on this holiday.'

Jean-Michel nodded, but Senga sensed that he didn't believe her. 'It is not usual to find young English girls touring the country alone and at this time of year.'

'I am Irish,' Senga said automatically, and groaned inwardly. Any description of her would probably say that she was of Irish extraction.

'Aaah,' Jean-Michel said, nodding, as if that explained everything. 'But your mother ... she must be a very liberated woman.'

Senga dipped her head to hide a smile. 'Yes, one could say that.' Katherine Lundy might be many things, Senga reflected, but she certainly wasn't liberated.

'But perhaps it is a trifle foolish to travel these roads unchaperoned. This is a wild part of the country ... the peasants can be ... rough.'

'My companion became ill on the road, and had to turn back,' she said quickly, 'I knew if I went back I would have to go home, and I did so want this holiday.'

Hugo's thin lips curled in a smile. 'Aaah, I understand. One of the reasons I came down here was to be on my own for a while, to get away from the city. Sometimes it is good to get a break.' He pulled a small watch from his vest pocket and thumbed back the cover. 'Now, you must excuse me, mademoiselle, but I have an appointment. Perhaps we can talk later on?' He bowed stiffly, and then turned towards the door, stopping with his fingers touching the handle. 'There is one thing ...' he looked at her expectantly. 'Your name – you have the advantage of me?'

'Oh ... of course. It's Senga ... Senga Corcoran,' she said carefully, suddenly unwilling to use the Lundy name.

Hugo nodded. 'Senga Corcoran,' he said, pronouncing her surname carefully. 'I took the liberty of purchasing some new garments for you – your old clothes were quite ruined with the mud.' He pointed towards the cheap wardrobe. 'They are within.'

Senga was dressing when the door opened and a young dark-haired, dark-eyed maid appeared carrying a wooden tray. Ignoring Senga's semi-nakedness she put the tray on the end of the bed and then turned to regard the girl with obvious interest. Senga stopped dressing and returned her stare.

'English?' the maid asked eventually.

'Irish,' Senga said immediately.

'He likes English.' Her accent was thick, barely comprehensible. 'He liked you.' She nodded to the clothes. 'He buy you clothes.'

'There was mud ...' Senga began, and then stopped, realizing that she didn't have to make any explanations to this maid.

'You will be careful of him. There have been other women. He likes young women.'

'I'm not sure what you mean,' Senga said, although she had a very good idea what the girl was talking about.

The maid crossed to Senga and sorted through the clothes which hung in the wardrobe, her blunt chapped fingers lingering on the silks and soft cottons. 'They are nice,' she said softly, almost to herself.

Senga nodded. Whoever had chosen the clothes had had good taste.

'He will be nice to you. Make promises. Be kind. And then ... then he will expect payment. With some he takes a little longer than others. The foolish ones he breaks easily,' she added with just enough bitterness in her voice for Senga to recognize some sort of personal experience.

'What happened?' she asked, pulling a silk chemise over her shoulders.

The girl blinked rapidly, moisture sparkling in her eyes. 'I am fifteen,' she said eventually, 'sixteen next birthday. I have a child by him.' She turned on her heels and walked out, leaving the young girl in stunned silence. Had she heard correctly; her knowledge of French was improving every day, but even so, she was still capable of making stupid mistakes, and the girl's provincial accent had ... She shook her head. She had heard correctly. All she had to do now was to decide how this information affected her.

So that's who she was.

Jean-Michel Hugo folded the paper and tucked it under his arm: the Irish girl, Senga Lundy – he smiled at the name Corcoran, wondering why she had chosen it – runaway from the posh school on the other side of the border, the Chateau. And a sizeable reward offered for her too.

When he had first seen her sheltering beneath the bridge, he had guessed that there was something

457

wrong, something amiss, with her. Sometimes the offer of a drive in a car – especially for a peasant girl – worked, and then a little drink ... a few soft words ... It was a game, and Jean-Michel Hugo was an expert player.

Although Jean-Michel Hugo was only twenty-three he had been married five years. It had been an arranged and loveless match that had caused nothing but bitterness and resentment from the day he had walked down the aisle to marry the girl he had met on three previous occasions. It had been a marriage of convenience, allowing his father, who earned a sizeable portion of his income by smuggling contraband in and out of Marseille and Algiers, to divert some money into a legitimate enterprise. It had also allowed his wife's family, whose money had been invested in hotels and bars, to amalgamate their business with the Hugos'. Once the formality of marriage had been complete, Jean-Michel rarely saw his wife. Her interests lay in different directions to his, and she spent six months of the year touring the galleries of Europe. He preferred slightly more earthy amusements. For him there was the chase, and his youthful good looks and charm allowed him a certain measure of success.

Now this young girl was an interesting exercise. She had run away from school, was alone in a strange country, with no money and only the vaguest knowledge of the language. She was innocent certainly – and a virgin. Jean-Michel Hugo smiled at the thought. Why, it would almost make the last few boring weeks worthwhile.

Michelle, the dark-haired hotel maid, stood by the window of her topmost room, with the child in her arms and watched the man below open the door for the young girl. Michelle wondered how old she was ... fourteen, fifteen, sixteen? Well, she had done the best she could; she had tried to warn her. She could do no more than that. Monsieur Hugo may have taken her virginity with his soft words and fancy gifts, but she had had his child. She hefted the bundle in her arms, and reckoned that perhaps she had had the better of the deal.

Senga Lundy looked out through the rear window of the car. Had she imagined it or had she actually seen someone at the topmost window? A pale face holding something – a child perhaps. She turned away and glanced at Jean-Michel. Catching her eyes, he smiled warmly, and for a single moment she was deceived into thinking that this man would do her no harm. And then she looked into his eyes – and realized she had seen that look before. She had seen it in her mother's eyes – the same, cold, calculating expression. And Senga Lundy understood then that there was a very real possibility that Jean-Michel Hugo was every bit as dangerous as the unnamed maid back in the hotel had warned. She returned Hugo's smile, and asked, 'Where now?'

'Next stop Paris,' he said brightly.

CHAPTER THIRTY-FIVE

The journey to Paris took four days, and in that time Jean-Michel Hugo behaved impeccably, always treating Senga with the utmost courtesy and respect. Initially, they travelled in silence, and then, as the hours rolled on, he began to ask questions, gradually drawing her out into speaking of herself, her past and her family. Senga was extremely careful what she told him, editing her comments carefully, falling back into the fiction she created while she had been in the Chateau, reluctant to disclose too much of her past.

Senga too learned a little of the Hugos and their extraordinary business which had started in hotels and pensions and then moved into supplying materials – principally food, wines and linen – for the hotel trade, and thence into the entertainment business. Jean-Michel also claimed to be a distant descendent of the great French writer, but Senga couldn't make up her mind whether he was serious or not. He was unlike any man she had ever met before; charming, intelligent and good-humoured, and yet, underlying it all, she sensed that there was something else, as if all his charm and good humour could be instantly replaced by something darker. In that respect he reminded her of her mother; she too was able to wear the mask ... perhaps that was why Senga had been able to recognize it in others. Perhaps that was why she had distrusted Maria Leiber; she had sensed that she too had been wearing a mask, pretending to be something that she was not.

At some stage during the journey, or on one of the stops along the road, she was expecting Hugo to make his move – from listening to the older girls in the Chateau, she had a vague idea just what to expect – but it seemed as if he was disinterested in her. And his very disinterest annoyed her, and in a vague and curious way, stung at her pride. She was pretty she knew – when she was older, she expected she would be beautiful – her body had already begun to develop its womanly shape, and she had inherited her mother's hair. Although she usually wore it curled into a bun at the back of her head, or twisted into a long plait, when she left it unbound, it flowed down her back in a silken wave, almost to the base of her spine. It was her finest feature she knew. And, as the journey progressed, she took to leaving it unbound, a simple band across the top of her head keeping it away from her eyes.

Was Hugo disinterested because he saw her simply as a child? But she was a young woman now, and entitled to be treated as one. Hugo's composure nettled her, and eventually, towards the end of their journey, she lapsed into a sulky silence, and it was only as they neared their destination that she perked up.

Senga knew they were nearing Paris because the very texture of the air seemed to change. After the crisp country air, with its sharp keen smells, this air was now tainted, pungent in a vague unidentifiable way that told of too many people living too closely together. Senga breathed in deeply, recognizing the same city smell that she associated with London and Dublin: the odour of civilization. Traffic became heavier now; carts and bicycles, cars and coaches thronging the streets as they moved on through the suburbs towards the heart of the city. Whatever pretence Senga Lundy had created pretending to be a sophisticated young woman vanished as she watched with childish amazement the crowds thronging the boulevards, spilling out onto the roadway from the cafes.

She dimly remembered Dublin, and she knew London, but this was different: the city seemed so alive, so vibrant ... so exotic. Her mouth opened into an 'O' of astonishment as she spotted a negro couple walking arm in arm through the crowd. She had never seen black people before, and what was even more astonishing was that no-one seemed to be taking any notice.

'Musicians,' Hugo said, following her astonished gaze. 'Probably American jazz musicians.'

The car finally came to a halt in traffic on the Rue du Temple. The tree-lined avenue was completely immobilized by two trams which had collided and then slewed sideways, shattering one of the ornate lampposts in the centre of the street. Hugo hissed in annoyance and consulted a small-faced wrist watch. Leaning forward, he tapped on the glass partition separating him from the driver. 'Turn there,' he pointed to the right.

'The traffic, monsieur ...' the man began to protest.

Hugo swore in a dialect Senga didn't catch, but his meaning was clear. The driver didn't say another word. Placing his hand on the horn – the sound creaking and asthmatic – he turned the car and drove at a sharp angle across the street towards the Place de la Republique, amidst a chorus of shouts and car horns. Pedestrians darted for the pavement, cyclists wobbling into the kerb to avoid the careering vehicle. The white-knuckled driver finally turned to the right and slowed down.

Hugo was laughing quietly.

Senga looked back through the window, but they had left the traffic snarl-up far behind.

'Is something amiss?' Hugo enquired.

'We could have killed someone,' she breathed, aware that her heart was pounding painfully in her breast.

Jean-Michel Hugo considered for a few moments. 'I suppose we could,' he said eventually, almost as if the idea had never occurred to him before. He reached out and squeezed Senga's hand gently. 'But we didn't, and that's all that's important, eh?' He leaned forward and pointed to the top of a tower that was just visible above the buildings. 'The Eiffel Tower.'

'I want to climb it,' Senga said immediately, full of enthusiasm.

'And so you shall. Tomorrow, we shall tour; I shall show you the Paris few tourists see.'

'But I want to see everything: the Eiffel Tower, Sacre-Coeur, Notre-Dame, the Hotel de Ville, the Louvre ...'

Hugo held up both hands. 'Everything, I promise, all the museums, all the churches, all the galleries. I promise. But that is for tomorrow. Something to look forward to, eh? But first we shall rest and refresh ourselves, and I think we must find you clothing slightly more suitable to your class and station.' He looked at her with a directness that she found embarrassing. 'Your figure is right; your bosom is small, and your features are regular. The look this season is vaguely masculine; we shall have to have your hair cropped, bobbed and then shingled ...'

'No,' Senga said, suddenly forceful. 'Not my hair. I will not allow anything to happen to my hair.'

'Aaah,' Hugo seemed nonplussed and then finally said, 'but it is the fashion.'

'I am not a follower of fashion,' she said quickly.

'Every woman is a follower of fashion,' Hugo said, sounding almost puzzled. 'Do not allow the cost to influence you, I will gladly ...'

'Monsieur Hugo, I was not thinking of the cost.' She turned to look at him, her deep, dark eyes catching and holding his gaze. 'My hair has never really been cut, it has been trimmed, but never cut. I feel it is my best feature, and I am loath to have it cut now – especially just because it is fashion.' She smiled slightly, 'My mother always said that we must instigate fashions rather than follow them.'

Her very directness shocked him speechless, and for the first time since he had lifted her unconscious body out of the mud, he looked at her closely. He had seen her naked when she had lain unconscious in the bed in the small hotel, and had even touched her body, marvelling at its flawlessness. But now he looked at her face and watched her eyes, and they suddenly seemed far too old, far too knowing for such a young girl. And he realized now that her hair was indeed thick and lustrous and he recalled seeing it unbound on occasion over the past few days. She had a mind of her own – and Hugo wasn't sure he liked that in a woman. He liked his women willing and compliant. But perhaps it was time for a little sport, a change. And a change was often more beneficial than a rest, he had heard. At the back of his mind he knew he would sleep with this young woman, but there had been no urgency, no immediacy in the thought. Until now. Here was a challenge ...

'Well of course, it is your decision. Will you allow me to present you with some clothing more suitable to Paris?'

Senga touched the clothes she had stolen from Maria Leiber. They had been old to begin with and were beginning to show their age. She smiled. 'I think that would be nice. I'd like that.'

Hugo sat back into the seat, relieved to be back on familiar territory. He wasn't used to women who refused his offers of presents. Squinting in the dim interior of the car, he realized that this girl certainly had possibilities. Initially, he had thought her too young – but they are never too young, eh? – but now he wasn't so sure.

'Well then, some clothes, and then I think we shall dine at La Rotonde in Montparnasse. It is in the Quarter and attracts the bohemians. You will like it there,' he assured her.

Senga wasn't so sure.

Katherine Lundy hated Paris. She stood at the tall bay window of the apartment on the Rue de Vaugirard in sight of the Palais de Luxembourg and the Luxembourg Gardens, surprised that the emotions still ran so strongly in her. When she had first come here ... what, more than twenty years ago now, she had been working for the notorious Dublin Whoremistress, Bella Cohen, and she hadn't been back more than twice in all that time.

The Whoremistress had taken her in when she had

been homeless and pregnant and treated her almost as a daughter, and in return Katherine had gone to work for the woman, organizing her books and her business ... and the woman at that time had run one of the largest brothels in Dublin. But Katherine had persuaded her that times were changing and that they needed to improve both their stock and their presentation, and so Bella Cohen had sent the woman she most trusted on the first of many trips to the capitals of Europe to examine how they ran their houses, and it was with the information she gleaned on these fact-finding trips that Katherine eventually created what was acknowledged to be one of the finest brothels in Europe.

Initially Paris had held a special place in her heart. It had been the first stop on her European tour, and the first 'foreign' capital, with the exception of Dublin, which she had visited. She had found it fascinating and exciting, exotic and more than a little sinister ... although she realized that very few other people saw the same Paris she had. She had seen the brothels, the squalid houses, the salons; she had talked to the street-girls, the cabaret girls, the dancers, and she had come to the conclusion that this was a dangerous and occasionally lethal city for the ladies of the night. At that stage she used to fool herself that Dublin was different; now, she knew it was not. But she had learned a lot in Paris; she had first discovered that houses kept 'specialists', women who performed specific functions and whose fees, of course, were proportionally higher. It was in Paris that she had first learned that certain houses kept women whose sole function was to attend to other women. The idea had both shocked and intrigued her, and although Bella Cohen would never allow her to instigate it during her tenure as the Whoremistress of Dublin, when she retired it was one of the innovations which Katherine introduced into the house – and one of the most lucrative. In many respects Katherine had been an innocent when she had come to Paris in 1900 ... but she had left the city a wiser person.

The woman smiled bitterly, watching her reflection in the glass twist its mouth in mockery. Perhaps that was why she had come to loath the city. She had lost her innocence here. She had lost her virginity in Dublin and her innocence in Paris. Even when she had been living in the brothel in Dublin she hadn't really felt part of the 'life'. But when she had left Paris she had come to realize that she was indeed no different from the girls who sold themselves on the street corners or in the cafes.

Paris had made her realize that she was a whore.

And now her daughter was in this city. And Paris swallowed the young ... especially young women. There were a hundred ways for them to fall into the 'life', and all of them were insidious, and if Katherine Lundy had one ambition left in life, it was that her daughter would not follow her own tainted footsteps. But if Senga was in the city – and she had to be ... she could be nowhere else ... Katherine would not accept that she could be anywhere else – she would find her. She had to.

'Madame? Madame?'

Katherine turned, realizing that Martha Tilke was talking to her.

'There is a gentleman to see you, Madame. He said he has an appointment.'

'A name?'

The tall thin woman frowned slightly. 'When I enquired Madame, he simply said, "Tattoo".'

Katherine nodded. 'I will see this man. Please ensure that we are not disturbed.'

The woman nodded and backed from the room, leaving the door open. Moments later a small, swarthy man stepped into the room and immediately moved aside to stand with his back to the wall. With his arms folded across his thin chest, he regarded Katherine Lundy carefully.

'You are not what I expected,' he said in perfect English, with just a touch of an American accent.

Katherine remained standing by the window, knowing the light coming in from behind her would blind the small man, making it difficult for him to distinguish her features. 'You are not what I expected either,' she said quietly, keeping her voice neutral. 'Perhaps you should convince me of your identity.'

The small Frenchman smiled, a flash of white teeth in the gloom, and moved quietly across the room towards Katherine. Her face was schooled into an impassive mask, and so she didn't react when she discovered that the man wore a black eye-patch over his left eye. Without saying a word, he shrugged off his jacket and rolled up both sleeves. His forearms were a mass of ornate, mutely coloured fleur-de-lys tattoos. Without a word he rolled down his sleeves.

Katherine stretched out her arm and he took her hand in a firm, dry grip. 'So we meet at last,' she said quietly.

'It is an honour to meet the famous Madam Kitten,' Tattoo said, admiration evident in his voice.

'The honour is mine.'

Katherine indicated a seat, and they both sat down facing one another across a small side table. The small Frenchman folded his hands together, fingers interlocking, and looked into her eyes. 'How may I be of assistance to Madame?'

'I am looking for someone,' Katherine said quietly.

The Frenchman smiled. 'But Madame is always looking for someone ...'

Katherine Lundy's association with Tattoo went back nearly twenty years, although this was the first time they had actually met. He procured suitable girls for her Dublin and later her London operation. Her requirements were simple: the girls had to be pretty – but not beautiful – and had to speak English with a pronounced French accent. Tattoo recalled the occasions when he had had to train his girls to corrupt their perfect English with a pseudo-French accent to satisfy the Madam's customers.

'It must be very important to bring you all the way to Paris?' Tattoo persisted, when Katherine didn't answer his question.

'It is,' she said, almost distantly.

The Frenchman frowned. This was not what he expected. When he had been dealing with the woman by letter, her instructions had always been crisp and concise, totally unlike this reticent, stumbling woman.

'A woman, Madame,' he reminded her.

Katherine looked up at him, and the Frenchman almost recoiled with the look of anguish in her eyes. 'I am looking for my daughter, Senga.'

Senga hadn't realized she was hungry until the food started to arrive, and then she realized she was starving. At first her self-consciousness at sitting at an open air café made her eat with all her proper table-manners, and then she realized that the people sitting around her, crowding the boulevards, seated six and seven to a table designed to hold four, were eating and drinking with gusto. Jean-Michel Hugo was devouring a chicken leg cooked in herbs and wine, holding it in both hands and gnawing at it, whilst his eyes were constantly moving over the huge crowd that filled La Rotonde to capacity. His eyes caught Senga and he grinned, grease glistening on his lips.

'Is it always like this?' she asked indicating the crowds with a sweep of her head.

'Always.' He dropped the chicken leg to his plate and wiped his fingers enthusiastically in a large napkin. 'This is Montparnasse, part of the bohemian quarter,' he said, pouring himself another glass of thick red wine, topping up Senga's glass. 'In Paris it is simply known as the Quarter. And this is the heart of the Quarter.' He nodded across the street to three other large restaurants that were situated on the corners of the crossroads where the Boulevard Montparnasse met the Boulevard Raspail. 'If you look yonder you can see the Dome and the Select and here, beside us, is the Coupole. It is said if you sit here, you will see all Paris walk by your table; but if you eat here, then sooner or later, all Paris will join you at your table.' He sipped some more of his wine. 'But you haven't touched your drink,' he said in astonishment.

'I must admit I have very little taste for wine,' Senga said, 'and I fear I drank too much coffee earlier today.'

Hugo struck his forehead with the palm of his hand. 'Of course, at the couturier's. You must forgive me, I had forgotten.'

Senga bent her head to hide a smile. Hugo had taken her to a tiny couturier in a narrow, sloping cobbled side-street, not far from the restaurant earlier that afternoon. She had then spent the next two hours standing stiffly to attention while two tiny old ladies outfitted her with everything from underwear to shoes. Her protestations had gone unheeded and although she hadn't seen money change hands, Senga had seen similar operations in London, and knew that the service the two women provided did not come cheaply. She had finally settled on a pair of peach satin cami-knickers worn under a stark white silk blouse, a bright red cardigan sweater and white wrap-around skirt. Her shoes were high-heeled and laced, and added three inches to her height. The simple red and white set off her raven hair to advantage, and she was aware – as was Hugo – that she was attracting a lot of attention at the cafe.

'What shall we do tonight, eh?' Hugo asked, catching her by surprise.

Senga looked at him blankly.

'Theatre, club, cinema or opera?'

'But ...'

Hugo held up both hands in a typically French manner. 'I will hear no buts. You are my guest, and it is my honour and my pleasure to entertain you.'

'Why?' Senga demanded, her very directness catching him off guard once again.

'Why? Because ... because ... I want to. I like you Senga Corcoran. You have charm and style. And I like a woman with style.'

'Let us assume for the moment what you say is true and

she does manage to reach Paris – and that would be no mean feat remember – well then she would face several dangers. Without money she will starve. Now there are ways for a young woman to earn money, but ...' Tattoo let the sentence lie; both he and Madam Lundy had made their fortunes in that direction. 'And then again, she could always end up as an artist's model. There is money to be earned there; it is not good money, but it can be regular, especially during the summer when there are many students who wish to draw ... or who wish to stare at a naked young woman. There is danger there too of course, but then it comes from a smooth-talking man who will make many promises, and deliver only lies.'

'Senga is no fool,' Katherine said quickly, 'she would see through those lies.' She hoped.

CHAPTER THIRTY-SIX

Jean Hugo's apartment was across from the Quai de la Tournelle, in sight of Notre Dame Cathedral. They had driven up along the quayside which was lined with bouquinistes – second-hand booksellers – who had displayed their books and pamphlets on carts and what looked like large wooden cases set atop the walls. Senga was amused to find that even though some of the booksellers were obviously preparing to finish for the day – and she was shocked to discover that it was close to ten o'clock – people were still clustered around.

'In Paris, bookselling is a vocation,' Hugo remarked, 'both the sellers and the collectors are a breed apart. They are dedicated to it with a passion that some men only reserve for the pursuit of women. The booksellers are like priests, their customers are the worshippers. I would venture to suggest that you would not find this in any other country.'

Senga suddenly thought of Patrick and the books he had often brought home from the bookshops along Charing Cross Road. 'It is much more widespread in London, where there are a large number of shops along the Charing Cross Road, and I suppose that would be considered the centre,' she said, 'but in Dublin it is concentrated along the quaysides like this.'

'You lived long in Dublin?' Jean-Michel Hugo asked casually.

'I was born there,' Senga said absently, and then immediately regretted it. She had deliberately avoided speaking of her past, and had thus far managed to divert the few questions he had asked.

'Your parents are wealthy then,' he said, not looking at her. He leaned across her, one hand touching her knee

471

while he pointed downriver. 'Notre Dame de Paris,' he said.

Senga twisted in the seat to look at the grand cathedral ... and used the opportunity to move a little further away from him. She had noticed that over the last few days – and in the last few hours – in particular, he had grown quite familiar with her, his hands touching, always casually, and always with good reason. He would touch her hands during conversation when he wished to emphasize a point; he would rest his fingertips on her shoulders when he wanted to point out something; and in the car, he had taken to tapping her knee when he wished to draw something to her attention. He had also taken to sitting directly across from her when they rode together, his knees almost – but not quite – touching hers.

'They are wealthy?' he asked again, and Senga noticed that his deep eyes had narrowed.

'Why do you say that?' she asked lightly, careful to keep her attention on the river and the distant cathedral.

'You have lived in Dublin and London and now you're travelling throughout France on an extended holiday outside of the school season, which indicates a governess or some sort of private education.' He waited, obviously expecting an answer.

'They are wealthy,' she said quietly.

'And your father, what does he do?'

'He is a ... writer,' she said quickly, and then bit her lip, anticipating what his next question would be. 'He writes under a variety of pseudonyms,' she added quickly, attempting to forestall the question.

'But how marvellous, a writer. Perhaps I would know his name or names.'

Senga turned and smiled sincerely at him. 'We are honour bound never to reveal his working names.'

'Aaah,' Hugo sat back into the seat just as the car pulled into the kerb and stopped. 'We have arrived.'

The concierge was a tiny wizened woman who appeared out of the shadows as soon as Senga and Jean-

Michel had stepped into the echoing marbled hallway. Even the brash Hugo stopped and wished her a courteous good evening. She nodded in his direction, although she didn't actually look at him, but she watched Senga through small glittering black eyes.

'This is Miss Senga Corcoran, a tourist; she will be staying with me for the next few days.'

The woman nodded, but said nothing and shuffled back into the shadows.

'This house is one hundred and fifty years old,' Hugo muttered, directing Senga over towards the stairs, 'but I believe she is older.'

Hugo's suite of rooms took up the first floor. Originally three families had occupied the floor, but the Hugos had bought out the other two and then proceeded to knock the rooms into one another. As he turned the key in the lock, and twisted the handle, he explained that the apartments actually belonged to his parents – although they rarely used them, preferring newer, even larger apartments close to the Rue de Berri overlooking the Avenue des Champs Elysees.

Senga stumbled as she entered the apartment; she was standing on a tiny balcony, surrounded by a brass rail, with four steps leading down to the huge sunken sitting room. The apartment consisted of four interconnecting rooms, the enormous large dining cum sitting room, an equally large bedroom with a bathroom complete with a sunken circular bath, shower, toilet and bidet off it and there was a small but complete kitchen off the sitting room. It had been recently decorated – she could still smell the paint – in a starkly modernist style, harsh sharp colours with severe and uncomfortable looking furniture. Even the ornamentation was modern, with the exception of a shelf of what looked like African carvings and a series of small Impressionist paintings on the bone-white walls.

Hugo saw Senga looking curiously at them and nodded in delight. 'Yes, they are genuine. You know it is still possible to pick up some of the lesser paintings

473

and lithographs of the acknowledged masters of the Impressionist period. I guarantee that they will prove to be a superb investment.' Senga nodded absently, crossing the room to look out through the long windows down onto the Seine. 'I had the apartment re-decorated recently,' Hugo chatted on, unaware that he had lost her interest. 'My parents had it cluttered with some antique furniture, dark heavy-looking stuff – ugly,' he added, sitting into a tall-backed white wooden chair. Senga thought it looked hideous. 'But no matter; they took most of it with them to their new apartment ...'

She was feeling trapped again. The feeling had been growing on her all day, and she had finally recognized it now. It was the same feeling she had had in the Leiber house, that impression that there was trouble brewing, she could almost taste it in the air like the odour of a distant thunderstorm. She stood before the window and refocused her gaze, looking at the reflection of Jean-Michel Hugo in the glass. The shadowy reflection robbed him of all humanity, leaving only a ghostly transparent impression on the glass. She thought it curiously apt.

'Are you married?' she asked, turning and asking the question at the same time.

In the long silence that followed, Hugo looked at the young woman closely, watching her, and he was surprised to find no trace of fear or nervousness in her voice or expression. 'Why do you ask?' he asked eventually.

Senga shrugged. 'Just curious.'

'I'm curious about you too, you know?'

'Answer my question,' she persisted.

'I was married.'

'Was?'

He shrugged eloquently. 'What do you want to know: my wife and I barely knew one another when we were wed; it was an arranged marriage. It didn't work out.'

'So you are married,' Senga stated flatly.

'We have parted …'

'Why are you treating me this way?' Senga asked quickly.

Hugo frowned.

'New clothes, food, wine, the use of your apart-ment …'

He started to shake his head.

'You know I cannot pay you now; I have no money. But when I return home, I will ask my mother … my parents to reimburse you for your expenses.'

'But you must allow me …'

'I cannot,' she snapped. 'You mustn't think me ungrateful,' she added immediately, 'because I'm not. If it hadn't been for you, I'd still be wandering the roads of southern France.'

'Yes,' he murmured.

'I've nothing to give you in return for all your kindness – except my thanks,' she said.

Hugo spread his hands. 'But I expected nothing else.'

They both knew he was lying.

'I didn't know girls worked around the tower,' Katherine remarked, joining Tattoo on the small walkway close to the top of the Eiffel Tower. Below them the night-time city spread out before them like the contents of a master jeweller's craft on black velvet. The noise of the traffic and the city was muted, a distant hum. They had the top of the tower to themselves; it should have been closed, but Tattoo knew the guards …

The small, swarthy man smiled crookedly. 'I won-dered if you would notice them … but I suppose I should have known better.' He turned to lean his elbows against the rail and looked up at Katherine Lundy. 'It is quite a lucrative beat. It is one of the prime tourist attractions; there are always a ready supply of customers and any number of cheap hotels hereabouts to bring them to. They are of course operated under "licence". Surely you did something similar with your Dublin operation?'

Katherine leaned against the rail, facing away from Tattoo. A warm, faintly noxious breeze tugged at her greying hair; without her glasses the lights below were vague haloes of coloured light. 'I must admit I didn't. I preferred to concetrate on the house and my other business. I never bothered with the free-lance girls.'

Tattoo shrugged. 'Just because they're not working in your house, doesn't mean they can't work for you. You "licence" the prime beats, and they pay you a percentage. You'll have to police it rigidly in the first few months, make an example of one or two if they get out of line and hold back some money, but once they know they can't cheat on you, it'll run well. It can be a very lucrative sideline,' he murmured, 'and if it does nothing else it allows you to control the population.' He caught her glance and grinned. 'Too many girls can cause a glut on the market and the price can drop. This is no business for amateurs.' A curious expression came into his eyes for a moment. 'I must admit I earn good money encouraging girls not to stray too far from the path, and I think I earn better money discouraging girls from even stepping onto it.'

Katherine said nothing. She was all too aware of Tattoo's reputation. He was a man who seemed unable to understand the concept of pain – when it applied to others, that was. He was a master of dealing pain.

'Have you any news for me?' she asked eventually.

The small Frenchman shrugged. 'Some – a little.'

'Good or bad?'

'Mixed. I got in the last reports from my people late this afternoon. I contacted people I knew in the towns and villages close to the school and the Leibers' farm. I have spent a fortune on telephone and telegraph messages.'

'Just present your bill,' Katherine murmured.

'I retraced your daughter's steps and started at the school as you suggested. Luckily, I knew someone in Neuchatel itself, and he knew both the school and its teachers. I talked to this man for over an hour on a ver' bad phone line. And I must tell you Madame, I know this is a fine school with a fine reputation but had I a daughter, I would not want to send her there. There must be eighty or a hundred girls there, but there is no joy there; my man said he would run away from it himself.' He shrugged again. 'But enough. I then sent some people to visit the Leibers.' Something like a smile touched his thin lips. 'They were reluctant to speak. Your woman, Tilke, had already spoken to them and money had changed hands; that money had made them greedy.'

'But they still talked to your agents?' Katherine pressed.

'Eventually,' he said slowly. 'Eventually, when they were asked questions, they answered – indeed, they seemed almost eager to answer.'

'Indeed?' Katherine murmured, leaning forward to look down, down onto the Boulevard St. Germain where the traffic crawled like giant insects. 'And how much did this information cost me?' she asked, although she already had a very good idea of the answer.

'They volunteered the information,' he murmured, 'and in the circumstances, I waive my usual fee.'

Katherine nodded solemnly. Tattoo may have waived his usual fee, but now she was indebted to him, and she knew that one day he would call in his debt.

'Then, working on the assumption that she was making her way towards Paris, I sat down with a large scale map and worked out all her possible routes ...'

Katherine ground her teeth together, locking her jaw into an angry jutting mask. 'I have no wish to doubt your methods, monsieur, but I am eager to know if you had any success.'

'Of course, Madame,' Tattoo said solicitously, 'you are concerned with your daughter's well-being and I have done nothing but boast. You must forgive me ...'

'There is nothing to forgive,' Katherine snapped, a hard edge creeping into her voice.

'There was an accident outside Villersexel, it is a town

477

not far from Lure. A young woman was hit by a car and spent a week in a small hotel there. She was attended by the local doctor – and her injuries were not serious Madame, so do not worry yourself. None of the staff at the hotel remember her – and that in itself is suspicious. There was one young woman there whom one of my men thought knew something, but she seemed almost too frightened to speak. However, our agents spoke to the local doctor and he remembered the girl and her injuries; he also remembered the driver of the car. It was Jean-Michel Hugo ... and Monsieur Hugo's family own the hotel the girl was kept in ... and Monsieur Hugo has a large automobile.'

'Coincidence?' Katherine murmured.

'I do not believe in coincidence,' Tattoo said quietly.

'Nor do I. Has he an apartment in Paris?'

'He has.'

Katherine Lundy smiled.

'Tell me about your wife?' Senga said suddenly, deliberately, startling him.

Jean-Michel Hugo looked up in surprise. 'Who, Madelaine? But I've already told you. Why do you want to know?' he asked.

They were sitting at either side of a glass table, a bottle of room-temperature red wine between them. Senga's glass was still almost full with her first serving, but Hugo had refilled his glass twice from the bottle.

'I was just wondering what sort of woman she was. I was just wondering if she realized how lucky she was to have such a considerate husband. There cannot be many men who would be so solicitous of a stranger's well-being.'

Jean-Michael Hugo accepted the compliment gracefully. He was finally getting someplace with this ice-queen. Her protective armour was beginning to break. Maybe she wasn't so different from some of the other women he had had. And once they started asking questions about his wife, he knew that they were already beginning to categorize her in their own minds, creating the excuses which would allow them to go to bed with him. This girl wasn't so different ...

He picked up his glass, running his finger-tip around the rim, and stared deep into Senga's eyes. Embarrassed, she dropped her gaze. 'Madelaine was – is – a very beautiful woman, and I remember thinking when we first met how lucky I was. I told you ours was an arranged marriage, and so I never actually met my bride until days before our wedding. My father wished to use my father-in-law's shipping connections to further his business, and my father-in-law saw some of the advantages of joining with my father. Unfortunately neither of them bothered to consult with Madelaine or myself.

'Madelaine was beautiful as I said; she had the sweetest smile I ever saw. I think I loved her the first moment I set eyes on her. And then I realized that she was a child ... literally. She had the mind of a child, a simpleton. Ours was a marriage on paper alone; two days after we were married, she was removed to a Swiss institution where they care for people like her.' Hugo dipped his head to hide his eyes. Some women could read sincerity in a man's eyes and he had an idea that Senga Corcoran might be one of those. He had three different stories that he told, depending on the girl he was talking to; he hoped that Senga would go for what he called the sympathy story.

'But how terrible for you,' Senga said quickly, not sure whether she believed him or not, not sure whether a man would tell such a monstrous lie about his wife. She stood up from the table and walked around the chair, almost unconsciously putting as much distance between herself and Hugo. She wished she were more experienced with men, so that she would be able to judge him, but all she had were her instincts, and her instincts told her that he was lying. She decided to trust her instincts.

'And what would you like to do tonight?' Jean-Michel Hugo asked suddenly.

Senga turned to look at him. She was standing in front

of a plain wood and metal bookcase set into a nook of the wall. There were about a dozen books on the shelves; the rest of the space was taken up with small African carvings and objects d'art.

'We could go to the theatre, the cinema, a club, the opera, a bistro … or we could just drive around, and I could show you Paris by night.'

'I'm not really hungry,' Senga said carefully, not wishing to offend, abruptly aware that she was on dangerous ground here. 'That meal we had earlier today was quite filling.'

'A show then? We could go to the Follies.'

'I would like to … but perhaps tomorrow night,' she suggested. 'I am very tired. It has been a long day for me. If it's all the same with you, I would like to stay in, and perhaps just read awhile or even talk, before going to …' she stopped before using the word bed, ' … before going to sleep.'

'Of course, of course, but you must forgive my thoughtlessness. I will have some snacks prepared, a light supper, and then you could retire to your bed. You know you have only to ask,' he said, watching her intently, trying to gauge her reaction, 'your wish is my command,' he added with a smile.

Senga smiled her thanks. 'A light supper sounds wonderful, just perfect.'

'I will arrange everything. A little light supper … and then to bed.'

CHAPTER THIRTY-SEVEN

La Bouche spotted the shape in the deepest shadows on the Quai de la Tournelle and moved across the street, heading towards it. It had been a slow night and she was both cold and tired, but if she managed one more trick off the streets before midnight, she'd call it a day and head for her flat for an hour or two's sleep before going out again around three to cruise the clubs. She wasn't as young – nor as pretty – as she had once been, and she found she needed those couple of hours sleep if she was to complete the club circuit successfully. The tall, dyed blonde usually pulled two or three tricks – usually drunk, but no matter – from the clubs in and around Montmartre.

She spotted movement again and a shape was briefly outlined against the light on the opposite side of the river. It looked vaguely manshaped and that was enough for her.

La Bouche was wearing flat-soled ballet pumps – at over six feet in her stockinged feet, she found her height sometimes put people off – and so she was able to approach the shape in the shadows completely noiselessly.

'A light, monsieur ...?' she tried her opening gambit.

There was a gasp and then the unmistakable sound of a gun being cocked. She felt her blood run cold. She had once had a pimp who liked to play with guns; he had blown a hole in the side of his head playing Russian Roulette one night. But that noise – the double click of a pistol being cocked – was a sound she would never forget.

'Go away,' the voice whispered in a bad accent.

La Bouche gladly obliged. In this milieu the gangsters

481

were perfectly welcome to kill themselves, as long as she wasn't going to get caught in the crossfire. She passed an older couple walking slowly up the street as she hurried away, and wondered briefly if she should warn them.

But why – it was none of her business.

There were now four empty bottles of wine on the glass topped table, and Senga still hadn't finished her first glass. Jean-Michel Hugo didn't seem to notice.

Senga was now standing as far away from the man as possible. It lacked ten minutes to twelve and she was deathly tired. All she wanted to do was to sleep, but she knew she couldn't go with Hugo in his present condition. All she could hope to do now was to wait him out and hope that he fell into a drunken slumber before she collapsed from exhaustion. She was hungry too; the supper Hugo had promised to send out for hadn't materialized. She looked across at the Frenchman. Although he was very obviously drunk, he still looked sober except for the ragged flush to his cheeks and the vaguely perceptible tremble in his hands, but he didn't slur his words and seemed perfectly lucid, and she knew then that he was the most dangerous type of drunk.

'I think I've shown you a good time,' he said suddenly, startling her.

'Yes ... yes, you have. You've been very good to me,' she agreed. 'I am truly grateful. Thank you.'

'Following our accidental meeting ...' he grinned inanely at the bad joke, 'I put you up – at my expense mind you, my expense – in one of my family's best hotels ...'

Senga remembered the dirty, shoddy room, and smiled grimly.

' ... paid for a doctor for you out of my own pocket. Then I drove you to Paris in my own car – again at my own expense – paid your hotel bills along the way, fed you, and then, when we finally arrive in Paris, I have you outfitted in the latest fashion, offer the run of my personal apartment, bring you to the best restaurants in the city, offer you the theatre, the cinema or even the opera, and what do you do? You say thank you ... thank you ... THANK YOU!' he spat.

'What do you want me to say?' she asked quietly.

Hugo finished the last of his wine in one long swallow. A pale pink rivulet trickled its way from the side of his mouth and down his chin, speckling his shirt. 'More than thanks,' he murmured, 'more than thanks. I expect you to express your thanks.'

'In what way?' Senga asked, although she already had a very good idea what he meant. She put the book in her hand back on the shelves and surreptitiously lifted an African carved wooden comb. It only had four tines, but they were each about two inches long. Holding it cupped in her hand gave her some confidence, but not much.

'Are you a virgin?' he asked suddenly.

Startled, she looked at him.

'Well?' he demanded belligerently.

'I don't think ...' she began.

'I don't care what you think,' he snapped, 'I asked you a question.'

'I don't think I want to answer it,' Senga said coldly, surprised that she didn't feel more alarmed. She had a vague idea of the act between a man and a woman, but some of the details were foggy; perhaps if she knew more, she'd know enough to feel frightened.

Jean-Michel Hugo stood up suddenly, swaying on his feet. 'Come, come now, you cannot be so naive ... surely you knew that all these favours, all these goodies would have to be paid for sooner or later. Why, everyone knows that.'

'And what about the servant in that first hotel of yours I stayed in, did she know the price?' she demanded.

'What ... what girl ... what are you talking about?'

'The girl who bore your child,' Senga snapped.

'Not my child,' he shook his head. 'Could have been anyone's. Sluts like that will lay with anyone.' He took a step towards her, and she immediately moved away. 'Aaah, ready for a little game eh? I like a little game, fires the blood. What shall we play?'

'Leave me alone,' Senga hissed, manoeuvring around towards the door.

Seeing where she was headed, Hugo scooped up a vase from the mantelpiece and flung it at her. It shattered against the door inches from her face. She staggered backwards with a scream. Another thrown vase exploded against the wall over her head, showering her with splinters and slivers of glass. Senga backed further away ... and then felt a doorway at her back. Still facing Hugo across the room, she felt with her left hand for the key, but in her haste it came out of the lock. An empty wine bottle thudded to the floor by her feet and Senga yelped and stumbled back against the door – and it clicked open, sending her staggering back into the room behind her. It was the bedroom.

She slammed the door shut and fumbled with the key which she still clutched in her trembling fingers. She managed to fit it into the lock and had half turned it when Hugo struck the door from the other side with all his weight. The blow sent Senga staggering back onto the floor, but the door held. With an almost desperate effort, she flung herself at the door and turned the key fully, the solid click of the bolt the sweetest sound she had heard in a long time.

There was another blow from the other room and the door vibrated in its frame. Hugo was screaming at her, and then what sounded like glassware shattered against the door. Senga darted across the room and grabbed a chair from in front of the dressing table and tilted it on its back legs to brace it against the door handle. She took a moment to take stock of her surroundings. The bedroom was as large and as sparsely furnished as the sitting room. The bed was enormous and circular – the first time she had seen a circular bed – covered with sheets of what looked like black silk. Senga touched the cloth with her fingertips: it was silk! There were two small cabinets on either side of the bed; one held an assortment of liquors and the other a collection of instruments which she didn't recognize – long thin, blunt-nosed objects, a pair of manacles, feathers, pots of oils and unguents. Across the room was a glass and metal dressing table; she caught sight of her reflection in the mirror and smiled at the wide-eyed startled look frozen on her face. There was a door directly across from her, and a quick glance confirmed that it let onto the large bathroom. There was only one window in the bedroom and it looked down over the back of the house onto a small refuse-littered yard. There was no way out – and nothing she could use as a weapon in the room. All she had was the bone comb clutched tightly in her right hand. She turned her clenched fist over and forced her hand to open. The tines had bitten into her flesh drawing blood; four dots of crimson nestled on her chapped flesh like tiny rubies. She wove her fingers through the comb, and clenched her fist so that the tines stuck out between her fingers. If she could hit him in the face or throat ... But she realized that all she could effectively hope for now was that Hugo would eventually sober up and come to his senses.

At first she thought it was another bottle breaking – a sharp, cracking pop – but then she saw the door shiver as if it had been struck a hammer blow. She stared open mouthed at the small ragged hole just above the lock.

She knew what was happening ...

Another crack, and a chunk of wood just below the lock snapped away from the door.

... but somehow she couldn't express it. It was unthinkable ...

The third crack ripped the lock away from the door completely.

... but Hugo was shooting ... a gun ...

Jean-Michel Hugo hit the door with his shoulder. The two back legs of the up-tilted chair slithered across the pale cream carpet, and then the right leg cracked and the chair spun away. The door snapped open hard enough to rip it from its topmost hinge, leaving it hanging at an angle.

Jean–Michel Hugo stepped into the room.

'You should have been grateful,' he hissed. He raised the pistol and pointed it at her. His hands were small, she noticed incongruously, but even so, the gun looked tiny, like a toy, a child's toy. 'There was a girl like you once,' he whispered carefully, with that precise enunciation of the drunk, 'and she wasn't grateful either, even though I treated her well. She had an accident,' he reminisced. 'But you don't want to have an accident, now do you?'

Senga shook her head in a mute 'No.'

He crossed to the bed and sat down onto it, leaning back on his left arm, the gun held loosely in his right hand. He tilted its barrel slightly upwards. 'Perhaps you'd like to tell me who you are … as you strip.'

'No,' the young woman said firmly.

Hugo leaned forward and his left hand dipped into his pocket. He lifted his hand from his pocket and, with a twist of his wrist, snapped open a straight razor. 'Now you can strip of your own accord, or I can cut the clothes from you … and it would be a pity to destroy such lovely clothes. The choice is yours.'

Senga looked into his eyes and saw no pity there, saw only the lust. Determined not to give him the satisfaction of seeing her weep, she stared at him as she unbuttoned the expensive dress he had bought for her earlier. What matter if she had to strip for him; eventually he would have to come close to her, and she would have him then. She squeezed the comb between her fingertips.

One by one, her clothing began to puddle around her feet, the white wrap-around dress, the silk blouse, the stockings and finally the peach cami-knickers … until she eventually stood naked.

Hugo had been expecting her to cover her groin and

her breasts with her hands, but instead she stood proudly facing him, her hands hanging loosely by her sides. He nodded slightly. He had always known that this one was different; she had pride. But he knew that while she may have said 'no' and protested a lot, she wanted him. He instinctively knew when women desired him, and once again he had been proved right. Look at her, flaunting herself at him, with her slender white body, her small breasts, her flat belly with just a touch of body hair. Yes, she wanted him, and he wanted her ... he wanted her so badly.

He did a quick calculation, wondering how much wine he had drunk. Not enough to hinder his performance.

He snapped the razor closed and placed the gun on the bed as he stood and quickly stripped off his clothing. The girl's eyes never left his face, she didn't look at his body, curiosity didn't tempt her to look at his erect manhood. He thought he detected two spots of colour on her cheeks: lust, embarrassment?

'This is your first time,' he asked, almost gently, 'you are truly a virgin?'

Senga nodded.

'I will be gentle with you. There will be a little pain ... but it will be compensated by much pleasure. You realize you are a lucky lady; not many women are initiated into the art of love by a master.' Completely naked now, he took a step towards the young woman, leaving the gun still lying on the bed.

And Senga stepped towards him.

Hugo reached out for her, his fingertips touching her breasts, her nipples, and then Senga had moved into the circle of his arms, and her own arms had come up, wrapping themselves around his head ...

The pain was like nothing he had ever felt before. It ate into his face like acid, beginning close to his hair-line, running down through his eyebrow, through his eye and into the soft flesh of his cheek. It was agony. He opened his mouth to scream, when he saw the girl's hand move again, saw the light glisten on what looked like needles tipped with crimson – his blood – and then felt the agony again as she stabbed something into his face, obviously attempting to gouge out his eye. He brought up his hands to protect his face, and the flesh was ripped and torn by four needles. Screaming aloud now, he struck out at her, a blow catching her across the side of the head sending her sprawling, the comb spinning from her hand. But instead of following her, Hugo – blood streaming down his face, speckling his body – threw himself back onto the bed, reaching for the pistol.

Senga staggered to her feet and raced past him, heading for the door. A bullet smacked into the wall by the light fitting, destroying it in a shower of sparks, plunging the room behind her into darkness. She had to get out of the apartment … there were other people in the house … Hugo wouldn't be able to do anything to her with other people around. Would he? She threw herself up the steps from the sunken living room and had her hand on the handle of the door, when Hugo screamed at her, 'STOP!'

Something in his voice made her turn around. The Frenchman was standing in the centre of the sitting room, the gun held tightly in both hands, holding it pointing steadily in her direction. Blood was still streaming down his torn face, streaking his body. Incongruously, he was still erect. He was shivering as he spoke, his teeth chattering wildly together.

'Why?'

Senga turned to face him, her hands behind her back, working on the doorlatch. All she had to do now was to keep him talking long enough to slide back the latch and then – naked or not – she would make a run for it down the corridor. 'Why?' she asked, puzzled.

'Move away from the door. Away!' The fingers of his left hand came up to touch his once-handsome face. 'Why did you have to do this? I only wanted what I was entitled to. I paid for you, just like any other whore, I paid for you. And you've marked me, scarred me. But do you know something?' His voice which had been reasonably steady and even, now rose to a screaming crescendo. 'Now I'm going to have you anyway, and when I'm finished with you, your own mother won't even recognize you!'

Senga looked into his eyes and saw only madness there. She crossed herself.

'Praying to your God won't help you now. Only a miracle could save you now – and I don't believe in miracles.'

'I do!'

Senga and Jean-Michel Hugo turned towards the voice. There was a figure standing in the doorway leading to the darkened bedroom, vague and indistinguishable in the shadows. But the light from the sitting room picked out the large black pistol held unwaveringly in the man's hand.

Hugo's expression changed and blood rushed to his cheeks, mottling his skin with rage. He opened his mouth – and the front door was literally ripped from its hinges by two terrifying explosions. Senga screamed and fell to the floor as the door careened down into the sunken sitting room. Smoke and dust swirled in the opening and then a small dark man wearing an eye patch over his left eye stepped into the room, a double-barrelled shotgun levelled at Hugo. He stopped in surprise, seeing the second man in the shadows also holding a gun on Hugo. A second shape moved in the smoke ... and Katherine Lundy stepped into the room.

'Mother?' Senga gasped, too numbed now by events to even begin to formulate a question. She looked at the gunman in the shadows and then to her mother standing beside the small man with the shotgun. She had never thought she would be so pleased to see her mother.

'What ...' Hugo began.

'Shut up!' Tattoo snapped.

'I know you,' the Frenchman said, blanching;

489

Tattoo's reputation was fearsome. He looked at the woman. 'I am ...'

'I know who you are, Jean-Michel Hugo,' Katherine said quietly, as she pulled off her coat and went to wrap it around her daughter. 'Do you know who I am?'

Hugo started to shake his head, when Tattoo said, 'This is Madam Katherine Lundy ...'

' ... The Whoremistress,' the figure in the shadows said quietly.

Everyone turned to look at him. Katherine glanced at Tattoo. 'I thought he was one of yours?'

The small dark man shook his head. 'I thought he was with this animal,' he nodded at Hugo.

Katherine tilted her head. 'Who are you ...?'

Hugo made his move at that moment. Spinning around he lifted the gun, bringing it around to level it at Katherine Lundy ...

The roar of a heavy pistol was drowned by the double blast of the shotgun. Hugo was dead before he hit the ground, the gaping hole in the back of his head matched by an equally enormous hole in the centre of his chest.

Tattoo made a move to break and reload his shotgun.

'Don't.' A slight movement of the gun emphasized the instruction.

Seemingly oblivious to how close she had come to death, Katherine Lundy turned back to the shadowed figure. 'Who are you ...?' she repeated.

The figure stepped out of the shadows into the light.

'Patrick,' both women gasped simultaneously.

'But you're dead,' Katherine whispered, ashen-faced.

Patrick Lundy smiled grimly. 'No mother, I'm very much alive, despite your best efforts to the contrary.' He glanced at Senga. 'I told you I'd come back for you someday.'

'Madame ...?' Tattoo murmured, hopelessly confused.

'Walk away, Frenchman,' Patrick said grimly. 'Leave the gun and don't even look back.'

Tattoo dropped the empty shotgun onto the floor and

490

walked away. He had looked into killers' eyes too often not to recognize the signs. He had been paid to bring the Madam to Hugo, and to kill him if necessary; well he had done both things, he had earned his fee. Whatever domestic troubles the Madam was experiencing were strictly her own problem, but from the look in that boy's eyes, he wouldn't be at all surprised to read in the morning papers that two bodies were found in that apartment.

Senga, wrapped in her mother's coat, hugged her brother. 'However did you find me? You came just in time; he was going to ... when I heard your voice ...'

'Sssh, sssh now.' Patrick's eyes – and gun – never left his mother, who had remained standing by the door. 'It's all over now.'

'How did you find me?' Senga murmured, turning to look at her mother, directing the question to both of them.

Katherine answered. 'I had some people retrace your steps. They discovered the hotel you stayed in, and from then it was a simple matter of identifying Hugo from his car.'

Senga looked at Patrick.

'I got the message you'd left for me at the bookshop,' he said softly, smiling at Katherine's sudden tight-lipped expression. 'I got to Switzerland only to discover that you'd run away and then, like our dear mother, I retraced your route. I spoke to the doctor who'd treated you following your car accident, and then it was a simple matter to discover this vermin's address.' He nudged Hugo's shattered corpse with the toe of his boot. 'I climbed up the drainpipe and got in through the back window ...'

'Just in time too. He was going to kill me,' Senga shivered.

'He had killed before,' Katherine said quietly.

Patrick squeezed his sister's shoulders. 'Go; get dressed. Your mother and I have some things to sort out.'

Senga looked from Patrick to her mother and then disappeared into the darkened bedroom. Moments later a small bedside lamp clicked on.

' "Your mother," ' Katherine said quietly, 'I am your mother too, Patrick.'

'You stopped being my mother a long time ago,' Patrick said, not looking at her. He opened the gun and pulled out the two empty cartridges, replacing them with two from his coat pocket. He snapped the gun closed with a metallic click. 'You know, I had sorted out in my own mind what I was going to say to you when I met you again. I had it all neat and orderly in my own mind; I would go through all the reasons I had to kill you, and then I would shoot you. A single, clean shot. And that would be that.'

Katherine said nothing.

'I hated you. You drove me from my home, you effectively destroyed my life; your interference caused the death of my wife. And then you set your assassins on me. I think I've reasons enough to kill you.' He brought the gun up in both hands, thumbing back the hammer, and pointed it at her face.

And then he allowed his arms to fall.

'And then I find you here. What brought you here?'

'I came for my daughter,' Katherine said simply. 'She was in danger and, whatever else you may say about me, I do love her. I loved you too, Patrick. You were all I had. Everything else, the house, the money, the servants ... all were as nothing. But you were my children, mine! And when I saw you re-making the mistakes that had destroyed my past, I wanted to stop you, and then ...' she shrugged, 'then things just got out of control.'

'Give me a reason not to kill you,' Patrick whispered. 'Me!'

Senga stepped into the room and went to stand between Patrick and Katherine. 'Patrick, I hated her too, God knows I hated her for what she did to you and to me. I hated her enough to run away from that school

492

she had sent me to. I was going to try and make my way back to Ireland to you. I never wanted to see her again. But when she walked through that door this evening, I was never so glad to see anyone in my life. I think I realized then that she truly loves me ...'

'I do,' Katherine said sincerely.

'And I know you love me, Patrick ...'

He nodded.

'You both came here for the same reason. This is the first time the three of us have been together in ... how long?'

'Too long,' Katherine murmured. 'You are my family,' she said to them both.

Patrick shook his head. 'I don't think so, Katherine Lundy. A mother doesn't kill her own son.'

'She does if it means protecting him.'

'You twist and turn things to suit yourself,' he snapped, 'you can even justifying ordering your own son's death. I said I hated you. But I'm not even sure if I've that depth of emotion left for you. I don't think I've any feelings left for you.' He glanced at his sister. 'But I'll tell you this, if I had come across you at any other time, at any other place, I would have killed you!' He dropped the hammer on the pistol and tucked it back into his coat. Patrick looked at Senga. 'I'm going back to Dublin. You can come with me ...' he nodded towards his mother, 'or you can go on to London. It's your choice.'

'There is no choice,' Senga said, her voice calm and steady. She stepped across the dead body on the floor and went to kiss her mother.

EPILOGUE

Katherine Lundy walked down the deserted quayside just as the first of the police began to arrive. She had come to Paris looking for her daughter; instead she had found her son.

Only to lose him again. And Senga with him.

But she was contented. She hadn't known how heavily the burden of his death had lain on her until she had seen him step into that room, and even if he had shot her then, she would have died happy, knowing that her two children were safe.

And even though she had lost Senga to Patrick, she was content. He would take care of her. He was so much like his father: hard and cruel, completely ruthless when the need arose … a sudden thought struck her and she smiled. And he was more than a little like herself too if it came to that.

And Senga? She too seemed to have adopted some of her mother's slightly less than feminine characteristics. Katherine had seen the marks down Hugo's face where her daughter had defended herself. And even though she had been at gunpoint, she hadn't been grovelling or screaming, nor had she given in to his demands. She was her mother's daughter all right. Perhaps it was time to let them go. They had proven beyond any doubt that they could take care of themselves.

She spotted the prostitute leaning against the quayside wall, looking back up the street where police and onlookers were milling about. There was a man standing beside her and as she drew near, she realized it was Tattoo.

'Madame …' he began.

She waved him to silence. 'It's over, Tattoo. My business here is complete.'

The small man nodded. Family matters. He touched Katherine's arm gently. 'Madame, perhaps you will allow me to introduce La Bouche, a lady of talent, who wishes to travel ...'

Katherine Lundy turned to look at the woman with professional eyes. Perhaps business wasn't entirely complete.

And in any case, Patrick had said they were going back to Dublin. But no matter where they went, they would never be entirely beyond her reach. Whatever happened, they would always be her children.

NOTES

Michael Collins was a real historical character, as are many of the minor characters portrayed in ANOTHER TIME, ANOTHER SEASON. It is unlikely that any of them acted in the manner portrayed in this book. This is a work of fiction, and their personae for this work are also fictional.

Far too many of the events are factual.

A THREAD OF GOLD

In 1865, when beautiful Laure Frémont marries Philippe Beynac, she believes the course of their love will flow as smoothly as the golden wine at their château in the Dordogne. But beneath the gaiety and splendour, a terrible blight is threatening their cherished vineyard. And then, with the outbreak of the Franco–Prussian War, Laure finds she is losing everything she holds most dear.

So begins one woman's struggle for both herself and her child's survival in an alien world, and a fight to restore the estates which are her heritage. She faces agonising choices, and conflicting demands: Henri Séguier, the rich neighbour who offers her a love which she can never return; Jean-Claude, the romantic painter, who loves with a passion that will haunt Laure forever; and the solemn, kindly Charles De Miremont, whom she realises she can use for her own desperate ends.

And even when the dark clouds of war again intrude and the threads of Laure's life are once more pulled apart, her spirit will never be broken . . .

Also by Helen Cannam in Sphere Books:
A KIND OF PARADISE

0 7221 2360 4   FICTION   £3.99

LORDS OF THE AIR

GRAHAM MASTERTON

When Herbert Lord was tragically killed in a plane crash in 1931, he left behind an aeronautical empire – and a personal legacy to his sons . . .

JAMES inherits his arrogance, his attraction for women, and the ruthless ambition that will pave his way to the top of the American airline business with scandal – and even murder . . .

RICHARD the stay-at-home, has the dependability to run the British company, the patriotism to adapt it to wartime needs, and the vision to prepare it for the jet age . . .

MICHAEL is endowed with his daredevil flying genius, and the romantic spirit of pioneer flying that will lead him to the lonely skies of Australia's North-West Territory . . .

And to all three, powering across continents through family rivalry and world conflict, glamour and danger, Herbert also left a secret – a secret they cannot learn until they have paid the price . . .

Also by Graham Masterton in Sphere Books don't miss

0 7474 0124 1   GENERAL FICTION   £3.99

Deeds

JOSEPH AMIEL

The world of real estate has dominated the lives of the
Behr family for three generations. And now the young,
dynamic Ralph Behr intends to ensure the family's
immortality in the shape of the Behr Centre – three 150
storey towers, to dominate the Manhattan skyline.

But overnight Ralph's elaborate plans and wild lifestyle
are brought to an abrupt halt. The unwelcome arrival of a
figure from the past throws Ralph into an intricate plot to
save the family name – and into a bizarre marriage with
Gail, a spirited, highly moral woman whose life has been
a crusade against everything Ralph has ever stood for.
His passion is to make money. Hers is to save the world.
They met once in childhood. They will meet again at
the altar . . .

Also by Joseph Amiel in Sphere Books:
BIRTHRIGHT

0 7474 0246 9   GENERAL FICTION   £3.99

THE
FIREBRAND
Marion Zimmer Bradley

'Still my fate: always to speak the truth, and only to be thought mad'

Kassandra, daughter of Priam the king and Hecuba the priestess, twin sister to Paris and prophetess of Apollo, her visions dismissed as lunatic ravings, is powerless to avert the fall of Troy . . .

'Marvellous . . . makes the mythological heroes seem human' – *Today*

Also by Marion Zimmer Bradley in Sphere Books – don't miss:

THE MISTS OF AVALON
THE CATCH TRAP
NIGHT'S DAUGHTER
LYTHANDE

0 7474 0126 8   GENERAL FICTION   £3.99

Nancy Thayer
MORNING

'THERE HE WAS, THE PERFECT HUSBAND, AND HERE SHE SAT, NOT PREGNANT, THE IMPERFECT WIFE. THE FLAWED WIFE. THE INFERIOR WIFE. THE RAPIDLY-MENTALLY-DETERIORATING WIFE.

SHE WANTED TO BREAK ALL THE DISHES OVER HIS PERFECT, UNDERSTANDING, LOVING HEAD.'

But it wasn't Steve's fault. It was nobody's fault that she couldn't have the child she so desperately wanted. So Sara channelled her energies into her work as an editor. And then she read a manuscript that led her to a creative life of a different kind; the autobiographical novel of a beautiful, terrifying recluse with a mysterious past . . . and a painful obsession.

Also by Nancy Thayer in Sphere Books:
NELL
STEPPING
THREE WOMEN
BODIES AND SOULS

0 7474 0104 7   GENERAL FICTION   £3.50

ZOYA

DANIELLE STEEL

One woman's odyssey through a century of turmoil
. . .

St Petersburg: one famous night of violence in the October Revolution ends the lavish life of the Romanov court forever – shattering the dreams of young Countess Zoya Ossupov.

Paris: under the shadow of the Great War, émigrés struggle for survival as taxi drivers, seamstresses and ballet dancers. Zoya flees there in poverty . . . and leaves in glory.

America: a glittering world of flappers, fast cars and furs in the Roaring Twenties; a world of comfort and café society that would come crashing down without warning.

Zoya – a true heroine of our time – emerges triumphant from this panoramic web of history into the 80s to face challenges and triumphs.

0 7221 8315 1   GENERAL FICTION   £3.99

The Winter Women

MARY ROSE-HAYES

The Winter women have everything!

ARRAN
a bestselling novelist with a social conscience, waif-like
beauty, and an unbelievable sex-life . . .

CHRISTIAN
the elegant jet-setting hostess, with a string of famous consorts
and lots of money . . .

ISOBEL
screen idol of millions, beautiful and gifted actress and
devoted mother to her enchanting twin children . . .

Yes, the Winter women have everything: talent, fame, beauty,
wealth – and a lot of secrets. Secrets that none can share until
their father's shocking death: secrets that bar them from one
thing they all truly want. Love . . .

*bright, vivid, well-written . . . oodles of action and a sense of
humour* – Kirkus

0 7474 0135 7   GENERAL FICTION   £3.99

STARK
BEN ELTON

Stark have more money than God and the social
conscience of a dog on a croquet lawn. What's more,
they know the Earth is dying.

Deep in Western Australia where the Aboriginals used
to milk the trees, a planet-sized plot takes shape. Some
green freaks pick up the scent. A Pommie poseur, a
brain-fried Vietnam Vet, Aboriginals who lost their land
. . . not much against a conspiracy that controls society.
But EcoAction isn't in society; it just lives in the same
place, along with the cockroaches.

If you're facing the richest and most disgusting
conspiracy in history, you have to do more than stick up
two fingers and say "peace".

0 7474 40390 2   GENERAL FICTION   £00.00

POSSESSION

PETER JAMES

Fabian Hightower was killed in a car crash. That's what
the police told his mother. She didn't believe them —
she'd seen him that morning. Fabian, the police insist,
is dead. But Alex's imagination keeps playing painful
tricks on her. It haunts her days; it breaks her nights
and it is turning her grief into terror. It drives her, in
desperation, to a medium. And it freezes the medium
into petrified silence. Because it isn't her imagination. It
is Fabian. He wants to come back . . .

'A psychothriller that eschews shock-horror tactics,
offering instead a more cerebral, more plausible
investigation of the paranormal'
Publishing News

0 7474 0336 8   GENERAL FICTION   £3.50